LORDS & LADIES
COLLECTION

*Two Glittering Regency
Love Affairs*

The Veiled Bride
by Elizabeth Bailey
&
Lady Jane's Physician
by Anne Ashley

The *Regency*

LORDS & LADIES

COLLECTION

The *Regency*

LORDS & LADIES
COLLECTION

Elizabeth Bailey & Anne Ashley

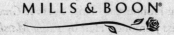
MILLS & BOON®

First published in Great Britain 2006 by
Harlequin Mills & Boon Limited,
Eton House, 18-24 Paradise Road, Richmond, Surrey TW9 1SR

THE REGENCY LORDS & LADIES COLLECTION
© Harlequin Books S.A. 2006

The publisher acknowledges the copyright holders of the individual works as follows:

The Veiled Bride © Elizabeth Bailey 2000
Lady Jane's Physician © Anne Ashley 1999

ISBN 0 263 84424 2

138-0206

Printed and bound in Spain
by Litografía Rosés S.A., Barcelona

The Veiled Bride
by
Elizabeth Bailey

Elizabeth Bailey grew up in Malawi, then worked as an actress in British theatre. Her interest in writing grew, at length overtaking acting. Instead, she taught drama, developing a third career as a playwright and director. She finds this a fulfilling combination, for each activity fuels the others, firing an incurably romantic imagination. Elizabeth lives in Essex.

Chapter One

An air of must and gloom shrouded the dimly lit interior of the narrow church. High walls entombed the line of wooden pews, and the sound of Rosina's footsteps on the cold stone flags seemed to echo round the vaulted arches above. At the sight of the dark figure awaiting her before the altar, the flutter in her stomach intensified.

He was half in shadow, a shaft from the simple rose window casting light in a diagonal across his back, so that only one stiff shoulder and a partial outline of his head were visible. There was a glimpse of waving brown hair tied back, a coat of sombre hue, and that was all.

Rosina felt sick. Her throat dried. Without intent, her fingers closed tightly on the arm of the man who walked beside her. He looked down, and she caught a kindly look of reassurance on the lawyer's face as he laid his hand briefly over hers, and pressed her gloved fingers. It was meant, Rosina thought, for comfort, but it had the effect of bringing a lump to her throat to add to her fervent apprehension.

Biting her lip, Rosina fastened her eyes once more upon the faded silhouette of the unknown gentleman into whose keeping she was about to pledge her life. He had not turned, though he must have heard her approach. It was all of a piece. Had he not rejected any desire to meet her before the wedding? She must suppose that he would not look at his bride one moment before he was obliged.

The aisle appeared endless, giving rise to a flurry of panic. She was making the most dreadful mistake! What was she about, to marry a man of whom she knew little more than his title? Probe how she might, there had been nothing of any significance given away. The lawyer who led her so stolidly to her fate had been uncommonly discreet. Anton, Lord Raith, remained an enigma.

Yet here she was, throwing herself headlong into intimacy with this stranger. Had any other course offered to afford her equivalent protection, she would have taken it. Indeed, as she neared the end of the aisle, she began to wish she had done so. If only she had not been tempted away from that other—so much less appealing!—solution to her hideous dilemma. It was too late. She was almost at the altar, where the pastor stood ready to bind her in wedlock to an obscurity.

Rosina was aware that she was shaking as she took her place at the gentleman's side. The most dreadful palpitations warred with an upsurge of nausea, threatening to choke her. It was all she could do to remain standing upon her two legs as the support of the lawyer's arm was removed. She drew raggedly on her breath, trying both to still the tumult of her bosom and to conceal its effects from the silent creature at her side.

Yet she could not resist a flying glance cast up at him. She was rewarded only with his stern profile. As well might she be marrying a statue, for all his interest. Curiously, this lack of attention had a slight calming effect, and a little of her panic subsided. She dared a second look.

At close quarters, the profile was personable enough.

As much at least as she had believed when she'd had the only glimpse of Lord Raith that he had permitted— through the glass of a coffee-room window. Mr Ottery, with whom all her dealings had been done, had arranged it at her insistence, for in this she had been adamant. Willing though she was to compound for a man she had never met, she would not marry one she had never seen. Not that she had got much good by it. Her prospective bridegroom had been as still then as now, she remembered, where he sat at the large table within the inn, only one side of his face turned in her direction—and that partly concealed by the sweep of loosely tied hair that looped upon his cheek, and the broad-brimmed hat that cut off any sight of his eyes.

Rosina could not see much more of him now, for he was taller than she had expected and her head reached only to just above his shoulder. It was enough to note the tight set of a firm jawline and the dip below a high cheek-bone.

All at once her attention was recalled to the priest, as he began the marriage rites. 'Dearly beloved, we are gathered here today in the sight...'

She stared blindly at the pastor. Dear Lord, it was happening! The heart rattled in Rosina's chest. She wanted to cry out to him to stop. She wanted to flee from the church. She could not do this! Was she mad to have consented? Dear Lord, let him not continue. She had no notion what the clergyman was saying, although snatches of the ceremony reached her ears.

Wild thoughts of denial chased one another through her head. She could wait for the impediment bit. Only there was no impediment beyond her own dread: she was of age, and free to marry. Why should she not refuse him? She had only to answer, when the vital question was asked if she would take him, that she would not. No, that was unthinkable. She must speak immediately—interrupt. But her tongue cleaved to the roof of her mouth, and she had no words.

Beside her, Lord Raith listened to the drone of the cleric's voice with even less attention than his betrothed. But, contrary to appearances, he was far from disinterested in his bride, though he did not look at her. When he had heard Ottery's murmuring voice, and the priest had said that he rather thought the bride was arriving, Raith had trained his gaze upon the statuary behind the altar, and fixed it there.

The light footfall that accompanied his lawyer's heavier tread had thrown him into his habitual tight control. Of all things, he must withhold himself until the last. Whatever the outcome, he could not endure the mortification of a last-minute withdrawal. More than that, he would not afford her any opportunity for regret. At least, not until the knot was tied. After—let it be as it might. He would know how to act. But he would not go through this ignominious process a second time. He would have this girl to wife, or none!

He pictured her as he heard her approach, the image strong in his mind. Fine-boned and delicate, with coal-black eyes in a face ashen with fear—or want? He had been unable to decide. A riffle of unease at his deception disturbed him. The advantage was all on his side. But then, Rosina Charlton need not have agreed to the bargain. She had chosen to sell herself. There had been no coercion. Her need, he must suppose, was as much a goad as his own.

Not that her story had been any more particular than that of others. It was common enough. An orphan without means, and no better future to which to look forward, he imagined, than the dreary prospect of tutoring other people's children for a pittance, or a drudgery of companionship hardly less appealing. Marriage, even to a man with whom she was utterly unacquainted, must be preferable.

Only Raith had seen something in her eyes that was out of the ordinary. Something indefinable, but a sense of mystery had struck him. It might have been attributed to that air of fragility, but he had thought there had been more to her story than she was willing to tell. On the second meeting, Ottery had probed on his instruction, but had got nothing by it. His fascination had intensified.

Yet Raith could not gainsay a trifle of self-disgust at his subterfuge, necessary though it had been. No matter how cogent her reason, he could not but feel that there was more than a touch of the sacrificial lamb in the waif that arrived at his side.

It was with difficulty that he refrained from risking a glance. He felt her eyes upon him, and was barely conscious of stiffening. His thoughts were swallowed up by a wholly unlooked-for surge of sensation in his chest. Like the rush of power at the onset of battle! It was a moment or two before he was able to command himself again. By the time he did so, the cleric was fully embarked upon his litany.

'Wilt thou, Anton, take this woman…'

For a moment of hideous suspense, Raith could not think what he was being asked. There was a breathless pause before the answer came to him.

'I will.'

He heard a tiny sigh beside him, and bit down hard against the flooding intensity of feeling. As the pastor asked the same question of the bride, he held his breath, half-afraid of her answer.

It came, a bare whisper on the air. 'I will.'

Tightly controlled, the breath slid out of Raith as the cleric's voice droned on. The ceremony seemed to drag.

'Who giveth this woman to be married to this man?'

From the corner of his eye, Raith saw his lawyer step forward and take the bride's left hand. He watched the slender fingers disappear into Ottery's large grasp, and reached out at the command of the priest. A weird sense of unreality took him as the girl's gloved hand was put into his.

The fingers shook perceptibly, and Raith was swept with a wave of compassion. He placed his thumb upon the fingers, exerting a slight pressure. They jerked once, as if she would free herself, and then stilled. Even through the silk, he could feel their chill.

'Repeat after me...'

Rosina winced a little as the fingers tightened. She watched the bare browned hand imprisoning her own, listening with only half an ear to the low-pitched murmuring beside her, conscious of the warmth emanating from the firm grip. Without warning, the shadowy figure had become real, and only one phrase penetrated her consciousness: *for better or for worse.*

It echoed in her head, tauntingly, as the parson turned to her. She was about to take that final, fatal step.

'I, Rosina, take thee, Anton...'

As she repeated aloud the words she was given, she had only one conscious thought. There was no going back.

Raith could not resist the impulse to turn slightly, that he might keep her under surreptitious observation. He heard only vaguely the words of her promises, listening rather to the hushed tone of her delivery, almost in question, as though she was not aware of the meaning of what she said.

She was as intriguing as he remembered. That elfin face, its pallor heightened by the mere wisps of black curl escaping from the confinement of a close cap. He had thought, that first day when he had watched her, himself unobserved, from his post behind Ottery's judas painting, that she looked younger than her given years. Of all the candidates, she had been the only one who had caught his interest. Something in her look had touched him. She had it now as she repeated the phrases that were giving her into his keeping. She seemed lost. There was a wistfulness, a vulnerability, which had struck with him an instant chord of sympathy. He could feel her plight, with the memory of his own.

'Have you the ring?'

Raith turned quickly back to the priest, looking to the man at his side. The plain gold band Ottery had purchased winked in the light. Raith watched the cleric take it, beset by an abrupt thrill of possession. She was his, come what may.

Rosina felt her fingers released, and emerged from the hushed daze that had enfolded her as she spoke the fatal words. She took in that the pastor was addressing her. The ring? Yes, she must take off her glove! She tugged at it, frantic as the silken folds resisted. Her fingers were all thumbs, feeble and unresponsive. A tiny sound of frustration left her lips.

Then she felt Lord Raith's hand once again close over her own. Removing her trembling and hopeless fingers, he turned the hand palm up with gentleness and undid the buttons she had forgotten at her wrist. The glove slid off, and was gone. Covered in confusion, Rosina kept her gaze lowered.

'With this ring…'

Only now did she see that her bridegroom was supported by a person on his other side, for her whole attention on coming up the aisle had been taken up by this man, who was sliding his ring carefully down her finger as he spoke the words of its significance. Riveted, Rosina gazed at the encircling gold as if in a waking dream, a fog wreathing her brain. All thought suspended, she heard herself pronounced a wife.

'Those whom God hath joined together, let no man put asunder.'

It was done. Trance-like, she turned to the man to whom she was vowed, and found his eyes upon her.

They were grey, and in their depths was a mix of apprehension and defiance. But Rosina did not see it. Her heart felt as if it had stopped. Time did not exist. The dream had turned to nightmare.

The only reality was the shock of the countenance that was at last turned full-face towards her. A countenance destroyed, hideously marred, by a disfiguring scar that ran from eyebrow to chin, cutting across Lord Raith's right cheek. Ridged and ugly, its harsh ragged line stood out white against the tanned roughness of his skin.

Rosina was still in a state of dumb stupor as she was led into the vestry to append her signature under that of her spouse. It lasted while she waited, standing to one side in the little room, through a low-voiced conversation between His Lordship and the lawyer. The cleric offered her a chair, which she took with a murmured word of thanks, sinking down upon its wooden seat, and staring directly before her. When Raith came to her at length, she did not even look up at him.

'Are you ready to go?'

Rosina got up, allowing him to take her arm without protest or acknowledgement and walking where he urged, her gaze blank and unchanging.

Raith felt acutely her withdrawal. He had been afraid of this. She could not bear to look at him! No doubt she was distressed by his trickery. She knew now why he had made an issue of their not meeting before this time. He was sure it must rankle with her for some time to come. It was a question whether she would ever forgive it.

Sighing a touch, he turned his attention to his groom as they reached the portals of the church. Parton had acted as his groomsman, for want of any other trustworthy person he might have introduced as a second witness. Ottery having been otherwise engaged, there was no one else. Raith remembered that, having signed the register, Parton had slipped away.

'Catterline has the chaise ready at The Dog over yonder, me lord. Would you wish to leave directly, or will Her Ladyship require refreshment before we set out?'

Rosina started out of her deep abstraction. *Her Ladyship?* It was a moment or two before she realised that the man was referring to herself.

'Ottery has arranged for coffee and cakes, I believe,' Raith answered.

'We'd best not leave it too late, me lord,' advised the groom, with a worried glance at the greyness outside. 'It don't look to me as if the rain'll hold off. Roads are bad enough as it is, and the nights drawing in an' all.'

It was indeed drab, even for late October, Raith reflected. They had only ten miles to reach Marton where they were to spend one night, but there was only a pair harnessed to the chaise—he could afford no more with his present means, though that was a situation shortly to be remedied—and it was already close on two. Parton was right. They must not dally.

He turned to Rosina and offered his arm again. 'Will you walk, ma'am?'

He was dismayed to find that, although she took his arm, she kept her gaze firmly turned away from any possibility of encountering his unsightly features. It was a relief when Ottery caught them up as they passed through the high gateway.

Raith glanced back at the austere outlines of the church. It was an ancient edifice dedicated to St Nicholas. Not large, with pretensions to the Gothic in its tall spired tower and arching interior. From Raith's point of view, its chief attraction lay in its situation, towards the outskirts of Coventry in a little-frequented area that had almost the atmosphere of a village. On a Tuesday, with the world busy about its concerns, the place was all but deserted.

'You chose well, Ottery,' he said, and turned to cross the road towards the small public inn so conveniently placed.

'I thank you, my lord,' said the lawyer, and moved to keep pace beside Rosina. 'I trust Her Ladyship will approve the light collation I have bespoken.'

Becoming aware that she was addressed, Rosina looked quickly up. The lawyer was smiling kindly at her, and a little of the deep abstraction in which she had been enwrapped began to leave her. Once more she realised how she had been styled, and the strangeness of it sent a shiver through her.

'You must be cold,' Ottery observed, and glanced over her head at his employer. 'Her Ladyship had a cloak. We left it in the church, I must suppose. I'll fetch it.'

Before Rosina could say anything, he had turned back. Her cloak? She remembered now. She had been wearing it when she arrived with the lawyer. Mr Ottery had taken it from her and draped it over a pew. Such was her state of mind that she had forgotten all about it.

'Lady Raith?'

She jumped. He was calling her by his own name! She had not turned before she saw that he was holding something before her. Her glove! He had taken it off for her when she could not. The memory of his gentle action returned.

She took the glove, glancing fleetingly up at him. He

was on her right and she could not see the scar. 'Thank you.'

She had barely drawn it on when Lord Raith ushered her into the inn. In a moment, the landlady was curtsying before her and offering the services of the house. Rosina allowed herself to be led away, hearing behind her the voice of the man to whom she had entrusted control of her life bidding someone bring to a private chamber the refreshments that had been bespoken.

It was with a rapidly growing feeling of heaviness that Raith awaited her in a cosy parlour. The nonsense about her forgotten cloak had depressed him, serving to remind him not only of her missing glove, but of the acute shock into which she had been thrown by his appearance, or else she would have recalled its existence for herself. Had he made a mistake not to allow her to see him before? Should he perhaps have met her several times so that she had grown accustomed? Only he could not have endured it! To be obliged to spend time fidgeting in the company of a girl whom he hoped might find it in her to stomach his disfigurement. Small hope of that—as was all too obvious. But it was a pointless exercise to engage in such thoughts. It was no use to cavil. He had taken what measures he had taken, and must live with the consequence.

He stiffened as the door opened. But it was only Ottery. He let his breath go. He need not dissemble for the moment. The man was more than his lawyer, he was a long-time friend.

'It all went off reasonably well, I thought, my lord,' said Ottery, laying the dark cloak across the back of a straight chair set in a corner of the room.

Raith laughed harshly. 'Is that what you thought? I wish I might say the same, by thunder! Did you see the way she looked at me?'

The image of her shocked countenance came back to him, the coal-black eyes enormous in her white face.

'My dear sir, a touch of astonishment was to be expected,' the lawyer pointed out gently.

'A touch!'

'I believe the young lady was somewhat overwhelmed by the whole business, my lord. I cannot think it was merely a reaction to—'

'Don't try to spare me, Ottery,' Raith said wearily. 'I have seen quite enough of a like reaction in females to be sure of the cause.'

He moved to the table where the landlord had set the light repast which had been ordered. He picked up the coffee pot in slightly unsteady fingers, and felt Ottery's hand upon his shoulder.

'Don't refine too much upon it, my lord. Even if you are not over-sensitive, as I believe, I am sure you will find that custom will ease the difficulty.'

It appeared, when Rosina presently entered the room, that there might be truth in this. Raith braced himself as she glanced at him, but it seemed to him that her gaze did not flinch. Rather it travelled from his face to the table. He was glad, however, when Ottery took it upon himself to supply her with a cup of coffee, which was all she would take.

'Will you not eat something as well, ma'am?' said the lawyer persuasively. 'It will be several hours before you are able to do so again.'

'Thank you, but I am not hungry.'

In fact, Rosina was feeling a trifle sick. When the landlady had left her in a bedchamber, she had sat down abruptly on the bed, overcome by faintness. A little water splashed on her face had eased the sensation after a short rest, and she had not troubled herself to do much more than cleanse her hands after making use of the house facilities.

She had straightened the set of the dove-grey chemise gown, which was the only one she possessed with any suitability to the occasion. It was of damask, close-fitting at the bodice with a low round neck sloping to a V-shape in front, where the edged lacing of her underdress afforded modesty. The skirt was full and long, with a plain hem, the sleeves tight to the wrist. She wore no sash, and had added one of her habitual enclosing caps, of silk and lace.

The rest of her meagre wardrobe had arrived in a small trunk, along with herself and Mr Ottery, in the hired carriage in which he had fetched her from The Crown at Brinklow, for she had not wished to advertise her departure from Gatty's cottage in the little village of Withibrooke. The trunk was now, she must suppose, bestowed in Lord Raith's chaise.

Lord Raith! And she was now his lady, for better or for worse. She was recovering from her stupefaction, and could even sympathise with His Lordship's reluctance to show himself prior to the wedding. If this was his secret, so also had she hers—and one susceptible of a more acute reaction than her own had been to his.

Once refreshments had been consumed, Raith was inclined to hurry, bearing his groom's pessimistic forecast in mind. In short order, he was handing his bride into his chaise, and turning to speak brief words of farewell to his lawyer.

'I will come to Raith Manor as soon as the legalities have been formalised, my lord. Your signature will undoubtedly be required on several papers, but I do not anticipate any difficulty with the procedure.'

Rosina had noticed the coat of arms on the door of the chaise, and remembered how fortunate she had thought herself to have secured a haven with a peer of the realm. It must assure her safety, so Gatty had said. But would her old nurse, to whom she owed so much, have let her go so readily into this had she known of Lord Raith's unfortunate affliction?

He had told her during their brief sojourn at the inn that, his estates being about twenty miles distant, they would make the journey over two days. His own horses, it appeared, were stabled at Marton, where he had made a change this morning when he was driven up for the wedding. He did not wish to put them through a second such journey on the same day.

'Besides, it will be growing dark by the time we arrive there, and it will not be comfortable for you to travel by night. I have secured accommodation at the Bell Inn. It is not the posting-house,' he had added quickly, 'so we need not risk running the gauntlet of curious eyes.'

Rosina had immediately had a vision of a bedchamber such as the one she had left upstairs, with a bed easily able to accommodate two persons. She had felt herself grow hot, and had quickly looked away, forgetting in her agitation to wonder at his not wishing to meet acquaintances.

She thought of it again now, for she had leisure enough to think. Having stepped up into the coach—electing to sit upon her right hand for a reason which was not hard to seek—the companion of her future life had loosened his bulky drab greatcoat, enquired civilly of his wife whether she was comfortable, and thereafter turned his gaze upon the restricted view from his window.

He was sticking closely to the letter of the agreement, Rosina reflected, for no further word had been spoken inside the carriage. She was glad that he did not expect her to engage in polite conversation. She would have been hard put to it to think of anything untoward to say. Their brief acquaintance had already crammed her mind with questions which she would shrink from asking—not least concerning the fearful gash, the unexpectedness of which had thrown her into shock.

To her shame, she felt herself burning with curiosity. She had forced herself to look at him casually, afraid of betraying herself, but she had wanted so badly to stare! How had he come by it? It was so vicious a blemish. She could not blame him for concealing it. Nor for not wishing, as he put it, to endure the gaze of the curious. Or was it because he was bent upon keeping the manner of their marriage secret?

Rosina supposed that a man might not wish the world to know that he had felt himself obliged to advertise for a wife. She had been considerably taken aback upon first seeing the advertisement. Before, that was, she'd had any thought of applying for the position herself.

It had become a ritual for the apothecary's boy at Hopsford to trudge the half-mile from his employer's shop to the cottage at Withibrooke where Gatty had taken her in, to bring the *Gazette* for her. Toly Aughton had befriended poor Gertrude Hoswick some years ago, Gatty had told her.

'It was when I could still see a little, my dove,' had said her old nurse. 'I'd sent to the shop to get something for my rheumatics, I think it was, and Toly brought it over. Well, when he saw what a sad and sorry state I'd got myself into, not being able to manage quite with the fire and what not, he took pity on me, bless the boy.'

Rosina had been poring over the newspaper, looking for a post that might suit a female with few accomplishments and no references, while her old nurse slowly felt her way about the kitchen making a meal of sorts, when her eye had been caught by the oddity of the advertisement.

'Dear Lord, Gatty, here is a gentleman advertising for a wife!'

At first she had been inclined to be dismissive when her nurse, once the extraordinary announcement had been read out to her, had suggested that perhaps Rosina should write in reply.

'Gatty, are you mad? I have not escaped one tyranny to put myself into another! Why, who knows what sort of a man this person is?'

'You won't find out, my dove, if you don't write,' had urged her nurse prosaically. 'It may be as he's perfectly amiable and respectable.'

'A man who is obliged to advertise, Gatty? He cannot be respectable!'

'Could be all kinds of reasons. No harm finding out. It ain't needful to do more. He won't know where you are— no more than that other—if you only give the Receiving Office at Brinklow for your direction. If you don't wish to take it no further after, that'll be the end of it.'

'But, Gatty—'

'I know it ain't what your poor mother would have wished for you, my dove, but things ain't turned out nowise the way she hoped. And it might be the saving of you.'

Rosina had been sceptical. But the slim chance that Gatty could be right persuaded her to do as she suggested. She wondered now whether they had made a horrible mistake that day. She glanced across at her lord, and discovered that he had, to all appearances, fallen asleep. How could she know if she had been wrong? If she had, it was in that first moment of putting pen to paper. Because once she had set events in train, she had found it hard indeed to halt them, for the opportunity had rapidly become too advantageous to pass up.

To her surprise, she had received, in response to her letter, a request to come for an appointment, her credentials—such as they were—apparently meeting the requirements. She could not, she thought, have withdrawn at that stage, for curiosity had got the better of her. Within a matter of days, she had found herself travelling the relatively short journey on the stage—for which, to her surprise and gratitude, a ticket had been sent—to Banbury, where a clerk had met her, and conducted her to the offices of Mr Ottery, situated in the business quarter of the town.

The exterior of the building had been pleasant enough. But after climbing two sets of narrow stairs within, she had entered an outer office of chilling formality. Two further clerks sat writing at desks, which were piled with beribboned parchments and folded documents. Open bookcases of dark wood, fairly stuffed with voluminous and hefty volumes, groaned against every wall, rendering the atmosphere so dull and gloomy that Rosina felt immediately intimidated.

She was shown directly through into a slightly less austere apartment, where two large windows at least let in light, and a couple of paintings adorned the walls between similarly overburdened bookcases. One was of the hunt, the other a particularly dark portrait with a pair of eerie eyes.

Mr Ottery, with whom she had been corresponding, proved to be a pleasantly avuncular man of middle years, besuited in plain black, with a grey tie-wig atop a friendly face. He had a kindly smile, and a manner that put Rosina as much at ease as the awkwardness of the situation would allow. He had done what he might to allay Rosina's quivering anxiety.

'There is no cause for alarm, ma'am,' he said calmly. 'My client—the gentleman in the case—is merely desirous of gaining access to his fortune.'

Was that all? She had ventured a question. 'Must he marry to do so?'

'The inheritance has been so arranged, ma'am, yes.'

'But, why?' It slipped out, but she retracted the question at once. 'I beg your pardon. It is none of my affair— only, it seems so odd.'

'Such clauses are not uncommon, ma'am,' Mr Ottery offered reassuringly. He gave a slight smile, his voice dry. 'Marriage is thought to have a sobering effect.'

Rosina was betrayed into a laugh. 'I hope you would not wish me to understand that the gentleman in question is wild?'

'Quite otherwise.'

This was so cryptic that Rosina felt herself tense up again. What sort of man was he, then, that he must needs advertise for a wife? She eyed the lawyer. He was not very forthcoming. He waited rather to see what she might have to say. She bit her lip, and took a determined breath. If he would not tell her, then she must ask.

'Forgive me, sir, but I do not quite understand. If his only motive is to gain his inheritance, why should the gentlemen use this means of finding a wife? There must be eligible females enough to suit his purpose.'

'There are reasons,' the lawyer answered, 'why my client would not wish to make his choice among the females of his acquaintance.'

So she had supposed! But what were they? Were all her questions to be treated to evasion? A hollow opened up inside her, as the enormity of the whole proceeding came home to her. Had she taken leave of her senses, to be considering this course of action? She should not have listened to Gatty. For all she knew, the man in question was a monster!

'What is wrong with him?' she blurted out suddenly.

The lawyer looked blank. 'I beg your pardon?'

Rosina glanced away, feeling suddenly acutely uncomfortable. Exposed—as if she were being closely scrutinised. She brought a hand unconsciously to rub the back of her neck under the chignon that held her black curls in place below the confining cap. Her gaze darted about the room, and she slid her hand down, clasping it with the other and entwining her fingers. Mr Ottery's face came back into view, and she stared at him, hardly aware of what she said, or that her voice was shaking.

'It s-seems logical to s-suppose, sir, that if your client does not wish to marry from his acquaintance, that they must find him in some way…unacceptable.'

She thought the lawyer's eyes narrowed a trifle, and her discomfort increased. Illogically, she felt guilty—as if she had said something hurtful. More than ever the conviction crept over her that someone—he, it must be, for there was none other in the room!—was watching her, seeing into her very thoughts. Mr Ottery was speaking again, and she tried desperately to focus her mind again.

'My client wishes for nothing more than a marriage certificate. He is not willing to offer other than that. It is to be an arrangement purely for convenience. That, he believes, is *unacceptable* to the ladies of his own circle.'

The underlying antagonism below the flat tones penetrated Rosina's anxiety. It had, strangely, the effect of calming her a little. There was more than loyalty here. She had felt from the first that Mr Ottery was to be trusted. If he was the gentleman's champion, then neither his person nor his character could be quite devilish.

She gave a tiny smile. 'He is fortunate in your friendship, I think.'

The lawyer looked taken aback. He said nothing for a
moment, looking her over in frowning silence. 'Miss
Charlton,' he said at last, 'you are a shrewd observer. Is
there anything else you have seen that I have not been at
pains to tell you?'

A little of Rosina's tension eased, and she gave a self-
conscious laugh. 'I might guess at some things.'

'Pray enlighten me.'

She bit her lip again, but the temptation to unburden
her mind of its puzzles was too strong. 'I think your client
is a man of means—or this fortune will make him so. Not
rich, perhaps, but comfortable enough.'

The lawyer smiled. 'Well reasoned, ma'am. Anything
else?'

'I imagine he has property, for a wife would only burden him if there was nowhere for her to live.'

'You are correct,' said Ottery. 'There is an estate in
Warwickshire, your own county.'

Rosina's spirits rose. Come, this was more encouraging.
At least she was eliciting some detail. Her own desperate
need urged her to probe further. If she could only know
enough of the gentlemen, perhaps she might be emboldened to think of—or hope for?—such a solution. She gave
him a speculative look.

'You have not mentioned the circumstances of his birth
beyond the fact of his gentility.' She paused, but Mr
Ottery had nothing to say. Rosina's fingers travelled unknowingly to her upper chest, as if to quiet the uneven
flutters there.

'I would guess that your client is titled,' she suggested,
'or there would be no need for this—charade. Nor, if his
degree was very high, would he marry by this means,
risking his name with the Lord only knows what obscure
family connection.'

The lawyer, Rosina saw, was beginning to look amused. She could not help smiling. 'You are surprised?'

'That fairly describes it, ma'am,' he returned, with a laugh. 'I have not met with this level of deduction in any other candidate.'

Rosina's eyes clouded. 'Perhaps they had none of them as insistent a need to glean the truth.' The reminder of her purpose here threw her into acute consciousness. Dear Lord, she was falling into it so easily! Abruptly, she rose. 'I think I have wasted enough of your time, Mr Ottery.'

The lawyer had stood, coming quickly around the desk. 'Pray don't go, Miss Charlton. I assure you, there is no cause either for alarm or distress. You are young, and perhaps you do not know that circumstances now and again so arrange themselves that a gentleman feels himself forced into taking a course of action that might be considered unusual, to say the least. But as to my client's reasons, they are intensely personal. I beg you to believe, however, that his proposition is both simple and honest. May I beg you to sit down again?'

So much understanding sounded in his voice that Rosina allowed herself to be persuaded. But as she re-seated herself, she was once again struck by that unaccountable feeling of being observed. Almost involuntarily, she cast another searching glance about the room. No, they were alone. It must be the lawyer's own regard that was making her nervous.

Or perhaps, she thought, catching sight over Mr Ottery's shoulder of the portrait, it was a trick of those charismatic painted eyes. She shivered and dragged her attention back to the matter at hand.

The lawyer was outlining the details of the gentleman's stipulations. 'My client proposes, upon my advice, that his wife should be passed off as a female to whom he has been betrothed by a long-standing arrangement made between the parents or guardians of both parties. The lady in the case will be supposed to have lived retired in the expectation of his addresses being paid in due course. It will therefore not be considered particularly odd, my client believes, should his wife continue to live in a quiet way upon his estates.'

Rosina frowned in painful concentration, trying to follow the thread of his discourse. It did not quite ring true. And it was a matter of acute importance in her own case.

'Forgive me, but why should his wife do so, if she is marrying the man of her expectations, whose social standing cannot be in question? Would she not rather suppose that the marriage would bring her into contact with the circle of his friends?'

'A just observation,' agreed the lawyer. 'But the case is that my client has been abroad for many years, and his acquaintance with such a circle is but slight. He has no desire to increase it, and will himself therefore be content to live in a similarly restricted manner.'

This was so exactly what Rosina herself wanted that anxiety rose up once more. She did not wish to become so deeply enmeshed in this affair that its attraction became great enough to tempt her. Only—a marriage of convenience, which would ensure a lifetime's security at the trifling cost of marrying a stranger, with the added advantage that she might live in the obscurity she craved—it would be difficult indeed to find anything to equal it. What in all conscience was there to be said against it, beyond her own deep-rooted dislike of selling herself for profit?

Oh, but there was one thing. Her heart sank. How could she have overlooked the one aspect of the matter that would, at a blow, render it impossible? An uneven beat started up in her pulses. She looked at Mr Ottery, and was obliged to swallow on a dry throat. Could she bring herself to speak of it? She must. It was unthinkable to continue ignorant of the answer.

'There is one thing…' Her voice died. She drew another painful breath and tried again. 'The gentleman must wish, I suppose, to be provided with—'

Dear Lord, she could not even say it! Even less could she look at the man across the desk. His eyes—worse, the hateful eyes of that horrid portrait!—must see clearly her confusion, for she felt heat rising in her cheeks.

The lawyer's voice came, devoid of all expression. 'Naturally, my client will wish to be provided with an heir.'

Rosina's breath sighed out. He had guessed it! Relieved of the necessity of speaking of the matter, she almost forgot her reason for asking it. Until Mr Ottery spoke again.

He coughed delicately. 'Such a matter will be arranged at the convenience of my client. There is to be no aspect of the marriage vow excluded in the agreement.'

What did that mean? Her eyes flew up, meeting the blandness of Mr Ottery's gaze. No doubt that she would be expected to obey—in all things! At the convenience of a stranger who was obliged to advertise for a wife? Oh, she could not! It was to escape one vile trap only to fall into another. She said nothing, forming mentally the resolve to leave this place at the termination of this horrid interview, and apply immediately instead for a post as housekeeper, which was all the occupation she felt fit to obtain.

'There is one further proviso,' said Mr Ottery, as coolly as ever. But his eyes watched her narrowly, Rosina thought. 'It will be impossible for my client's prospective wife to meet him prior to the wedding.'

On her return to Withibrooke, it had been this last that had formed the chief topic of discussion between Gatty and herself.

'Can it be that the gentleman's age is against him?' had wondered her nurse.

'It cannot be that, for Mr Ottery gave me to understand that he has a year or so yet to reach thirty. No, he must be deformed, or crippled,' Rosina had insisted. 'Perhaps he is a dwarf.'

'It does seem so, my dove, I must say. Mayhap the man has a horror of women. One of these fellows they call a molly.'

'Or he is merely ugly, or extremely fat.'

Whatever it was, they had been agreed that this reluctance to meet a female with whom he expected to spend his life must betoken some deficiency of person. Which meant, as Rosina had pointed out with a shudder, that the conjugal duties involved constituted a fate more undesirable than the one for which she had been intended.

'Nor,' had said Gatty worriedly, 'since I can't settle it in my mind that this housekeeper business will perfectly answer the purpose, can we yet be certain you have escaped it.'

A fact of which Rosina was only too well aware. But if this was the alternative—! Dear Lord, let her not be recommended to this unknown gentleman's attention.

'I have only to hope, Gatty, that Mr Ottery found me so probing that he will cross me off the list without a second's delay.'

Rosina had so convinced herself that her application must be unsuccessful, that an invitation to a second interview had thrown her into acute indecision. A vehicle was to be sent for her conveyance, which indicated to her old nurse's mind—if not to Rosina's—that her candidature had been approved.

A lurch in the road brought her out of her reverie. Startled to find herself in the coach, for the memories had been all too vivid, she glanced at the man beside her. Dear Lord! She really had gone through with it. Despite all her misgivings, she had thrown herself upon the mercy of this unknown man whom she must now call 'husband'.

The thought caused a tiny sound of distress to escape her lips, and Raith looked round. It was dim now in the chaise, but even in the half-light, he could see that the elfin face was pinched and strained, the dark eyes luminous. Concerned, he said the first thing that came into his head.

'I thought you were asleep.'

He heard her indrawn breath, and noted that her voice shook a trifle. 'No. I—I thought you were.'

There was silence for a space. Raith could not think what to say to ease her evident discomfort. Perhaps there was nothing to say. He fell back upon convention.

'We will be at Marton very soon.' He glanced out of the window again. 'Dusk will be upon us in a trice. It must be well past four.' His gaze came back to the piquant features. His voice dropped. 'Are you tired?'

The gentle note drew Rosina's tears at last. 'I believe I am still in shock,' she blurted out, and put her fingers to her eyes, pressing them there.

His voice came again, rougher, a species of pain within it. 'I should not have sprung the thing upon you. I know how repellent are my features.'

Chapter Two

Rosina was struck by the bitterness of his utterance. She had not been referring to his scar; the remembrance of it had not penetrated her roving thoughts. But it was in her mind now, all too vividly. How deeply he must feel it, to imagine that it was the one thing he must conceal at all costs. Equally, to suppose that it was the focal point of her distress. It loomed, evidently, all too large in his mind.

The desire to weep was receding, and she was conscious of sympathy. Her hand fell, and with deliberation she turned her head to look at him. Lord Raith was facing the window. She could see the outline of his hat, the queue of his brown hair, and the edge only of his chin, dark and indistinct in the gathering gloom.

Rosina realised that this was the first time she had given a thought to his feelings. Was it as hard a thing for him to be saddled with an unknown female for his wife? He had chosen it. But so had she—necessity having forced the decision upon her. It had not made it any easier. Why should Lord Raith feel it less acutely? Her words came without intent.

'How did you come by it?'

She heard the echo of her own voice with dismay. She

should not have asked so tactless a question. She thought
he stiffened, but he did not look at her. His head straightened and his profile stood out strong against the light from
the window. Rosina thought he was not going to answer.
When he did, she found that she had been holding her
breath.

'I have been soldiering these many years.'

Then he had been wounded in action. She did not like
to ask how he had received such a blow as this must have
been. But why such bitterness?

'My father was a soldier,' she said impulsively.

He turned to look at her, and Rosina kept her eyes on
his face. She could barely see the blemish now, in any
event. Without allowing him an opportunity to respond,
she quickly resumed what she wanted to say.

'Had he come home thus tarnished, neither Mama nor
I would have thought less of him, nor loved him the less.
We should not have cared how he looked—only that he
had come back.'

Her voice cracked on the last words, and she turned
from the intentness of his gaze. She had meant to offer
comfort. Not to remind herself of that difficult loss. She
strove for control.

'I did not know that you had lost your father to war,'
came from the man at her side. The tone was gentle, all
trace of bitterness vanished. 'I am sorry.'

'It was some years ago,' Rosina managed to say.
'Mama took it badly. She did not long survive him.'

'Which is why you find yourself in this unenviable situation,' he said drily. 'Life deals harsh blows.'

The bitter note was back, and Rosina turned again to
look at him. She found herself moved by an unaccountable desire to ease him, if she might. Too eager to question it, she broke instantly into speech.

'Lord Raith, forgive me, but you do yourself too much

injury! This is your battle scar. It is an honourable wound. You should wear it with pride.'

A harsh laugh escaped him. 'Indeed?'

Even in the dim interior of the carriage, Rosina saw his eyes glitter strangely. Danger emanated from him, and she drew back into her corner of the chaise.

'And if the wound is dishonourable? Should I not then wear it with shame?' His tone was low but rancorous. 'You know not of what you speak, therefore don't speak of it at all!'

It was a moment or two before Raith regained control. When he did, he was equally distressed by his own outburst, and the effect of it on the blameless girl beside him. She had not spoken again. He dared to look at her, and his spirits dropped the more to find her not sunk into her corner, as he had half-expected, but sitting bolt upright on the edge of the seat, one hand grasping tightly the looped handle at the side of the chaise. Her head was firmly turned away, but the stiff outrage of her shoulders was sufficient reproach.

'That was unforgivable,' he uttered raggedly. 'I beg your pardon.'

The silhouette of her features were turned towards him, but he could not see her expression. He was unprepared for what she said.

'For better or for worse, my lord.'

Then she sank back against the cushions, and did not look at him again.

Raith cursed inwardly. He had made a mull of it. He would have to school himself to better control, if he was not to alienate her altogether. What had she done, after all? Tried to mitigate the virulence of his own response to the welt across his face. He had drawn it on himself, leading her to suppose that he had received the wound in battle. Better that than the humiliating truth! Only the deception rankled. Why quibble, Anton Raith? It was as much a lie as leading her to believe that he had no interest in seeing her, when he had done so from the first. His choice had been almost instantaneous!

Since he must adopt this method, even Ottery had believed that he had chosen well. Despite the fact that his lawyer—his truest friend!—had disapproved of the entire proceeding.

'God only knows, my lord, what sort of dreadful female you may attract by such an advertisement!'

'Which is why I am relying on you, my friend, to weed out the graspers and whores,' he had replied frankly. 'She must be genteel, I grant you that.'

'Genteel!' Ottery had scoffed. 'I dare say we may count ourselves fortunate not to be besieged by an army of maiden aunts and governesses.'

His guess had not been far off, Raith reflected. The majority of some fifty replies had been from ladies old enough to have mothered him, a number of whom were already engaged in employment. Others were poor dependents, eager for release. Of all the applicants, there had been only six or seven whom Ottery had deemed worthy of interview. They had all been sad women, Raith thought, and more than one might have done for his purposes—if Rosina Charlton had not applied.

Even her letter had been different from the others. Without exception, all the rest had dwelled upon what they conceived to be their own attractions. Catalogues of beauty had battered at his eyes as he had sifted through the sheaf of applications handed to him by Ottery.

'"Item: two lips, indifferent red,"' Raith had quoted, laughing, as he came upon yet another effusion.

Ottery had smiled, but had then picked up one letter set aside from the rest. 'This one, my lord, has nothing to say of her own appearance.'

Raith had run his eyes down the sheet. It was obviously penned with care, the characters looping gracefully. There was no embellishment, no embroidery to a simply stated list of facts. She was an orphan, obliged to earn her living, and had been seeking for some few weeks a position suitable to a female of gentility. She gave her age as two and twenty, and added the names of her parents to her own. The only indication to her character came in the final sentences. She had no wish, she said, to intrude upon society, and would be content to be earning her board by the bargain.

She had offered no references, unlike most of the others, who listed in the main names of title or repute. In a word, she had given nothing away—a reticence that had its own attraction. Which was why Ottery had been surprised that he wished to see her.

'My dear sir, there is no recommendation whatsoever, beyond her age.'

'That is precisely my reason,' Raith had insisted. 'She is a mystery, and therefore the more tempting.'

Ottery had been sceptical, but he had admitted, after that first interview, that he was drawn to Miss Charlton. Raith had been lured by his first sight of her, despite the intervening gauze screen of the central portion of Ottery's convenient portrait. It was cleverly designed, for one saw as if through a veil, yet from the other side the deception was undetectable. Ottery believed it had been used for darker purposes in former times during the years of the Civil War, for it had come down in his family through generations. Raith had been glad of its provision of his anonymous presence—else he would not have chanced upon Rosina Charlton!

He had instructed Ottery to check her credentials after that first occasion. The lawyer had located records of the Charlton family, of which one member's name tallied with that of Rosina's father. There were living members, and he supposed there must be reasons why Miss Charlton did not sue to them for help. He was the last man to question that. But her mother's family proved for the moment untraceable.

Rosina had been evasive on the subject at her second interview, saying that her mother had been an only child of genteel, but insignificant, parentage.

'And when she died?' Ottery had asked.

There had been hesitation. That vulnerable look had come into the black eyes. Raith had seen, with a lurch at his chest, the quiver of her lips.

'I was fifteen. I had…guardians.' Again she had looked away, moistened her lips. Then she had brought her gaze directly to bear on his lawyer. 'They—died.'

Raith had been convinced that she had fabricated that last. But he had refused to let himself be troubled by it, for he had already instructed Ottery to make the offer.

'Let us see how she reacts. We can always reject her.'

Not that he'd had any intention of doing so! It would have taken much to push him to it. He had thought the better of her for not jumping at the opportunity.

She had fidgeted in some degree of nervousness, he recalled, looking about rather wildly. Almost as if she sensed his presence! Ottery had been patient—more so than he would have been himself, had he been sitting at the desk.

'Take your time, Miss Charlton.'

The black eyes had darted to his face. She had seemed to gather herself. 'I cannot agree to it—until I have at least had a sight of him.'

Ottery had hesitated. Raith had shrunk away from the portrait, moving into the little room behind his lawyer's office. He heard Ottery excuse himself, and was not surprised to see him come through the intervening door.

'What do you wish, my lord?'

Raith had striven within himself. His ingrained instinct of hermitage battled with a dawning respect. In her place, would he not have held out for the same? How could he blame her, when he had himself made certain that he did not wed where he had not examined the wares? Yet if it would make her retract! He had faced the lawyer squarely.

'I cannot afford to let her go, Ottery. I must agree.'

But not the whole! That had been far too risky. He had been aware of his own urgency, delivered in a low tone so as not to reach through into the next room.

'Let her see me from a distance. Go. Ask if that will content her. If she is in agreement, we will arrange it at Brinklow. After—I rely on you to secure her consent.'

He had posted himself once more behind the portrait, deeply anxious. It had been evident that Rosina Charlton resented the recognition that Raith had been in the next room all along. She had said little, but her manner was enough.

'Can one hear through that wall?' she had asked, a flash of something like defiance in the black eyes.

Raith could only be thankful that she had not known how closely she had been both heard and observed. Ottery had ignored the question, instead putting the proposition Raith had outlined. To his relief, she had agreed. But not without further reference to his proximity.

'It would be simpler, would it not, if the gentleman would only walk through that door?'

Ottery had smiled, he remembered, but had not answered. The girl had become agitated.

'Does he not wish at least to see me, Mr Ottery?'

'It is immaterial to my client what you look like, Miss Charlton.'

A response which now made him writhe at the memory. He had deceived her at every turn! Even more, because of his conviction that a mystery attended the female who had today become his wife. Had he selected any other of the candidates, he might have revealed himself, for he would have taken an oath that his disfigurement would not have deterred them. Their intention had been plain: to better themselves and their position in life, at any cost. But Rosina? No, she was far too intelligent, too shrewd. She had taken this step to secure some other goal. But what?

She had given nothing away. And Raith had not dared to risk her disgust. He had ensured that she could not see him full-face, for fear that she would refuse the contract, which would have been unendurable! He was forced at last to realise the truth. Once Rosina Charlton had entered the lists, he had wanted no other wife.

The private parlour Lord Raith had hired at the Bell was comfortingly ill-lit. A glow fell from two wall-sconces either side of the room, but neither reached the table where the new-married pair were dining. By the light of the single candle placed in its centre, Rosina saw only the gleam of her spouse's face rather than its features. The stresses of the day had so exhausted her, that she welcomed the relief from a too intimate tête-à-tête.

She had been relieved, on arrival at the inn, to discover that His Lordship had arranged for her accommodation in a separate bedchamber to his own. The intimation that he did not intend to insist upon his rights this first night did much to ease the strain of being obliged to dine with him. She had been a trifle apprehensive—after the acerbic exchange in the chaise!—but Lord Raith had thus far behaved impeccably.

At his suggestion, neither of them had changed. Rosina was grateful, wondering if he had done it out of deference to her undoubtedly meagre wardrobe. She had noted his

own fresh cravat, and being at last sufficiently composed
to be able to take in his appearance, had been relieved to
find him not at all fashionable in his dress. His coat and
breeches were of a blue so dark as to be almost black, the
sobriety relieved only by a cream waistcoat of brocaded
silk. Were it not for the facial defect, he must be counted
not ill-favoured.

Once the covers were removed, and dishes both of fruit
and sweetmeats placed upon the table, Raith had, to his
bride's consternation, told the landlord that he did not
wish to be disturbed again until he rang the bell.

Rosina's breath caught in her throat as he looked across
at her. But his first words were not at all alarming.

'Have you eaten sufficient?'

'I thank you, sir, yes.'

Rosina had in fact made a good meal, for she had found
herself to be hungry. She had begun with a little difficulty
upon a steaming bowl of pease pottage. But at the first
remove, her appetite had quickened, and she had managed
to consume a portion of pigeon pie, together with stewed
mushrooms and pickled French beans. A white fricassee
of chicken had followed, of which Rosina had taken but
a mouthful, only to obviate the need for persuasion from
across the table. But she had rejected a Bath pudding,
opting instead to partake of a little fruit.

Lord Raith, she noticed, had been almost as sparing,
instead refreshing himself liberally from a bottle of claret
that was provided along with the food. Rosina had taken
only water, but now her husband reached out to the wineglass that stood to one side of her place, and filled it half-
full of the red liquid.

He laid it down in front of her. 'It is appropriate, do
you not think, to drink to our nuptials?'

Rosina did not think so at all, but she was chary of
saying so. Lifting the glass, she sipped a little of the wine.

Raith followed suit, watching her. She looked, he thought, a trifle more relaxed, if a little wary. He was glad, for he felt impelled to make amends for his earlier lapse.

'It is early days, I know,' he said carefully, 'but we may as well go over our expectations for the future.'

Rosina gazed at him blankly. *Our* expectations? Dear Lord, was she supposed to have any? He must be referring to his own. To show willing must be her first concern.

'I will be glad to know what you require of me.'

'Let me rather ask first what you expect,' he countered.

She was goaded into instant response. 'Why, nothing, sir.'

For the first time, Lord Raith smiled. Oddly, the scar changed with the smile. He looked far less sinister, Rosina thought. Unless it was due to the poor light?

'Come,' he said gently, 'that is quite unreasonable. You must have some thoughts of what you would wish your life to be. More now than ever, I would suppose.'

But Rosina was not fully attending. The word she had thought of echoed in her head. Sinister. Was it appropriate? Yes, it had been so, the first moment that she saw him. But not now. Not when he was gentle, when he smiled.

He was eyeing her, and she suddenly realised that he had been speaking. What had he said?

'I beg your pardon, sir. I was distracted for the moment. What did you ask me?'

The smile faded, as did the cordiality of his voice. 'You must have expectations, ma'am. I would be glad to hear them.'

Rosina sighed. If he was going to be this difficult, any expectations she might have had were vain! It was as well that she had none.

'I gave up all thought of deciding my own future a long

time ago. I would rather you tell me what you wish, so that I might school my conduct accordingly.'

'How dutiful!'

'Is that not what you wanted?'

'I don't know what I wanted!'

Raith controlled himself with difficulty. This would not do. He was only driving her further away. But before he could say anything less abrasive, she forestalled him.

'My lord, I am grateful for your protection.'

Raith caught at the word. 'Protection?'

He thought the dark eyes flickered, but he could not be sure in the uncertain light.

'I—I meant only to s-say,' Rosina faltered hastily, 'that—that I am happy to be given this much improvement in my life. I only wish to keep my side of our agreement.'

Raith had not missed the flurried cover-up. Protection was exactly what she had meant. His suspicions were aroused again. Protection from what? Or was it, from whom? Better to pretend not to have noticed it. At least she was talking!

'Pray tell me what I must do,' she said. 'I know you have made precise plans for this marriage. It is, after all, for your convenience.'

She was right. He'd had very precise ideas about how he was to live with the mythical wife of his imagination. She would, he had supposed, keep the household running smoothly, be at his call when nature so demanded, and in due time bear his children. He had seen them lead all-but-separate lives while existing side by side. But that was before this girl entered his ken. The prospect appeared to him bleak beyond words, now that he was married to Rosina Charlton.

Impossible to state anything of what was in his mind!

She was waiting for a response. He smiled again, unconsciously.

'We will have to work it out as we go along, Rosina.'

Rosina's attention caught on his use of her name, coupled with the smile. Her breath tightened. He really did look quite different. Only what had he said? Was she to have no guidelines? Must she tread blindly? And with a man so prickly that every utterance could make him withdraw into his shell.

'What are you thinking?' Raith asked softly.

She looked quickly away from him. 'I had hoped that I might have an indication—some hint of how I should go on. I do not want to draw your fire…' She faded out. What had possessed her to say that? Now he would grow cold again.

But Raith was shamed. She was right. He had shown himself disgracefully apt to snap—and on her wedding day. He looked her over while her gaze was averted. She had removed the cap, leaving her head so dark in the dim glow of the room that the white elfin countenance looked still more vulnerable. He had noted the old-fashioned gown. It had made her look the more delicate, drawn in to her small waist. Something would have to be done about her wardrobe. She must be possessed of little suited to her new station. Not that she needed anything to enhance her allure, he reflected.

Becoming aware of his regard, Rosina glanced back at him, and met his eyes. There was that in them which she barely understood. But the message spoke to her depths, and the image of her bedchamber came to her, shortening her breath. He had ordered separate rooms. But what if he chose to enter hers tonight? She would have to receive him! Only she had rather they had been better acquainted first. The notion of being bedded by a total stranger was almost as nightmarish as the fate she had previously faced.

Curiously, she did not feel him so much a stranger still, though she had known him less than a day. But she could hardly feel sufficiently acquainted with him to be indulging in that particular intimacy.

Raith noted the changes of expression that flitted across her face, and wondered at what caused them. She was afraid of him, he thought. Small wonder!

'You have no reason to fear me,' he said quickly.

'I don't!' she returned, but much too pat.

'You need not dissemble. I can see it in your face.'

Rosina looked down, and then away, as if she would hide her features from his too-penetrating gaze. 'If—if I am a trifle apprehensive, it is not to be wondered at.'

'I agree with you,' he returned unexpectedly. 'It is a situation any young woman would find intimidating. The more so—under the circumstances.'

What circumstances? Was he again referring to the blemish of his looks? She was tempted to mention it, to say that it was not that which held any terror for her.

'You are doing it again,' he accused.

Rosina frowned. 'Doing what?'

'You look as if you will ask me something, and then— through apprehension, I must suppose—you withhold it. Be plain with me, Rosina. I am not a monster!'

'Then why,' she asked, goaded, 'did you think so badly of yourself to wish to become riveted only to a stranger?'

'Because I could rather bear the cringing revulsion of a stranger, than that of some society damsel!' he flashed back before he could stop himself.

Rosina threw her hands over her face, her breath unsteady. Her eyes closed, and she shook her head against the hurt. He was impossible!

'Forgive me!' he uttered hoarsely. 'I did not mean to throw that at you.'

Her hands dropped, and she regarded him hopelessly. 'I did not cringe, Raith. I was only shocked to see it.'

It warmed him that she had dropped the title, if only because he had driven her too far. 'I know. I beg your pardon.' He gave an unconvincing laugh. 'Ottery will have it that I am over-sensitive. Perhaps he is right.'

Rosina bit her lip, and gave him a direct look. 'No, you were right earlier. It is better if we do not speak of it.'

She meant that his sensitivity made him too difficult to discourse with on the subject, but she was unsurprised— even after this little acquaintance—to see him retire again behind his wall of bitterness. She felt too tired to deal with it.

But Raith had been aware of his own stiffening. He made a deliberate effort to pull back. She had meant nothing untoward. He must not take needless offence. He recalled her question, and amended his answer.

'The truth is, I think, that most society damsels would be affronted if I were to offer for the reasons I have given. And what is worse, they would expect me to alter my whole way of life to suit them.'

'I am hardly in a position to do that,' Rosina conceded, adding darkly, 'and the last thing I wish for is to flaunt myself in society.' To encounter that man? No, Lord help her!

Raith was again struck by a queer intensity in her response. She had a particular reason for that remark, he was sure of it. Dared he probe?

'Why so?'

Rosina shifted in her seat, and took up her wineglass, not looking at him. 'I am not equipped for it, my lord.'

'In what way?'

She sipped at the wine to gain time. What could she say? How she wished now that he might have remained withdrawn! She dreaded such questions almost as much as he dreaded any mention of his lacerated cheek.

'I have been out of the expectation of anything of the kind for many years,' she said, prevaricating. 'I should not know how to go on.'

To her relief, he did not pursue the subject. A silence fell. To Rosina, it was more difficult than conversation with him had proved. She glanced at the timepiece on the mantelshelf, its dial lit by the glow from candles in the near wall-sconce. It was growing late. She could not avoid the dread question of the coming night for much longer. She sought for a neutral subject, anything bar what was in her mind.

'Is—is your home a large place?'

It was, she thought, innocuous enough. But it appeared that the sensitivity of Lord Raith extended even to this.

'It is vast,' he said flatly, and there was an edge of bitterness in his tone, 'but I dare say you may find the situation there less attractive than you anticipate. I think I will let it speak for itself.'

Which left Rosina in greater mystery than before. She had not had any particular desire to know about his home. To her it had signified nothing more than a haven up to this moment. But his attitude, together with the faintly derisive note in his voice, gave rise to the liveliest apprehensions.

It was all too much for one day. She wanted very much to leave him, but the consciousness of his right to enter her bedchamber at any time he chose kept her glued to her seat. She toyed with the wineglass, fidgeting.

Raith saw it with a growing sense of disappointment. Yes, she might disclaim her fears, but he was no fool. What had he expected? Let him at least try to keep his unamiable tongue in check. He tried for a soft approach.

'You must be tired. Why do you not retire?'

He noted the faint colour that rose to her cheek. Hell and damnation! What in thunder did she suppose he was going to do? Did she truly believe him such a monster? Hurt rose up, and he could not help himself. A mocking laugh escaped him.

'Don't look so dismayed! I will not inflict myself on you tonight. You may go to bed with a quiet mind.'

Rosina got hastily to her feet, tears stinging her eyelids. He rose also, but she barely noticed.

'Good night,' she said huskily, and made rapidly for the door. She had almost reached it when his voice checked her.

'Rosina!'

She halted, biting her lip, but she did not look round. She heard rapid footsteps behind her. Then his hand was on her shoulder, and she had perforce to turn.

The candlelight was stronger near the door, and Raith could see the wetness under the coal-black eyes. His chest caved in. He groped for her hand, and brought it to his lips, kissing it lightly.

'I've made you weep. A bride should not weep on her wedding day.' A slight smile curved his mouth. 'Save it for tomorrow. I have no doubt I'll give you cause.'

The rueful tone warmed her. She thought he was for once unconscious of his disfigurement, for she could see the scar clearly in the brighter light, and it did not dismay her. It struck her that with the smile some might even think it attractive. So strange a thought! She smiled back at him.

'Sleep well, my lord.'

'And you,' he answered, and released her.

For a moment or two he looked despondently at the closed door. Then he returned to the table, and once more took up the bottle of claret.

* * *

It had rained again in the night, and the roads were soggy. The journey was necessarily slow. It seemed slower to Rosina, for the heavy fact of her husband's relapse into taciturnity. She was not much refreshed, for she had slept little, her mind full of unquiet prospects of the future and beset also by a tiny fear that Lord Raith would change his mind, after all, and visit her bedchamber.

She had heard, she thought, his footsteps on the stairs, for they had passed her door. Rosina knew his chamber was adjacent, and a latch had clicked somewhere behind her head. She did not know what time that had been, except that it must have been very late. That her lord was asleep now in the coach seemed to bear out the conjecture.

At breakfast, he had been civil, but reserved. Rosina, in whom the night's cogitations had engendered no small degree of curiosity about her spouse, was conscious of disappointment. Small hope of getting to know him if he was bent upon retiring into his shell in this disagreeable fashion. The prospect of long years of increased loneliness stretched ahead of her.

Not that she had ever known anything else. These few short weeks with Gatty had been all the heaven that she had known since her mama's demise—and even these had been clouded by the ever-present fear of discovery. She must suppose that her hateful guardian could not imagine that she had taken refuge relatively near at hand. Or else he was never sober enough to work the matter out!

If only Cousin Louise had not died. She had been a faded and sickly creature—and no wonder, married to a drunken sot whose gambling must have fairly ruined her life!—but her presence had afforded protection. And her advice had been sound, if singularly undutiful.

'Keep out of his way, my dear. Say nothing to draw attention to yourself. Take your cue from my example, Rosy. I see him as little as possible, and if I am obliged to be near him, I never give him cause to notice my presence. It answers very well.'

Since Louise Cambois spent most of her days in her bed, Rosina was not much surprised that she was able to evade her husband's attention. She had herself chosen to avoid him by taking on the duties of housekeeper, which her mother's cousin was happy to relinquish. Her efforts had met with success for close on seven years. She had been one and twenty when Louise had faded away completely one day. Astonishingly, Herbert Cambois had been distraught at the death of his wife. Rosina had been moved to attempt to console him. A fatal mistake. For it had brought to his notice that he had in his charge a young girl of—in his own words, Rosina remembered, wincing—'no mean worth in the marketplace.'

She had not understood at first what he meant. For a short time, she had supposed that he was referring to finding her a husband. An unexpected and not unwelcome prospect—anything was better than to continue in his house! By the time she had realised her error, her guardian had already enmeshed her in his foully cruel design.

Shuddering, Rosina came out of her thoughts as the chaise halted. She started up, and looked from the window. An inn sign swayed in the wind.

'Ladbroke,' said Lord Raith's voice beside her.

Rosina turned quickly. He was lying back against the squabs, but his eyes were open.

'Are we stopping here?'

'Briefly. We turn off the Banbury Road beyond this village. I imagine Parton is checking whether the horses are in need of rest. You may get down if you wish.'

'I thank you, my lord, but I am comfortable enough.'

He said nothing more, and Rosina sank back into her seat, consciousness returning, for she was aware that his eyes were upon her. It was hard indeed to behave nor-

mally in any respect in his presence, now that she knew
he was awake. Recalling her late remembrance of what
she had left behind, she wondered if indeed she was any
better off with Anton, Lord Raith.

A tap came at Raith's window. He turned his head and
saw Parton signalling. He let down the glass.

'They'll do for a few miles yet, me lord. Catterline and
me reckon to go on to Itchington Bishops and bait them
there before we tackle the Heath.'

'Very well, Parton. Do as you see fit.'

'Likely Her Ladyship will be in need of a bite by then,
an' all, me lord.'

Raith agreed to this and shut the window. In a moment,
the chaise was on the move. He turned his head to look
at his bride again. What thoughts had they been that so
disturbed her? She had been lost in abstraction, staring at
the bobbing backs of the horses through the window in
front—though he could swear she did not see them!—
seemingly unaware of the fidgety movements of her
gloved hands, flicking incessantly at her fingers' ends.

They were quiescent now, tightly clasped in her lap,
her head downcast. But that was because she knew that
he was observing her. The thought caused a wave of unrest that was already becoming familiar. Such an unsettling effect as she had upon him! He eyed the neat profile,
with its wisps of black escaping from the close cap. Did
she always wear that thing? Raith saw, with satisfaction,
that she had left her hair loose beneath it, so that one long
waving tress hung down the centre of her back. So black
against the grey of her gown where her cloak had slipped
away behind. He was tempted to reach out and touch it,
stroke it, curling it about his hand.

A shaft of heat shot through him, and he shifted
abruptly, turning away. Enough! He must crush all such
thoughts. It was too soon to be pressing her to that duty.

She had expected him to be demanding it of her last night, by thunder! He trusted he was enough of a gentleman to curb himself until she'd had a little time to adjust. He closed his eyes, intending once more to feign slumber. He had proved his hasty temper too unpredictable in conversation with her to risk indulging his fervent wish to engage her attention.

But Rosina had other ideas. She had not bargained for it, but she found herself yearning for companionship. To be travelling with a man to whom she was now tied for the rest of her life, and to behave as if they were each alone in the chaise, seemed to her absurd. If Lord Raith would not make an effort to establish cordial relations, then she must. It would not be easy, for he was so very unapproachable—not to say touchy! But the prospect of the years stretching ahead of her, in genteel isolation, were too lonely to be contemplated.

She cast about in her mind for a safe topic that she might introduce. Rejecting as dangerous the notion of asking him whether he had seen much action—or indeed anything about his soldiering life—Rosina settled for a question about Mr Ottery as being the least potentially harmful.

'My lord?' she began.

He opened his eyes. 'My lady?'

'Oh, that sounds so odd!' Rosina said impulsively, on a breathless laugh. She turned and found his eyes upon her, in mute question. 'Of all wild possibilities, I never dreamt of hearing myself thus styled.'

Raith's features relaxed a little. 'That I can appreciate. It is still new to me also.'

'You have only recently inherited?' asked Rosina, her curiosity aroused.

'It was wholly unexpected.'

She waited, but he volunteered no more, looking away

from her again. Dear Lord, but it was uphill work with him! She would have to use the ploy she had already thought of.

'You have known Mr Ottery for some while, I gather? He seems a very good sort of a man.'

Raith knew not how to reply. What sort of a question was that? Did she wish to know, or was she merely trying to engage him in conversation? He glanced round at her, and found the dark eyes trained upon him. Was there a trifle of wistfulness in their depths? Whatever it might be, its effect was to cause him to answer automatically, though little conscious of what he said, for her countenance took up all his attention.

'He is an excellent fellow. I hold him in very high esteem. Indeed, I know not what I should have done without him—on occasion.'

The memory his words evoked jerked him into consciousness. He looked quickly away. No—he must not. Anything but that. He did not want to provoke himself into again losing control in her presence. Hell and damnation! She was trying. The least he could do was to follow suit.

'How have you been living?' he asked at random. And then thought it might be taken wrong. 'Ottery said you were with your—nurse, was it?'

'She had been my nurse,' Rosina confirmed. 'Only when—when Mama died, and I was obliged to...' She faded out, realising where her words were tending. That would not do. She would be bound to evoke questions about just that part of her life that she wanted to keep secret.

'Obliged to?'

Dear Lord, must he hold her to it? Necessity brought inspiration. 'Obliged to leave Gatty—my nurse. She was going blind, you see.'

There could be no harm in revealing that much. No need to state how Herbert Cambois had refused to have the elderly dame in his household, believing poor Gatty to be useless at her work. Which she was, poor lamb, but through no fault of her own. Rosina had begged in vain, appealing to her cousin. She had not known at that time how little influence had Louise.

'Fortunately, Mama had provided her with some little means. Not a pension, but small savings that she had acquired over many years of service. She was Mama's nurse before me, and she came with her as maid upon her marriage. I believe it was Papa who insisted upon it, for he knew that Mama would be often alone.'

'She did not follow the drum, then?' Raith asked, finding himself eager even for this scrap of her history.

'She could not, for she had a weak chest, and Papa would not permit her to endure the rigours of campaigning.' Rosina had become lost in her own tale, almost forgetting to whom she spoke. 'Mama knew her own frailty, and with the dangers attendant upon my father's profession, she saw to it that my guardianship was assured.'

'Who was your guardian?'

Rosina started, gazing wildly round at him. She might have known she would make a slip! Her breath caught, and she wished fervently that she had not so foolishly begun on this course. Why could she not have left him to his close-tongued reserve? But she was giving herself away every second that she refrained from answering.

'My—my mother's cousin. At least—not her, but her husband.' She did not dare look at him for fear that her disgust and hatred would show in her face. 'When I went to him, Gatty bought a little cottage. I took refuge—' stopping with a gasp, and hastily correcting herself '—I mean, I went to her there...after his death.'

She fell silent, and Raith eyed her profile with a good

deal of misgiving. Had he not suspected all along the apparent commonplace of her story? What in thunder had occurred? The guardian must be the key. That he was dead, Raith highly doubted. *Refuge,* she had said. One did not take refuge from a dead man! The suspicion filtered into his mind that he had taken to wife a runaway.

Rosina could have cursed herself for inadvertently letting out so much. That was what came of making conversation! She resolved not to do so in future. But it appeared that she had aroused the curiosity of her husband.

'Why did you not go to your father's family?'

A shadow crossed her face. 'The Charltons did not approve the marriage, for they considered Mama to be beneath them.'

'Surely they would not visit his mistake upon you?' objected Raith.

'My mother's cousin did not think so either,' Rosina said drily. 'I did write, at her instigation, when I was eighteen. I received no reply.'

'It would seem that you have been unfortunate in your relatives. Was your guardian at least good to you?'

Rosina's pulses jangled. Dear Lord, how could she answer him? To say anything at all would be to invite further question, yet more probing. How could she extract herself? One thing she decided: if Lord Raith chose to be inaccessible in future, she would not attempt to lure him out.

She avoided the question. 'His wife was a friend to me.' Then she yawned ostentatiously. 'I beg your pardon, my lord, but I am still a trifle tired. You will not mind if I sleep?'

'Not at all,' Raith returned politely.

As little as he believed in his own pretence did he believe in this. She had betrayed too much, and now she was withdrawing. If he had hoped to catch her out, he had been cleverly deflected. She was determined to be secretive. He foresaw a string of stilted interchanges between them.

When they stopped at Itchington Bishops a short while later—he was as little fooled by Rosina's artless awakening as he had been by her pretence of sleep!—he was disheartened to discover that he had been right. The consciousness of distance gnawed at him all through the simple luncheon at the Hart and Hounds. His wife made play with a selection of patties and fruit, which conveniently prevented her from engaging in anything but the most desultory remarks.

The weather was inclement enough to provide food for some of them, the state of the roads and the distance still to be covered offered the rest. Raith found himself irritated beyond words, although he initiated no subject himself.

On the whole, he was glad that his lady chose to pretend sleep for much of the remainder of the journey. Had they attempted to talk, he knew he must have been provoked into ill-temper. He could see nothing for it but to keep well out of her way.

Rosina had reached much the same conclusion. It had not been easy to remain aloof. Were it not for her dread of giving anything more away, she might have burst out a number of times. It seemed to her that, under the calm exterior, Lord Raith smouldered. She could feel it emanating from him, like a black fog. It was almost as if the bitterness exposed in him last night was now directed at her.

She was nettled the most by the deliberate manner of his choosing always to place himself to her right, that she might see as little as possible of his rent face. He did so when he escorted her into the inn, and again when he took a seat at the table. Had he not gone to elaborate lengths to hide the thing from her, Rosina was convinced that she would not have given it a thought. The initial shock over, she was growing as readily used to it as one did to any new countenance. Several times she was obliged to bite her tongue on a protest. It would be better, she decided, if they were not too often together. She could only hope that her new abode would prove large enough to allow her to avoid him.

It was dusk by the time her husband told her that they were turning into the gates of his home. But there was still light enough for Rosina to see that her hope was not misplaced.

Raith Manor was a huge grey mansion, standing four-square to the long, open approach. It had an air of total isolation. Shuttered windows, bare grainy walls, discoloured in places. A huge arched frontage stood out from the central section that was slightly inset to the square bays at either side. Black wooden double doors opened directly on to a stone-flagged porch almost level with the ground. To either side was a mass of lumped trees, like a hungry forest, bushy even in their sparse winter garments, stretching away into distant acres.

Bleakest of all, where green lawns should have been, lay a sodden sea of black that gave off an acrid stench. Gazing in growing dismay from the chaise window, Rosina perceived that the whole area was covered in ash.

Chapter Three

'I must apologise for the state of the place,' said Raith, as the chaise came to a stop before the entrance doors. 'I hope soon to remedy some, at least, of its ills, now that you have enabled me to obtain control of my fortune.'

Rosina could find nothing to say in answer to this. The chaise door was opened and the steps let down. An elderly male servant was waiting to hand her out.

'M'lady,' he said, bowing.

The oddity of being thus addressed upon her arrival was swallowed up by the realisation that the servants had gathered on the porch. She climbed down from the chaise, staring in perturbation at the little knot of persons in uniform. What was she supposed to say to them all?

'I am Kirkham, the butler, m'lady.'

'How do you do?' she murmured, glancing back almost instinctively to Lord Raith, as if seeking guidance. He had jumped down, and came forward to offer his arm.

'This will not take long,' he said quietly, and to the butler, 'Good evening, Kirkham. Be so good as to make the introductions, if you please.'

Rosina felt like a fraud as she was drawn to the porch and presented to a gaunt, harassed-looking female in black, who turned out to be the housekeeper. There were two footmen, three maids and a cook, besides a few others of evidently too menial a station to be given more than a wave of the hand, together with the cryptic addendum that they were from 'below stairs'. Rosina's mind became fully taken up with the impossible idea that this gallant little band comprised the entire domestic staff. How could so few possibly manage to care for a house this size? She knew enough of housekeeping to be appalled at the amount of work they must each accomplish.

Within minutes, she had entered a draughty hall, and the domestics had dispersed, with the exception of Mrs Fawley, who was detailed to show her to her personal quarters, while Lord Raith went off with the butler.

Rosina did not know whether to be glad or sorry to have been deprived of his support. But as she followed the housekeeper through the hall into a central lobby, and began to mount the stairs there to the upper floors, she could only be thankful that her husband was not there. She doubted whether she could have disguised the crushing despair that gripped her.

The place was so empty! It was clean enough, but austere. She caught glimpses through doors of draped huddles—of furniture? The walls were painted rather than papered, in muted tones. And from the few framed pictures hanging from them stared disapproving ancients from classical myth.

In the bedchamber to which she was led, however, an effort had been made to create a homely atmosphere. There was a fire in the grate; a vase of greenery dotted with a tiny collection of flowers had been placed upon a wide bulky table set in the window embrasure which fronted the dead lawns; and a painting depicting a lady on horseback in a charming landscape had been placed upon one of the walls.

'The master chose this one to be put in here, m'lady,' offered Mrs Fawley, coming to stand behind her as she examined the painting. 'It's His Lordship's mother on the horse.'

Rosina looked at the female with new interest. But the features were too indistinct in the gathering darkness for her to be able to make out any resemblance. She was intrigued by the thought of Lord Raith having made this choice, however, and resolved to look at it more closely in daylight.

She turned back into the room, and felt her spirits drop. No amount of prettifying could serve to alter its depressing solidity. The walls were drab, the bed hefty and old-fashioned, with a high ornate tester and thick turned posts, its blue velvet curtains heavy and dark, matching the drapes at the windows.

The housekeeper moved to an inner door by the outer wall. 'Your Ladyship's dressing-room is through here.'

Dressing-room? She went through the door indicated and found a room only a little smaller in size to the bed-chamber. Here was a dressing-table and stool, a long pier-glass, and a washstand. Two large presses stood at one side, along with a chest of drawers, a small armoire and a chest.

Rosina stared about her, fascinated. What would she do with such a place? Who could have sufficient clothes to fill all these receptacles? Not she, certainly. Her entire stock would fit into less than half the armoire and a single drawer!

'And through here,' the housekeeper said, crossing this room to a further door on the other side, 'is the antechamber adjoining His Lordship's similar apartments.'

A sick feeling settled in Rosina's stomach. Why had she not anticipated as much? With unwilling feet, she moved slowly to follow Mrs Fawley. The antechamber

was a small no man's land, placed directly over the front
door of the mansion, where a large window let in light.
It contained a fireplace, with two plain chairs either side,
a little table against the wall.

Rosina stared at the door that opposed her own. It was
mercifully closed, but she could readily picture the rooms
beyond. Rooms that at night contained her husband.

She moved to the fireplace and stared down into the
empty grate. For what purpose was this used? To make
assignations, perhaps? The cynical thought was pushed
away. Lord Raith needed no assignation. Four doors only
separated him from taking up his marital rights at any time
he chose. Of what use to think of it? She had agreed to
this of her own free will, and there was nothing she could
do about it.

'Will there be anything further, m'lady?'

She turned quickly, and forced a smile. 'No, I thank
you, Mrs Fawley.'

The housekeeper curtsied, and withdrew through
Rosina's own apartments. She stared after the woman,
feeling acutely assailable and unprotected. Not that she
could imagine how Mrs Fawley might save her from
nightly raids!

Rosina fought down her discomfort. She must not think
like this! Only…how else was she to think of it? The
whole dread notion had loomed hideously into view
again—the worse for the situation of these carefully convenient arrangements. Rosina felt more distanced than if
she had been presented with the *fait accompli* of having
to share her spouse's bed from the outset. It had been the
way Mama and Papa had lived. And Cousin Louise had
only taken a different bedchamber to her husband's out
of choice.

But she was no longer Rosina Charlton, of no account.
She was Lady Raith, a baroness, and she must learn to

accommodate herself to the different circumstances attending that life.

The only difficulty was, she thought dismally, as she moved towards the door to her apartments, that she did not feel remotely like Lady Raith. That female was some fabricated individual, with whom Rosina had nothing to do. She felt like an intruder. It was inconceivable that this was her home, and that the man who occupied the suite of rooms across the way was indeed her lord.

Arrived in her dressing-room, she discovered that her trunk had been brought up and placed upon the chest. It was already opened, and one of the maids was engaged in removing her garments from it and bestowing them in the various receptacles about the chamber.

'Oh!' she uttered, startled. 'I can do that myself.'

The girl looked astonished, but she bobbed a curtsy. 'Begging your pardon, m'lady, but Mrs Fawley instructed as I should do it for you.'

Dear Lord, she was become a lady indeed! No one but Gatty had ever waited upon her before. She felt excessively uncomfortable. Particularly to have a servant go through the unprepossessing collection of her clothing. For the first time she wondered with what fabricated tale Lord Raith had fobbed off the domestics. The story Mr Ottery had outlined? Unlikely that any of them had believed a word of it! And if they had, they certainly would do so no longer once this girl gave out the details of her belongings, as she undoubtedly would.

Unable to endure the humiliation, Rosina went through into the bedchamber, only to find a second maid preparing the bed for her occupation. A lit candelabrum was set upon the table in the window, which had the odd effect of darkening the room. Another curtsy was offered. She would have to become accustomed to that. She, who had been upon cordial terms with Toly Aughton, the apothecary's boy, and innumerable persons of all conditions these seven years, servants and traders alike.

'I'll bring the warming-pan, m'lady, if you'll ring when you wish to go to bed,' said the girl, turning down the sheets. She curtsied again, and made for the door. Then halted with a gasp, and turned. 'Begging your pardon, m'lady, I forgot. His Lordship's compliments, and he'll do himself the honour of dining with Your Ladyship in an hour, if that is convenient.'

It was as much as Rosina could do to assent. Before she could recover herself, the other black-clad maid came in from the dressing-room, bobbing again.

'Will Your Ladyship select which gown you choose to wear this evening?'

It was too much. Rosina sank down upon the bed, and clasped her hands tightly together in her lap, her eyes fixed upon the maid.

'Pray…what is your name?'

'Joan, m'lady.'

'Joan—' She took a steadying breath. 'Pray don't ask me what I am going to wear. You must see for yourself that I have few gowns. Indeed, this is my best, and I have worn it since yesterday. I am sure His Lordship will not expect me to make any change this evening.'

Joan looked nonplussed. She was small, plump, and apple-cheeked. Likeable rather than pretty. Not much older than Rosina herself. She curtsied again.

'As Your Ladyship pleases.'

Rosina sighed. 'That is all, thank you. You may go.'

Joan curtsied again, and left the room. Rosina got up and went into the dressing-room. The trunk was tucked in a corner. It was empty. Rather wildly, Rosina opened drawers and closet doors, looking where her things had been stowed. She felt as if nothing belonged to her any more. Her life was at the beck of others. Even her clothes

were no longer hers to use as she chose. And as for that—
that despicable little room next door! She wished she
might lock it and shut herself off from invasion.

Pausing, Rosina straightened as a daring thought struck.
Was there a key? She darted to the bedchamber door—
and found none. Neither within nor without. Fairly running back across the dressing-room, she looked in the lock
of the door to the antechamber. Nothing.

Fiercely, she grasped the handle and dragged open the
door. An intense feeling of relief swamped her. There was
a key on the other side. Not pausing to consider her action, she moved into the little room and triumphantly extracted the key from the lock.

A latch clicked behind her. Gasping, Rosina turned.
Entering the antechamber from his own dressing-room
door was Lord Raith.

Raith looked at the key in her hand, all thought suspended. His glance travelled to her face. What he saw
there threw a shaft into his chest. Revulsion! He had
known she must feel it. She had tried to gainsay it yesterday. Tried to make him think that she did not regard
it. But here was proof, if he had needed it. One had only
to look at her!

In fact, Rosina was consumed with consciousness. She
could not fail to notice his flawed features, for light from
the window fell directly upon that side. But anything she
might have felt at the sight of it was overborne by an
absurd sensation of guilt, as if she had been caught out in
wrongdoing. Without thinking, she put her hands behind
her back, as if she would hide the key. To her consternation, her spouse's eyes followed the movement, and the
bitter look of cynicism became pronounced.

'Don't trouble yourself to make a secret of your feelings. You are welcome to lock the door and pocket the

key, if it will make you sleep safer at night. I am unlikely to break down the door, no matter how strong my desire to molest you!'

Rosina heard the words with resentment, despite an increasing sense of guilt. Need he be sarcastic? Was it surprising that she should be apprehensive? Last night he had acknowledged that she had reason. She eyed him. He stood stiff and tight-lipped in the doorway, grey eyes glinting. There was no trace of melting—as there had been last night.

She straightened, bringing the key from behind her. Fitting it into the lock again from the side where she had taken it, she looked back at him.

'I married you for better or for worse, my lord. I will abide by the terms of the contract.'

He leaned against the door jamb and folded his arms. 'Am I expected to thank you? You set inordinate store by that part of the marriage vow, I take it. Let us hope that my gentlemanly instincts may prevent me from forcing the worse upon you before we have had time to become better acquainted.'

Irritation flared. 'Oh, Raith, must you be so—so naggy?' she uttered in a fretful tone.

She moved into the antechamber and crossed to the fireplace, tweaking at her fingers. Raith watched her, the fire dying out of his eyes. She was right to reproach him. What in thunder ailed him, to be picking on her in this brutal way? He had driven her into disquiet again, and it was the last thing he had intended. But what he had said, he reflected soberly, was not so far from the truth. He had been married to her for little more than four and twenty hours, and already he was chafing at the necessity for patience. If he did not take care, he chided himself savagely, he would lose her utterly.

There was little point in excusing himself yet again.

She would grow weary of his apologies, even if she believed—as he did not!—that it excused his offences. He moved into the room. She must have heard him, for she turned.

'If you wish to speak to me at any time, you have only to send your maid to consult with my valet.'

Rosina was wary of the change of tone. He was so apt to alter at a second's notice. He looked no less dangerous, despite the relaxation in his voice. The light was at his back, and his face was shadowed. But the white gleam of his scar could be clearly discerned. Like a tiny streak of lightning in the dark! Now he did indeed look sinister.

What had he said? Her maid? 'I have no maid,' she said on the thought.

'I was forgetting that.'

His words rose to her consciousness, and she suddenly took in what he had meant. Send her maid to consult with his valet? A flash of anger sparked. She was not yet so great a lady!

'If I should wish to speak with you, my lord,' she said in a tight voice, 'I shall use no go-between! Such a course could do nothing but increase the distance between us.'

She passed him quickly and, with an ostentatious gesture, removed the key from the lock and replaced it on the inside of her own door. He had turned, and she looked at him with some degree of defiance, but he did not speak. Rosina waited a moment. Then she went into her dressing-room, and shut the door behind her.

Rosina woke to strong daylight. She lay blinking in the huge bed, unable for a few moments to recall where she was or what she was doing there. When it came back to her, she started up on one elbow, glancing about the bed-chamber in quick alarm.

The place was much less disturbing with the velvet

drapery drawn back. Rosina remembered that she had come in last night to find that the chambermaid, whom she had met coming out of the room armed with a warming-pan, had closed the curtains about the bed. It would have been like sleeping in a tomb! In a frenzy, Rosina had flung them all back, and, regardless of the cold, done the same at the windows, opening the chamber to the night.

She had been warm enough, snuggled in well-dried sheets, several blankets and a down coverlet. Her sleep had been fitful, however, and she had woken several times, and found herself listening out, straining her ears for some sound from the interconnecting rooms. Her husband had shown himself so changeable that she had found herself unable to rely upon his assurances—flung at her with such abrasion! Particularly in the light of his attitude at the dinner table last night.

The thought drove her out of the bed. A fire had been lit in the grate, and in the dressing-room next door the ewer was already full. The water in it was tepid, and Rosina guessed that she had woken late. Forgetting that she had only to ring the bell to acquire freshly hot water, she made use of what was there, and began to ready herself for the day.

Not that she had any idea what she would do. Her spouse, she recalled, had told her that she was unlikely to see much of him. Judging by last night's encounter at the dinner table, Rosina felt it to be unlikely that she would have much chance to talk to him either.

Having washed off the stains of the journey and tidied herself, Rosina had left the room to find the butler waiting at the top of the stairs to show her the way. If she'd had any apprehensions about dining once again tête-à-tête with Lord Raith, they had been put to flight the moment she had entered the dining-room below. A table of inordinate length had been set with places at either end. She could not have conversed with His Lordship if she had tried!

Her husband had already been at the table, but he had risen civilly and bowed as she took her place. Rosina had looked down the long gleaming wood surface, and then at his face. Was this how he intended they should live? They might as well be on separate islands!

She had glanced about the room. Two chandeliers hung from the ceiling, but they were unlit, illumination being provided only by candelabra set upon the sideboards, and single candles in ornate sticks placed at intervals down the table. This was the main item of furniture in the long room, apart from a couple of sideboards where the food was waiting. All the other chairs were set against the walls. It was the most absurd arrangement. But if that was what her spouse wished for, she had supposed it was not for her to cavil.

At least she had anticipated him aright. He was dressed, as she was, in his wedding gear, with a less formal waist-coat of plain blue silk that he had been wearing from that morning. His hair had been combed and retied, looping casually.

The meal had been well prepared, if a trifle heavy. A ragout of veal, served with artichoke hearts, mushrooms and forcemeat balls, and a gravy of meat broth. It had been removed with a rabbit pastry, a dish of scallops and stewed cucumbers, followed by a blancmange and red-currant tarts.

Rosina had eaten a little from each dish, not wishing on her first day to cause offence to the cook. She knew well the amount of work that went into the preparation of dishes of this calibre, and had often been called upon to console the Cambois cook for the frequent waste of her

efforts. Neither her guardian nor his wife had been health-
ful enough to display hearty appetites.

But the food before her had taken up less and less of
her attention, as she had become aware of her spouse's
fixed regard. He had hardly taken his eyes off her. He had
eaten and drunk steadily, barely glancing either at his
plate or his glass, apparently bent upon watching every
move she made. She had felt exposed. As time wore on,
her consciousness had increased, giving rise to an irreg-
ularity both in her breathing and her heartbeat. She had
been drawn and repelled at one and the same time, and
her fingers had stolen up more than once to touch her neck
briefly, or rest lightly upon her bosom.

But Rosina's consciousness had at length given way to
indignation. What did Lord Raith mean by glowering at
her from his end of the table? There had been a kind of
hunger in his gaze. A well of emotion that she had barely
understood had accompanied that sense of danger she had
felt in him before.

She had been glad at last to be able leave him to his
port, and had half a mind to go straight upstairs to bed.
Only Kirkham had ushered her into a large saloon at the
front of the house, where a cheerful fire and a quantity of
candelabra about that end of the room had given off a
comforting feel.

'Tea will be served in half an hour, m'lady,' he had
said, and left her there.

Rosina had taken a chair by the fire, and looked about
her, unimpressed. The furnishing was sparse, the walls
dull, and the dark wood overmantel of a piece with the
austerity of the whole house. The place was denuded of
frills, and there was no touch of elegance. All was heavy
and old-fashioned. Rosina had wondered what in the
world she was going to find to do in a place like this with
the endless empty days that stretched ahead of her.

It had been less than a quarter of an hour later when her spouse had joined her. She had dreaded his coming, unable to determine how she was to respond to the moody intensity that he had displayed throughout dinner. But when he entered, there had been no trace of it in his countenance.

He had greeted her with a calm air of courtesy, asking whether she had enjoyed the meal. Rosina had been tempted to inform him that his behaviour had ruined any possible enjoyment, but she had been so relieved that she had chosen prudence, cautiously following his lead.

'It was very good, I thank you.'

He had taken up a place before the fire, choosing, Rosina had noted with scant surprise, a stance that kept his right side turned away from her. Looking about the saloon, he had said in a disparaging way, 'I am sorry to say that there are only one or two rooms suitable for use at this present. This is one of them. I will hope to remedy that in due course.'

Rosina had tried to think of something inoffensive to say. 'Most of the rooms seem to be very large.'

'Yes,' he had agreed, 'and draughty. They can be made habitable. I have known this house when it was a sight more pleasant to live in.'

Surprised, Rosina had gazed at him. 'I thought you had only just inherited.'

For a moment, his features had drawn in tight, and forbidding, and Rosina had felt her heart sinking. Not again!

'I grew up in this house,' he said shortly.

It was his harsh voice. She was intrigued, but she made no reply, fearing one of his lightning changes of mood. But he had made, Rosina thought, an effort to relax. When he spoke again, it had been in a more natural tone.

'It will be some days before Ottery has freed my trust fund, and in the meanwhile there is little that can be done within the house. I am presently engaged, however, in a great deal of inspection about the estate. My agent calls every day.' He had looked at her, an air of apology in his face. 'I regret, ma'am, that I must leave you very much to your own devices for the moment. I dare say we shall meet, for the most part, only at meals.'

Rosina had been secretly dismayed by the formality of his manner. Almost she had preferred him to be jibing at her. There had been too much coldness in it—at one with the alien nature of the living conditions demanded by the social standing of this house. She had answered him, however, with equal formality.

'What would you wish me to do, sir?'

She had thought he had looked a trifle impatient. If so, he had curbed whatever natural response he might have made, returning to the cool withdrawal of his earlier utterance.

'I recommend that you get upon terms with Mrs Fawley, ma'am. She will, I don't doubt, assist you to know your way about the place. You may, of course, give her any instructions that you choose.'

'Oh, I shan't do that!' she had protested involuntarily.

Her husband had glanced briefly at her. 'You are mistress here now, ma'am.'

Rosina had been betrayed into an unwise response. 'In name only!'

Lord Raith's unamiable temper had flared. He had turned, and the livid laceration matched the fierceness of his grey eyes. 'Yes, you have made your preference abundantly clear! Don't imagine I will sue to you to change it. Good night!'

With the curtest of bows, he had strode from the room, leaving Rosina to bury her face in her hands with a groan of frustration. The tea, which came shortly thereafter, had done a little to revive her. But she had gone to bed in a deeply pessimistic frame of mind, troubled for the future.

But Thursday morning found her a trifle less down-hearted. Perhaps it was the fact that the drizzling rain, which had thus far accompanied her venture into matrimony, had ceased, so that a weak October sun peeped through disintegrating clouds when she looked from the window.

She was about to leave the bedchamber when her eye was caught by the painting of Lord Raith's mother. She moved to examine it. The female on the horse was younger than Rosina had expected. There was not a great degree of beauty, though she had a sweet smile. Rosina could discern no resemblance to her husband. But it was not a large painting, and the features were small. Why had Lord Raith caused it to be placed here?

The door opened, and Rosina looked round to find on the threshold the maid Joan, who had unpacked her belongings. The girl curtsied, looking with surprise at Rosina's habited state. She had dressed herself in an old gown of blue kerseymere, made high to the throat, feeling the big house was likely to be chill despite the change in the weather.

'Good morning, m'lady. I was waiting for you to ring.'

'Thank you, but I was quite able to manage.'

Joan looked hesitant, fidgeting with her apron. 'Yes, m'lady.'

Rosina frowned. 'What is the matter?'

The girl bobbed again. 'Mrs Fawley said I was to wait upon you, m'lady, according to His Lordship's orders. Until, that is, Your Ladyship should hire a real abigail.'

She had been somewhat out of charity with her spouse, but this mark of thoughtfulness touched her. She remembered that scrap of conversation they'd had in the antechamber. Rosina smiled at the maid.

'That will be helpful, Joan. For the moment, however, I don't think there is anything—' She broke off. 'Stay! Do you know how to iron?'

'Oh, yes, m'lady,' said Joan eagerly.

'Then—perhaps you might do what you can with my gown? It is of damask, and sadly crushed from the journey, I fear.'

It was clear that Joan was delighted to be given even this minor task. Rosina, familiar as she was with the hierarchy of the servants' hall, guessed that her promotion to lady's maid, if only temporary, was a giant leap up the domestic social ladder. She resolved to curb her own instincts to look after herself and allow the girl to enjoy the just employment of her new status.

'Perhaps you would first show me where I may be served with breakfast, Joan?'

With alacrity, the maid led her downstairs to the same vast dining-room, where the butler supplied her needs. She learned that it was after eleven o'clock. She discovered, upon enquiry, that her husband usually breakfasted at ten. Rosina was tempted to use this information to make certain of *not* encountering him in the mornings. Only she knew it would cause inconvenience to the servants—especially the cook, obliged to keep food warm—who must wait upon the pleasure of the gentry, when they might have been better employed elsewhere.

By the time she had eaten in solitary state in her single chair, with only the sight of Lord Raith's empty place at the other end, Rosina was further tempted to make herself mistress of the house as her spouse had suggested. She would give much to institute changes that might lessen the dreadful formality of Raith Manor.

Raith had recommended her to talk to Mrs Fawley, but Rosina chose rather to wander about the house by herself, forming her own impressions. They were not favourable.

The house was enormous, and as she wandered through interconnected rooms, the drab silence of the empty spaces depressed her. There was everywhere dullness, an air of neglect and isolation.

Holland covers were laid over furnishings which had been pushed together in the centre of rooms. Those few paintings that remained upon the dun-coloured walls were inferior in execution. The wood mantels were clean, but unpolished—she supposed no one had time to make them gleam—and utterly free of ornaments. Chandeliers hung dully, their glass droplets long unwashed. There were perhaps two timepieces in the whole house. And as for silver—bar that in the dining-room and the various candelabra—there appeared to be none.

Walking around the first floor on the back face of the mansion, Rosina arrived in a long gallery populated by a number of ancestral portraits, obviously of former Raiths.

Her interest quickened, and she wandered slowly down the line, becoming wholly absorbed. A gentleman in an Elizabethan ruff stared back at her. The first Raith, perhaps? She had not seen any earlier style, though there were a number of later date, becoming indeed so recent that this last must be within a decade or two. Then she came upon one so startling that she almost jumped. It was of a gentleman who bore an uncommon likeness to her husband.

His hair was of a similar brown hue, worn in a ragged cut that rested upon the shoulders. He was older, she thought, but there was the same set jawline, the high cheekbone. Here, in the dip below it, was a deeper cleft perhaps, and the lips more thinly carved. Most striking of all, the grey eyes looked out upon the world with the exact air of cynicism that so characterised Lord Raith. Only there was no scar.

'Is it like, do you think?'

Rosina jumped violently. Turning, she beheld her spouse standing behind her, near a window. Her heart jerked into life, and she was unable to speak for a moment for the turbulence in her chest.

For all he was booted, Rosina had not heard him approach. He was in riding dress, a long frock of dark green over buckskin breeches, but he had discarded his gloves and hat. His hair, though tied back, was dishevelled, accentuating the resemblance. He was looking particularly bitter, glancing from her to the portrait, and back again.

Rosina found her tongue. 'It—it is like, but it is not you,' she managed, as calmly as she could.

Raith turned his gaze to the portrait. 'You are observant.' He strolled past her, and went to stand beside it, turning. 'Pray continue your investigation.'

He spoke quite coolly, but Rosina felt the bile welling within him. It caught at her curiosity, and she found herself less affected than usual. Had this significance in his virulent self-hatred? She looked from his face to the portrait, and saw at once that the resemblance was not nearly as strong as she had thought.

The unknown man on the wall had, she now saw, a look of—yes, dissipation—that had been drawn by the artist, perhaps without intent, in a swarthy shadow that edged the jaw and ran down in strong lines from nose to mouth and below the eyes. It was only, she realised, looking back at Lord Raith—whose far less mocking eyes were regarding her with concentrated attention—the addition of the ridged and ragged white lesion which gave him that sinister air. It was that which increased the similarity. The other, she decided, looked sinister without any adorning cut.

'Who is he?' she asked.

Raith came away from the portrait, and turned to look at it with her. 'My brother.' His jaw tightened. 'My half-brother, to be exact. My predecessor, the tenth Baron Raith. And to whose untimely demise you may count yourself indebted, for I would never otherwise have thought of marriage.'

Indebted! Was she not rather cursed? But to say so would be to provoke precisely the sort of contretemps that she wished to avoid. Besides, he had faced her without hiding the scar, and she guessed it had taken an effort for him to do so. Moreover, when he had moved back he was standing on her left, leaving it exposed. From this side, and so close, it was indeed cruelly ugly. A shaft of emotion seemed to crush her chest, and she wanted to weep for him.

'I am sorry if you were distressed by his death,' she ventured, faintly husky.

He glanced at her briefly, but his gaze returned to the portrait. 'Only because it meant that I must inherit this doubtful windfall.'

'When did he die?'

'In the summer.'

Rosina felt suddenly desperate to ask more, but she was already too strongly aware of the dangers of probing too far with her touchy spouse. His nearness was having an unsettling effect. Was it the sight of that graven cut?

To her surprise, Lord Raith appeared disposed to talk of the matter, though he continued to study the portrait.

'Ottery had written to me, warning me that Piers was travelling all too swiftly on the road to perdition. But I was in the midst of a campaign against the French, and paid no heed. Besides, I had no wish to watch him breathe his last. He would not have thanked me for it.'

His voice was even, but Rosina could read beneath it a wealth of unspoken emotion. Again she was swept with the oddest flood of feeling. It must be pity! And here must be the reason for his bitterness. She forgot caution.

'I am of the opinion that you did not care for your half-brother.'

Raith looked at her. 'Astute of you!'

She eyed him, unaware of the emotion that showed in her black orbs. Raith took it for reproach, and gave himself a mental kick. How could he have spoken to her so? After all his good intentions!

'Pay no heed to me,' he said quickly. 'It is not your fault that I was at enmity with Piers.'

Her eyes became questioning, and he avoided them, moving to the window. Easier not to look at her. The effect upon him of her expressive countenance was his undoing. Last night's petty bungling had ruined his sleep. He had tossed and turned, fighting the desire to go through to her chamber and beg her forgiveness for his ill-mannered departure. Had he not feared that she would think he had the intention of taking his pleasure of her, he would have done it. She could not possibly trust him. Nor, for that matter, did he trust himself!

He had spent the entirety of that interminable dinner in a state of anguish, so badly did he want her. On her departure from the table, he had gone across to the window and flung open the shutters, letting in the freeze of the night to cool his ardour. He had tossed off his port, resolved to give her no cause for distress, and broken the resolve within minutes of being in the same room with her.

This morning, her non-appearance at breakfast had been to him a relief, and he had set out with his agent on horseback, determined to remain out of doors until sunset. But memory—that intrusive betrayer!—had fed him images of his conduct, and he was riven with remorse. He had come back expressly to find her, and make amends. He drew a breath, and spoke without turning round.

'Rosina.'

'Yes, my lord.'

There was a quality in her voice—of sympathy? That was the last thing he wished for! Never mind it. This was not about what he wanted, but about what she deserved. He did not turn around, but kept his eyes on the view from the window: a deserted formal garden, the stables and outhouses just visible beyond, behind a belt of trees.

'I have behaved abominably since our marriage. More so since we arrived here. I do not know what to say to you. If I were to make you a promise to mend in future, I know I should break it. I am not fit company.'

Her voice came from behind him, a trifle diffident, he thought. 'It has, I think, to do with your half-brother. Your bitterness, I mean.'

'Bitterness,' he repeated dully. 'It was his own disease. I had it not, until he gave it to me.'

'But he is dead,' she pointed out. 'Can you not forget it?'

Would that he could! But how, when the very core of it had brought him to this pass? Else he would not have put himself on to the market—and purchased an impossible dream. But that could not be said. Easy enough to find another reason. They were all of them valid.

'It is a trifle difficult,' he said, turning so that she received his good side. 'His legacy surrounds me.' His hand threw an arc that encompassed the house and grounds. 'You've seen the place. It was never thus when my father was alive. Piers has brought it to this pass in the space of seven years.'

Rosina came to join him at the window, puzzling over his words. 'Was it then done to thwart you?'

He gave one of his harsh laughs. 'Not until he knew at the last that I must succeed him. He had only to marry and beget an heir to keep me out. Only his reputation was so besmirched that no female of any standing would have him. And Piers would never have stooped to the sort of bargain in which I have indulged.'

He saw her wince, and quickly put out a hand. 'That was not meant to insult you, Rosina.'

'I take no offence,' she replied, that wistful expression creeping into her elfin face.

It wrought havoc within him. 'You should!' he replied forcefully. He moved to her, and grasped her hands, holding them hard. 'Rosina, I meant to make a marriage of convenience, but I find myself with something quite different. I don't yet know what it is.'

A smile wavered on her lips, and the black eyes softened. 'It must be what we make it.'

He drew her closer, and Rosina found herself looking directly up into his disfigured countenance. There was a vibrancy in his tone, a throb of something she did not understand.

'Can you truly stomach this?'

Her voice shook, for her pulse had begun a slow thump that made it difficult to utter. 'If I am permitted to become accustomed, why should I not?'

He met the coal-black of her eyes, and almost gave in to the temptation to kiss her. But then he saw that her lip quivered, and felt the trembling in her fingers. She would let him do it, but she was intensely afraid!

Releasing her fingers, Raith stepped back. For a fleeting moment, he had forgotten. He turned aside, giving her again the one acceptable profile. He fought to remain where he was, though he wanted to walk away. It had cost him an effort to mention it, to ask. She had shown willing. Hell and damnation, was that to be all?

Rosina watched him, oddly bereft. For one wild instant, she had thought he was going to kiss her. A rush of heat had enveloped her, and her knees were still shaking. For the first time, she found herself wondering what it might be like to give herself to her husband's caresses.

There was a lengthy silence. Rosina cast about for something to say. Her mind was all chaos, but she wanted more than anything to hold him here. Let him not leave her flat—as he was wont to do—after rousing in her so tempestuous a reaction! All at once, she remembered.

'Speaking of paintings,' she said quickly.

He started, frowning as he looked round. 'Yes?'

'The one you caused to be put in my bedchamber,' she pursued. 'It is of your mother, I understand?'

Raith stared at her, hardly aware of what she meant, so intensely had he been involved with the too-close step towards disaster. Too close, by thunder, for comfort! He had made the highly inconvenient discovery that he could not satisfy his desire at the expense of her dignity. To know that she was forcing herself to accept his caresses? No, a thousand times.

'My mother?' he repeated vaguely.

'She seemed not to resemble you, but then I could not properly see her face. Is there no larger portrait?'

Rosina felt as if she was babbling. His abstraction had not escaped her. He was retiring into his shell again. She became aware that she could not bear it.

But Raith had caught up with her train of thought. 'There was no portrait done of her. I have a miniature.'

The vulnerable look was back in her face, and he had to turn away. Her voice came again, hushed.

'Why did you have it put in my room?'

'I thought it suitable. It is the most attractive painting in the house. Besides, it was her room once, and I re-member her with—affection.'

The word drifted between them, poignant and wistful. Rosina had no words.

Raith glanced at her. 'I must go. I came only to…say

what I did.' Reaching for her hand, he lifted it; keeping his gaze on her slim fingers, he caressed them lightly with his thumb. 'If I give you further cause to hate me, Rosina, remember that it is the last thing I desire.'

Then he dropped a light kiss on her fingers, released her and walked quickly away down the gallery. Rosina gazed after him, aware of a tingle at her fingers where his lips had pressed. She stayed thus for a long moment, thinking. Then she gave a determined nod, and went in search of Mrs Fawley.

Raith spent the day battling with his memories. His agent, Longridge, led him to Ratley, one of the villages on his estate a couple of miles away, where he lunched in the local inn, in a deliberate move to show himself. He then visited each of the farms and cottages in turn, as he was doing in all areas, day by day, meeting every tenant and listening to their grievances. They were many, increasing as word spread of his activities, and more took courage to come out with the list of wrongs.

His brother Piers had been the worst of landlords, squeezing from the estate every penny that he could, and putting nothing back. Raith made no attempt to defend him, and accepted instead the words he heard time and time again.

'T'weren't like this in your father's time, me lord.'

'I am aware of it, my friend,' he told them. 'I hope to mend matters in time, but you must have patience. It cannot be done all in a minute. Now, what is it you need? Longridge will take down a list, and we will do our best to accommodate you by and by.'

The time he had to spend with each one was lengthening, the more so today, for the news of his marriage had got about. He was obliged to accept felicitations, and answer questions about his lady. An exercise which added a new dimension to the drift of thoughts at the back of his mind as he listened with spurious attention to what were more or less the self-same complaints from end to end of his domain.

Hearing of the deprivations that had attended the tenure of his half-brother served to increase the bitterness. If Piers had deliberately chosen this way of revenge, by thunder, he could not have done it more thoroughly! Their father must be turning in his grave.

But the remembrances evoked by thinking of Piers led him instantly to visions of Rosina's delicate face. He had inflicted that bitterness on one who least deserved it. Yet she had generosity enough to forgive him, to understand. And he, ungrateful dog that he was, did not want her understanding. What he wanted, she was unable to give him, small blame to her. What female could? Which led him directly back to Piers.

It was a churning, useless circle that well-nigh exhausted him. It must have shown. They were not finished at Ratley, but his agent called a halt.

'My lord, you look fagged to death! Besides, it will be growing dark soon. There is no point in attempting to complete the task here today. We can return tomorrow, if you will.'

Raith had nodded wearily, glad enough to fall in with this scheme. They rode back to Ratley Grange together, where he parted from his agent and then cantered back to the Manor grounds. By the time he had left his horse at the stables, it made sense to change for dinner. He was early enough to call for a bath that he might wash the accumulated dirt from his person.

He dressed casually in deference to his wife's meagre wardrobe, in a coat of snuff-coloured cloth, with matching breeches, and a bronze satin waistcoat. By the time he started down to the saloon, he found himself to be in a

fever of impatience to see Rosina again. She was before
him, waiting.

'Good evening, my lord,' she said, with a smile.

Raith was taken aback. He replied in kind, watching
her warily. Was this submissive friendliness her notion of
disporting herself as a dutiful wife? Her countenance was
as enchanting as ever, but his suspicion increased when
he saw that she had made an alteration in her dress.

She had put off the gown of blue stuff that she was
wearing earlier in the day, and had instead donned a gown
of chintz. It was of a pale pink which little suited her, and
from the way it fitted looked as if it had been made for a
larger lady and altered down. It was, moreover, as old-
fashioned as the rest, Raith realised with a rise of annoyance. He knew little of female costume, but he could tell
that much. Where in thunder was Ottery with his funds
so that he might alter that? That she had worn it at all,
however, was a gesture that betokened a change in her
attitude towards him.

He watched her rise from the chair and come to his
side—the left side. She had noticed, then. Why would she
not, she was intelligent enough?

'Shall we go in, my lord?'

'As you wish.' He offered his arm, and led her through
into the dining-room.

Kirkham was holding the door, his face wooden. Raith
took this in vaguely, ushered Rosina before him and
walked in after her. He stopped short, staring.

The table had been reduced by at least half. A single
candelabrum was placed to one end, lighting where two
places had been set. One was his usual position, at the
head of the table. The second place, obviously for Rosina,
was set directly to its right. She would be seated so that
she must spend the meal looking at the mutilation on the
right side of his face.

Chapter Four

For a few breathless moments, Rosina thought Lord Raith was going to explode. His eyes blazed, and he shot a look at her that spoke volumes. Inwardly quaking, she turned from him and moved to the table.

'If you please, Kirkham,' she said quietly.

The butler made haste to pull out her chair for her. Rosina seated herself, as nonchalantly as her fast-beating heart would allow. Then she looked at Kirkham and nodded towards her husband's chair.

He drew it out, and coughed. 'My lord?'

Raith was within an ace of marching straight out of the place. How could she trick him so cruelly? Now he saw why she had been conducting herself in that deceptively wifely manner! He heard Kirkham cough again, and saw that a maid and both the footmen were entering the room, laden with dishes. To make a scene before the servants would hardly accord with his desire to create an impression of marital harmony.

He moved across to the table, noting that the sideboards, where the staff were busily employed, had been shifted also, so that they were closer to the table. The light was all concentrated in one area, making the room cosier.

The relief Rosina felt on seeing him approach was short-lived. He had no sooner seated himself than he leaned towards her, taking advantage of Kirkham's moving out of earshot. The grey eyes flashed, and she jumped.

'If we were alone, madam wife, I should be strongly tempted to use you in a manner that you would scarce find to your taste!'

Rosina's hands were shaking with fright, but she gripped them together in her lap, and answered him with low-voiced defiance.

'You have f-forgotten, sir,' she said, barely able to control the tremors in her voice, 'that you t-told me to m-make myself mistress here.'

'I did *not* tell you,' he returned savagely, 'to make of your husband a mockery!'

'Will you take wine, my lord?'

'What?' He turned quickly to the butler, saw that he was proffering a bottle, and snapped, 'Yes!'

The butler poured, and moved round the table.

'I will take water, if you p-please, Kirkham.'

Raith looked at her with narrowed eyes. 'You had better have wine. You may find that you need fortifying.'

She eyed him. Dear Lord, but he was angry! She looked at the elderly butler, who was still waiting. 'A l-little wine, if you please.'

Kirkham poured the wine, managing at the same time to convey to her a look of avuncular reassurance. Rosina smiled at him gratefully. He had been aghast when she had put forward her request to him and Mrs Fawley. Neither retainer had anything to say against her desire to reduce the table but, severally and together, both had advised her most earnestly to place herself upon Raith's left side. Rosina had been adamant.

'It is a risk, I know, but one I am willing to take. You

need neither of you fear His Lordship. He will have no hesitation in laying blame at the right door!'

An apprehension which had now been proven. For the moment Rosina was protected by the presence of the servants. She could only hope that by the time they withdrew, her spouse's temper would have calmed a little. Knowing already how lightning were his changes of mood, Rosina averted her gaze from his face in the hope that this might ease his consciousness. It availed her nothing.

'You need not try to mitigate the offence,' came at her in a derisive undertone.

Rosina looked to find the grey eyes smouldering. She steeled herself to meet them squarely. Her jumping nerves were steadying a trifle, and she was glad to find that she was once again able to command her voice.

'This morning, sir, you asked me if I could stomach—'

'I remember,' he uttered harshly. 'And you chose this method of forcing yourself to become accustomed. That much I had deduced.'

'Then how can you accuse me of mocking you?'

Raith stared at the soup bowl that had appeared in front of him as if he did not know what it was. 'Could you not have found a less public expression of duty?'

Rosina was hurt by the implication that she had done it from a sense of obligation to her married state. Her tongue sharpened. 'I fail to see how I might do so else, since you are shy of my regarding it even when we are alone.'

She received a look that made her quake. But since Lord Raith chose to retire into a silence choked with tension, she was not obliged to attempt to speak again. Let him fester all he wished! As long as he refrained from throwing his tongue at her, she could endure it well enough.

But her spouse became increasingly ill at ease as the meal progressed, drawing at length her reluctant admission that her wild scheme might have been misplaced. While he ate, partaking more and more sparingly of the viands that were put before him, he was subject to shifts of discomfort from moment to moment. He could not be still, and now and then his hand stole up—unknowingly, Rosina thought—and hovered, as if it sought to conceal that misshapen side. Recollection made him reach out swiftly for his glass, tossing back the wine. He drank a good deal more than he ate, and Rosina became more distressed for him each time he signed to Kirkham to pour.

His vulnerability was pitiful. By the time the last course had been set upon the table and the covers removed, she was deeply regretting having put him through this enforced exposure. It was for him, she now saw, a purgatory.

'Pray leave us, Kirkham,' she said, the moment the butler had set down the final dish, unable to help a note of urgency.

The elderly butler bowed correctly, and Rosina watched him leave, driving his minions before him. The door closed behind him and she turned in dismay as, beside her, her husband let out a groan of utter despair.

Raith's breath came thick and fast as he leaned his right elbow on the table, pressing his hand tight against the offensive wreck of his features, and closing his eyes. Blood and thunder! He had never been so near to disgracing himself with unmanly tears. Curse the wench, and her well-meaning interference! She little knew what she had put him through. He felt wrung out. Every instance of insult and ignominy that his mutilation had made him heir to had come crashing in upon him.

A whisper reached him. 'Raith…'

He shook his head with violence, unable to respond. Let her not attempt to condole with him—or plead, whatever she intended. Not yet awhile. He could not answer for his own responses.

But Rosina was too affected to be wise. His aspect was heart-rending, and she could not endure it. Her own eyes were moist, her voice husky with emotion.

'Raith, I know how you must be feeling…'

He reared up. 'No, you *don't* know! God send you never will!'

She flinched. 'I b-beg your p-pardon, I never meant—'

'Spare me, I beg of you!' he uttered raggedly. 'I know well enough what you meant.' He passed a hand roughly across his brow, and jerked out, 'It is not your fault. In your innocence, how could you know—'

'But I want to know, Raith,' she broke in desperately, driven by she knew not what need. 'I am your *wife*. You say we have a marriage other than you intended. Help me to be the wife you would wish for. Give me something of yourself.'

Raith dragged his fingers down his cheek, and his eyes, haggard in the candlelight, turned upon her face. 'This? You want to know of this?' He drew a breath loaded with anguish. 'Then for a beginning, picture to yourself a whore, for whose services I had paid, running screaming from the room upon first catching sight of it.'

Rosina put a hand to her mouth as tears sprang to her eyes, but she did not speak. He had turned his tormented gaze upon the candles, and did not see her reaction.

'And she was not alone. I took to wearing a mask—for such occasions.' His tone had roughened, though his voice was pitched lower now. 'I had reason to wish that I might do so at other times. There was a ball once, in Spain, where a bevy of ladies were obliged to use their fans for protection. But I saw them while they shunned me—whispering and pointing.'

Silent, the tears that trickled down her cheeks evoked

more by the evidence of his pain than by the words he said, Rosina listened with her eyes fixed upon the wicked injury that had made of him something of an outcast.

Raith spoke on, as if his tongue, once loosened, must run with the narrative. 'Once I thought I had found the inconceivable. A female—not respectable—with whom I became involved, who seemed indifferent. Until I found out that her particular penchant was to seek out those with deformities for an obscure fancy of her own. My disgust then equalled that which I evoke myself in women.'

He was spent. Leaning his elbow on the table again, Raith dropped his chin in his hand, only half-aware of concealment. His eyes moved to his wife, and he saw the tears on her cheeks.

'What, do you weep for me, Rosina?'

'Yes,' she said simply. She sniffed, and wiped away the stains with her fingers. 'It is cruel.'

Raith grimaced. 'It is human nature.'

There was a silence. He watched her, feeling a swelling in his chest for the recognition of her tender heart. A considerable lessening of his suffering had been afforded in the telling. He had said it all without intent, driven by her mad action. But now he could not be sorry for it. He felt instinctively that Rosina's compassion was not born of pity for his wound, but rather for his anguish. Was there that in her past which enabled her to comprehend his humiliation?

'You should weep rather for yourself,' he said unthinkingly. 'You must now live with it as well as I.'

Rosina turned her luminous black orbs upon him, and the wistfulness was pronounced. 'If you will let me.'

His chin was still resting in his hand. As of instinct, he shifted his fingers, to cover the whole scored side. 'So that you may pity me? Allow me some small measure of pride.'

She bit her lip, and a hint of mulishness crept into her face. 'I agree that you have pride—and a good deal of it false.'

'I have false pride?' Raith sat up, dropping his hand, and shifting to face her, hardly aware as he did so that he effectively removed the maimed side from her view. 'I will be glad if you will tell me how you know so much, when we have been but three days married.'

Rosina sighed with impatience. 'What has time to do with it? Today you came to me with a mouthful of gentle sentiment. Yet when I ask you for this one thing, you will not oblige me.'

Was she still at that? Had she not seen enough? 'You did not ask. You took it! And to my cost.'

'Yes, and for that I am deeply regretful,' Rosina said earnestly, twining her unquiet fingers together. 'But I am asking you now, Raith. And it can only be pride that will not let you give in to me.'

Raith drove his fingers into his hair, and groaned. This was so unfair. How she played upon his feelings. 'Rosina, I beg of you, change your seat tomorrow to the other side!'

The coal-black eyes registered acute disappointment, and her lip quivered. 'If you so command me, my lord, I must obey.'

'Hell and damnation!' Raith swore. He reached out and grasped her twined fingers, holding them hard. But his voice was soft, its menace a caress. 'How dare you put me at so vile a disadvantage, you unprincipled wretch?'

A tiny smile curved her lips. 'Well, but you are there, sir, and by your own effort.'

He had to smile. 'You are in the gravest danger, my lady. You should learn to mistrust my temper!'

Rosina's eyes softened, and his heart lurched. 'My lord,

it is my pleasure to obey you in all things—before you
order me. I have already learned it.'

Raith laughed out, releasing her, and Rosina warmed
to the natural sound of it. What joy to see him in humour
at last! The danger had been averted. She dared not press
him further. She would like to have stayed talking with
him, but she knew too little to risk inviting a relapse over
some chance misstep. Better to leave him now, inducing
a wish for reunion.

She got up, smiling with unconscious allure. 'I will go
to bed, sir. My sleep these last nights has given me little
of rest, and I am sorely in need of it.'

Raith had risen when she did. He saw her smile with a
rise of expectation, though her words belied it. Was it an
invitation? He spoke at random, the most obvious thing.

'You must be tired.'

'Somewhat,' Rosina agreed. 'I am unused to be in so
vast a chamber quite alone.'

What in thunder did that mean? Nothing, in all probability—bar what his fervid desire wished to make it. Raith
offered his arm.

'Allow me to escort you to the stairs.'

She took his arm, but with a laugh. 'I dare say I could
find my way. Or is that another of the formalities obtaining in my new status?'

Raith led her to the door. 'Do you find it so formal?'

'Excessively.'

'Enlighten me. What is the difficulty?'

'For one thing,' Rosina told him confidingly, 'the business of having a maid. And my previous situation has
made me apt to consider more the convenience of the
servants than my own. Then, too,' she added, as they entered the lobby, 'there is the elaborate arrangement of a
bedchamber, a dressing-room and that antechamber that
must be crossed before—'

She broke off abruptly, suddenly conscious of what she was saying—and to whom! Where had her wits gone begging? To be speaking in such a way to Raith, of all things. She felt herself grow hot, and taking her hand from his arm, made a swift dash to the stairs. She turned there, and found her spouse regarding her with question in his face. Oh, dear Lord, what had she done?

A smile, a quick 'good night,' and, picking up her skirts, Rosina fled up the stairs.

Raith watched her with an increased tempo in the pattering of his pulses. Was it possible? Could she truly have been indicating a wish for his attentions? It might have been a slip. He had noticed several times that Rosina was apt to let her tongue run away with her, and stop in haste when she realised that she was giving away what she had rather not.

But his own yearning was so strong that his instinct of caution wavered. Prudence dictated that he hold aloof a while longer. For all her protestations of willingness to endure his grotesque countenance, it must take a high degree of courage to undergo the intimacies of the marriage bed. A difficult enough experience for any young wife. In their situation, it must be an ordeal Rosina dreaded.

Hell and damnation! Swinging away from the stairs, he went quickly towards the one habitable saloon, with the intention of ringing for Kirkham to bring him brandy. On arrival, he found the butler already there, placing a tray upon the table by one of the chairs near the fire.

'Your port, my lord,' he said. 'I thought perhaps you would be more comfortable in here.'

Raith thanked him, deciding that port was quite as effective—and less obnoxious. It would hardly ease the difficulty if he were to go to Rosina reeking of brandy! He cursed himself, and seized the bottle and a glass.

'I will serve myself, Kirkham. Go to bed!'

The butler bowed and withdrew, leaving Raith to pace the length and breadth of the saloon, absently sipping at the glass which he was nursing between his hands.

In the heat of his imagination, he had taken infinite enjoyment in the image of Rosina's face, watching her responses—which must undoubtedly be as unlike reality as one could well imagine! He might forgo that pleasure. Do the thing in the dark? It would spare her blushes. He need not see the efforts she would make to conceal her aversion. And she would have the advantage of not seeing him.

A ripple of distaste went through him. She would not see, but she would feel! If he kissed her, she could not avoid the abrasion of his ridged cheek. The thought of kissing her threw spasms of want into his loins. Raith crossed to the tray and refilled his glass, tossing off the wine. Enough! He could not do it, and there was an end.

But the argument persisted in his head, and he remained downstairs for a further half-hour, with a vague thought at the back of his mind that if he left it late enough, Rosina would be asleep—and only a monster would disturb her then.

When his valet had completed preparing him for bed, however, he dismissed the man before climbing between the sheets.

'That will do, Paulersbury. Good night.'

The valet bowed. 'Very good, m'lord. May I suggest a bed gown, if Your Lordship intends to remain out of bed? The night is chill.'

When the man produced a silken morning gown with a handsome blue print, Raith felt his cheeks darken. Paulersbury had guessed his intent. Of course he must present himself before his bride decently clad! It took all his resolution not to snatch it from his valet and throw it aside. He allowed the fellow to assist him to don the thing, and then paced impatiently about his bedchamber as he waited for the man to finish dealing with his clothing in the dressing-room.

At last he heard Paulersbury's discreet cough, and the click of the outer dressing-room door that let onto the corridor. Yet now that the way was free to Rosina's bedchamber, Raith still hesitated. She would be asleep by this time. What was he doing, pursuing this course tonight? Only if he did not, perhaps he might disappoint her expectation—if she had indeed meant to issue a guarded invitation.

Bracing himself, Raith took up the single candle from the bedside table, and went through to the antechamber. Stealthily he opened the door to Rosina's dressing-room. He listened within, but could hear no sound. The door opposite was shut, but a gleam under it indicated that there was light within the bedchamber. By thunder, she was expecting him!

Touching an unconscious hand to his cheek, he softly opened the door. To his dismay, its hinges protested with a mild shriek, and he quickly entered the room, shutting the door again with unprecedented haste.

He turned. The bed-curtains were drawn back, and by the candlelight that came from one side, he could see Rosina sitting up in bed, an open book in her hands, staring across at him. She was without a nightcap, her dark hair falling about her shoulders. Her bosom rose and fell rapidly, and Raith broke quickly into speech.

'Am I disturbing you?' No, that was stupid. Of course he was disturbing her. And with intent! 'Don't be alarmed!'

Rosina was more than alarmed. She was frozen with terror. He had come! In an instant, she forgot how she had worried that he might, after her incautious words. Forgot, too, how she had persuaded herself into believing he would not.

An image sprang into her mind. That dread image that had haunted her these many weeks. Her guardian, stumbling through her bedchamber door, the candelabrum in his hand lighting up the coarse, drink-sodden features.

For a hideous moment, she did not see Raith. She was back in her drab little room, in the house where she ought to have been inviolate, with Herbert Cambois—come, he said, sputtering the words, to teach her what awaited her in the future he planned for her—with that hateful man.

Her breath pumped as she stared at him, and a measure of sense returned. This was not her guardian, she reminded herself, over the frantic eruptions at her pulse. This was Raith. He would not fall sobbing on to her bed, and crawl his loathsome way towards her. That was past. This—this was her legitimate husband. He had a right.

Raith had not moved from the door. She looked away from him, snapped shut the book, and laid it quickly aside, sitting up. But her jangling nerves would not settle, and her fingers travelled unknowingly over her bosom to the back of her neck.

'F-forgive me…you s-startled me,' she managed to say.

His own discomforts forgotten, Raith came quickly to the bed, laying his candle down. Next moment, he was seated beside her, taking her trembling hand into his warm clasp.

'Don't, Rosina! Don't be afraid. I will do nothing to frighten you, I promise. You have only to say the word, and I will retire again this instant.'

'N-no,' she quavered. 'It—it is not you, Raith. Pray— pray don't l-leave me.'

Deeply concerned, he watched the tremors of her white face, his mind thronging with questions. What did this betoken? There was something here that could not be explained by all the careful arguments that he had made with himself. This reaction had no reference to his arrival. If that were all, she would have greeted him with wary uncertainty—not this stark fright. The black eyes were dilated, a nightmare in their depths. Even his disfigurement did not warrant this, considering her attempts to adjust to it.

Her fingers shook pitiably within his own, and her whole frame shivered. Raith saw the tears on her lashes, and without thought, he shifted forward and drew her gently into his arms, holding her close.

'Hush now, sweetheart, hush,' he murmured, wholly unaware of the endearment he used, intent only upon easing her. 'All is well. There is nothing to harm you. Hush!'

Insensibly comforted, Rosina felt her jumping pulse begin to subside. She sagged against him, letting her head fall upon his shoulder. His hold was warm, and completely unamorous, one hand stroking down her back in a rhythmic movement that readily increased her relaxation.

But her proximity started at length to disturb Raith, coupled with the feel of her nestling thus within his arms and the warmth and scent of her skin under the thin stuff of her nightgown. His senses swam. The quality of his embrace began to alter. The motions of one hand took on a sensuality that delineated her contours, while the other shifted upwards, allowing his fingers to run and writhe within her hair. He laid his lips to the wispy curls and kissed across her forehead, travelling downwards as he brought her face up.

For a moment or two, Rosina felt the subtle adjustment of his ministrations as natural, and accepted them. Warmth pervaded her, but it was a pleasant sensation, unalarming.

Then his lips reached hers. The warmth intensified with

a rapidity that mirrored the sudden increased pressure of his mouth. She heard his indrawn breath, and fire streaked down her belly. Panic took her. Her hands came up, struggling, and she thrust away from him, pulling back into her pillows.

'N-no,' she uttered breathily. 'I cannot, I cannot.'

But the taste of her had overwhelmed Raith, and he forgot everything but his own need. His hands reached for her, pulled her back into him. He brought his mouth down on hers again, drawing hungrily at her lips, forcing them open.

Sensation flooded Rosina, melting her bones, burning her deep with a febrile throbbing that was too intensely vivid to be borne. She fought him, striving for release, her hands flailing at him, her fingers reaching frantically to drive his face from hers. They came, all unknowing, into contact with the scar. Its rough edging brushed Rosina's fingertips, and a vision of it burst into her head. Shock made her whimper.

An instant later, she was released, half-flung upon her pillows. Raith threw himself to his feet, a weal of agony in his breast. He felt her revulsion as acutely as if she had spoken of it. The fluttering touch against his mutilated skin, followed by a muted squeal of protest, had been enough to jerk him into awareness. He knew it to be his own doing, even as he extricated himself from the intensity of his passionate demand upon her. He had lost control—and come by his deserts.

'I beg your pardon,' he jerked out hoarsely. 'I forgot myself. It will not occur again.'

He thought, as he turned from her, that she reached out to him. Her voice followed him as he got to the door.

'Raith, wait!'

He halted there, but he did not turn. 'It is of no use, Rosina. I cannot do it!' Then he was gone.

* * *

The day being a degree finer than any that had gone before, Rosina took herself outside for a breath of fresh air. She told herself that she must do so while she might, for November was almost upon them. She did not truly expect that Raith would come riding in. And if he did, and she caught him thus unawares, it was unlikely that she would be treated to anything other than the distant civility to which she had been subject for the last several days.

It struck her that it was Monday, and she had been married for a week. If those first three days had been tempestuous, at least that had been better than this dull emptiness which made the time pass slowly. She could not even enliven her existence with an attempt to render Raith Manor more homelike. Her one effort had been crushingly rejected.

Upon the morning after her husband's abortive entry at her bedchamber—for which she had railed in turn at her own irrational fears and at his absurd sensitivity!—Rosina had come down to breakfast to find that her place had been changed so that she must sit upon Raith's left hand.

'His Lordship's orders, m'lady,' Kirkham had said apologetically. 'He instructed me on no account to allow it again to be altered.'

Pride had driven her back to the original terms of the contract. She was here on sufferance, merely to provide a means to an end. That Raith could countermand her request to the servants proved that he did not consider her to be mistress of his home. Her interference was not wanted.

As for that other matter, she must assume that His Lordship's requirement for an heir was to be put aside indefinitely. That one attempt—which she had bungled disastrously!—was to be the end of it. If only he had warned her of his coming. She would not have been shocked into remembering. She would have prepared herself to receive his caresses. So different from the foulbreathed fumblings of her guardian. Lord, the fever of Raith's kiss! How could she know that it would flame thus in her most secret depths?

The loss when he left her had been unbearable. The intensity of the sensations he had aroused had alarmed her, but the instant he had let her go, a tempest of longing had erupted within her. If only he had kissed her once more! She knew she would have responded quite differently. But he had instead taken hurt, and his withdrawal was complete.

They met only at dinner, and once at breakfast. Rosina had tried to reach him, but his barrier was of ice. He was polite, treating each overture with courteous attention—which did not extend to looking at her beyond an occasional glance of cool detachment. Rosina wanted often to hit him! Anything to break through that aloof isolation. She missed his violent outbursts, even his cynically bitter remarks.

Rosina had abandoned her efforts to thaw him out. She had hoped that Sunday would keep him at home, thinking that a whole day together must break down his reserve. But he had instead driven out, and Kirkham had told her that he had gone to spend the day with his maternal relations. Disheartened, Rosina had feigned sickness, refusing to appear at dinner last night, and requesting a tray to her bedchamber. Joan had attended her, and she had indeed felt so low that her poor appetite had lent colour to the fabrication.

A half-formed hope that her absence might rouse her husband to enquiry was found to be vain. He neither sent to her, nor ventured—as Rosina had secretly dared to envisage—to enter her bedchamber to find out how she did.

This morning, driven by loneliness, Rosina had written

to Gatty. Her old nurse would be anxious, and she had promised to let her know as soon as she could that all was well. She could hardly do that. But since Toly Aughton would be reading the letter, Rosina was obliged to write in coded phrasing, trusting that Gatty would read between the lines. She mentioned cagily that her lord had an unfortunate scar on his cheek about which he was a trifle sensitive, knowing that her nurse would instantly realise that this was the deficiency over which they'd had such earnest cogitation. She said that a degree of understanding might have been set up but for this circumstance, and that she wished it might not prove a barrier to an achievement one day of that sort of happiness that had attended the marriage of her dear mama and papa. Gatty would know from this that her feelings had become involved, and that her path was strewn with difficulties.

Rosina was glad that it was outside of her power to explain the extent to which she had allowed herself to warm towards her lord, for she did not know the answer to that herself. She knew only that she had started out with the intention of living a separated existence in a cold marriage meant only for her protection. Instead, she was beset by yearnings that she barely understood, and remembered glimpses of a ravaged creature whose distresses had played upon her heartstrings. She could not conceal from herself that Raith had engaged her sympathies.

She had ended her letter with an oblique reference to the state of the house and grounds, adding that she was glad at least to be the means of enabling His Lordship to make much-needed improvements.

The reminder of the ills that Raith had intimated were due to the activities of his half-brother had caused her to wonder again about the ash-strewn lawns at the front. Rosina had sealed her letter, written the direction to the

Brinklow Receiving Office and laid it aside, intending to ask her husband for a frank. She had sent Joan to fetch her a shawl, and, donning it over her blue kerseymere gown, had come outside.

She had been strolling for about fifteen minutes, puzzling over the state of the grounds, when the sound of horses reached her from behind. Turning, she perceived a phaeton turning in at the main gates. It contained one gentleman, heavily coated against the cold, and a liveried groom. A trifle of apprehension stirred in her breast. It was the first visitor she had seen since she had arrived. How was she to greet him? She watched the approach of the vehicle down the long central drive, and realised as it came closer that the gentleman driving was none other than Raith's lawyer.

She moved back towards the house, experiencing a rise of delighted anticipation at the prospect of seeing a friendly face—and one she knew at that.

'Lady Raith!' uttered Mr Ottery in a tone that gladdened her heart.

In a moment, he had handed the reins to his groom, and jumped down, doffing his hat. Rosina felt her proffered hand taken in a strong clasp, and found the well-remembered kindness in his face as he smiled down at her.

'How do you do, ma'am?' he asked, with real interest. 'I am very glad to see you again. How do you go on?'

'Mr Ottery! Oh, you cannot imagine how nice this is! I am safe enough, I thank you.'

'Safe!' He eyed her in frowning question. 'I hope so indeed.'

Rosina blushed, stammering out, 'I d-did not m-mean to say that. I am v-very well, I assure you.'

'I am glad to hear it, ma'am. You are settling in, I hope?'

'Settling? In some sort, yes.' What was she saying? In an attempt to gloss over this ticklish subject, she hurried into speech again. 'You have come to see my husband, I dare say. He is out riding. He does so every day. Indeed, I never see him but at meals.'

She thought she detected concern in his face, but he said nothing untoward. 'Ah, yes. I know His Lordship to be extremely occupied about the estates. It is often the case, when first a gentleman takes possession of an inheritance.'

Rosina smiled waveringly. 'I know nothing about it, Mr Ottery. The bargain is being carried out—in most respects.'

He looked as if he might probe the matter, but just then the sound of hoofbeats, travelling fast, interrupted them. From between the trees on the other side of the house, a horseman came cantering through on to the drive. It was Raith.

He saw the lawyer and reined in to a trot, riding up to where Ottery and Rosina stood. He touched his hat to his wife.

'Ma'am, your very obedient.' Then he turned to the lawyer, and smiled, holding down his hand. 'A thousand welcomes, my friend! Do you bring glad tidings? Do not tell me that your cursed legal complexities are any longer to keep me from my purposes.'

'By no means, my lord,' responded the other, laughing. 'I am come with papers a-plenty for your signature, but no quibbles, I assure you.'

'Excellent!'

The marked difference in his greeting of his lawyer, to that which he had extended to herself, had worked powerfully upon Rosina's feelings. He was insufferable! How dared he treat her so? After all his protestations, his tender mouthings, thus cruelly to shut her out. She could not think how she had accepted it for so many days. What, was she to be thus slighted by the man who had shown her so violent a passion? He was not indifferent to her, as it would seem he would have her believe. Why should she endure it?

Vaguely she heard Raith advising his lawyer to send his equipage round to the stables. 'I will meet you in the library, Ottery.'

He rode off towards the rear of the house, and she waited in a state of quivering indignation while Mr Ottery instructed his groom. She had no intention of betraying herself, but only to say that she expected to see him later in the day. But the lawyer most unfortunately said quite the wrong thing.

'My dear Lady Raith, forgive my interference, but I know His Lordship of old. His mask is a shield. He will lower it in time.'

Tears stung her eyelids. 'Oh, it was not always up so stiffly, Mr Ottery. Only I am lumped among those evil crones with whom he had past dealings, with no opportunity to redeem myself.' She caught herself up. 'I should not have said as much. Forget it, pray!'

He took her hand. 'Don't mind me, ma'am.' She thought he was going to say more, but he evidently checked himself. He pressed her hand instead. 'Take courage!'

Releasing her, he went off, heading for the front door. Rosina bit her lip, blinking away the threat of weeping.

The library at Raith Manor was, unlike the rest of the house, a room almost fully furnished, with cases wall-to-wall filled with books, and a sturdy oak table that served for a desk. Two long windows let in plenty of light, and a cheerful fire burned in the grate, flanked by two large chairs, with seats and cushioned patches of leather at both head and arms.

In these, Raith and his lawyer had settled, once a quantity of papers had been read over and signed. Raith was conscious of an easing of his inner tension—not entirely due to the happy nature of the business that had brought Ottery.

He poured them both Madeira and handed one of the glasses across. Then he stretched his booted legs out and crossed them at the ankles, sighing deeply.

'You must be relieved to have the business settled, my lord,' remarked Ottery, with the smile that always warmed his employer.

'It is so very much needed, Ottery, that I must say I am.'

'Do you really mean to use the substance of your means to bring the place about?'

'You are afraid that it may swallow the whole, I dare say,' guessed Raith, catching his concern. 'No, Ottery, I hope by good management to restore the estates into decent repair so that they may pay for themselves again. But I have warned everyone that this will take time. We will only put the most urgent of requirements into immediate effect.'

'I am relieved to hear it, sir. What of Longridge? Do you wish me to look about for a new agent, as we discussed?'

Raith shook his head. 'I am perfectly satisfied that Longridge was not to blame for the deteriorations. Indeed, he is obviously delighted to be able to offer better prospects to my tenants. And they trust him, Ottery. I have heard over and again how he tried to halt the decline, or play off the income from those with less to lose against that missing from the poorer element.'

He was glad of Ottery's approval. 'That is good to hear, my lord.'

He was surprised then to see that his lawyer dropped his gaze to his glass, and turned it, looking at the ruby liquid within. What ailed him? This was unlike Ottery. Had he something on his mind? He was about to question it, when the lawyer forestalled him.

'What of your marriage, my lord?' he asked, looking up.

Raith felt a hollow enter his chest. 'What of it?'

'Is it satisfactory?'

Eyeing him narrowly, Raith thought he detected a trifle of consciousness in his lawyer's gaze. He recalled that Rosina had been speaking to him before he arrived. He had known that Ottery was coming today, for he'd had his letter yesterday. But she had not known! Raith sat up sharply.

'What has she said to you?' he rapped out.

Ottery's eyebrows rose. 'Lady Raith, my lord?'

'Who else? Come, Ottery, I am no fool! My wife is apt to blurt out anything that is in her head—and then be sorry for it. She is not, I know well, in good spirits, and you caught her unawares.'

To his consternation, his lawyer gave him a look of rare severity. 'Why is she not in good spirits, my lord?'

Raith set down his glass and jerked to his feet, pacing away a little, the unruly beat of his pulse overloud in his own ears. He halted, turning to face Ottery.

'Why ask me? It is my fault—you've guessed that much.'

'Then why will you not mend it, sir?'

Before this one true friend, Raith could throw off the burden of concealment that he had put upon himself in the presence of his wife.

'Would that I knew how, Ottery! Or whether indeed I

should.' He came back and re-seated himself, sighing deeply as he took up his glass again. 'My friend, have I made the most terrible mistake?'

The lawyer looked deeply concerned. 'I warned you against a too-hasty decision, my lord. You will recollect that you were adamant. If it is a mistake, you can only now rectify it by pursuing your course. As for Miss Charlton—or rather, Lady Raith—I fear her interests are not being served as perhaps they might.'

'What do you mean?' demanded Raith narrowly.

Ottery folded his lips. 'I would not wish to presume upon my position, my lord.'

'By thunder, Ottery, don't do that! You know how I value both your advice and your friendship. I do not forget what I owe you. Say what you wish to me, but be plain, I beg of you!'

The lawyer set down his glass. 'Has she deserved of you such coldness? She does not know, I presume, that you chose her—above any other, my lord.'

'Do you blame me?' Raith protested. 'Only think what the others were like!'

'My lord, you did not select Miss Charlton merely because she was a cut above the rest,' said Ottery gently.

Raith gave a bitter laugh. 'You see too much, my friend.'

'Yet—your pardon, but you bade me speak plainly— you have not, for want of a better way to say this, taken advantage of your rights.'

Impossible to answer that! He could think of nothing to say, so he remained silent. No doubt Ottery would guess from it that he was perfectly right.

'Perhaps,' went on the lawyer, 'the lady in the case may be wondering why this does not occur.'

Raith frowned in quick suspicion. 'Did she say anything? No, she cannot have spoken of that!' He rubbed his forehead in painful concentration. 'Ottery, there is some mystery. I felt it from the first and, from things she has let fall, I have become convinced that this is so.' He met the lawyer's eyes. 'She married me for a reason other than the one she gave.'

'So also did you,' Ottery pointed out.

'True, my friend. But I fear my wife's reason is less palatable than my own.'

It was the first time he had put it into words—and it was as far as he could go. He had left Rosina that night, driven by the depth of his own self-disgust as she struggled to free herself from his grasp. He had been unable to pursue his need of her, even though she had called out to him. Her revulsion, as he had then thought, was born purely of her recoil from the ugly blemish of his face.

It was only later that he had, in calmer mood, become slowly convinced of his error. She had recoiled, but there had been more to it than that. He had found himself going through the events of that night, in moment-by-moment detail. Rosina's first inexplicable terror. The shivering limbs. The anguish of her utterance: 'It is not you, Raith.'

Who, then, had it been? Whose presence in her bedchamber had been in her mind? What vile happening had she remembered that caused her to fight against his caresses—*before* her fingers felt his face? He had been recalled to his senses—as how could he not be when her fingers fatally touched his cheek?—and had retreated from her presence. But what if some other man had not retired? What if he had forced his entry, and sullied the purity of the future Lady Raith?

Chapter Five

Rosina was glad to encounter Mr Ottery at the breakfast table on Tuesday morning, for she had been afraid he might leave before she had an opportunity to say farewell. She had met him at dinner, where, to her chagrin, he was seated opposite herself, and on Raith's right hand. Her husband could tolerate his lawyer's gaze without difficulty. But his wife was not permitted to look at that side of his face, for fear of her non-existent disgust of it!

No opportunity had offered for her to be private with Raith, despite the fact that he had been home all day since Mr Ottery's arrival. Perhaps it was as well, for her emotions towards him were so tangled that she felt certain she would only destroy all hope of breaking down his reserve. He had been a trifle less remote at dinner, not quite thawed, but certainly not as formal. Not, she dared swear, for any other reason than the presence of his lawyer.

Rosina had chosen to wear the damask grey gown that had served for her wedding, realising only after she came down—and by Mr Ottery's widening eyes—that it was scarcely appropriate. Her spouse had on a cloth suit of blue, while the lawyer's usual black had been augmented only by fresh linen.

She had thought, from the way Raith suddenly shifted to the fire a moment after her entrance, that she had angered him. But his slightly softened manner towards her seemed not to bear it out. But perhaps Raith had changed only because Mr Ottery took pains to secure her participation in any conversation—an effort for which she had been grateful.

Ottery had spoken of the estates as they had been in the time of Raith's father, recalling his early association with the family. He had taken over the practice from his own parent, pleased to be honoured with the continued trust of most of his father's clients.

'If he was anything like you, Ottery,' Raith had said, smiling, 'I am sure the honour was more on our side.'

Ottery had disclaimed, and talked of another of his clients, and an acquaintance with Lord Brook of Warwick Castle. This led to a discussion on the history of Warwick, which lasted until it was time for Rosina to leave them. She had not gone to the saloon, saying that no doubt they had further business to discuss and that she would only be in the way.

The fact that Raith was also at the breakfast table when she entered this morning was not entirely unexpected. He was dressed in his green riding frock and buckskins, but he would hardly go out before his lawyer had left. Rosina was instantly conscious of nervousness, for it seemed to her that he regarded her somewhat narrowly as she came to the table. It turned out that both men had finished their meal, and Mr Ottery was upon the point of departure. Recalling her letter to her nurse, and expecting that Raith would leave immediately after seeing him off, she stopped him as he made for the door.

'A moment, my lord.'

He halted, turning with a slight frown. 'Yes, ma'am?'

She was daunted, but said with a little diffidence, 'I only wished to ask if you will frank a letter for me, sir.'

'Ah.' He seemed to hesitate. 'Certainly. If you will bring it to the saloon, I shall do so as soon as I have seen Ottery to the door.'

'Thank you, but there is no hurry.'

'When you have done with breakfast, then,' he said. There was a pause, then he added quickly, 'I wished, in any event, for an interview with you.'

An interview! Dear Lord, for what purpose? The formality of his announcement chilled her, and she sank into her chair.

Mr Ottery came up to her, and took her hand. She thought there was reassurance in his smile. 'I will hope to see you very soon again, Lady Raith. Keep well.'

She was obliged to clamp down on a rise of emotion. Would that he could stay! He had brought a change to the atmosphere of Raith Manor—and that softening on her husband's part. If only it might persist! The two men went out, and she took up her fork to address a plate of baked eggs. But the consciousness of the coming interview with Raith had destroyed her appetite, and she could only manage a mouthful or two. She drank a cup of coffee, and then rose with determination. If she must face it, she had better get it over with.

She went swiftly upstairs to fetch her letter. By the time she returned to the saloon, Raith was already there. He was standing at the window, looking out over the desecrated lawns. He turned as he heard her enter.

Rosina steadied herself, and walked boldly across to him, holding out the letter. He took it from her, and looked at it. Dully, she thought.

'I have not a pen to hand,' he said. 'I will sign it later, and give it to Kirkham to send to the post office.'

He moved into the room, and laid the letter on the man-

telpiece. Then he stood for a moment, silent, looking
down into the fire.

Rosina could see only the loop of his tied-back hair
against the tanned skin. She felt her pulse start up, and a
flutter at her stomach. What did he want? The waiting
began to chafe her. She crossed to a chair—careful to
choose one that would admit of his being able to turn his
bad side away from her—and sat down, gripping her
hands together in her lap. Still he did not move. She could
not endure this! She had to speak. She could not help the
tremor in her voice.

'What is it you w-wanted to see me about, my l-lord?'

A groan escaped him, and he flung a hand up to his
forehead. 'Oh, dear God, Rosina!'

He dropped his hand after a moment, and turned. His
ravaged countenance drew from her a swift indrawn
breath. He looked haunted, and she knew instantly that
his barrier had been dictated by suffering.

'What is it, Raith?' she asked, anguished.

He threw up a hand. 'Don't ask. I cannot answer you.'
He made an effort to pull himself together. Hell and damnation! He had known how hard it would be to be with
her, and obliged to discuss more than the commonplace.
His feelings threatened every moment to get the better of
him. And he could not let that happen. He would not gain
her trust by ranting at her. On the other hand, he was no
nearer to gaining it—as Ottery had pointed out—by his
persistent withdrawal.

He wished that his lawyer had not thus advised him,
though he knew well that he was right. Ottery had been
adamant that he must seek out the mystery, whatever it
might be. And he should do it, not through his lawyer's
enquiry—as he had himself suggested—but by asking his
wife.

'It is your best chance of securing your own happiness,

my lord. To have me spy upon Lady Raith will serve only to alienate her affections. Try, if you can, to get upon terms that will bridge this iniquitous divide. Then you may ask her, and she will trust you enough to tell you.'

Well, let him begin with the business at hand. At least it would open the way to conversation—without entering dangerous waters. He moved to take a chair, noting with mixed emotions as he did so that Rosina's selected position gave him the advantage of sitting with his right side away from her. So much for her wish to accustom herself. Now that she had successfully driven him from her bedchamber, what need was there to put herself through that particular discomfort?

And she had succeeded in driving him off. No matter how strong his desire, he was unlikely to risk a repetition of the farce of the other night. He had discovered, to his cost, that he could not bed Rosina, if she could not accept him with more than mere duty—overcoming revulsion to do so. She must want him. Worse, she must care. What price that for a marriage of convenience?

But it afforded, he had admitted to himself, a sop to his conscience. Any of the candidates might have come to him tainted. It was unlikely that he could find, by means of advertisement, a lady of unimpeachable virtue. Ottery had warned him of it, and he had accepted the hazard. But he had not anticipated Rosina. He had not bargained for his emotions becoming involved. It was hard indeed to accept the disagreeable possibility—likelihood, even?—that another man had been before him. Even though his suspicion tended to the idea that she had been an unwilling participant in the act.

Until he had found out the truth, he could not deal with the inordinate difficulties confronting him. God knew his ardour was as strong as ever! Seeing her last night in her wedding gown had near been his undoing. But to take her—with, if he read her aright, the utmost care and gentleness—he must control his passion, and overcome both her reluctance and these misguided seedlings of jealous possession.

Enough! Futile to dwell upon it. Let him rather pursue this attempt to follow Ottery's advice, and get upon better terms with his wife. Terms—yes, there were other terms to be looked at. He was to begin with those.

'Ottery has secured the release of my fortune,' he began. 'It will shortly be in the hands of my bankers, and it is time to formalize the financial arrangements between us.'

'Formality again?' Rosina's tone was cheerless. 'Very well, sir. Pray continue.'

'It is only the matter of your allowance, Rosina,' Raith said, a trifle less stiffly. 'It cannot, I regret, be as large an amount as I could wish, for—'

'My lord, I am in need of nothing,' she said quickly. 'I did not marry you for—'

'I am quite aware of why you married me,' he interrupted, with a faint rise of hostility. Deliberately, he amended it. 'Or, at least, of why you say you married me.'

Her breath caught, and she threw a wary glance at him. She had given too much away. What had she said to make him suspicious? She did not speak, fearing what he might ask.

But Raith was already regretting his manner of introducing the subject. Her defences were up. He would not reach the truth this way. He backtracked.

'There are bound to be items that you will need, apart from the obvious—'

'The obvious?' she cut in, dark eyes flying to his face.

'For God's sake, Rosina, do not take an affront into your head!' he begged, seeing her expression. 'I am talking of clothing. You are a peeress. You need gowns suited to your station.'

Involuntarily, Rosina looked down at the faded open robe of blue floral, worn over a dimity petticoat. Another of Louise's cast-offs that she had imperfectly altered to fit her trimmer figure. The implied criticism sent heat into her cheeks, and she fidgeted with the set of the garment.

'You need not look like that,' came Raith's gentler tones. 'It is not your fault.'

The black orbs rose again to his, defiance in them. 'Only in having married you.'

There was instant hurt at his eyes. She had wanted to hurt him! The realisation smote her conscience, and she looked away, her fingers wafting to the fluttering at her bosom.

'I d-did not m-mean that,' she uttered, low-voiced.

'If you did, I must be the last to blame you,' came the leaden response. 'However, it is too late for regret.'

'You can say that?'

His glance raked her. 'What does that mean?'

Rosina's hand crept up to her neck. 'N-nothing.'

'It was not nothing.' He waited, but his wife remained steadfastly silent, refusing to look at him. Raith fought down an inward sigh. 'Never mind. Let us return to the point of this discussion. An allowance is a simple necessity. You cannot be forever applying to me.'

'I have no intention of applying to you!' she flashed. Checking herself, she bit her lip. 'I b-beg your pardon.'

'You need not,' Raith said dully. 'I am aware that I have made it difficult for you to speak to me with any degree of ease.'

Rosina looked down at her hands, hardly conscious of her repetitive pulling at her fingers' ends. 'I brought it on myself, my lord. I overstepped the boundaries of our agreement.'

'Yes, you did, by thunder!' he returned. 'But you know well that we have long thrown that agreement out the window.'

There was reproach in her eyes. 'I thought so, yes.'

Raith sighed. 'You need not look at me so. I have already admitted that the fault was mine.'

Rosina kept her gaze steady on his. 'Do you regret our marriage, Raith?'

'Not that, no!' He took a step towards her, and checked. 'It has been only a week. We must give it time.'

'Willingly, my lord. But what is the use of assigning blame, if there is to be no change?'

A slight smile creased his mouth. 'That is why we are here.'

'Oh? I thought you said it was an "interview".'

There was a silence. He eyed her with a resurgence of the emotions he had been keeping in check. Those expressive eyes, with such power to move him. She could sweep him in seconds from desire, to fury, to remorse, to tenderness. She roused him in every possible way. So readily could he become her slave, if he had not so fervid a need to be her master! And yet he would have her confide in him, that he might free himself of restraint. As if he could free himself of his own chains! It would be laughable, if it were not so tragic.

'What is it you want of me, Rosy?'

It was involuntary, said with a sigh, and he did not know that he had shortened her name to a child-like endearment. To Rosina, it was as if the barriers were coming down. She answered with no thought of preconception.

'I want you to be yourself! I hate it when you retire into your shell. I had rather you railed at me, or threw at me your bitterest acrimony. Anything—than that you should treat me with this civil *indifference*. I know it to be a lie!'

He looked away. What would she say if he told her that it was the only way he could induce himself to keep his hands off her? Recoil, belike. And if she did not, and he gave in to temptation, the very touch of her would drive him into unwise accusation. Unwise—and unfair.

'Accept my apologies,' he said as gently as he could. 'I will try to do better.'

Rosina subsided in defeat. She felt quite as much shut out, and she did not know why. For all his changed tone, there was an indefinable barrier still. A withdrawal—but one even more difficult to penetrate. Instinctively she felt that it had less to do with his self-loathing than with her. In some way, he found her wanting.

Raith saw the vulnerability creep over her features, and she was again the waif he had married. Inwardly he cursed, and rose, crossing to the window so that he need not see her. He spoke without turning round.

'You may have more need of funds than you know. We cannot forever avoid meeting with our neighbours, and you must prepare for it. They will soon be returning from London for the winter break. We will have to put up some kind of show together, for the sake of appearances.'

He turned on the words, and saw, with a sense of shock, that Rosina was looking deathly pale, the coal-black eyes regarding him with stunned surprise. Her lip was quivering, and her hands were so tightly clasped together in her lap that the knuckles jutted out white. Concern gripped him.

'What is the matter?'

'You said I should live retired,' she uttered on a gasp.

Raith frowned. 'Yes, but I did not mean without any sort of intercourse.'

'There was to be no social life,' Rosina protested.

'That is quite impossible. A man of my rank cannot live as a hermit, especially not in the country.' He came a step or two towards her. 'It will not be so very bad, Rosina. There are, unfortunately, no other peers in this immediate vicinity, which means that I cannot help but attract the interest of the gentry hereabouts. Furthermore, I have put a notice of our marriage in the *Gazette*, and—'

'Dear Lord, the *Gazette*!' she echoed, aghast.

'It is usual, you know,' he said, on a note of puzzlement. 'I regret the necessity, but it had to be done.'

'Why had it to be done? Why must anyone know of it?' She sounded frantic, a rise of panic in her voice.

'What in thunder is the matter, Rosina? What objection can you have to be seen to be my wife?'

'It is not that,' she said in a tetchy tone.

'Then why should you care?'

Why? Dear Lord, but for a very good reason! Only she could hardly tell Lord Raith.

She was up, pacing the room. Raith watched her, tweaking at her fingertips one moment, the next throwing her hands to her face in another of her unquiet gestures. In growing alarm, he wondered at her thoughts.

They were frantic. Suppose her guardian were to read of it? Dared she hope that he would not make trouble? And what—Lord help her!—what of that other dread creature? If he did not see the announcement for himself, he was bound to hear of it, for he moved in circles where gossip was ever rife. What if he spoke of it? Dear Lord, she might meet with his acquaintances! Herbert Cambois was not his only gaming crony. And he was of this county, though in the northernmost part. She had naïvely thought it a sufficient distance from here.

'They were bound to know of it sooner or later,' she muttered. 'But later, please God! I had not thought the mischief would be out this early.'

Halting, she turned on her husband, and found him regarding her with a heavy frown. Of suspicion? Well might he think her behaviour deserving of it. But that was past mending. This was a disastrous turn.

'Who will come here? Who is it you expect?'

'My immediate neighbours,' he answered cautiously. 'There may be others from further afield. The curious are bound to wish to meet you.'

'You knew this!' she accused. 'And you never warned me. I asked you what you expected of me, and you would not say.'

'I said, if you recall, that we would have to work it out as time went on,' he pointed out.

It was true, Rosina conceded, but it did not help. 'This is not what I bargained for.'

'What did you bargain for, Rosina?' he demanded sharply. 'You have spoken of protection. Who is it you fear?'

'No one.' She whisked about, pacing rapidly away from him, pulling at her fingers. 'It is only that I did not wish for such a life. Had I known of it, I should not have married you. I do not wish to be obliged to indulge in that sort of social interaction.'

Raith curbed his impatience with difficulty. Better to reassure her, than demand enlightenment. She was clearly too afraid to give him any rational answer.

'I am sorry if the necessity upsets you. I have no more wish than you to engage in social activities. But the surest way to invite excessive interest is to try to avoid such contacts. If we accept social intercourse, but do not ourselves initiate it, we will soon be classed as dullards, and people will be glad to leave us alone.'

Rosina checked, a set look in her face. By that time, the damage would have been done. She did not dare to hope that either Herbert Cambois or his odious friend would leave her alone. At the least, their knowledge of her whereabouts was bound to lead to unpleasantness.

Yes, she had entered into this marriage for protection. Once securely a wife, she knew neither could physically touch her. But that did not mean that they could not harm her. Or, which was worse, her husband.

'Lord Raith,' she said flatly, but with a giveaway tremor in her voice, 'it was ag-greed that I should live r-retired upon your estates. And that is what I intend to d-do. I shall engage in no s-social intercourse. If anyone p-presents themselves here, I shall r-refuse to see them.'

'Oh, indeed?' he said, equally flat—and dangerous beyond words, the livid welt standing out on the stern line of his cheek. 'Then, by thunder, Lady Raith, you have much to learn of me! You will do precisely what I tell you.'

Rosina's bravado collapsed. She threw her hands over her face. 'I can't, Raith, I can't!'

Caution vanished. He crossed the room, and seized her hands, pulling them down. 'Why, Rosina? Tell me why!'

'I cannot! There is no other reason.'

'No other? You have given me no reason at all.' He took her shoulders and shook her. 'Rosina, I will not be denied in this! I must know what happened to you, I tell you. What skeletons have you in that closet of yours?'

'None,' she cried frantically, pushing against his arms. 'You have more skeletons than I!'

'Don't try to fob me off! I will find you out.'

She struggled vainly in his strong grip, thrusting at his chest. 'Let me go! You will tell me nothing of yourself— yet you expect me to give up my secrets.'

Raith pounced on this. 'So there is something! I knew it.' He shook her again. 'Tell me!'

'No! You are mistaken—there is nothing to know,' she uttered desperately, trying to pull away.

He would not let her. 'Who is it who frightened you so? Believe me, I am no fool. What is the explanation for your upset in your bedchamber the other night? The man, Rosina! Who was he?'

She gave a gasp, and stilled. 'What did you say?'

'You had some sort of encounter, did you not? What man was involved?'

Rosina wrenched herself out of his slightly slackened grasp, backing away, and looking up at him with sudden fierceness in her black eyes. 'What do you mean? How— *involved*?'

Raith paused. That had been foolish. Now she would believe him suspicious of her. He wanted to pursue the subject, but the change in her dictated caution. More in that strain, and he would alienate her utterly. He drew a breath to steady his pulse, realising only now how uneven it had become.

'I meant nothing untoward,' he said raggedly. 'Not on your part.'

He was suspicious! How could he think it? But of course he could. She had known how it must be, which is why she had been careful to conceal it all. Men could not be trusted in the matter of the honour of their women. Mama had taught her that, when she was preparing her for—as she then thought—a normal married life to be looked forward to. The least hint of lightness would arouse a demon of jealousy. Men, Mama had said, might be as unchaste as they pleased—had not Raith even spoken to her of his amorous adventures when he had talked of the effect of his scar upon women?—but their wives must be beyond reproach. Nevertheless, the intimation that he thought it, even if he believed her innocent of blame, hurt her so much that, in that moment, she hated him for it.

All at once she recalled how he had put her from him. Not physically, but mentally, earlier in this dreadful discussion. The barrier was now explained. He thought her impure, and he would not touch her. There was nothing she could say. It mattered little what she said, if she were to try to explain. Without proof, he would never believe her.

She looked at him, unknowing that her eyes were sombre. 'Well, you have made up your mind, I suppose.'

About her guilt, Rosina meant. But Raith took it differently. Yes, he had made up his mind. There was no escaping the burden. No matter her fears, she would have to face the inevitable.

'I will take you to Banbury tomorrow. It is the nearest large town, and there are one or two modistes from whom you may purchase gowns a trifle closer to current fashion.'

Rosina thought that he was wilfully misunderstanding her. There was no point in arguing.

'You command me, sir,' she replied, on a distinct note of sarcasm. 'I must obey.'

Upon which, she walked out of the room, leaving Raith fuming. Whether he was more angry with Rosina or himself, he did not know. He had bungled it thoroughly. Had he not guessed how it would be? All his careful plans for nothing. He had drawn Rosina's enmity.

The chaise bowled comfortably along the road to Banbury, for the lack of rain had left the ground dry. It was a dull day, which was why Raith had elected not to drive his phaeton. He was doubly glad of it after five miles or so, for his temper worsened every moment, and in an open carriage he would have been obliged to hold his tongue against the ears of his groom behind.

'Is it your intention to hold to this attitude indefinitely?' he demanded acidly.

Rosina refused to answer, maintaining her fixed gaze out of the window. He could make her come with him, but he could not make her speak. And how dared he complain of her 'attitude'? What of those days when he had withdrawn into his ice castle, refusing to deal her more than polite civility? Let him now have a taste of his own medicine.

'It is of no use to sulk, Rosina!'

Oh, and had he not sulked? With what unmitigated injustice had he not taken himself out of her orbit for an offence he could only have imagined? Rosina could not forgive him: for the unspoken accusation, for condemning her, for his lack of faith. Most of all, for withdrawing without the slightest attempt to communicate with her.

If he had been gentle, open with her, tried to win her trust—she might have told him all. Instead, he had thrown it in her face. And now he complained of her silence! Could he not see that she was too hurt and angry to converse with him?

'Rosina, I warn you, I will not endure this. You forget yourself!'

It was too much. She turned on him, white with rage. 'Do your w-worst, sir! I care not.'

'You will care soon enough, I promise you,' he returned, 'if I have much more of this.'

The black eyes flashed. 'Are you threatening me, my lord? What will you do, b-beat me?'

'I am sorely tempted!'

'It is no more than I would expect,' she threw at him.

Raith's own eyes burned, and he seized her wrist. 'I have done nothing to deserve that from you.'

A choked sob escaped her, and she dragged herself from his hold. She stifled the onset of tears, clutching her fingers together in her lap. Husky, she spoke without looking at him.

'The rules have changed, my lord.'

He was shamed by her burst of sobs, and a little of his anger died. The last thing he had wanted was to lose his temper with her. But at least she was talking again. Not that he understood what she meant.

'How so?'

Rosina swallowed. Her fury had dulled, leaving a dead weight in her chest. She wanted to say that he had forfeited her esteem, and therefore she had no longer any desire or purpose to be the conformable wife for which he had advertised. But she could not make her tongue say such words to him. Already she had wounded him by an undeserved rebuke. Better that she refused to answer. But if she again relapsed into silence, he would only provoke her out of it.

'How much of my allowance am I permitted to spend, sir?' she asked instead, her tone stiff.

Disappointment struck at Raith. He had hoped to bring her out of this intolerable alienation. If the rules had changed, it was by her hand. She was no longer the vulnerable waif he had married. From the instant he had mentioned that accursed contretemps in her bedchamber, he had lost her to some other creature whom he did not recognize—one who regarded him with hatred. If he thought it would answer, he would attempt a soft approach. Only that, in her present mood, was impossible.

He accepted the change of subject. 'The expense will not come from your allowance. You will need whatever it takes to create the right impression. Do not stint, and tell the modiste to send the bills to me.'

Rosina instantly resolved to spend as little as possible.

Ottery regarded his client with perturbation as Raith marched about his office, the drab greatcoat swishing about his ankles. Raith saw the doubt in his lawyer's face, but refused to allow himself to be deflected. He had explained the urgency of his need, reporting Rosina's reaction to the whole matter of being publicly seen. Not omitting, though without going into detail, how that had provoked such a divisive quarrel that he was now driven to this means of enquiry.

'I care not how you do it, but find out what you can. You can start, I suppose, with this nurse of hers.'

His lawyer frowned. 'I have no direction, my lord. Lady Raith and I corresponded only through the Receiving Office at Brinklow. What is more, I don't even know the woman's name.'

Raith cursed. 'And I had that letter in my hand, by thunder! I cannot remember it, for I was too much out of my head to pay any heed.'

'Out of your head, my lord?'

'You need not look at me like that, Ottery. I know I have ruined everything, and there is no immediate resolution to be hoped for. Which is why I am asking for your help. Think, man! What can you do?'

Ottery considered. 'Do you know anything about this nurse, sir?'

'Only that she is blind and lives in a cottage somewhere.'

'Then it must be within easy reach of Brinklow. I had best begin at the Receiving Office, and check the villages roundabout.' He paused, thinking. 'Is there no other lead, my lord? Have you found out nothing at all?'

Raith's lips tightened. 'There was a guardian in the case. My wife claims that he died, but I think she is lying.'

He hesitated. He had hoped to avoid broaching this, but if Ottery was to appreciate the significance of his need—!

'Either he—or some other man, I don't know—has had at least designs on her virtue, if not...' He faded out, tugging his breath on the rise of emotion.

The lawyer got up from his chair in a good deal of consternation. 'My lord, you are not suggesting—?'

'Ottery, I do not know! Something occurred—of that nature. You are the only person I could trust with such a confidence.'

'Who was the guardian?' said his lawyer, suddenly brisk.

'I believe the husband of one of her mother's cousins.'

'Then it behoves me, I think, to try to find him, assuming he is not dead.'

There was a brief silence. Then Ottery came around the desk, and put a hand on his shoulder. 'Are you certain, my lord, that you cannot find a way through the impasse you have described? I am of the opinion that the results would be happier if you pursued the question with your wife.'

'No doubt,' Raith said dully. 'But that road is, I fear, closed to me.'

'It will not help your understanding with her if she discovers that you have set me to this task,' he warned.

'Do it! I will deal with that when it comes—if I have to.' What other choice had he? Battle was fairly joined with Rosina, and nothing would serve him but this.

The emporium outside which her husband had set Rosina down was not by any means of the first stare. It was hardly, he had pointed out, to be expected in a town like Banbury. Rosina had made no comment until she'd heard that Nadine had been recommended by Mr Ottery.

'Mrs Ottery, he tells me, has taken her custom here, for the woman has the Parisian touch.'

'Is she one of those poor creatures who has escaped from the Terror?' asked Rosina, forgetting to be stiff.

'I dare say,' agreed Raith, warmed by her more natural delivery. 'She has not been here much above two years, I gather, and I must suppose that not all French seamstresses can be accommodated in London.'

However that might be, on entering the portals of Nadine, Rosina felt herself to have been transported to paradise. Never had she seen such a collection of delightful gowns. Not that she had much experience. She had only been previously to any shop of the kind as a messenger for Louise. Not since Mama's time had she gone to a modiste to buy anything for herself—and then she had been so young that only the most demure of gowns had been permitted.

Her reception, when she announced herself to be Lady Raith, was gratifying. Taking her cue from her spouse's words, and not wishing to appear gauche, she said that she had been recommended by Mrs Ottery. *Madame* had at once been sent for by the assistant, and Rosina had the honour to be served by Nadine herself. The woman was indeed French, but she spoke good English, and there was no difficulty in understanding Rosina's needs. No hint of disapproval was given of the obviously ancient fashion of the gown she presently had on—that made-over pink chintz which had belonged to Louise.

Rosina was led about the salon, and shown a quantity of elegant gowns, almost all made with an astonishingly high waist. Rosina had not seen anything like it even in the last of Louise's copies of the *Ladies' Magazine*.

'Ah, but it is de very latest mode, milady,' Nadine assured her, when she questioned this. 'It has come from Paris. All de mesdames at London are wearing it.'

No matter the recent upheaval in their land, it seemed the French were yet the dictators of fashion. The gowns were made up in plain, sprigged or spotted muslin, mostly of white. The modiste assured her that, as a married woman, she was not obliged to wear white, and might with propriety even wear silk.

Rosina was at first overwhelmed, but the lure of new clothes—and those uncommonly à la mode—proved too great. Forgetting utterly her quarrel with Raith for a space, she tried on a variety of gowns and pirouetted about before a long mirror, in a state of delightful enchantment. The new waistline felt odd at first, set a little below the bosom, the skirt falling loosely to the ground. It had less fullness than she was used to, but a deal more movement in the petticoat.

'But de fashion, milady, it is perfect for you!' exclaimed Nadine, and Rosina was indeed gratified to see how well it suited her slim form. She looked taller, and altogether more graceful, she thought. And when Nadine produced a ribbon bandeau, threading it through her hair, the result was much more attractive than her close caps. The modiste showed how her hair could be worn otherwise in a high knot, which gave her the elegance of a long neck.

Rosina had set four gowns aside, together with accessories suggested by Nadine—a green net cloak for the white muslin and a sarcenet scarf to accompany the sprigged walking dress—and was debating between a Turkish robe with lace trimming, and an open robe with a pleated bodice, when a chance remark of Nadine's recalled her resolve to her mind.

'If milady will be advised,' she said, 'de Turkish it is nice, but de pleat it is more becoming to milady's figure. And so,' she added with an arch look, 'shall be more interesting for milord, I think.'

Milord? Raith! Oh, no. How could she have fallen into such extravagance? She was not the young newly-wed Nadine imagined, courted for her charms. She was the wife of Raith's convenience, purchased by advertisement. It was not fitting that she spend so much money. She did not ask the price of the gowns. It might not be London, but she was well aware of the exorbitant cost of female attire.

If there was an undercurrent of another purpose in her decision, Rosina refused to recognise it.

'I am sorry, *madame*,' she said, with real regret, for it was hard to give them up, 'but I fear I must decline all but the white muslin I first chose.'

Nadine looked utterly confounded, but that could not be helped. She said nothing, and Rosina realised one advantage of her status. Traders would take care not to offend her. The modiste had one of her assistants pack up the gown in a bandbox, and carry it outside to where the chaise had been left to await Rosina's pleasure.

She shook hands with Nadine, left the shop—and found Raith waiting for her outside its door. He was looking extremely irate, and the grey eyes glinted as he addressed her in a sarcastic undertone.

'Where, may I ask, are the other bandboxes?'

Unprepared, Rosina bit her lip. 'There is only the one.'

'One?' he repeated ominously. 'One bandbox? And how many gowns does it contain?'

Rosina began to feel sick, wishing that her spirits had not been so uplifted that she was now unequipped to fight back. But it had to be said.

'One.'

Raith's eyes narrowed. His voice was acid. 'Your notions are so nice, I take it, that you could find only one gown to your taste.'

She was nettled by his sarcasm. 'On the contrary, there were several, but I do not need them.'

'How many?'

'I do not know how many!' she retorted, anger rising fast.

'*How many?*'

She jumped, quivering a little. 'Five or six—I think.'

He spoke with careful restraint. 'Then be so good, madam wife, as to go back into that shop, and purchase the other five gowns.'

'No, I—'

'Rosina!'

She fell silent, glowering at him.

'I am not going to argue the matter, Rosina. But I warn you that we will remain here—all day, if necessary—until you do what I tell you.'

Rosina hesitated. He watched the black eyes waver, and kept his own directed at her face. He had been blazingly angry with her, but it was only by sheer effort of will that he maintained the appearance of it. The waif was back, and he could not endure her distress. He saw her crumble, and his heart melted. But he was not going to show it.

With one last defiant flash of the coal-black eyes, she turned from him, and went back into the shop. Raith let his breath go, and moved back towards the chaise.

Rosina went slowly through into Nadine's salon, wondering what in the world she could possibly say. Her humiliation was intense. How could Raith make her do this? Fervently did she wish that she had not let her determination to thwart her husband override her good sense. She might have known that he would react thus. To her cost, she knew him to be uncommonly dictatorial, if not always as peremptory as this. She had no choice but to obey him. How she hated her marriage vow!

She must think fast, for Nadine was coming towards her, a look of interest in her sharp French features.

'Milady?'

'I think—' Inspiration failed her. Dear Lord, what could she say? 'The other gowns, *madame*… His Lordship…' Oh, but this was hateful! She would never forgive Raith.

A look of comprehension came into the modiste's face, and her eyes registered a quick flash of amusement before she veiled them. 'Can it be that milady has changed her mind?'

Rosina was torn between relief and embarrassment, but she seized the excuse. An idea came—too late, but still of use.

'His Lordship has—has reminded me that we have a number of engagements. I—I think it would be better to take all the gowns that I liked. Can you recall them?'

'But yes, milady.' The modiste moved in the direction of the back, clapping her hands at one of her assistants. She gave Rosina an understanding smile. 'Milady would perhaps prefer dat de gowns are delivered?'

To spare her further ignominy while the gowns were packed up? With gratitude, Rosina accepted the offer, and found that there was more to Nadine's solicitude.

'If milady will permit—' She offered the added assistance of arranging the purchase of suitable accessories—bonnets, shoes and gloves—to go with the gowns, and would ask the traders to send their bills to His Lordship. 'If milady will trust to my judgement?'

Milady was only too glad to do so. She had not thought of the inevitable need for accoutrements to go with the new styles. Lord help her, if it had struck Raith! Nadine ascertained the sizes required, and the matter was settled.

Rosina left the shop in a much happier frame of mind. Her heart jumped a little when she saw Raith waiting by the open chaise door. But, forestalling criticism, she spoke the instant she reached him, in a low voice meant for his ears alone—for Parton was in the act of letting down the steps of the chaise for her.

'I have no further bandboxes, but you need not scold. Nadine is to have the gowns delivered—together with anything else I may need.'

Raith nodded, and handed her up into the chaise. But once the door was shut upon them, he turned to her.

'I apologise for my treatment of you, Rosina—but truly, it was the outside of enough.'

She looked away, fidgeting with her fingers. Had she not borne enough? What sort of apology was it, that contained its own excuse? From the corner of her eye, she saw his hand reach out. It closed over her own, and the warmth of it sent a charge of violent emotion hurtling into her chest. Her breath stopped.

'Rosy,' he said softly.

A compression seized her heart. She felt him shift beside her, and then his free hand cupped her face, drawing it round to face him. The grey eyes were tender.

'I can't bear this between us,' he told her gently. 'Can we not find a way through it?'

Rosina fought against the riot in her bosom. Her voice did not wish to obey her, coming out in a husky whisper.

'It was not—of my making.'

'I know.' His fingers played absently with hers, and he grimaced. 'You did say you preferred me to rail at you than to retire into my shell.'

The faintest of smiles wavered on her lips. 'I did, my lord.'

Raith warmed, and there was a swelling in his chest. Then she grew serious again, and his heart sank at her words.

'But that was b-before. There were—things said, Raith. I do not know how they are to be got over.'

'Nor I,' he agreed. A heavy sigh left his lips, and he released her fingers.

The loss struck Rosina hard. A bleak look had crept into his eyes, and she saw it with pain. Oh, dear Lord! He must not think that she did not care. With barely realised intent, she reached out her left hand as if she would touch it to his damaged cheek.

Raith saw it, and reflex took over. His hand shot up,

and seized her wrist just before the fingers reached his face. He jerked her hand away, holding her so tightly that his own hand shook with the effort.

Rosina gasped with pain, unable to help crying out. 'You are hurting me!'

His pulse was thundering in his head. He had not meant to stop her. He could not help himself. He heard what she said, but for a moment he did not realise how he was hurting her. Then he saw her hand, the fingers splayed. He glanced at her face. Her lips were parted in a pose of agony, her eyes glued to her imprisoned hand.

Recollecting himself, he loosened his clutch, and let her go. Rosina snatched her hand back, and grasped it just below the point where he had been gripping it, the fingers still spread as they began to curl. She was staring at it, breathing hard, and Raith saw the angry red weal his fingers had made.

He groaned, dropping his forehead into his hand. 'Hell and damnation!' he muttered numbly. After a moment or two, he straightened, and looked round at her. She was nursing her wrist, her lips pinched together. It must be hurting her still. Remorse bit into him.

'There does not seem to be anything I can say, except to beg your pardon.'

'It makes no matter,' Rosina said in a subdued tone. 'It was foolish of me.'

'For God's sake, don't try to take the blame!' he said forcefully.

She was silent. Raith sank back into his corner of the chaise, and closed his eyes. It seemed that no matter how he tried, he was doomed to failure. What in thunder was he to do?

Chapter Six

Rosina was dressing with a good deal of care. She did not wish to provoke another such outburst as had greeted her last night when she had dared to appear for dinner in an old gown. Raith had flown into one of his rages, demanding to know whether she was determined on behaving in this rebellious fashion forever, and adding a rider to the effect that she might hate him as much as she pleased but she was his wife, and she had better dress the part, or it would be the worse for her.

'And don't dare to tell me that the gowns are not yet delivered, for you brought one with you!'

'Yes, but I did not think it mattered quite yet,' Rosina had defended herself.

'Why in thunder do you suppose I troubled to take you?'

'I know, but there is no one here to see me.'

'Except,' her husband had declared bitterly, 'myself. Spare me the insult of telling me that you don't care how you look before me, for that I know already!'

With which, he had stormed off into the dining-room, leaving her to follow how she might. A frosty silence had reigned at the dinner table, and Raith had vanished after she had left him to his port. Rosina had not seen him since—he was undoubtedly off about his estate business, a convenient excuse for his withdrawal from his wife. She had spent the day in a state compound of misery and resentment.

How had she been expected to know that he desired her to change her appearance when they were in private? Was she supposed to be able to read his mind? It was typical of Raith to take an affront into his head. She had not meant anything of the kind—though she might readily have done so had she thought of it. Well might she hate him! Only did he suppose her to have so little regard for her skin deliberately to provoke him? She did not truly believe that he would raise a hand to her, but in his wild moods his tongue was frightening enough. The memory of his face in quite other mood came back to her. Dear Lord, but he was, when softened, all too endearing—and, oh, so difficult to hate! Either side of him could make her pulse race. It was only the lightning changes that she found so unsettling.

It was better not to take any risks. Accordingly, she enlisted Joan's willing assistance with her toilette, bidding her put forth her best efforts. If there was a stirring at the back of her mind of a wish to know how her husband thought she looked in the new fashion, Rosina suppressed it. She was doing this only so that he might not rail at her again.

She was a trifle late, for Joan was as unhandy yet with her hair as she was herself, never having previously attempted to secure it in the topknot advocated by Nadine. At the first attempt it was a degree lopsided, and a vision of Raith's cynical look made Rosina tear out the pins. He would be bound to make some caustic comment!

'But, m'lady, I thought it looked very well,' protested the maid, sighing.

'It was not straight, Joan. I cannot appear before His Lordship looking like a scarecrow! Let us try it again.'

Thus adjured, Joan set to with a will, and Rosina presently arose from her dressing-table with a style that she considered to be at least respectable. She waited while the maid placed the green net cloak about her shoulders, and examined herself in the long pier-glass with a critical eye. The gown was deceptively simple, with a cross-over front cut low to the bosom, from which the skirt fell in soft folds, and with little sleeves ending in ruffled bands, worn over long tight undersleeves of muslin through which the glow of her flesh could be seen. The green net appeared superfluous.

'Not the cloak,' Rosina decided, slipping it off. 'In the daytime, perhaps, but not now. I hope I don't freeze to death!'

But her blood seemed altogether too active to permit of her feeling the cold, pumping rapidly through her veins as she tripped carefully down the stairs, holding up the unaccustomed looseness of her skirts. What if he was still too angry to meet her for dinner? All that effort wasted! Her heart jumping, she entered the saloon.

Raith was standing by the fire, leaning his arm along the mantelshelf. He was himself attired formally, in that dark coat and breeches from their wedding day, with blue silk to his waistcoat. He looked across at her, and straightened abruptly.

Rosina paused on the threshold, watching his reaction, half-hoping for some word of praise. He was staring, but she could not read his expression. Self-conscious, she averted her eyes, and moved into the room.

Raith's gaze remained riveted upon her. He was incapable of words. She took his breath away! If he had before thought of her as delicate, she was now doubly so. The air of fragility was pronounced, for the litheness of her form was accentuated by the strange style. There was elegance, enhanced by the lifting of her hair, which equally emphasised the elfin quality of her countenance. But above all, she exuded so much sensuality that Raith had only one idea in his head. To sweep her up into his arms, and carry her directly to his bed, there to overbear both her resistance and his own scruples, and make her irrevocably his—and his alone.

A disastrous desire! How could he possibly do it? Rosina would fight him with her last breath. Or would she? He had expected continued defiance, and braced himself to face her renewed enmity. Instead she had presented him with a show of obedience. Was it to mock him? If so, she was wonderfully successful, for he could barely contain his yearning.

It was several moments before he was able to command it. By that time, a hint of colour had risen in her cheeks, and he realised belatedly that he had not even had the grace to compliment her.

'You look—' he was obliged to hesitate over his choice of adjective, for everything he wished to say was ineligible '—charmingly,' he finished lamely.

How inadequate a description. He would have preferred to tell her that she was alluring beyond endurance, but he had not the courage. He watched her lips break into a smile, and found his breath unsteady. One moment more, and his control would break!

'Shall we go in?' he said hastily.

He ought to offer his arm, but he could not trust himself to approach her. He watched her hesitate, eye him uncertainly. Abruptly, he snapped.

Rosina felt him pass her as she made for the door. It slammed shut. Her heart jerked. Raith was leaning against it, the wildness of his features heightened by the livid scar, of which he seemed wholly unaware. He radiated danger—of a kind that made her pulses leap in an erratic dance. Thought fled. His hot eyes raked her, and a blaze of heat rose up inside her as the recognition of his intent drove the blood thrumming into her veins.

Then he reached for her, and she moved as one in a trance, drawn intimately close by his strong grip. She saw only the depths of his avid grey eyes, hauntingly near. Then they closed, and his lips came down on hers. He mouthed her teasingly, in so tender a minuet that her bones turned to water.

Raith felt her sag, and caught her close against him, increasing the pressure of his lips, while the heady delight of her here in his arms drove from his mind every thought but one.

'By God, but I want you!' he uttered gutturally against her mouth. 'From the first I have wanted you—desperately!'

Rosina heard him with a melting at her heart, and groaned within his kiss. Her limbs trembled uncontrollably as she became aware of the heat and hardness of the form against which she was so tightly held. Her breath shortened as his lips left her mouth to shift down her cheek, and breathe flame into the hollows of her neck. She shivered the more, and her hands came up without intent, grasping at his shoulders, at his face.

Her hand came in contact with an unexpected ridge, and on the instant that she took in its significance, Raith froze. For a few hazardous seconds, Rosina held her breath, as a chill seeped through the fervid heat between them, like an ill-omened breeze.

Raith fought against the impulse that bade him fling away her hand, while the driving force within him sought to speed him to his goal. Slowly he shifted a little away, bringing his hand up to cover hers against his cheek, holding it there. His eyes found hers.

'You feel it, Rosy?' he said, low-toned and husky. 'The worst of me under your hand. Can you endure to feel it?'

She answered him from instinct, her voice a shaky whisper. 'You d-do not let me f-feel it. Let go my hand.'

It was hard to invite her touch, but it struck him in that instant that to do so would be to invite also her trust. He removed his hand from hers, setting his teeth, unable to help his own stiffening. He watched the movement of her coal-black eyes, willing himself to remain still as her fingers traced along the lengthy ridging line from his eyebrow, down his cheek, and to the corner of his lip. Never had he been so aware of it!

Rosina could feel the resistance that he was holding in check. The wound under her fingertips felt alien, but not as loathsome as it looked. She felt no repugnance, no pity, even, but a kind of morbid satisfaction, as her curiosity, so long aroused, was at last permitted to be indulged. It was a fascinating contour—and so peculiarly Raith! As if the store by which he set his own worth were contained in this unevenly ribbed line.

She would have liked to dwell longer upon it, but she knew his discomfort was too acute. Regretfully, she removed her fingers, and saw, with an inexplicable pain at her heart, the immediate relaxation of his rigidity. Her eyes went to his.

'Well?' he said, and the tight-lipped demand shot her through with distress.

What was she to say? She could hardly reveal to him the obscurely pleasurable sensations of her exploration! She recalled, with a sense of shame, the story he had told of a female who had obtained some sort of sensual satisfaction from the blemish. His disgust had been patent. What would she think of his wife, if she were to confess to such a feeling? Not that she had been moved in *that* way. It had served rather to give her a sense of intimacy, that he had allowed her a share in his deepest agony.

He was waiting. She must find something to say—that would not cause him to retire behind his protective barrier. And fast, for already his eyes were darkening.

'It is not nearly as bad as you think,' she said quickly. She saw that this statement found little favour, and thought fast. 'And—and now that I have once felt it, there can be no shock in my encountering it again—by accident.'

Raith did not know what he had wanted to hear, but these words did not encompass it. His ardour was already damped a trifle, despite the intense allurement of her nearness. It sank still more. He had hoped for better than this, by thunder! What, had he subjected himself to the excruciating disturbance of her touch, to be rewarded with an assurance that she might no longer expect to be shocked? What was she then—a degree less repelled? He was obliged to her for the mitigation!

'Then I may take it that you would have no objection to allow me to take you?' he said, unable to help a sarcastic inflexion creeping into his tone.

A wash of discomfiture flooded her, and she felt her cheeks grow warm. She matched his acrimony. 'Since when have my objections been the subject of your enquiry? You have always assumed them, and conducted yourself accordingly.'

'Because I see nothing other than duty!' he threw at her. 'It appears that I can make you respond to me, but—'

'What more do you want?' she cried despairingly.

'More than you are prepared to give, it seems.'

Frustration sighed out of her. 'Raith, I have never been other than willing. I am at your service, if you wish for it.'

'At my service!' he echoed, hurt beyond endurance.

'Hell and damnation take you, Rosina! Do *you* wish for it?'

She could not answer him. No, she did not—not if he meant to make her a sacrifice to his bitter self-hatred! She bit her lip, mute defiance in her gaze.

'I am answered, I suppose,' he said roughly. 'Would I knew whom it is I have to thank for it. I swear I would throttle him with my bare hands!'

He moved aside, and opened the door, oblivious of the blaze of anger in Rosina's eyes.

'Go in to dinner. I will join you presently.'

She left him without a word, and Raith crossed to the fireplace and rested his hands upon the mantel, staring down into the smouldering logs.

How much more of a fool was he determined to make of himself? He was shocked to realise that, in his need of her, he would have forgone that jealous possession of her maidenhead to which his emotions made him heir. Blood and thunder! Had he not sworn that he would not make himself master of her before he knew the truth? She had been taken—if it was so!—without her consent by this villainous unknown. But he must have taken her roughly, for she responded—and to his cost!—all too readily to gentleness. She had shown herself more than willing— had not she said as much? But, to his chagrin, she would not invite him in! Had she expressed a wish for his caresses, he would have thrown all caution to the winds.

As well that she did not wish for it, for his resolve was just. He owed that much to his name. Yet the blame was his for the close call. Had he not taken her to task last night for refusing to wear the new gown? If he was bowled over by her appearance, it was scarce Rosina's fault. He dared swear he might expect to see her return to her old garments tomorrow. She was unlikely to invite his cursed insanities a second time.

He sighed wearily, as he turned for the dining-room. Their relationship was deteriorating. And he was no nearer to gaining either her trust or her confidence.

Rosina was so choked with upset that she could not eat. She was glad of the excuse afforded by the delay of Raith's appearance, telling Kirkham curtly, as he came to serve her, that she would await His Lordship. His hateful, impossible Lordship! But she did not say it.

How could he be so unkind? Let him wallow in his bitterness, if he chose. Was she supposed to care? If he wanted her, he might have her at any time. It was his right. She had nothing to say to it. He knew as much. And if he hesitated, she was perfectly aware that it was not through any reluctance on her part, but from the dictates of his own masculine pride.

He had confessed, in the heat of the moment, his desire for her. But she had already known it—if not in her head, in the frenzied fire of her blood in response to him. A lump constricted her throat. Such tenderness as he had shown tonight when first he kissed her! It was that she wished for, if he only knew. If he used her thus, he might overcome all the hideous remnant of her guardian's rude betrayal.

Kirkham had poured her wine, and she reached out a quavery hand. A few sips of the red liquid sent a comforting warmth inside her. The slight relaxation released her tight thoughts, and the truth of her distress seeped into her mind.

She felt isolated by Raith's rejection. He was her husband. She would have taken him only for protection, but he wished for more than that. Yet in her darkest hour, she could not look to him for succour. Both his condemnation, and his insistence that she should enter into public acknowledgement of her position—the occasion of her wearing this horrid gown and its wretched sequel!—were alike to blame.

A thought struck her. What if Raith should not be content with showing her to this small public circle? He had already proven that the arrangement she had believed them to have made had not marched with his own understanding. Did she dare to trust him? Might his decision in this not be as changeable as the fiery friction of his moods?

Her fears rose to the surface as Raith entered the room and took his seat. She tried to quiet them for, as things stood between them, the last thing she needed was to let him see her apprehension. If only she could think that she might have overestimated the dangers. She might hope that Herbert Cambois was too drunk to read the journal. And that other? Why should he take time from his gambling to seek her out now? If it were only true that her acquaintance would be confined to the coterie of this small area, she might be less concerned.

'My lord?' she said impulsively.

He glanced at her. 'Ma'am?'

Her heart sank. Were they back to that? 'I wished only to ask—just how public a life you want me to lead?'

What was she at now? Had his unthinking reference brought on a reminder of her fears? Who in thunder was the fellow? But he must not ask that—not before the servants. Let them at least maintain some semblance of rational behaviour!

Yet Raith found himself unable to help an acid note. 'You can hardly call it leading a public life to be toadying to a parcel of neighbours.'

Rosina breathed a little more easily, nodding at the butler who was offering her a serving of artichoke pie to accompany the baked sole nestling on her plate.

'You will not then seek to take me to London?'

'London!' he repeated with loathing. 'You may be sure I shall not.'

But Rosina was not satisfied. 'Raith, do you swear it?'

He found the black eyes upon him in that vulnerable look that had always power to melt him. He fought the sensation, responding with impatience.

'Have a little sense, Rosina! Do you suppose anything would induce me to lay myself open to the sort of vulgar curiosity that I would be obliged to endure there? The very sight of me would set tongues wagging. No, you need not be afraid that I will drag you into London society.'

Rosina doggedly held his eyes, an unyielding compulsion in the black depths of her own. 'But do you swear it?'

Raith could not withstand her. His chest tightened, and he spoke without hesitation. 'I give you my word.'

He watched a measure of relief creep over her features, and saw her draw in a slow but unsteady breath, sighing it out. Then she turned away, and began to address her food. Raith followed suit, a stabbing at his gut for the hideous certainty that attacked him. If she was this much afraid, how could he doubt of his suspicions? She would tell him nothing. Was it because she feared to meet the villain—to her undoing?

Rosina stared at her maid in ill-concealed dismay, and requested her to repeat herself.

'His Lordship's compliments,' said Joan again, her slow delivery showing how careful she was to recall the precise wording that had been relayed to her, 'and please to join him in the antechamber before you retire.'

Rosina had already been halfway out of her clothes when the knock had come on the dressing-room door. She had leaped with shock, but recollected after a moment that

Raith could not yet have come up. Besides, the knock had come from the door that led to the corridor, not to the antechamber.

Joan had already gone to answer it, opening the door a crack and peering out. 'It's Mr Paulersbury, m'lady,' she had announced, and slipped out of the room. By the time Rosina had recalled that this individual was her husband's valet, Joan had come back into the room with this disturbing message.

Rosina was thrown into an agony of apprehension. What now, dear Lord? Was it possible that he had changed his mind? Did he mean this for an assignation? No, it was too absurd. If it were that, he would wait for the servants to leave, and then come himself to her bedchamber. Realising that she was halfway undressed, she began automatically to resume her gown, and then stopped, horrified.

Wear that again? And invite his abortive caresses? No, Lord help her! Hastily, she instructed Joan to help her to change, beset by horrid sensations. They had not talked again at dinner, after she had extracted that promise. Yet Raith had not disappeared, as she had thought he must. Instead, he had come into the saloon where they had taken tea together, and sat in a chair at a distance, looking abstracted. He had not once glanced at her, not even when she said good night. And now this! What did he mean by it?

When she was attired in her nightgown, and covered with a wrapper of blue linen, tied firmly at the waist, Rosina felt several degrees more secure than she had in the new muslin gown. Her hair was already loosened, and she combed it through and placed over it a mobbed nightcap. The ensemble must, at the least, discourage her spouse from any resumption of physical intimacy.

She dismissed her maid, and went to the door of the

antechamber. Her breath caught, and she put her ear to the wood, listening intently for some sound from within. Perhaps he was not yet there. What if she did not appear? Would he let it be, or come to find her? She fought down the flutters in her stomach. What use to defy him? Even if he did not pursue her, she would not escape a raking on the morrow. Better to get it over with, whatever it was he wanted.

She took hold of the door handle, and cautiously pulled it towards her, peeping around it.

'There is no need to be so shy of me—I will not bite!' came Raith's irascible tones.

Rosina stepped gingerly into the room, closing the door, keeping her back against it, and her fingers about the handle.

Raith was standing by the fireplace, where a two-pronged candelabrum threw light on his face from the mantel. It spread over the area immediately before the grate, in which a small fire was throwing up a lick of flame. The chairs had been set facing each other, in evident preparation for a tête-à-tête.

She looked warily at him. He was also clad in his night gear, a green-lined banyan of yellow silk belted loosely over his long nightshirt. His hair was untied, falling raggedly to his shoulders. Light flickered on his scar with the motions of the candlelight. He looked excessively attractive, and warmth flushed in Rosina's depths. His attitude, however, was far from amorous.

'Come here and sit down,' he said in a tone that brooked no argument. 'I want to talk to you.'

Rosina took a single pace towards him. 'Why could you not talk to me in the saloon?'

'Because I don't want to be disturbed. And there is no necessity to keep the servants awake.'

How long did he mean to keep her awake? Her heart

began to thump. Oh, she knew what this betokened! There was no intent of love-making here. He meant instead to question her, she was sure of it. And he had chosen this place so that she was thoroughly at a disadvantage. For to where could she escape? With the servants abed, he might keep her here all night—and none the wiser.

'Rosina, come here, I said!'

Her lip trembled, and tears sprang to her eyes. 'I d-do not w-want to.'

'Oh, good God!' he exclaimed, and moved quickly.

She backed, fumbling again for the door handle, but Raith was quicker. He took her by the shoulders, and she looked up, white-faced, into his shadowed features.

He brought one hand up and cupped her cheek, quite gently. 'Are you crying? Don't be a little fool, Rosy. I mean you no harm, I swear it! Now, come.'

The threat of tears receded. She allowed herself to be drawn to the fire, where Raith obliged her to sit down. She did so, primly, hugging her wrapper about herself.

Raith stood over her for a moment, watching these signs. How ill-at-ease she was! And no wonder. He moved to the other chair, and shifted it so that he sat at an angle, where the candlelight could only fall upon the good side of his face. He had himself well in hand, but the sight of her had given him a jolt. If she had looked enchanting in her new gown, she was unbearably sweet in the blue wrapper and mob-cap. But mercifully less seductive, although the consciousness that she was naked under the thin chemise that peeped below the bed gown had a deleterious effect upon his concentration.

Enough! He must control his thoughts. There was to be none of that. He hastened to come to the point.

'I want to talk to you, Rosy,' he repeated.

Rosina was a little cheered by his persistent use of the

pet name he had recently adopted for her. It augured a benign beginning at least. Yet still she eyed him askance.

'So you said. What about?' As if she did not know!

A faint smile curved his lips. 'You look at me with so much suspicion. The truth is that I am at a loss, dear wife.'

Rosina's gaze became even more suspicious. 'I do not understand you, sir.'

He relaxed into the chair. 'We know so little of one another.' He threw up a hand as she drew back. 'No, I don't mean to pry into your secrets—not yet. I thought I might rather give you some of mine.'

Indeed? He took her for a fool! She eyed him with a touch of scorn in her dark gaze. 'So that you may induce me to open my closet of skeletons in return?'

'At least you admit the existence of skeletons!'

'I admit nothing!'

His features tightened, and her pulse skittered a little. Let him grow angry! She was equally angered by his trickery. He would get nothing from her by this means.

Raith knew not how to proceed. She had found him out. He had arranged this with just that intent. Over dinner, with the persistent allure of his wife's presence at his side—and the goad of that cursedly suggestive promise she had extracted from him—he had begun to chafe at the restrictions of his marriage. How in thunder could he wait until Ottery delivered his findings? It might take weeks to unearth Rosina's history. Even then, how could he know it was the truth? Only Rosina knew that. Impatient, he had instructed Kirkham to have this room prepared, and ordered his wife's attendance. It began to seem as if he was wasting his time and effort.

The thrust of disappointment spurred him. By thunder, he would get what he wanted from her—and tonight!

He leaned forward again. 'Rosina, we cannot continue

in this way. And by God, there is no need for it! If you will only tell me the truth, we can—'

'What truth?' she broke in. 'That which you have built up in your mind? Oh, I know well enough what you think of me!'

He reached out and caught at her unwilling hand. 'If you truly knew it, you would open your mind to me!'

His fingers came in contact with the wrist he had man-handled on the previous day, and Rosina winced, giving an involuntary hiss of pain, trying to pull away.

'Be still, can't you?' Raith said, looking down. He saw a mark, and loosened his clasp, but tried to draw her hand towards him. 'Let me see!'

'It is nothing,' Rosina said quickly, again attempting to withdraw her hand.

He would not let her, and looked up. What he saw there made him respond with less than gentleness. 'Look at me with resentment in your eyes, if you will, but it is of no use to struggle, Rosy. I will not let you go until I have seen it.'

Her breath shortened. He had so much power to control her! Was she to have no will of her own? She let her hand lie in his, but a burning seed of rebellion grew in her breast.

Turning the hand in his fingers, Raith pushed back the wristband of her nightgown. A thin bruise was exposed there, in the soft flesh of the inside of her wrist. The memory flashed in his mind. In the chaise, when she had moved to touch his cheek. This had been her reward!

'I had no notion that I had hurt you so badly,' he uttered remorsefully.

Had he not? And he so apt to hurt! If not her body, then her heart and mind. But yes, her body. What of the sensations he had aroused in her by the intensity of his passion? And then rejected her only because she could not answer him on his terms. Did he ever stop to consider the distress he was inflicting? No—his temper was too ungovernable.

As if he read her thought, Raith sighed. 'I am a brutish husband, am I not?'

Yes, he was! But she did not say it. Yet almost Rosina suffered a reversal of feeling, as he lifted the wrist to his lips and pressed them gently to the wound. Oh, but he could be tender! Then why had he ever to carp at her? She dared swear that in another moment, if she did not do or say as he demanded, he would be railing again.

Raith covered the wrist, keeping her hand imprisoned within his own, and looked at his wife's face. She was eyeing him again with that wary suspicion in her eyes. How could he blame her?

'Why should you trust me?' he uttered, a harsh note in his voice. 'I said I might give you my secrets, did I not? Will you believe then that I know what it is to be in the power of someone who can force you to do what you would not?'

'You know it?' Rosina snatched her hand out of his, and tucked it into the folds of her wrapper. 'And yet you persist in treating me as if I have no power of my own.'

He was startled at her tone, and as of instinct shifted back, away from her. 'That is untrue! Did I force you that night I came to your bedchamber?'

Rosina stood up abruptly, incensed by his obtuseness, by the single track of his thoughts. 'Is that all that is in your mind? What of your insistence upon my staying in this room to be subjected to your questions? What of the manner in which you seized upon me in the saloon when I came down—'

'You need say no more!' he interrupted. He had risen when she did, and the consciousness of the truth of what she said drove him into defence. 'You may reproach me for that if you will, but as for my questions—I am your husband, Rosina. I have a right to know my wife's history.'

'Then why did you not obtain it before you married me?' she demanded, moving away from the chairs towards the window. 'You cared little enough what I might be—or who, if it comes to that. You did not even wish to see me. Why should you have troubled yourself about my past life?'

Raith felt himself to be on acutely assailable ground. How could he tell her that he had seen her, and not deserve the most righteous rebuke? He was obliged to prevaricate.

'What would you, Rosina? I am a peer of the realm, and that has its obligations.'

She turned on him, the black eyes snapping in the gloomy edges of the pool thrown by the candles. 'Obligations, Raith, which you were ready enough to ignore when it suited you.'

Her chest was so constricted that she could barely breathe, but the tide of burgeoning resentment that had so long been held in was overwhelming. She saw him open his mouth to speak, and forestalled him, her voice trembling with the force of her emotions.

'You t-took a wife from ad-advertisement. You c-cared only for the advantage of your f-fortune. Now—because you choose to—to set store by some incautious w-words that I let fall, I am made the—the scapegoat of your jealous fury!'

Raith followed her a step or two, racked by her distress, but hounded by his own need into defending himself further. 'Do you think I want to believe it? Blood and thunder, Rosina! Can you not see how I am tortured by these doubts?'

'Doubts!' she echoed, husky now, the words coming

thick and fast as the dam of anguish burst the barriers of her characteristic diffidence. 'Do you not see how your doubting t-tortures me? If there were any truth in that t-tenderness with which from time to time you move me—with which you touch my heart!—there would be no room in you for doubting. But it is *false*—and I hate you for it, Raith!'

He was aghast, moving to her. 'Rosina—'

'Do not come near me!' she cried, dashing the welling tears from her eyes, and backing away. 'I do not w-want to hear your cozening words—your soft approaches. They can mean nothing—or you would have faith.'

Raith stopped short. 'Blind faith? Is that what you expect?'

'I expect nothing. I have been given nothing!'

'How can you say so?' he demanded, hurt overriding the turmoil of dismay and guilt to which her grief had given rise. 'Is my regard nothing?'

'What regard? You have no regard for me, but only for yourself!' she threw at him. 'And for your arrogant pride.'

'Is it arrogance that a man should wish to assure himself that his wife is chaste?'

'It is arrogance to assume otherwise.'

'I do not assume it!'

'But you suspect it—and that is enough!'

Raith's fingers clutched at his hair. 'Hell and damnation! That you persist in this refusal to enlighten me can only increase my doubts. Why cannot you see that, Rosina?'

She uttered a mewl of equal frustration, throwing her hands to her face. 'Dear Lord, but you are blind! Raith, if you doubt me, you will do so whatever I tell you, unless you have certain proof. Can you deny it?'

Raith seized her right wrist, and pulled her close, a blaze of anger in his eyes. 'I deny it utterly, though I well might have fallen to so base a level. I have been too many times betrayed by the perfidy of women. You play the innocent all too convincingly, but so may the lowest whore!'

The breath was stopped in Rosina's throat. A white heat of rage drove the blood coursing through her veins. There was no thought in her action. Her right hand was imprisoned, but she pulled back a little. Driving with the whole force of her other arm, she dealt her husband a ringing slap, full on his scarred left cheek.

Raith reeled with the blow, releasing her, and throwing an instinctive hand to the stinging sensation on his face. He recovered in a few seconds and, with the realisation of what she had done, he turned astounded eyes upon his wife.

'Why, you vicious little vixen!'

With automatic intent, he advanced upon her. But Rosina threw up both hands, and the violence of menace in her coal-black eyes gave him pause.

'Strike me at your peril!' she uttered, low-voiced and vibrant. 'You have deserved that of me.'

Then she turned from him, and whisked herself through the door into her dressing-room. With shaking fingers, she turned the key in the lock, and then leaned against the door, panting and spent.

Rosina watched the departing coach from the window of the saloon. The local pastor was the third caller that she had received in the last few days. She was relieved to have rubbed through the ordeal of explaining her non-appearance at church, and could not help reflecting that the absence of her spouse had provided an adequate excuse. Besides, had he been here, she would have been so wrought up that she could not have thought of anything intelligent to say.

She dreaded his return, each day expecting that the evil hour could not be any longer delayed. How was she to find the courage to face him? It seemed incredible that here she was in November, almost two weeks a wife, with no idea where her husband was, or how much longer he meant to be away. She knew only that the last she had seen of him had been his face of thunderous astonishment after she had struck at it.

How had she dared? Her heart misgave her whenever she thought of it. Her moment of triumph had been short-lived. Within a very few minutes of that fatal impulse, every ounce of courage had dissipated with the realisation of what she had done. She remembered the sag of her knees, the sudden horrific thought of the pregnable outer doors. Terror had gripped her at the fierce inevitability of Raith's revenge. She had flown to the door that gave on to the corridor from her dressing-room, and locked it with frantic fingers. It had not been enough. *Her bedchamber.*

Her feet had grown wings as she sped through, fleet as the wind, in her mind a startled question. Was there even a key? Her relief, on discovering it in the lock, had been stupendous. She had fallen upon it, like an animal upon its prey—and had such extreme difficulty in making it turn, that she had cried aloud in her frustration and haste.

Once secured within her own apartments, Rosina had backed from the door to sink down upon the bed, her pulse fluttering wildly in her throat, listening intently for the sound of her husband's approach.

But no footsteps disturbed the eerie quiet of the night. There was no rattling at any of the door handles. She had sat for a long while, mumchance, while the teeth chattered in her head, and her whole frame quivered and shook as she cursed and lamented that hideous loss of temper, and wondered at her own foolhardy audacity.

Actually to hit Raith! Had she run mad? What brazen

defiance had driven her to so insane a proceeding? Oh, but he would make her suffer for it!

But when it had appeared that there was to be no immediate reprisal, Rosina had collapsed in a heap on the coverlet, the inevitable tears coursing down her cheeks. Dismayed guilt had warred with dread, buoying her defences.

How could she have done it to him? She had not meant it. No, dear Lord, that was a lie. She had! He should not have driven her so hard. But what had induced her? Never in her life had she lost herself to such an extreme. Only, how could she bear it? Recalling his words, she broke into a fresh storm of weeping. Oh, but it was shameful of him! To equate her so cruelly with a woman of that sort.

But here the deep voice of conscience prodded her. Raith had right on his side. He deserved that his wife be pure. Only if she had not been—if that evil pair had succeeded in their base design!—Rosina would never have given herself in marriage. Not to any man—let alone one whose bruised spirit had commanded the tenderest promptings of her heart. A fresh deluge of tears accompanied this thought. He ought to have trusted her! Oh, cruel—to withstand every impulse that bade him overcome his doubts. She could not but recognise the portent. He could not possibly care enough. Let him not therefore speak of his *regard*. How could he use her so? She was glad she had assaulted him!

But this fierce resurgence of spirit could not long endure. She knew she had been wrong to do it—bitterly wrong. She could not wonder at her spouse's furious intent of retaliation. She had balked him for the moment. But for how long? Unless she were to run away—which was not an option that recommended itself, for where could she go?—she foresaw that she was doomed to run the gauntlet of his just vengeance. The best she could pray for was for the night to cool him, and mitigate the manner of it.

It had been long before she had been able to rouse herself to get into bed. Even longer before she had slept. For whatever hopes she might secretly have cherished, for the resolution of the difficulties of her marriage, were at an end. Whether or not Raith chose to punish her, he would never forgive her. If he could allow the blow— how could he forget the place where it had struck? She had dealt it to him at his most vulnerable point, and he was bound to suppose that she had done so on purpose.

Her dreams had been unhappy, full of ill-omened fragments where Raith and she were ever at outs. Except once, when she had dreamed that he kissed her—and had been awakened by a heavy-handed knocking at her door. She had started up in alarm, the remnants of the dream fading, to be replaced by the cruel memory of last night.

For a dreadful moment, she had imagined that her husband was come at last, to take his revenge. The vision in her head was armed—with a vengeful stick! Her voice had cracked.

'Who is it?'

'It's me, m'lady. Joan.'

Relief had flooded her, and she had struggled out of bed, and staggered across to unlock the door.

'Why, m'lady, are you ill?' the girl had asked, bobbing.

Rosina had seized at the straw, gratefully. 'Yes. At least, I am faint—and have the headache. I will—I will remain in my bed.'

She had accepted with gratitude her maid's assistance to clamber back between her sheets, for she did indeed feel dreadfully weak. She had lain there all day, afraid to get up for fear of encountering Raith. No message or demand had come from him, and she had not dared to ask concerning his whereabouts. She could only hope that he had gone out about the business of the estate, as usual.

By the following morning, however, she'd had time enough to screw up her courage. How she was to face him, she knew not, but the thing had to be done. Better to do it sooner rather than later.

Nevertheless, she had got up late, and dallied over her toilette, dreading the moment of meeting. And then, when she had come down to breakfast, her pulse jumping with fright, she had not known whether to be glad or sorry at the news with which Kirkham had greeted her enquiry.

'His Lordship, m'lady? Why, he has been gone since yesterday.'

A hollow had opened up inside her, and her blood had seemed to stop. 'Gone? Gone where?'

'His Lordship did not say, m'lady. He told me only that he would be from home for he knew not how many days, and that we should not look for him to arrive at any particular moment.'

Rosina had been at first overwhelmed with relief. The evil day had been postponed. But the waiting was proving a good deal worse. Her nerves were beginning to fray, and just three days after that quarrel, with still no sign of Raith, she was fretting herself into a state of unalloyed affliction. Between apprehension that an accident had befallen him, and the fear that he would walk in unannounced at any moment—and belike treat her to a thunderous scold!—Rosina was in constant dread. She was losing flesh, and her wan looks drew comment even from the butler.

As if sent on purpose from the gods to increase her distresses, Saturday had also brought visitors. Fearful of one particular individual, she gave orders that no one was to be admitted without their name having first been brought to her. She was tempted to deny herself, feeling

unequal to the task of meeting anyone without her lord's
support. But recalling how little support she was likely to
feel in his presence after what had passed, she suffered a
change of front, deciding that she would do better without
him.

As it chanced, the callers were of so much humbler
station—expressing their fervent wish not to be backward
in paying Lady Raith a visit—that Rosina was not put to
any impossible or impertinent questions. Not even the
pastor had remained today longer than strict propriety of
taste dictated. Rosina saw him go with a sensation of relief, hoping that she would not be obliged to receive many
more visitors before Raith's return. Which thought served
only to depress her with the remembrance of what must
await her when her husband chose to come home.

It was as well for what little peace of mind she was
able to command that she did not know how her spouse,
in company with Mr Ottery, was scouring the countryside
around Brinklow in search of an unknown blind woman
and her cottage.

Chapter Seven

'This is ridiculous, Ottery!' said Raith impatiently, setting down the tankard of ale with which he was refreshing himself from the dust of the country roads. 'It may take weeks to cover the ground. Where in thunder are we, by the way?'

'Paylington, my lord,' answered the lawyer, with a slight smile which Raith found distinctly irritating. 'I do not wonder at your finding difficulty in recalling the name of the place. We have covered so much ground.'

'Yes, and much good have we got by it!'

'Patience, my dear sir. We will find the needle, if we take apart the haystack.'

'I'm beginning to believe that we are in the wrong area altogether,' Raith said, sighing as he attacked the vast sandwich with which he had been supplied by the landlord of this particular hostelry. 'And I can't for the life of me remember where we have been.'

'Have no fear, my lord. I have kept a careful account,' said Ottery, taking out a pocketbook and consulting its pages. 'We have so far searched through Conib Abby, Newnham Regis, Fifsenhill, and—'

'Spare me the list!' Raith broke in.

He did not wish to hear it. Suffice it that they had hunted high and low—relentlessly, even through this Lord's day, disturbing simple folk at their well-earned rest. He was sick of jolting over rutty tracks. Parton was loud in disapproval of the wear and tear on his phaeton. But had they found hide or hair of Rosina's blind nurse? No, they had not!

'Well, we have made some progress, my lord,' said Ottery soothingly. 'People have been helpful. We have been regaled with local histories by at least three sightless old women, and as for cottages—'

'If you are seeking to raise my spirits with a pleasantry, Ottery, you may spare your breath. If we have seen one cottage, we have seen fifty. I am full to the brim with cottages!'

He saw, with despair, that his lawyer was regarding him with that knowing look. There was no fooling Ottery. He was well aware of the cause of his client's frustration. How could he not be?

'I am but poor company, by thunder!' he said, laying his hand briefly on the other's arm. 'And you are patience itself, my friend.'

'Why do you not go home, my lord, and leave the business to me?'

Raith looked away, picking up his tankard again. 'You know the answer to that.'

He had been entirely open with the man. After that disastrous night, he had been in need of solid guidance from a well-disposed source. And Ottery was the only person he could trust. He had fled his own home, and driven to Banbury, where he had found his lawyer almost upon the point of setting forth to begin his enquiries on Raith's behalf.

Ottery had ushered him into his private sanctum—that hidden little room behind his office, from where Raith had first secretly seen the disastrous enchantment of his vulnerable waif. Oh, how vulnerable! So destructive had been his treatment of her that she had been driven to lash out.

'She said that I had deserved it of her, Ottery, and by thunder I had!' he had confessed, wrung by his own conscience.

'If you drove her to hitting you, my lord, I must say that I agree with you,' had been the lawyer's uncompromising comment. 'You are not married to a termagant.'

'Far from it.'

He had called her a vixen, in the heat of his shocked response. But he had not meant it. Within two seconds of the door closing behind her, he had been smitten with horror at the remembrance of what he had said to her. She had taken it to herself. He had become confused by the memory. Had he applied that vicious word to her? Surely he had not meant to suggest for one moment that she was herself a whore? How had he put it, that she should take that meaning from his words?

For he could not doubt but that it was what she had thought. His cheek had smarted for some moments, but that was a small affliction. Much worse was the dread consequence of that bitterest of quarrels. Whichever way he looked at it, he could see no possibility of mending.

Rosina had escaped from him, and locked the door. He would not pursue her. To what end? His state of mind was too uncertain to permit him any rational resolution. He knew only too well how uncontrolled was his temper. A family failing. In Piers, it had been vicious. His half-brother had made no attempt whatsoever to control it. In his father, he had seen it only once, although Ottery had told him that this was due to a steadfast rein that had curbed it through the years.

For himself, he knew it to be a curse, aggravated by the bitter blows to which fate had subjected him. No, he had not been able to unleash himself on Rosina that night. He had slept ill, his mind dwelling upon the undoubted unrest with which he guessed his Rosy was spending the night. And all to be laid to his account.

'I must put an end to it, Ottery. Until this matter is resolved, I cannot trust myself to deal with her as she deserves.'

'And if the matter is resolved to your discontent, my lord?' Ottery had asked, with an accuracy of aim that pierced his defences.

He had sunk his head into his hands. 'Don't. That is the grief under which I hang suspended. It is killing me, Ottery!'

'And Lady Raith no less.'

Raith had jerked up again, his heart twisted by the reproach in his lawyer's voice. 'I know it. You are right to take her part. There are times when I wish fervently that she had not written that accursed letter—and put herself irrevocably into my hands.'

Ottery had leaned across the small desk and placed a hand over those Raith gripped together on its surface. It had afforded him a small degree of comfort—to be understood.

'My lord, if I believed you meant that, I would be advising you this moment to put her aside.'

A wry smile had creased Raith's lips. 'You know me too well.' His hand had turned up and gripped the one above it. 'Help me, my friend. Yet again, I beg of you to help me.'

'You know I will, my lord. What do you wish?'

'I cannot go home,' Raith had said with urgency. 'I cannot face her. At least, I must go back—if only to fetch some toggery and other necessaries. But I need not fear an encounter. If I know Rosina, she will be only too eager to stay out of my way.'

'But where will you go, my lord? You cannot walk away from your own home.'

'Of course not!' he had retorted impatiently. 'For what do you take me? No, no, Ottery. I will go with you to search out this nurse of hers. Until I have the truth, there can be no peace for either of us.'

But the hunt was nearly three days old, and they were no nearer to finding their quarry. His lawyer, however, had been thinking.

'My lord, I wonder if we might do better to go back to the Receiving Office.'

'For what purpose?'

'We have assumed a place within walking distance. I had been holding to the notion that Lady Raith, when she was Miss Charlton, had collected her letters for herself. But figure to yourself this, my lord. Now Her Ladyship is gone to Ratley, how does the nurse receive any letters, if she is blind? Did you not say that Lady Raith had written to her?'

'Blood and thunder! Why did we not think of that before?' exclaimed Raith, half-rising from his seat. 'I franked that letter for Rosina not a week since.'

As they were staying at The Crown at Brinklow while conducting their researches, it was no difficult task to find their way to the Receiving Office upon the morrow, and effect an interview with the individual in charge. This worthy remembered their first visit, when Ottery had asked after 'Miss Charlton.' No one had known from which village she had hailed.

'A blind woman this time, is it?' mused the postmaster, scratching his chin. 'I don't recall no blind woman a-coming here to fetch no letters.'

'But someone might have called on her behalf,' Ottery pressed him. 'A friend, perhaps.'

The postmaster eyed them both dubiously. 'You don't have no name, then?'

'No,' replied Ottery with a patience that Raith could only admire, 'that is why we are asking. We know that the woman concerned lives in a cottage, at no great distance from here. At one time Miss Charlton, about whom we asked previously, was staying with her.'

The postmaster was shaking his head, a frown creasing his brow. There was no recognition here, and Raith's heart sank.

But one of the clerks whose function was to sort the mail had been hovering in the background, apparently waiting on a query. He spoke up suddenly. 'Your pardon, Mr Briggs, but would it be Mrs Hoswick as the gentlemen is after?'

Hope quickened in Raith's breast. 'Who is she, fellow?'

'I don't know no Mrs Hoswick, lad,' objected Briggs.

'I were thinking of Toly Aughton, the apothecary's boy down Hopsford way, sir.'

'Oh, young Toly?' said Briggs, his face clearing. 'Ah, yes, gentlemen, maybe that'll be it.'

Raith was on the point of exploding, but he was checked by Ottery's hand on his arm. As well his lawyer had so ready an understanding of his moods.

'How does this boy Toly come into the picture, Mr Briggs?' Ottery asked gently.

But it was the clerk who answered. 'He come and fetch the letters for Mrs Hoswick, sir, as is blind and lives in a village 'bout a half-mile from his master's shop.'

'That's right,' agreed Briggs. 'Now I think of it, sir, he come in not a few days agone. There was a letter seemingly, wasn't there, lad?'

'Aye, sir,' said the clerk, looking awed. 'Franked by a lord it were!'

Raith exchanged a glance with Ottery. By thunder, they had it! 'What name?' he demanded.

'The lord's name, lad,' Ottery said, clarifying the matter. 'Do you recall?'

'Couldn't hardly read it, sir,' uttered the clerk disparagingly. 'A scrawl it was.'

His Lordship gave a wry smile, as he asked, 'Was it "Raith"?'

'Aye, that would be it.'

Ottery became business-like. 'Right then, my lad. Where may we find this Toly Aughton?'

The cottage was minute. Was it from here that Rosina had written that fateful letter? The woman who opened the door had her eyes, but they moved constantly, in the way of blind people, and it was clear that they saw nothing.

She was a pudgy female, of less than average stature, with a wrinkled face under a large mob-cap, and a slightly grimy apron tied about her middle. She looked, Raith thought, exactly like a nurse.

'Who's this you've brought, Toly?' she said gruffly, just as if she could see them both.

'It's two gennelmen, Mrs H. Come to find you. I didn't rightly know if I ought to have brung 'em. Only I didn't like to refuse, seeing as—'

'I think, ma'am, that we can speak for ourselves,' Ottery interrupted. 'May we come in?'

The nurse raised her chin, moving her head from side to side as though she took in something of the look of her visitors. Almost Raith would swear that she could see. After a moment, she nodded, somewhat grudgingly opening the door.

It led directly into an incommodious kitchen, which must nevertheless, Raith thought, be the biggest room in the place. The two of them, greatcoated as they were, seemed to dwarf the place. The nurse bade them all sit down, herself moving to an open range where she set a copper kettle to the fire. Raith noted how she felt her way about, marvelling at her resilience.

He seated himself on a plain wooden chair at one end of the table, while Ottery took his place next to him. The boy hovered by the door. The elderly dame then turned from the fire, and came to the table. She did not sit.

'You're the one, I think,' she said, turning her face in Raith's direction.

'The one what?' he asked, in quick reaction.

'As wants to see me.'

'Your guesses are uncanny.'

She shook her head. 'It ain't guesswork, sir, not by a long way. When you've lost one sense, you find you can use others a deal better.'

'I have heard it said so,' Ottery put in. 'It is reassuring to discover that it is true.'

'Now you, sir,' said the nurse, turning to him, 'are one as comes along o' the other. It ain't nowise your affair as you've come for.'

'You are perfectly correct,' said Ottery, with a lift of the eyebrow and a smile for his client.

Raith was experiencing the most extraordinary sensation of premonition. This woman knew just who he was.

As if she read his thought, she turned her sightless eyes towards the door. 'I thank you, Toly, and you can leave the gentlemen safe here with me. They ain't nowise harmful.'

'You sure, Mrs H.?'

'Yes, you run along, boy. 'Tis private business as this gentleman has with me.'

She waited only until the young lad who had been their

guide had left the cottage and shut the door. Then she moved back to the range.

'Now, my lord, you'll take tea?'

She did know! Had he not thought it? Raith exchanged a glance with his lawyer, and found his own amazement reflected in the other's face. The nurse was busying herself with a pot and a set of cups and saucers.

'How did you know?' he asked.

'Ah, that would be telling,' said the elderly dame over her shoulder. She spooned tea-leaves into the pot.

Raith grimaced at the lawyer. Ottery grinned. He looked at the woman's back.

'How long have you lived in Withibrooke, Mrs Hoswick?'

'Since just after Mrs Charlton upped and died,' she said, without turning round. 'I'd a deal better have stayed with my dove, but it weren't to be. He wouldn't have me, not as my sight were going.'

Raith mouthed at Ottery, 'Who?' and received a lift of the eyebrows, and a quick shake of the head. Perhaps it was too soon to probe.

She was extraordinarily handy with the teacups for a blind person. Raith jumped up to accept them from her, passing a saucer with a cup containing the steaming brew across to Ottery. It was not a beverage to which he was partial, but it would be politic to drink it. He would not wish to offend this woman's sensibilities. He watched her place her own dish carefully in front of her, some distance from the edge of the table. Then she pulled out a chair and sat down, facing Raith.

'Now, my lord, tell me. How is my Rosy? Fourteen days it's been! Is she well? Is she happy?'

Raith could not speak for a moment, silenced by his consciousness of the distress to which he had reduced the girl for whom this female obviously cared deeply. And she had been counting the days! What in thunder was he to tell her?

He hesitated too long. Mrs Hoswick's head drooped a trifle, and she sighed.

'I knew it. Her letter was all too silent, poor lamb.' She tutted for a moment, sipped her tea, and then looked up, suddenly brisk. 'Well, and what do you want of me, my lord?'

On impulse, Raith reached out to touch one of the work-roughened hands. 'Your help, Mrs Hoswick. I am as anxious as you are for Rosina's happiness.'

She allowed his hand to rest upon hers for a moment without speaking. He removed it, and she stood up.

'Will you allow an old woman a liberty, my lord?'

Raith shot a glance at Ottery, who shrugged expressively. 'Of what nature?'

'Let me feel your face.'

Instinct caused Raith to shrink inwardly. What had Rosina told her in that letter? The thought of those pudgy hands playing over his scarred face was acutely uncomfortable. But if that was what it was going to take! He looked at his lawyer, whose features were creased with concern.

'It is a blind person's way of seeing, my lord,' he murmured, setting down his own cup, and mouthing further on a whisper, 'Will you risk it?'

Raith drew a breath, and mouthed back, 'I have no choice.' Ottery nodded, and Raith turned back to the nurse.

'Very well.'

She moved around the table, obviously so familiar a motion that she did not need to use her hands. Raith shifted his chair, and waited, rigid with tension, as she stood before him.

The fingers that came to rest upon his face were gentle.

He had an immediate vision of Rosina under these hands, stroking comfort. The touch was featherlight, and his rigidity lessened—until it came in contact with his disfigurement, and hesitated. Unlike Rosina, whose finger had traced the line, the nurse's played a rhythmic stroke back and forth across it, at the same time as she did as much on his other cheek.

He sighed out his breath as her examination ended, and saw her nod. 'You'll do,' she said.

Raith was betrayed into a laugh. 'I thank you.'

Ottery intervened. 'Do you feel inclined to help His Lordship, ma'am?'

'I'll tell him only where to find out what he wants to know.'

Raith could take this no longer. 'How in thunder do you know what I want? How did you know it was I?'

The nurse laughed comfortably. 'Ah, you mustn't run away with the idea that I'm a seer, nor nothing like that. Deduction, my lord. You weren't *him*, I'd take my oath. He'd not have come here with no pleasant words for such as I, he wouldn't. Nor he wouldn't bring no one with him—unless it were t'other. Him I'd know, though we ain't met. One whiff of his breath is all it 'ud take, my lord, and that's a fact.'

So that was what she had been doing on the doorstep. Sniffing at them. He glanced to his lawyer and found the same deep appreciation upon his features. But this passage had been all too confusing—besides sending a riffle of that jealous flame burning through him. Two of them, by thunder! Which of these was the man whose throat his itching hands sought to surround and strangle?

'I pray you, Mrs Hoswick, could you sort out one ''him'' from the other?'

There must have been an indication of his unquiet thoughts in his voice, for she shot her face towards him,

and a frown creased her brow. Raith felt impelled to reassure her.

'Don't be alarmed. I have need of this information—I
will not use it ill, I promise you.'

Mrs Hoswick clasped her hands together on the table.
'The only thing I care for, my lord, is that my Rosy is
safe,' she declared with hostility. 'Now, if you can't make
her so, then you'd best bring her back to me.'

'I want to keep her, Mrs Hoswick,' he uttered raggedly.
'Only I cannot—if I do not…' He faded out, unwilling to
put into words the hideous truth of his intended findings.
He wondered how much she knew. He dared swear she
would not say.

'I can't tell you nothing, my lord,' said the nurse, folding her lips together, and rising. 'You'd best go now.'

Raith leaped up, casting an anguished glance at his lawyer. To his relief, Ottery took over. Rising, too, he moved
to lay a hand on the nurse's shoulder. She must have heard
him approach, but she flinched, throwing it off.

'His Lordship is anxious to find out the truth, ma'am,'
he said gently. 'You cannot wish for Lady Raith—I mean,
for your nurseling, for that is now her name—to find herself back in the hands of the man whom she fears above
all others.'

For the first time, Mrs Hoswick began to look anxious,
kneading her hands in her apron. 'If only I knew what to
do for the best.'

'She is my wife, ma'am,' uttered Raith desperately.
'Neither of us knew, when we wed, that we would find
ourselves with a marriage utterly other than that we had
planned. But it is so. Help me to make it safe for her.'
He hesitated, watching uncertainty ripple across the elderly dame's features.

'I don't know, my lord,' she said, the sightless eyes
shifting with the uneven tenor of her thoughts.

Raith moved to her, and sought her hands, holding them hard. 'Mrs Hoswick, if it turns out otherwise, I promise you faithfully that I will return Rosina to you—intact. And provide you both with means to secure what haven you please.'

'He means it, Mrs Hoswick,' Ottery put in, adding persuasively, 'If you wish, I will write it all out for you, and His Lordship will sign it, that you may be certain of a right in law.'

But the nurse put up her chin, and nodded at last. 'That ain't needful, sir. I couldn't read it nohow, in any event.' She let out a sigh. 'You'd best go and parley with that there Herbert Cambois, as was her guardian.' She turned again to Raith. 'But if you'll take the advice of an old woman, my lord, you'll leave the doing to this 'un, and go your ways. It ain't good for my dove to be left alone, and it's your business to protect her.'

The caller was becoming extraordinarily difficult. The visit had started well enough. A little practice had given Rosina poise, which, blended with her natural air of civil deference, had won for her the amiability of those far less comfortably circumstanced than she now was herself.

But Lady Doddinghurst's baronet husband placed her only marginally lower in the social scale than her hostess, yet Rosina found her quick to demonstrate her superiority of worldly knowledge. Not to say fashion.

Until her arrival, Rosina had been satisfied of the modality of her sprigged muslin gown, with its long sleeves and gathered bodice, a frill adorning the hem. But this matron, fresh from the metropolis, wore a gown of violet crêpe of exquisite cut, enriched by a cloak of purple velvet. A feathered turban completed this formidable toilette, under which a sharp pair of eyes looked down an impos-

ing Roman nose, surveying her hostess from her head to
her heels.

'Charming,' she uttered with a spurious smile. 'A trifle
countrified, but quite charming.'

Lady Doddinghurst was of an age to claim acquaintance
with Raith's own father, and lost no time in putting
Rosina in her place. Beginning with this doubtful compliment, she asked who of the surrounding gentry Rosina
had already received, and proceeded to a comprehensive
lecture upon their strengths and frailties. Rosina listened
in amazement, but without any apprehension on her own
part, until the visitor switched her attention to Rosina's
personal affairs.

'And how did you and Lord Raith become acquainted?'
she demanded, with a smile that did not reach her eyes.

Rosina fought down sudden panic. 'In—in the usual
way.'

'Is there a usual way?' enquired the dame.

Abruptly Rosina recalled the tale which Mr Ottery had
once said should be the preferred report of their union.

'Why, yes. The—the marriage was arranged. Our respective parents had—had planned it. A long time ago.'

A haughty stare was bent upon her from the chair to
the window side of the fire. 'Who are your parents?'

'They are both dead,' Rosina stated, hoping that common civility would prevent further questions on this head.

'Ah, how sad,' said the lady, with a pitying smile as
she sat back. 'However, it is interesting to hear that
Anton's father took pains to ensure his betrothal. Particularly in the light of subsequent events.'

Rosina knew not what to say. Lady Doddinghurst spoke
as if she did not believe in the tale Raith had concocted.
What did she know that Rosina did not? Everything, since
she knew so little! She saw the woman's smile increase—
at her discomfiture no doubt—and hurried into speech.

'I believe it was the wish rather of my lord's mother,' she said at random, and hastily borrowed Mr Ottery's amused comment. 'Marriage is thought to be a steadying influence.'

'And yet His Lordship is from home.'

'There is—he is engaged upon business that cannot be laid aside,' Rosina said crisply, beginning to be angry. 'My lord has only just come into the inheritance, you must know, and there is a great deal to be done.'

The other woman laughed with a touch of scorn. 'So I should imagine, after the way Piers treated the place.'

She cast a disparaging glance about as she spoke, and Rosina found herself roused to resentment on her spouse's behalf. She threw out a challenge.

'You seem to know a great deal about the family, Lady Doddinghurst.'

'So much, my dear,' agreed the other, meeting the attack head on, 'that I find it hard to imagine that the second Lady Raith could have thought it necessary to secure the betrothal of a mere boy. After all, he was not yet into adolescence when she was taken off by a fatal illness.'

Raith's mother had died when he was a child? Dear Lord, but he might have primed her on these matters! Now what was she to say? Should she confess her ignorance? No, she would not. This female was altogether too patronising to deserve her confidence. She opted to retire from the lists.

'I am not in a position to comment, ma'am,' she said frostily. 'However it may have been, I was given myself to understand that Lord Raith and I were to be married in due time, and so it proved to be.'

Lady Doddinghurst, looking like a cat who had been at the cream, did not hesitate to harry the retreat. 'How odd that your parents should secure you to a second son with no hope of inheriting, whose sole income derived from the army.'

Rosina was effectively silenced. The best she could do was to eye her visitor with head held high, hoping that nothing of her deep disquiet was visible. For a moment, the elder lady gazed down her nose, as if she dared her to respond. Then she relaxed, sitting back and smiling in a winning way.

'My poor child, I had no intention of putting up your back. If you take my advice, you will persuade your husband to think up a better tale. I am sure he will oblige you. I cannot think that Anton Raith will be eager for yet more scandal to be attached to his name.'

Incensed, Rosina threw aside all caution. 'I am afraid I know nothing of any such stigma. Perhaps Your Ladyship will care to enlighten me as to the meaning of these hints?'

'Oh, my dear Lady Raith, do you mean to say that you do not know? But how foolish of young Anton to have kept you in ignorance. Though I dare say he had hoped that there were few persons old enough to remember the truth about his mother's marriage. And indeed, perhaps the later disgraces, being of a more personal nature, are of closer concern to him.'

An icy voice spoke from the doorway. 'I see, Lady Doddinghurst, that you have not lost your penchant for probing into the private affairs of others.'

Rosina's heart felt as if it sprang almost out of her chest, and she was unable to stop herself leaping from her seat. Dear Lord, Raith was back! He was standing just inside the room, his eyes upon the visitor, his damaged countenance wearing its most cynical look. He had discarded his outer garments, though he was still in travelling dress: a double-breasted frock-coat of rust-coloured fustian with a stand collar, and waistcoat to match, over buckskins and boots.

Rosina was stricken with an abrupt sense of his virility. But it was driven out of her head by the instant remembrance of their last meeting.

'My l-lord!' she uttered faintly, conscious of a tremble starting up in her limbs.

He was coming towards her. What was she to do? She shot a glance at Lady Doddinghurst, and saw that dame's eyes passing from herself to her husband, and back again. She must not let this dreadful female see the true state of their relationship.

'You—you startled me, my lord,' she managed, forcing a smile to her lips as he reached her.

She felt him take her hand, and lift it. It quivered, utterly outside her control, and Rosina met his eyes as he bent his head to kiss the fingers. She read a message of warning in them, and realised—with a flash of resentment in her breast—that he meant to put on a show for the benefit of her visitor.

'A thousand pardons, my love, to be bursting in on you without warning in this way,' he said smoothly, and slightly pressed her fingers.

Rosina withdrew them quickly, and sank back into her seat, conscious of an overwhelming desire to weep. Hateful to have him behave in that familiar fashion, when the truth of their dealing was so very unlike it. *My love,* indeed!

His voice had hardened. 'You have much to forgive, I perceive. I should never have left you to the mercy of your neighbours.'

Glancing swiftly up at him, Rosina thought she detected reassurance in his eyes. Easy to see that this remark had been directed at Lady Doddinghurst. A peal of patently false laughter breaking out behind him confirmed the notion.

Raith turned to confront the most vicious of the local gossips. He was appalled to see her here, and his conscience writhed for Rosina having been obliged to face her alone.

'Very well attempted, my dear Anton,' said the woman, with the smile he detested. 'But you know, it is difficult to be set down by a young man whom one has known since he was in short coats.'

'Difficult, ma'am, but not impossible,' he said, deliberate menace in his tone. 'As you will find, if you persist in troubling my wife with your ill-considered remarks.'

'Oh, pish!' scoffed the matron. 'You do not frighten me, Anton. Recollect that I have brought four sons into the world, and am a grandmother several times over.'

'Then you should have more consideration for the sensibilities of a young lady who has not your worldly knowledge and experience,' he returned.

Rosina saw a flush stain the woman's cheeks, and the smile vanished. She could not but be conscious of satisfaction, and she was cheered by Raith's having championed her. She had dreaded his coming, but this front he had put up to dampen the impertinence of her visitor might give her a respite. He seemed not to have the immediate intention of seeking revenge for her dreadful lapse. Might she dare to hope that the intervening four days had dulled his anger?

But his presence, despite that horrid charade, was sending her heart into high gear. She had feared his return, but she could not withstand the realisation that she had missed him in spite of it. Missed the very sight of him—wrecked features and all. If only circumstances had been different. If she had been able to offer him a history wholly untarnished—if not as tainted as he feared.

'Well, and how are you faring, Anton?' the creature was saying, glossing over the earlier exchange. 'Doddinghurst had been of the opinion that Piers must have brought the place to the verge of ruin.'

Raith had taken up a pose near the fire, ensuring that Lady Doddinghurst, rather than Rosina, was subjected to the unsightly side of his face. But at this, he turned his mocking grey gaze upon her.

'And hoped to purchase it for a song at the last? I regret, ma'am, that the estate is under entail. It is out of the power of any incumbent to effect a sale.'

He was well aware that since Sir Humphrey Doddinghurst's land marched with his own, the addition of the Raith estate—at a price well under its value— would have been highly desirable. He was glad to see his old enemy redden again under the hit. She rose to retreat, much to his relief.

'I have stayed too long.' She crossed to Rosina and held out her hand as Raith tugged on the bell-pull. 'My dear Lady Raith, I will say farewell for the moment.'

Rosina took the hand as briefly as civility would allow. She was less immediately concerned with the woman's departure, than with the fact that it would leave her alone with her spouse. Her pulse started up the dreadful tattoo that so often attacked her in his presence, and the flutter in her stomach made her feel sick.

The woman turned at the door, and Raith discovered, to his chagrin, that she was not out of venom. 'One last morsel of advice, dear Anton. Don't leave your wife in ignorance, when a little knowledge will prevent her from making a complete fool of herself.'

Raith swore as she swept through the door, which the butler was holding open. He strode into the centre of the room, looking after her.

'That female is the most disagreeable of my acquaintance. Damn her for being so absolutely right!' He turned, his eyes going to Rosina.

At once he forgot Lady Doddinghurst. How white and strained was his waif! She looked thinner. Or was it the effect of the charmingly simple gown? No—for her elfin countenance was drawn. What had he done? He wanted to go to her, draw her up into his arms and hold her comfortingly close. But the consciousness of his own duplicity prevented him.

What would she say, were he to tell her of his activities during his absence? If she were to know that Ottery was even now on his way to Nun Eaton, bent upon bearding the fellow Cambois, who had been her guardian. Raith had hired a chaise for him, and himself driven home in the phaeton with Parton. He had not precisely followed the advice of Rosina's nurse, but rather his lawyer's forceful representations.

'In your present frame of mind, my lord, I must and will conjure you to leave these enquiries to me. I do not wish to be obliged to bring you off from a charge of murder! Besides, you do not know that there is truthfully any occasion for your wrath. Let me handle the business, as Mrs Hoswick suggested.'

It had taken some discussion, but he had at length capitulated, spurred more perhaps by Ottery's further argument. 'You left Lady Raith, as I understand it, in a distinctly perturbed frame of mind. Picture to yourself, my lord, the aggravated distress occasioned by your long absence—with neither explanation, nor opportunity to make up the quarrel.'

And Ottery had been right, by thunder! She looked so much the worse, that he could never sufficiently blame himself. And to crown all, he had left her unsupported to an ordeal which she dreaded, subject to the damned impertinences of Lady Doddinghurst and her like.

'I am sorry that I left you alone like this,' he said rapidly. 'I would not for the world have had you suffer that creature's rudeness.'

Rosina's jumping nerves settled a little at this evidence that he did not mean to upbraid her—at least, not yet. She was tempted to offer her own heartfelt apology for that dreadful blow, which she could never sufficiently regret. But she was too afraid of re-awakening his anger with the memory.

At a loss for anything inoffensive to say, she cast about in her mind, and recalled what he had just said. There was material a-plenty here. Without thought, she plunged in.

'She would not have it that our betrothal had been arranged, as Mr Ottery told me was the planned story. She said that your mother died when you were a boy—and then she spoke of scandal, and…' Her voice died.

What had she been thinking of? That was what came of trying to keep off the subject uppermost in her mind. Now he would retire again behind that impossible barrier of ice.

'I b-beg your pardon,' she uttered in a low tone. 'I d-did not mean to p-pry.'

Raith heard the tremor of her voice with a further twist of the knife in his sorely tried conscience. So strong was the impulse to go to her, that he was obliged to turn away, moving to the window and looking out. But here, at least, was one thing he could remedy.

'You have a right to ask, Rosy,' he began, using the name involuntarily.

Rosina heard it with a melting at her heart. Had his anger then indeed died? When he called her by that nursery name—though it might be in impatience—it seemed always to betoken affection. Was there not a degree of fondness? He had said so—on that fatal night. He had spoken of his regard. And she had rejected it. His gentleness on occasion would indicate it. Only it was not, she reminded herself sadly, strong enough a feeling to withstand what lay between them.

She glanced at him, and found Raith observing her. But the instant he caught her eye, he looked away. Her gaze went to her fingers, unquiet in her lap. Oh, if things could only be other than they were.

'Lady Doddinghurst spoke no less than the truth. I should not keep you in ignorance.'

What was he talking of? Then she remembered. 'Do you mean that there was a scandal?'

'Long ago. It forms, in large part, the basis for my brother's unrelenting enmity.'

Her curiosity aroused, Rosina turned to look at him. 'Was he so much your enemy?'

'Have you not wondered why the lawns are all of ash?' He was staring out at the desolate frontage of the house. His tone was flat. 'Piers had them fired.'

Rosina gasped. 'You cannot mean he caused them to be set alight!'

Raith shifted away from the window, and came to the mantel, looking down into the charring logs below. 'Ottery thinks he had some hope that the flames might spread and burn the house. But since he was in it, he could scarce set the house on fire directly.'

It was stated flatly, but Rosina's shock was intense. 'But how could he—how could anyone do such a thing?'

'A final act of revenge,' said Raith, without moving from where he stood, nor looking round. 'Everything in the house that was worth a groat had been sacrificed to his gambling. The estate was a wreck. I must suppose that he wished for nothing to be left intact.'

To learn that the man had been a gambler was oddly not much of a surprise, although it caused a shiver to run through Rosina's frame. In just such a fashion had her guardian been driven to reduce his own home. But the gambling of Herbert Cambois had been a sickness. This, Raith seemed to suggest, was a deliberate wasting of resources.

'Why should he do that to you?' she asked.

Raith turned, and the bitter look was pronounced. 'Because he chose to believe in the gossip that suggested that I was not my father's son.'

Rosina stared at him blankly. 'Was he blind, sir? Could he not see how you resembled him?'

'He was nine years my senior. The likeness was not readily apparent until I grew to manhood.'

'But why in the world should he think such a thing?' she demanded, caught up in this first hint of the origin of her spouse's deeply felt hurts. This must be the scandal of which Lady Doddinghurst had spoken.

Raith sat down in the chair lately vacated by that dame, and glanced across at her. He was himself so taken up by his memories that he saw his wife's features without taking them in. They were overlaid by the vicious curl of his half-brother's mouth, the taunting voice.

'Spawn of a strumpet! Anton whatever-your-name-is, you are no brother of mine.'

He set his teeth, and his gaze went back to the fire. 'My mother eloped at sixteen, and my grandfather brought her back only on the following day. Papa was a widower, and a close friend of my maternal grandfather. He offered to marry her, to save her name.'

Rosina heard it with mixed feelings. She ached for the pain in his voice. Yet she saw how his history was affecting her own. Small wonder he cared so for the purity of his wife.

'Piers had me almost believing that I was born of that other union, but my father made a point of teaching me that it was not so.' He drew in a breath, and let it out in a sigh of despair. 'I don't know why Piers persisted in the belief. He was the elder son, there was no possible way I could inherit. Perhaps my father petted me too much, or showed me preference because of my mother's youth. I know he was ever kind to her.'

'Some men,' Rosina ventured, out of a yearning to ease his hurt, 'are disposed to evil, I believe. They will use any excuse.'

For a moment or two, Raith came out of the memories. He spoke without thinking, with no intent of upsetting her or probing for a truth that he was in a fair way to find out for himself. 'You speak from experience, no doubt.'

She did not answer, and he relapsed into reverie. He hardly knew that he continued to talk of it aloud.

'Piers was quite inventive. His tortures were inflicted under a cunning guise. The older brother inducting the younger into the sports of boys. He taught me how to shoot and to play at cricket—and other such pursuits. He took me riding, and bird's-nesting. I hated every moment of it!'

'Why did you go with him?' Rosina asked. 'Could no one have stopped him from taking you?'

Raith laughed mirthlessly. 'It was rather encouraged. And one was ever taught that the worst sin was to rat upon one's brethren. Who would have believed me? Piers was impatient of my inability to climb with sufficient speed, or to ride on as fleet a hoof—' the words spitting from him '—and took opportunity to school me for every mistake.'

Rosina shuddered at the horrors she envisaged him suffering. Had he not hinted at this that night? That he knew what it was to be in someone's power. But a child. It was inconceivable that it should have gone undetected.

'But was this your lot for all of your childhood?' she asked, quite aghast.

Raith shook his head. 'Piers was away at school for much of the time. As we grew older, and I was sent to school in my turn, I used to long for the term and loathe the holidays when I must encounter him at home. And it did end at last.'

'How?'

Raith got up from his chair and returned to the fire, supporting his hands on the mantel. 'Ottery caught him at it. Piers was—administering one of his lessons. I suppose he had grown careless. At twenty a man feels invincible, and he'd had me at his mercy for years. He had tied my hands for the purpose, and so there was no possible way that he might persuade Ottery of the legitimacy of his actions.'

'What did Mr Ottery do?' asked Rosina, finding herself unsurprised to discover that gentleman's hand in these events.

Raith's head turned, and there was a wealth of satisfaction in both face and voice. 'He struck Piers to the ground. You cannot conceive with what delight I saw him fall.'

Into Rosina's mind flew an instant vision of her hand slamming into Raith's own cheek. Shame burned into her. Oh, she understood only too well. How she had enjoyed the sensation! Only it was unworthy. There had been no vindictive intent in Raith's treatment of her. If he had earned of her the blow, he had not deserved her rancour.

'What happened?' she asked hastily, to rid herself of the unpalatable memory.

Raith turned fully, and moved restlessly back to the window. 'Ottery haled us both before my father. Piers was loud in denial, and my father, I think, did not wish to believe his son capable of that sort of petty cruelty.' He winced with discomfort at the memory. 'Ottery forcibly stripped me of my shirt to show the evidence.'

He recalled in his mind the lawyer's words, delivered in a voice of leaden fury. '"My lord, how else did the boy acquire these wounds? He could not have inflicted them upon himself."' Ordered by his sire, and encouraged by Ottery, he had been induced to give a halting account of his brother's activities.

Rosina eyed the stiff shoulders, and the set line of his jaw in profile, the white ridging laceration where he had forgotten to turn the other cheek. The certainty gripped her that she had not been told it all. Wherein fitted that blemish, which lay at the root of his bitterness?

'It is the only time I have known my father to lose his temper,' he said evenly. 'It was terrifying to see him extract a confession from Piers. Then he forbade him the house. Had it been within his power, I believe my father would have disinherited him in my favour. I am glad he could not, for the banishment was enough to secure all the justification my brother needed for his enmity.'

There was a silence. Rosina was moved by the story. This last must indeed have caused a deal of talk. Was it that which Lady Doddinghurst had called the 'later disgraces'? That Raith had felt able to share it with her both touched her, and threw her into a fever of anxiety. She was tempted to reciprocate, to give of herself in return. Only she dreaded the inevitable change in his mood—if she were to speak of it. It was his own mother's unchastity that had brought upon him such undeserved punishment. How could she doubt of his being as sickened as she was herself, if he knew the full sum of her own history? She looked down at her fingers, unseeing how one pulled at another.

Was this the truth at last? She had blinded herself to her fears. She had turned her own deep disgust of the event into righteous wrath, and hurled it against Raith. So deep was her shame, that she could not endure the thought of her husband knowing the substance of it. Let alone telling him all. He must turn from her in utter contempt and revulsion. She could not tell him—*she could not.*

'Rosina?'

She leaped with shock, looking up. She had not seen him approach. He was standing near her chair, his hands clasped behind his back, regarding her with a concerned frown.

'My l-lord?'

He reached down and cupped her chin in his hand. 'You are looking haggard. Have you been so distressingly troubled?'

The black orbs darkened. 'How can you ask me?'

Raith's heart twisted. 'I am sorry for it.'

'You are sorry?' On impulse, she reached up and grabbed at his hand, clasping it within both her own. 'Raith, I—'

'Your pardon, my lord.'

Rosina slipped her hands away, and Raith moved swiftly to one side, turning. 'Yes, what is it, Kirkham?'

The butler came into the room, and shut the door carefully behind him. 'I beg your pardon, my lord, but a gentleman has called, and Her Ladyship has requested that no visitor should be admitted before she had been given a name.'

Glancing at Rosina, Raith saw that the interruption had thrown her back into discomposure. Hell and damnation! Must there be a visitor just then? She had been within an ace of offering him something—perhaps her confidence. Now the moment was lost.

But Rosina was almost glad of the butler's unexpected entry. What had possessed her? She had very nearly thrown caution to the winds.

'Who is it, Kirkham?' she asked tightly.

'Lord Forteviot, m'lady.'

Raith cursed. 'Forteviot? That fellow was a friend of my brother's, if I am not mistaken.'

'True, my lord.'

'What in thunder does he want with me?'

He glanced at Rosina as he spoke, and his thoughts stopped dead. She was gazing at Kirkham in dumb horror, her face draining visibly of colour.

Chapter Eight

Rosina was dying inside. He had come! Had she not known that he would? Every moment of her wedded life had been but a prelude to this one. Fate had a hand in it, and the gods were cruel.

'Admit the gentleman, Kirkham.'

Her eyes flew to Raith's face. He had spoken in the hardest voice she had ever heard him use. His eyes were on the door as the butler departed, the wrecked side of his profile hidden from her. The good side was set, the jawline stern, the high cheekbone standing out white against his tan. He did not look in her direction, and Rosina knew that she was lost. She had given herself away—and not a word said.

If she could have fled the room, she would have done it. But her legs were like lead, her heart likewise. Time had no meaning. Numbly, she waited for the entrance of doom.

'Lord Forteviot.'

Into the saloon he strolled. Arrogantly at ease, the thin cruel line of his mouth curled in that well-remembered smile that mocked even as it signalled his intolerable self-satisfaction. He was dressed more conformably and neat than she had been used to see him, presiding over the card table in her guardian's house. There he had sprawled, even in her enforced presence, with cravat untied and waistcoat unbuttoned, eyeing her with that lascivious assurance of ownership.

'My dear Lord Raith,' he uttered, silky-smooth, crossing to her spouse and holding out his hand. 'Or may I call you Anton? It seems excessively strange to be addressing you by your title.'

'No doubt,' said Raith shortly, shaking hands as briefly as he could. 'I was not much more than a youth, when last we met—was I?'

There was an edge to the words that caught Rosina's attention. Raith knew him? Dear Lord, it was worse than she had supposed! They were not of an age, for Forteviot was near forty to her husband's eight and twenty years. What a hideous mischance that he should be acquainted with the man.

'Ah, yes,' Forteviot was saying easily. 'You went into the army, did you not? A worthy career. I am sure you acquitted yourself as heroically as ever.'

Rosina heard his words with a sense of disassociation, as if her mind had become detached from her body. For an icy coldness had so entered her that she was unable to feel anything beyond it. But her thoughts formed clearly, as if she watched a pantomime unfold before her eyes, convinced of its utter falsity.

She looked again at Raith, and saw his own cynical look pronounced. But the next moment, all thought suspended again as Forteviot turned his lizard eyes upon herself. She had ever felt him as reptilian, and the green slits that surveyed her from his invariably half-closed eyelids had borne out the impression. She shuddered inwardly.

'Present me, my dear fellow, I conjure you. This must

be—I feel sure I cannot be mistaken—this must be Lady Raith.'

Without intent, Rosina's glance went to her husband. The chill barricade of his eyes thrust through the protective shell of numbness that had momentarily encased her. Her heart plummeted. She became conscious of faintness, and had to concentrate hard to keep herself from a swoon.

Resistless, she let her lifeless hand be kissed, staring up into that hated face with a complete absence of expression.

'My very dear Lady Raith,' purred softly from his lips, while the contemptuous mockery of his eyes taunted her with an entirely different message. 'I am altogether delighted to make your acquaintance. How fortunate is my dear friend Anton to have secured so elusive a prize.'

Raith's attention caught on the word. It had been so odd a thing to say of her, had he not been already certain of the villain's identity in Rosina's life. This was undoubtedly the man from whom she had sought protection. That tiny clue—or had it been planted deliberately?—confirmed it. *Elusive.* Had she been so to Forteviot? That he had come here seeking her could not be in doubt. Bile rose in Raith's stomach as his imagination painted for him what must be the truth of their previous relationship. Was there to be no end? The fell hand of providence was once more at his throat.

Rosina paced up and down her bedchamber. It was horribly late. Would the creature never go? What was he saying to Raith? Had he betrayed her? Not that it mattered. She had all too clearly betrayed herself!

The nausea in her stomach intensified. Oh, to what torments of horror and despair had she been subjected! Gone was the gentleness that had characterised Raith only moments before Forteviot's arrival. Gone forever, she did not doubt. After the veiled hints that the wretch had thrown out, how could she blame her husband? They were deliberately vague, designed to prey upon the sensitivity of a jealous mind.

'Your features are uncannily familiar, Lady Raith,' he had said at one point, in his silkiest tone. 'Yet I feel sure I would remember meeting you. Is it possible that I am acquainted with one to whom you are related?'

Rosina had not known how to answer him. Had hesitated too long, while Raith's tight-lipped tension grew— to her increasing distress.

'I have few relatives,' she had said, hoping to deflect the man.

Forteviot had smiled upon her in a knowing way, and returned his attention to her husband. How like a snake had been his approaches. He had behaved as if his acquaintance with Raith's half-brother gave him claim upon Raith himself.

'So many years since we met, my dear Anton. And I so fond at one time of your dear brother Piers. How could I fail to take opportunity to renew our acquaintance?'

As if she could be in any doubt as to why he had come here! But to Rosina's consternation, Raith had chosen to accept this, if with a stilted manner of studied civility that had sat uneasily upon him.

'How, indeed? I was not of an age at the time to lend sophistication to your gatherings.'

Then Forteviot had pretended to fall into a mood of reminiscence. His smile had increased, but Rosina had read contempt in his gaze.

'You afforded us a deal of entertainment, I recall. Piers was perhaps less amused by it. But then, there is often that little frisson between brothers where there is a great disparity of age.'

'That *little* frisson, yes,' Raith had responded, so lightly that Rosina was moved to stare at him in perplexity. 'Un-happily, it has proved vain. For there is my poor brother so early in his grave, while I am here in his place.'

'An instance of the strange workings of fate,' had agreed the other man smoothly.

What had they meant by it? She had listened to the give and take of words, breathless with apprehension. An undercurrent of suspicion lay beneath Raith's every utter-ance, despite the cynical air he had adopted. Forteviot had been all too quick to foster it.

'And here is another instance, my dear Anton,' he had said, turning his mocking eyes upon Rosina again. 'What chance was it, I wonder, that gave into your hands this particular delight? Piers would have wondered at your good fortune.'

Rosina glanced quickly at Raith, and saw the muscle twitch in his jaw, making the scar ripple. But his voice was smooth, as he turned the question back on his op-ponent.

'Piers would have envied me, I make no doubt. As surely you must, sir, to see me master of this pretty en-chantment. Must he not, my sweet life?'

She had shrivelled inside to hear that false endearment on his lips. He had raked her with the cold grey of his eyes, and then turned with a scornful laugh back to that hateful man.

'Modesty forbids my wife to speak.'

His deliberate cruelty had crushed her. And she had vowed to withhold herself from giving him the satisfac-tion of knowing anything of her story.

But that resolve was fast dying. Forteviot had long out-stayed his welcome, yet to her horror, Raith himself had encouraged him to remain.

'We have talked so long, and it is growing dark. You must remain to dine with us, Forteviot.'

Dine with them? So that he might hint and conjecture interminably? No, Lord help her!

'My dear Raith, why not dine with me instead at Kington?' had said Forteviot. 'I am staying at the Cross Keys. We will only bore Lady Raith with our memories. And we might try a hand or two of piquet afterwards, if you should care for it?'

She had felt Raith's glance, and held her breath, unknowing whether she feared more to be left alone with her husband, or to be relieved of his presence, not knowing what Forteviot might say to him.

'No, why should we venture into the cold? We can as well play here, sir.'

In that moment, Rosina had wanted desperately to intervene. To scream that if Forteviot were to remain in the house, she must leave it. But that would have been fatal. Dinner had been a nightmare, never knowing from moment to moment what Forteviot might not say to undo her utterly.

'Since Forteviot and I are going to play cards, my love,' Raith had said as she had risen, 'you may as well go to bed. I am sure His Lordship will excuse you.'

Excuse her to the freedom of his tongue, no doubt! She had been on tenterhooks ever since. Did Raith truly suppose that she could sleep, having no notion what might be said down there in the saloon? Or knowing that her husband had so tight a control on his temper that it could not fail to erupt—doubtless upon his wife's luckless head.

Rosina began to wish that she had swallowed her pride, and found the courage to confess all to Raith. However hideous, it could not have been as bad as this, for whatever fondness he had begun to cherish for her would undoubtedly be swept aside.

In a state of mounting tension, she waited to hear the sound of the front door. Her perambulations brought her within sight of the painting of Raith's mother. Pausing, she brought her candle up to the figure on the horse, as if seeking for that vanished gentleness that he must have acquired from this source, for he had it not from the Raiths.

The front door slammed, and she jumped with shock, her heart thudding. She ran to the window, putting the light behind her so that she might see out. A coach was approaching from the stables, and a shadow moved towards it.

Rosina's pulse began to thunder in her head. He was gone, and Raith was done! He would be coming up in a moment. Now that the time was upon her, she wanted to hold it back. She went with lagging steps through to the antechamber door.

Why was she doing this? Raith had told her to go to bed. She was still dressed in the Turkish robe, the most modest of her new gowns, its scalloped folds of the neckline covering the area about her bosom. Would he berate her for having remained up? Why for that, when he had a more cogent reason?

She heard footsteps in the corridor. Her heart fluttered. For a craven moment, she was tempted to withdraw. But her fear of having been betrayed was too strong. She must know!

Drawing a breath for courage, she opened the antechamber door. The room was empty, and in darkness but for the feeble light from her own candle. She moved to Raith's dressing-room door, and hesitated, feeling sick. But it would not do. She lifted her hand to knock—and the door opened.

Rosina stepped back quickly as Raith moved into the doorway. He was stripped to his shirtsleeves and his hair was untied—a *déshabillé* that enhanced his masculinity.

Rosina's throat dried. But the candelabrum in his hand fell upon taut features. Her heart sank.

'Has he gone at last?'

The response was cold. 'He has gone.'

Raith moved to the fireplace, and set the candle holder on the mantel. He was conscious more than anything of fatigue. The effort to contain himself, to beat Forteviot at his own game, had exhausted him. Like that numbness after battle, before reaction set in. Yet he had heard her moving in here as he had begun to undress, and entered on impulse. The questions must be asked, though he dreaded her response. He turned and looked across at her shadowed face by the window.

'Were you afraid that he would tell me everything?'

Rosina's defences went up, overriding the intensity of his attraction. He was unnervingly right. But she was angered to think that he assumed her guilt proven. She refrained from answering.

Raith's voice hardened. 'You had as well tell me as not, ma'am. It makes no difference now. What is this man to you?'

She bit her lip. How could he be anything when Raith was by? Impossible to say that. Yet she must speak, or she would draw his temper.

'Nothing.' It was scarce adequate. She swallowed and added flatly, 'I do not like him.'

'That does not answer me,' he said, an edge to his voice.

Rosina was disinclined to answer him. He had made his own judgements—the more hurtful in light of the sensations his own appearance was invoking. If it made no difference, why should she say anything at all? He would not believe her.

Raith waited a moment. Was she still so stubborn? Why, when she must know how futile a gesture it was to defy him? He turned his eyes away, unable to bear the glinting pallor of her features as they flickered in the light of her candle.

'The man is a gambler. Not as reckless as my brother, but quite as determined. He consorts with men of ill repute, and I know him for a loose-living rake. He is tolerated by the world for his social veneer of charm, I imagine. But men of my father's stamp would not give him the time of day.'

She heard it with resentment, crushing down her awakened senses. Whence this catalogue? To make her feel how low she had sunk in his esteem?

'Why do you tell me this?'

The barb of his bitterness sounded in his voice. 'How do you imagine it makes me feel, to know that you have had dealings with a man of that sort?'

Rosina stiffened in the shadows. 'Dealings? What, pray, is your meaning?'

'You know well enough,' he said roughly. 'You have had some…acquaintance with him.'

Acquaintance! Why did he not say it outright? 'You will have to be more explicit, my lord, if I am to understand you.'

Raith moved swiftly, and Rosina instinctively shrank back. The candle guttered as her hand shook, drawing his attention. He took it from her and set it on the sill of the window, his eyes on her face as it darkened with the removal of the light. His chest felt as though it must burst. He wanted to crush the life out of her!

He hissed in a breath. Had he run mad? He took her throat between his hands, pushing up her chin with his thumbs. He spoke in a guttural whisper.

'Do you know how easily I could break your neck, Rosina?'

She did not flinch, but he could feel the tremble of her

limbs. Her black eyes glittered in the dark. 'If your hatred is so v-vengeful, you had b-better do it.'

A groan escaped him, as his fingers loosened, altering his touch to a caress. 'You think I am driven by hatred? By thunder, I wish it were so!'

Rosina met his eyes, a fierce pulsing war within her, engendered by his proximity. Spasms of need gripped her depths, while a flame of resentment fired her mind, urging her to hit him. Yet as desperately did she yearn for his kiss, the feel of his fingers burning at her flesh.

Raith read the confusion of messages, and his loins flared. His gaze fell to the shiver at her lips, and his mouth came down. But the image of Forteviot's mocking eyes intruded, and he jerked up again.

He took in an unsteady breath, and his hands slid to her shoulders. 'Rosina, I ask you again, what is that man to you?'

His withdrawal shot pain into Rosina's chest, overriding the rest. She pulled back, brushing his hands off. 'Nothing! He is nothing to me.'

'Blood and thunder, *don't lie to me*!'

Her breath caught, and she could not keep her voice from quaking. 'You can m-make me afraid b-by these means, Raith, but you w-will not loosen my t-tongue.'

Raith flung away. His conduct was disgraceful. Hell and damnation, how she aroused him! And he had not wanted to lose his temper. How dangerous in every way it was to be near her!

'Your pardon,' he said, curt and crisp, moving back to the empty fireplace and thus out of range of touching her again. But frustration rapped out of him. 'What is the point of concealment? You know as well as I that you gave yourself away the moment you heard his name. And if you had not, he has said enough to incriminate you.'

Rosina took a hasty step towards him, her voice husky

with dread. 'What did he say to you? What did he tell you?'

'Nothing beyond what you heard,' Raith told her. 'The moment you were out of the room, he was as closed as an oyster.'

Then he had got nothing by his efforts. Rosina sighed with relief. She could not doubt but that Forteviot, had he said anything at all, would have said it in such a way that she was indeed incriminated.

'But that is nothing to the purpose,' Raith pursued. 'You can no longer deny it, Rosina, for God's sake! You are acquainted with this man.'

Rosina's head came up. 'What of it? So also are you, sir.'

A jolt seemed to kick at his chest. 'Then you admit it!'

She threw her hands up to her face, her chest hollowing out. Oh, dear Lord! She had not intended to admit anything. Dared she say that she had meant that her acquaintance with him had begun today? To what purpose? He would never believe it. She sighed, capitulating.

'Yes, I have met him before.'

Raith did not move from where he stood. He could not have done so had he tried. The hurt was too acute. Dully, he repeated his earlier question. 'What was he to you?'

Impatience seethed out of Rosina. 'What do you imagine, Raith? You have seen how I regarded him. Can you then suppose me to have been in love with him?'

'Not—in love.' God, how the word taunted him! 'But I'd stake my oath that he was the man towards whom you exhibited such fear. He was—in despite of your wishes, perhaps—your lover.'

He had said it at last. Had she not known that this was what he believed? But to hear it from him was more wounding than Rosina could ever have imagined. Her heart bled. She had as well have endured her guardian's lust, and allowed herself to be sold into Forteviot's possession. What had it availed her to escape? She had snatched at some other life, and been found wanting. In the process, she'd had a glimpse of tenderness, of what love might be—and lost it.

She picked up her candle, and showed him an ashen countenance. 'There is no more to say, Raith. I am going to my bed.' Then she turned to her door, and quietly left him.

Raith spent the night in an agony of affliction. When he remembered back to those moments prior to the fated arrival of Lord Forteviot, he could not but be struck with a burning sense of the unfairness of it all. He was ashamed of his treatment of Rosina. He had come home to make his peace with her, and had ended in a worse quarrel. A curse upon the villain! What was his association with Rosina?

He wished fervently for Ottery's return, knowing he could not hope for it for another day or two at least. Yet how might the guardian's testimony help? Only it must, or Rosina would not have left his house. Had not her nurse intimated that there were two men involved? Forteviot must be the other. What was the connection between them?

He had resolved to curb his impatience, and to treat his wife with the civility that was her due. He must refrain from questioning her further, and let her be. Though how he was to do either of those things when the sight of her threw his hurt into high relief, he did not know.

He could only be glad that she did not appear at breakfast. He had determined to resume his inspection of the estate, and had accordingly donned riding dress. It was Wednesday, and his agent did not yet know he was back. But he would send to Longridge, and meet him wherever the man had currently reached in their investigations. He needed occupation, by thunder!

'Your pardon, m'lord.'

He looked up from the coffee he was drinking. 'What is it, Kirkham?'

'Does Your Lordship plan to use Parton this morning?'

'Why?' frowned Raith. 'I was going to send him to my agent, but what do you need?'

The butler coughed. 'You know how short of staff we are, m'lord, and I would be obliged if I might ask Parton to ride to Kington to deliver a letter for Her Ladyship.'

A cold hand seized upon Raith's chest. 'Kington?' He stared at the man, a startled query in his mind. The question rapped from him. 'Where is the letter?'

Kirkham went to the sideboard and picked up a salver. It was of pewter, there being no silver remaining in the house. He brought it to Raith, who snatched up the sealed missive and read the inscription. All thought of inspections went out of his head. He leaped from his chair.

'Have Parton saddle my horse. I will take the letter myself!'

Within ten minutes he was astride his mount, cantering cross-country, making for the bridle path that led over some three miles to Kington. He had taken a snap decision, but as he rode, he had leisure to find justification for it.

If he had felt murderous towards Rosina last night, he was now doubly so—but against Forteviot! He might have broken the seal and read the letter. As her husband, he had the right. What man would not choose to open a letter penned by his wife to another man? And one of whom he entertained the gravest suspicions? He might have confronted her, but that would make her even less inclined to part with her secrets.

No, this was the best solution. It would afford him infinite pleasure to be able to take Forteviot at fault. It would serve him out for at least some of the foul wit he had exercised at Raith's expense.

He had himself played a loathsome part last night. He had acted in much the manner of Piers, and Forteviot had begun, he thought, to believe in it. Why should he not? It was seven years since they had met—for Forteviot had formed one of the party on the fiendish night when he had suffered that final humiliation at his brother's hands. That he had fought back had earned him Forteviot's jeering remark about heroics.

Raith set his teeth, turning the horse onto the bridle path, and letting him have his head. He was no longer a raw youth. Let Forteviot beware him this time.

He covered the ground in some fifteen minutes, cantering easily into Kington, and rode into the yard at the Cross Keys, bidding the ostlers good day. He was already known at this inn, and the landlord greeted him with offers of refreshment.

'I want nothing, I thank you, Tarbert,' he said, divesting himself of hat, gloves and whip. 'I came only to see Lord Forteviot. I trust he is still with you?'

'Oh, yes, my lord. He has just rung for his breakfast. Would you wish me to show you up to his private parlour?'

Forteviot was lounging in a cherry-striped morning gown, a nightcap covering his unwigged head. He was reading a newspaper, but he glanced up as Raith entered the room. A startled look came into his face, but he summoned a smile, and spoke with all his usual urbanity, rising from the chair.

'My dear Anton, what an unexpected pleasure!'

Raith made no attempt to disguise his acute dislike. He stared at the man, and watched with satisfaction as the smile faded. Was that wariness in those slitted eyes? Raith withdrew the letter from his pocket and held it up. He allowed the disgust he felt to sound in his voice.

'This is from my wife. It is addressed to you, Forteviot. Perhaps you would read it, and then be good enough to tell me why my wife is writing to you.'

The other's eyebrows went up. 'Is she, indeed?' He resumed his seat, crossing his legs in an attitude of nonchalance. 'Why don't you read it for yourself, my dear Anton? I feel sure it can contain nothing that cannot be seen by a husband's jealous eye.'

Raith looked him over with contempt. 'Don't attempt to trifle with me, Forteviot! The game is up. I know that you have had dealings with my wife.'

'If you know, my dear Anton—'

'If you once more address me in that supercilious fashion, you lying cur, I shall knock your teeth down your throat!' interrupted Raith with heat.

The other smiled in an infuriating way. 'Yes, I rather thought that your manner of last night was assumed. This is much more like you. My dear—but I must not call you that! Really, how difficult it is to know quite what to—'

'Will you cease this prevarication?' Raith crossed the room, and threw the letter down on the table. 'Read it!'

Forteviot picked up the letter and turned it over, examining the seal. 'You amaze me, Raith. You really have refrained from opening the thing.' He laughed gently, and Raith set his teeth at the sound. 'You know, your chivalry is quite misplaced. Perhaps I would even say, wasted.'

A chill swept through Raith. His eyes narrowed. 'Do you care to explain that remark?'

'Do you know, Raith, I don't care to,' Forteviot said apologetically, breaking the seal on the note. He ran his eyes down the single sheet, and his smile broadened. 'Well, it is what I expected.' He held it out. 'Will you read it now? Or are you still bent upon being noble?'

Raith did not take it. 'I will rather have you tell me the substance.'

Forteviot tutted gently. 'Very foolish, sir. Would you expect me to betray a lady?'

'Spare me your affectations!' Raith twitched it out of his hand, and pocketed it. 'Write a reply, and I will take it to Rosina myself.'

A pitying look was cast upon him. 'Thus forcing her to recognise the unparalleled nature of your forbearance, in the hopes that this will induce her to confide in you. My poor Raith, you must be gravely mistaken in her character.'

Raith felt his temper rising, and reminded himself that the man was bent upon provoking it. That he had doubts himself was one thing. To hear Forteviot impugn Rosina was quite another. He was hard put to it to refrain from striking the villain where he sat. If he did so, he must prepare to be challenged. He had the intention of calling Forteviot to account in due time—but on his own terms.

'You do yourself no good by these hints, sir,' he said instead in a cold tone. 'Unless you can substantiate them, be assured that I will believe no ill of my wife.'

The eyebrows rose again. 'Yet you come here in a righteous fury, demanding to know why she is writing to me. Permit me to tell you that I find you a trifle inconsistent.'

'Call for pen and ink,' said Raith impatiently. 'I have no mind to listen to your smooth-tongued insinuations.'

'As you wish.'

Forteviot rose, and moved across to a small table set in the window embrasure. Upon it rested an inkstand and several leaves of paper. He took up a pen, and dipped it in the ink.

'I did wonder how you had become inveigled—I hesitate to say entrapped—into marriage,' he said, throwing the remarks over his shoulder. 'But I realised how unwitting had been your involvement when I found out about your advertisement.'

Raith heard his words with alarm and puzzlement. He knew about the advertisement? 'How did you find out?'

Forteviot turned slightly to survey him, holding the pen poised. 'I have my sources. An apothecary's boy was extremely helpful.'

Concern for Rosina's nurse attacked Raith. She had half-expected, when he and Ottery called upon her, that her visitors might have been this man or the guardian, he recalled. He did not wish to ask whether Forteviot had seen Mrs Hoswick, for fear of alerting him to her whereabouts if he did not know them. Yet what of the boy Toly, whom he had certainly seen? Had Forteviot bribed him—or used some other method?

'Where did you find this apothecary's boy?' he asked.

'At Hopsford. And by the same method you did, I fancy. Those fellows at Brinklow Receiving Office appeared unsurprised at my enquiries. I suspect, my dear Raith, from the boy's guarded remarks, that my visit followed hard upon your own. What he had to tell me was most interesting.'

'Indeed?' Raith eyed him with growing suspicion. What need had he to make such enquiries, if he had seen—as must be supposed—the announcement of Rosina's marriage in the *Gazette*? And why give her husband this information? What mischief was he brewing? Like a fool, Raith had fallen straight into his trap!

Forteviot was folding his letter. 'I have not a seal with me. No doubt you will carry your nobility so far as to contain your curiosity until you reach home.'

Rosina paced the saloon, in much the same state of tension as she had paced her bedchamber on the previous evening. Had Forteviot yet had her letter? Would he respond instantly? She had known he meant to make trouble! But she was not prepared for the dreadful nature of it.

With her chocolate this morning, Joan had brought the fell tidings, contained in a note from Forteviot that had been brought over from the Cross Keys. She had passed over his sarcastic felicitations upon her marriage, and read quickly to discover what he intended. It had been an unhappy moment.

Since she had deprived him of his prize, he said boldly, it behoved her to repay him what she had been worth to him. Now that she was so advantageously placed, he had no doubt of her being able to do it. She had better find a way, or he would be obliged instead to request it from her husband—and she must know what that would mean.

Blackmail! How could she pay a tithe of such a sum— even had she a mind to do it? It was not her debt, but her guardian's. She had sent Joan for pen and paper, and sat down immediately at her dressing-table to answer him as much. She said nothing of Raith, nor deigned to say that she could not afford to pay him. She recommended him to apply to Herbert Cambois, and let her alone.

Once the letter was despatched, she had become prey to tension, wondering what might be the outcome. Hearing from Joan that Raith had ridden out, she'd had the maid dress her again in the simple sprigged gown and come downstairs to await Forteviot's response.

She dared not suppose that he would accept her refusal to pay him. What would she do if he told Raith everything? Would his version of events march with the truth? She doubted it. It would be better that she tell Raith the whole. What did it matter any longer? Her marriage was all but over.

Raith walked in on her unexpectedly halfway through the morning. He had evidently just ridden in, for he was in his green riding frock and buckskins, his boots a trifle mud-splashed. His aspect was forbidding, and the memory of last night's uncomfortable interview sprang into her mind. She stared at him as he shut the door—and locked it.

'I have no wish to be disturbed,' he said curtly, by way of explanation. He saw alarm enter her eyes, and added, 'I am not locking you in, Rosina. You may leave here at any time that suits you.'

Rosina knew not what to say. Did he mean to renew his questions? 'What is it you want?'

Holding her eyes, he removed both letters from his pocket, and coming forward, held them out to her. 'These are your property. I have not read either.'

Numbly, she took the letters, and knew on the instant what they were. The seal of the one she had written was broken. She spread it open. 'Dear Lord, whence had you this?'

'It came to my hand this morning.' He saw the horror creep into her features, and was conscious of a feeling of guilt. He repressed it. It was time and past that the lies were exposed.

Rosina was opening the other letter. She ran her eyes down the short message it contained. She barely took in the words as the implication sank into her brain. She felt sick.

'You took it to him! My letter—you took it to him yourself. Why did you not read it?'

'Because I wanted him to tell me himself what it contained,' Raith told her flatly. 'When he would not, I told him to write that reply for me to bring back.'

She heard him, but she did not take in much of what he said. Raith had not read the letters—either of them. What should stop him making himself master of their contents? Did he believe that in this extremity she would at last tell him the truth? If so, he was right. What choice had she?

Her breath was ragged. 'I did not s-seek to contact him, Raith.' She dug into the hidden pocket of her gown and produced Forteviot's first letter. 'I wrote in reply to this.'

For a moment she held all three papers within her fingers. Then she thrust them upon him. 'Read them. Read them all!'

Turning, she moved quickly away to the fireplace, and leaning her hands on the mantel, rested her forehead upon them, trying vainly to control the quickened breath that accompanied the palpitations of her bosom.

Raith watched her with a wrenching at his heart. In despite of all, she drew his compassion. His resentment of Forteviot grew, and he unfolded the letters as he moved to the window to read.

So Forteviot attempted blackmail? Hell and damnation! That presupposed that there was some disgrace attached to the matter of this sum of money he demanded, and said Rosina had been worth. In what respect? God send it was not what he was beginning to suspect! What had it to do with the guardian's debt to Forteviot? It began to seem that Rosina had been caught up in a situation which she had no power to control. Had he not suspected as much? Only how far had it gone?

His chest caved in, as he felt the dread certainty of his wife having been obliged to succumb to Forteviot. With unsteady fingers he sifted through the man's last communication. It was a brief statement of his own visit to Forteviot, stating only that Raith had challenged him to account for his correspondence with her, and asking whether she dared to tell her husband the truth. Raith looked up to find Rosina's eyes upon him.

She had turned to watch, finding it more bearable to

see his reaction as he read, than to wait for it in words. He was frowning heavily, and a muscle twitched, shifting the rent of his cheek. But Rosina could not tell what he thought.

He eyed her in silence for a moment. The waif-look was pronounced, and altogether touching. He laid aside the sheaf of letters upon a side table, and came up to her. He reached for one of her hands, and brought it to his lips.

Softly then, he said, 'Can you not trust me, Rosy?'

Tears sprang to her eyes. 'Lord knows I want to, Raith!'

He said nothing, but only enclosed the quivering fingers within his own, holding them tight. Rosina met the tenderness of his gaze, and sighed. She wanted to fall upon his chest, and feel his arms encircle her. She was seized with the urge to touch her fingers to his blemished features, so close, and open to her sight. But to win the right to that—if he could find it in him to forgive the shame of the indignities she had endured—she must open her life to his inspection.

She looked down. 'Very well. Loose me now, if you please. I will tell you it all.'

As Raith released her, the wash of relief that flooded him was tempered by the visible paling of her features. He stood aside, and watched her move to take a chair. She did not look at him, but sat stiffly upright, her fingers pulling at each other in unconscious expression of her inner disquiet.

'You believe,' she began in a tone of forced calm over her tautly held-in tension, 'that it was Forteviot who—who violated my honour. But it was not he, though he is guilty of the intention. It was my guardian who made that attempt.'

'Attempt?' queried Raith quickly. 'Do you mean to imply that he did not succeed?'

Rosina threw up a hand. 'Pray, let me tell the tale in my own way. You will know all—by and by.'

Raith curbed his impatience with difficulty, gripping the mantel with one hand. He set his jaw, and Rosina saw it. She kneaded unconsciously at the muslin folds of her petticoats.

'You are eager to know if he took me,' she said low-toned. 'He did not—' closing her eyes tight shut '—penetrate.'

The word stabbed in his gut. He gripped his underlip between his teeth, his eyes fierce upon her delicate elfin face. What rude invasions had been attempted? How far had been taken this despoiling of her virgin innocence? He saw the black eyes open, and their luminous sheen threw him into acute disorder—and murderous intent. Her guardian was a dead man!

Rosina could not look at him. 'Of what p-purity I may still be p-possessed,' she uttered shakily, 'I must l-leave you to be the judge.'

He flung over to the window, unable to trust himself. Much more, and he would seize her in his arms, and tell her that she need give him no more of this. He had wanted to hear it. But even this little telling was a species of torture. He had wanted to know her to be pure—and she was, it seemed. But at what cost? Behind him, Rosina spoke again.

'I must tell you how it came about. And—and the part played in this by Forteviot.'

Raith set his teeth. This was not helping her. With deliberation, he turned again, and went to sit in the opposite chair. 'I will hear you with patience.'

She cast a look at him, and a tiny smile wavered for an instant on her lips. Then she withdrew her gaze, and clasping her hands tightly together, began her tale, explaining how her pity of her guardian's grief had made him see her as an asset. She twisted her fingers.

'I believed at first that he intended me to marry. He instructed me to be present at his gambling sessions, intimating that I would meet suitable gentlemen. He would not hear of my refusal, though I did refuse. At length he threatened to throw me out if I did not do it. I had nowhere to go. It seemed to me then a lesser evil to comply.'

Raith listened in a steadily increasing state of tension. Guessing what was coming, he ached for the rude shock of awakening that Rosina must have experienced. Too well did he know how unmannerly a thing was the sight of men at play—their behaviour indecorous, their drinking excessive, and using language unfit for feminine ears.

'There were some five or six each night. I was required to refill their glasses, or bring fresh cards. Only Forteviot paid me much heed.' She shifted with discomfort, one hand going up to touch her neck as if she sought to brush away the memory of his lascivious eyes. 'He looked me over in a way that made me feel—unclothed.'

One night, she had gone to the parlour to discover only Forteviot and Herbert Cambois. The mask had been stripped off.

'My guardian told me that a bargain had been struck.'

Raith held his breath. The image of Forteviot's mocking features hovered at the forefront of his mind. He wanted to smash his fist between those slitted eyes!

'I was to be the p-payment for his debts to Forteviot.'

Rosina's voice failed, and she was obliged to put a hand up to her mouth. Raith rose quickly, and took a step towards her. But she threw out a hand, shrinking back.

'I can only say this once, my lord. Pray let me finish!'

But her tears choked her. Raith cursed. He stepped swiftly across to a baize table in one corner of the room, where a decanter and glasses had been forgotten from his game of piquet with Forteviot. Pouring a measure of Madeira, he brought it back to Rosina, bidding her drink it.

'It will calm you.'

She put out a trembling hand, and took the glass, throwing a brief glance up at him as she sipped at the liquid. She felt the warmth of it spreading through her, and was presently able to speak again. Raith took the glass from her and placed it on the mantel, where he remained, watching her face.

'I cannot describe to you my feelings upon the event. Forteviot was very frank. I was to be his mistress. When I failed to—please him, he would cast me off. He thought I should have no difficulty finding myself another protector.'

But the worst part of the tale was yet to be told. Rosina moistened her lips, and her fingers writhed about each other. Raith watched her with mounting distress, and black fury in his heart as he learned how, when Forteviot had gone, Rosina had cast aside all pride, and pleaded with her guardian to free her from this intolerable future.

'He was adamant. Nothing would serve him but this. I did not know what to do. If I'd had a way of finding a post, I would have taken it. But without references, my situation was impossible. And there was no time.' Her voice sank. 'I tried to school myself to accept it. But when I saw how Forteviot eyed my person—I knew I had rather die by my own hand!'

Raith's fist was clenched so hard that his knuckles ached. He forced himself to straighten his hand, and clamped his mouth tight shut on the hot protesting words that rose to his tongue.

'I resolved to be gone from my guardian's house before the plan could be put into execution. I had in secret received my nurse's direction, and I knew she would give me refuge.'

She had made her plans and enlisted the aid of those two of the servants who were her particular friends. But that night her guardian had stumbled drunk into her bed-chamber.

'He looked just as you did—standing in the doorway with a candelabrum,' she said huskily.

'That is what threw you into the memory, and made you so afraid?'

Rosina nodded, drawing a sobbing breath. 'He meant, he said, to teach me submission. He—he laid down his candle, and—fell upon me. I managed to throw him off, but he pulled at the covers. He caught me, and he is a big man. I thought I was done for.'

She recalled struggling, and the loathsome wetness of his slobbering kiss as she had tried to evade his mouth. He had torn at her nightgown, and she had flailed half-naked in the cold night air. She had felt him thrusting at her thighs, while his hot hands had seized at her flesh.

She had been saved in that moment when he raised himself up in order to effect an entry, for the wine had gone to his head and he had paused, swaying. She had pushed into his chest, driving him off. As he had fallen among the disarranged covers, Rosina had struggled out of the bed, and run as for her life, slamming the door upon his infuriated grunting. She had fled to the attic room of one of the maids, where she had remained for the rest of the night.

'In the early dawn,' she finished, 'we crept out when the other servants had ascertained that he was abed in his own room. He had stumbled about looking for me, we thought, for the place was a wreck. Aggie helped me to pack as much of my belongings as I could carry in a portmanteau, and she promised to send the rest secretly by carrier to Brinklow.'

There was silence for some moments in the saloon. Raith was too harrowed by the tale to speak. The near rape so appalled him that he wished fervently that he had never asked her for this truth. Was not his the cruel demand that had thrown her time and again back into this memory? How hurtful must it have been for Rosina, to be reminded of it each time that he had harried her to tell him.

But Rosina, he saw, was quiescent now. In the telling of it, had she exorcised something of the ghost? Or was it merely that exhaustion now prevented her from feeling anything? It was a sensation he could appreciate.

'How did you get to your nurse?' he asked.

Rosina heaved an unconscious sigh. 'In disguise. A groom stole for me a greatcoat, a slouch hat and a pair of boots from the stables. I looked less like a country wench than a farm boy. I had no money, so I had to make my way by asking lifts from carriers.'

She fell silent again. She felt both exposed and empty. How might Raith be less disgusted than she was herself? She was not impure, nor was it her fault, but she was nevertheless tainted. Had their marriage remained a convenience, he might have been expected to tolerate it. But they were long past that. How could he possibly bear it? If she could only know his present intentions towards her!

'What will you do now?'

Raith straightened abruptly. 'I am going back to Kington.'

Rosina blenched. 'To see Forteviot? To what purpose?'

His jaw was set, danger in his eyes. 'To challenge him with this story—and to dare him to answer me!'

Alarmed, Rosina rose from her seat. 'You will not call him out, Raith?'

'Have no fear! I mean to settle this affair. Do not forget that he has come here with the intention of extorting money.'

He went purposefully to the door, and turned the key in the lock. Rosina followed him, laying one hand upon his arm.

'Raith, wait!'

He turned. 'I must go, Rosina. It is useless to try to stop me.'

'One moment only, I pray you!'

The plea was intense. Raith hesitated, his fingers about the handle of the door. 'What is it?'

Her fingers left his arm, travelling to her bosom as the coal-black eyes searched his face. 'Raith, do you believe what I have told you?'

He frowned in puzzlement. 'Of course I believe it. Why should I not?'

Rosina's lip quivered. 'And when F-Forteviot gives you some twisted v-version of it, to make you think ill of me, will you believe it then?'

Raith's heart contracted. He let go the door handle, and caught her hand. 'How can you suppose otherwise? Do you imagine I would take that fiend's word before yours?'

'Why should you not?' she uttered. 'You know me little better than you know him. How long have we been married?'

'I don't know,' Raith said roughly. 'Two weeks— three? What does it matter? It feels like a lifetime!'

Her fingers clung to his. 'But it is not, Raith. It is little more than two weeks. And that man is persuasive. I have no proof that I am telling the truth. And you have entertained doubts of me from the beginning.'

Raith cupped her cheek, the grey eyes remorseful. 'For which I hope you can learn to forgive me.' Then he drew her to him and dropped a light kiss on her hair. 'But you need have no apprehension. Ottery is even now at the house of Herbert Cambois. I will wager that he will extract the truth. He is no fool.'

But Rosina was pulling away from him, shock in her eyes. Realising what he had said, Raith gave himself a mental kick. It was too late. The murder was out, and his wife's outrage was patent.

Chapter Nine

'Mr Ottery is at Nun Eaton? Dear Lord, you have been spying upon me!' Rosina swung away. 'You have plagued me beyond endurance to tell you these things, and all the time—' Halting in the middle of the room, she turned upon him. 'How could you know where to find my guardian? How did you know his name? Whom did you bully to—' She stopped, checked by a horrifying thought. 'Gatty! You have found my nurse!'

'Yes, we found her,' Raith admitted, torn between guilt and the conviction that his actions had been justified. 'We were searching all the while I was away from here.'

'And you returned to me with soft words and…' She faded out, choked with chagrin. 'How could you use me so?'

'I had no choice, Rosina! You would say nothing. What was I to do? I had to find out the truth in any way I could.'

'But to set your lawyer to spy upon me! And Gatty. What did you do to her to make her betray me to you? She would never have done so without force.'

Anger flared in Raith's breast. 'Is that what you think of me, by thunder? There was nothing of that sort, Rosina.'

The black orbs burned at him. 'What did you do to her?'

'For what do you take me?' he uttered frustratedly. 'I found a poor, blind creature whose sole concern was for your safety. She was only induced to confide the name of Cambois when she understood that I was more fitted to provide your safe keeping than Forteviot himself.'

Rosina's eyes flashed. 'But you did not tell her your suspicions of me. She would have demanded that you return me to her.'

'Which indeed she did,' Raith confirmed flatly. 'I gave her my promise that I would do so, should it turn out…' He paused, realising how infelicitous was this trend.

But Rosina had divined his meaning. The blood drained out of her face, and he saw the waif returning.

'You had as well d-do so at once,' she said huskily. 'There can be no t-trust between us.'

Raith moved to her, and tried to take her hands. She whipped them behind her, stepping back. A weight of anguish hovered above him. He was going to lose her!

'Rosy,' he uttered raggedly, 'don't do this, I pray you!'

She met his eyes full, and the pain within them was echoed in his own breast. 'I d-dare not give in to you, Raith. Your suspicions have wrought h-havoc within me—as they have in you. You think it is over, but I know it is not. Mr Ottery will gain nothing but lies from Herbert Cambois. Between him and Forteviot, they will re-awaken your doubts—I know it!'

'No, Rosina!' he said forcefully. 'Trust me!'

'How can I trust you?' she demanded, anguished. 'You have blown hot and c-cold upon me since the first moment of our union.'

Raith was silenced. He knew it to be true, and knew not how to reassure her. Desperate, he uttered, 'Rosy, we are married, for better or for worse. Nothing can change that.'

Rosina let out a laugh that cracked in the middle, and turned away from him. She found herself unsteady on her feet, and grasped at the mantel of the fireplace for support. She did not look at him. She spoke in the flat calm of despair.

'You speak always from impulse, Raith, and fail to see your own contradictions. But a moment since, you said you had told Gatty that you would return me to her. Now you quote me the marriage vow, and expect me to believe in it.' She took a breath, and looked across at him. 'I must face it, if you will not. We are on the brink of separation.'

A shaft sliced into his chest, and his heart cried out against it. He wanted to seize her in his arms, and over-bear her conviction with the fire of his lips. But she had drifted too far away from him, and a voice at the back of his mind whispered that there was truth in what she said.

'If it should come to that, then know that it will be to my everlasting regret.'

The torment of his heart was in his voice. Rosina heard it with a twisting in her own breast. 'Oh, why did you not meet me before we married?' she cried, distraught. 'Why did you not ask me then?'

He flung it back at her. 'Why did you not tell me at the outset?'

Her lip quivered. 'Would you have m-married me, if you had heard then what I have t-told you today?'

Raith looked at the delicate elfin features, at the lumi-nous appeal of her coal-black eyes, and knew his answer would ever have been the same.

'Yes,' he said simply.

Then he turned on his heel, and left the room, wrench-ing open the door, and slamming it behind him.

Rosina stared at the shut door, frozen as the sound of

his footsteps died out of the hall. Into the numbness of her mind floated the only possible realisation. Raith did care! He would have married her, in spite of all. What could that mean but one thing? She had long suspected it, but had not dared to believe.

Yet how was it possible? He had not known her—not seen her!—until they married. Had his ardour grown so rapidly? Why should it not—when her own had been almost as swift? She could no longer tell at what instant of time her spouse had thus fatally pierced her heart. Might it be that Raith was similarly affected? Oh, he wanted her! But so also did Forteviot, and—

Her thoughts slammed to a halt. Raith was going back to that man! Dear Lord, why could he not see the danger? So small a twist as it needed to turn him against her once more. If it was indeed the case that his heart was touched, then she was lost indeed. For she saw how vital to him must have been the declaration of her chastity. Forteviot would change him. She knew he would. Raith had bade her trust him, but how could she, knowing how subject he was to those lightning fluctuations of temperament? It would take so little!

How was she to bear his renewed hostility, if it was true that he loved her? She could not! Raith—*Raith!*

She did not know whether she cried aloud, as she tore open the door to run from the saloon, crossing the hall on winged feet. Driven by desperate need—some wild half-formed hope of detaining him!—she flung wide the front door, and ran out on to the porch, gulping in the frosty chill of November.

Before her yawned the empty ash-strewn lawns. A sob escaped her, and she ran out on to the drive, forgetting the open front door, the only thought in her mind that she was too late. Raith was already gone!

The certainty of impending loss gripped her. What use

to have confessed it all, when her enemy's cunning could only play on her spouse's jealous heart? If she better understood his anguish, she was doomed to be the poorer for that knowledge.

Only half-aware of what she did, unheeding of the cold that penetrated through the thin muslin of her sprigged gown, Rosina took off along one side of the mansion. As she went, her mind roved without intent, images pricking at her. Visions of Raith's features, the ugly scar slashing his cheek. Ugly? Yes, it was so, and yet she could only regard it with tenderness. Impossible that there had ever been a time when she could see its savagery upon that beloved countenance without a swelling of affection.

Impossible even, that she had fallen in love with him. Had Raith set out to woo her, he could not have done it with more success than he had achieved with his abominable swings from violent rage to tenderness. Why did she care so for him? He had done his best to make her hate him! Only it was the wounded soul within the tiger that had lured her heart. Dear Lord, how was she to bear his loss?

Her breath caught, and tears sprang to her eyes, half-blinding her. She tried to halt them, but the overwrought bursting of her sorrow would not be contained. Choked sobs stifled her throat, and she stumbled on without intent, pushing through stark wood branches that came in her way. She lost all sensation of direction, and had no idea that she had wandered into the woody retreat that abutted the grounds of Raith Manor.

All at once, a violent pain gripped at her womb. She gasped out, grabbing at the nearest tree for support. It came again, and the occasion of it burst into her mind. Oh, no. To be caught unawares with this? Not now. Not here. She must get back to the house.

But the pain intensified, and Rosina felt the first eruption of her flux. She looked wildly round, trying to gather her bearings. She was in a forest, but she could not be so far from the mansion. A sensation of cold came upon her, and she realised belatedly that she had come forth without so much as a shawl. Another violent wave of agony overcame her. Hanging on to the tree, she waited for it to pass.

Raith remained by the parlour door, willing himself to remember the rules of gentlemanly etiquette. He had not stayed to lay aside his hat and whip, and his right hand struck a rhythmic beat of the weapon against his boot. Much as he longed to do it, he could not march across the room and lift the villain from his seat with an iron grip about his throat. Nor smash his fist into that complacent countenance! By and by, he would have satisfaction—and enjoy it. But not now.

'Well?'

Forteviot's eyebrows lifted. 'My dear Raith, I do not deny that there is some substance in the tale.'

'Substance! Do you dare to imply that there is any vestige of a lie?'

'Nothing so blatant, my dear fellow,' tutted the other, crossing one leg over the other. He had found time to dress between Raith's two visits, sporting a neat tie-wig atop a fashionable suit of green broadcloth over a flamboyant striped waistcoat. But he lounged still at his ease.

'Enlighten me,' Raith said curtly, moving to throw down both hat and whip upon a chair. 'What is amiss with my wife's story?'

A knowing smile curved Forteviot's thin lips. 'Oh, she warned you, did she? I imagine she might well suppose that my version of events did not quite mesh with her own.'

Raith's ire rose the more as he stripped off his gloves.

How poisonous a tongue had this scoundrel! For he could feel the insinuating pull of his own suspicion even from this slight turn. He flung down the gloves and his voice became snappish.

'Be specific—and do not attempt to suborn me with artifice.'

Forteviot spread his hands, his smile broadening. 'I have no wish to do so, Anton.'

'I know what you wish, Forteviot. You think to extract money from me. You will find me an ill subject for extortion.'

The other looked pained. 'So ugly a word, Anton. No, no. If I seek recompense, it is not to be wondered at. Twenty thousand is a goodly sum.'

'Which you won fairly at play. But not from Rosina.'

To Raith's surprise and distrust, Forteviot heaved a sigh tinged with melancholy. 'I thought to win her, you see. You have succeeded—inadvertently, I know—where I could not. I suppose I am too old for her.'

Disgust coursed through Raith. 'Spare me your shams! You are not trying to make me believe that it was marriage you intended? By thunder, but you take me for a fool! You sought to make a harlot of her.'

He all but ground his teeth, and his long riding frock rippled with motion as he jerked across the room.

'You would have taken her innocence, and dropped her without compunction when she no longer suited your purposes.'

Forteviot's eyebrows rose again, and he laughed gently. 'My dear Anton, nothing could have been further from my mind. Naturally I could not marry a girl who came with no dowry or connections. I have a position in society to keep up.'

'Which is as much as to say that I have not.'

'You entirely mistake me, Raith. But you misunderstand. When I say that I failed to win her, I mean that she did not favour me. That did not imply that she was unwilling to take up the role I had outlined. Rosina had no objection to the bargain of itself. It was sealed with her agreement. Indeed, she was very frank with her requirements.'

Raith set his teeth. 'Take care! If you knew how my fingers itch to close about your throat—'

Forteviot threw up a hand. 'Believe me, I appreciate your feelings. But you have come to me with accusations, my friend, and I have my reputation to consider.'

In one violent movement, Raith swung over to the table where the man sat, and slammed his hands down upon it. 'Your reputation is not at stake here, sir. We are discussing the reputation of my wife! I say to you again—*take care.*'

For a brief instant, he saw the flare of retaliation in the other man's eyes. Then they were veiled again, and the habitual urbanity returned.

'I see that you have not lost that hot-headed temperament that was so much your undoing all those years ago.'

Raith did not move from his position. 'No,' he said deliberately, 'I have not lost it. If you value your skin, Forteviot, you will beware of it.'

His tormentor held up one well-manicured hand. 'Consider me warned.'

His jaw tightening, Raith stood upright once more. His tone was biting. 'Very well, then. Tell me this, if you please. If Rosina was willing to become your mistress— I do not mince words, I!—why did she run away?'

Forteviot looked blank. 'Is that what she said?'

Once again, Raith found himself almost caught by the expression of innocent enquiry—as if Rosina had been trapped in a lie. Hell and damnation, but the fellow was wily! Well, then, let him set his head in a noose. He clamped his lips upon a sharp retort.

'You have another explanation?' he asked evenly.

'I hesitate to say this, my dear Anton,' said Forteviot in a rueful fashion, 'for I know how it must wound you. But the boot was on the other leg. Had I accepted her for the debt at the last, I should have been obliged to hand her back. I had not bargained for receiving damaged goods.'

By extreme effort of will, Raith contained himself. A muscle twitched in his cheek, and he could barely get out the words. 'How would you know if they were—damaged?'

Forteviot's lips pursed, and his features became pinched in an expression of displeasure. 'I am sorry to say that my partner in the exchange betrayed me.'

An oath left Raith's lips. The wretch knew of that? 'He told you?'

There was scorn in the other's smile. 'You do not know Cambois. What would you? He was drunk, as ever he is. The fellow confessed all to me.'

In spite of himself, Raith could not help the question. 'How do you know that he succeeded—carried out the attack?'

'Oh, did Rosina say otherwise?' queried Forteviot innocently. 'Dear me.'

He sighed again, and Raith met his eyes, despising himself for the dread rise of uncertainty in his breast.

'Well?' he demanded roughly. 'What is your inference this time?'

Forteviot spread his hands again in his characteristic way. 'I hesitate to say it, Anton. You have several times offered me violence this morning, and—'

'Say it, and be damned to you!' Raith flung at him, thrusting away to the window.

'Then do not blame me, for I am quoting another.' His voice was matter-of-fact. 'Cambois gave me to understand that someone had been before him. A footman belike. She consorted, he said, a great deal with the servants.' The tone lowered to one of hushed compassion. 'Rosina did not run away, my poor Anton. Cambois was obliged to throw her out.'

For a moment Raith stood just where he was, gazing unseeingly out of the window, struggling with his baser self. How cunning was this history! Marching readily with Rosina's tale, and yet parting from it in just those details that were guaranteed to strike precisely at his questing jealousy. It had to be intended! He strode away, pacing across the little parlour, and back again. Then he faced Forteviot. He spoke in a low tone that was laced with a vibrant chord of hatred.

'You black-hearted devil! I don't believe a word of this!'

A laugh escaped Forteviot. 'How should you?' he said pityingly. 'Who can blame you, my dear Anton? Your affections are deeply engaged.'

'So deeply,' Raith returned, his breath taut, 'that I will trust my own knowledge of her before your trumped-up fictions.'

'In your place, my dear fellow, I should feel precisely the same,' said Forteviot gently. 'You are bound to wish to think the best of her. And she is so very innocent and sweet, is she not? On the surface.'

'*Enough!*' Raith drew several tight breaths before he was able to command himself. 'I know what you would be at, Forteviot! I tell you now that you will not succeed. Neither in this, nor in your vile scheme. If you persist—' with a raking glance that made the other flinch, his voice dropping to a menacing hush '—I will kill you.'

*   *   *

Raith cantered his sweating mount into the stable yard, and brought him to a standstill. Leaning forward, he caressed the beast's warm neck.

'I have ridden you too hard, old fellow. You will have to forgive your master's blue devils this accursed day.'

He had galloped the animal, in an attempt to rid himself of the seed of doubt planted by the wilful evil of Rosina's enemy. There had been enough of suspicion in his marriage. She had been too much injured already. He would not be cozened into belief.

Dismounting, he looked in concern at the stallion's heaving flanks, the steam rising from his coat. 'We must get you properly looked to, my buck.' Turning, he called into the stable block. 'Parton!'

There was no reply. What in thunder ailed them all? If his groom was not present, one of the two stable lads always came running forth on his approach. He set his hands to either side his mouth.

'Ho, there! What, is no one by?'

He was obliged to call out several more times, before the sound of running feet at last answered him. They came from the side of the mansion, and belonged, he saw in a moment, not to either of the stable boys, but to one of the maids.

'M'lord!' she gasped, as she caught sight of him. 'Oh, m'lord, thank goodness you are come!'

Quick alarm gripped him. Keeping hold of the horse's rein, he moved forward. 'What in thunder is amiss, girl?'

'Her Ladyship!'

Raith's heart stopped. With a claw-like hand, he seized the maid's arm as she came up. 'What has happened to Her Ladyship?'

Wincing, the girl panted out her frantic news. 'Gone— m'lord!'

Hoarsely, his mind blank, he repeated it. 'Gone?'

'Aye, sir. Mr Kirkham—he found the front door open. He asked us all—if we done it. Only no one didn't know nothing about it, m'lord. Then Mrs Fawley—she thought of Her Ladyship. Joan went looking for her, m'lord—and she weren't nowhere to be found. Every one of us has been out this half-hour and more—searching.'

Raith heard her with a mind incapable of any form of action. Only one solid thought drummed insistently in his head. Rosina had left him!

Vaguely he noted the maid's round eyes popping at him. He must seem a very ninny. But her amazement was differently explained. 'You've gone all white, m'lord.'

Raith made an effort to pull himself together. He held out the bridle. 'Take this! Where are they looking?'

The maid accepted the horse's rein from him, and pointed towards the front of the house. 'All the way along the woods, m'lord.'

A sudden distant shout arrested Raith's attention. He strode forward a few steps, and heard answering calls. The maid, he found, had kept pace beside him, leading the horse.

'Likely they've found her, sir!' she said excitedly.

'Keep hold of my horse! I'll send one of the boys directly,' he said. Then he was running.

He was operating on the instinct of command, the long years of campaigning shifting into play. An officer in battle did not think. He took an instant survey and acted. Raith met the oncoming figures of his servants, and took in what they said without stopping to consider what they meant, or to bandy unnecessary words.

He barked orders, handing away his whip, hat and gloves. With effortless remembrance, he sent someone to attend to the needs of his horse back at the stables. And he followed without question the direction indicated towards the apparent whereabouts of his wife.

But unlike a charge in the field, where the same burst of energy was demanded by the exigencies of warfare, he was driven here by an undercurrent of desperate need because Rosina's safety was in question. When at last he came upon the woeful figure, huddled in a heap against the trunk of a tree, he froze for an instant of stopped time, torn between relief and dread.

She was shivering, and her hair had come loose. But she panted as if with heat, and the black eyes were glazed. She was bent forward over herself, her hands hugging her stomach. And then he saw the blood.

'Rosy!' he uttered hoarsely. 'Rosina, what ails you?'

Her head turned at the sound of his voice, and Raith dropped to one knee beside her, reaching to cradle her. She was ice cold. His voice gentled.

'Rosy—sweetheart!'

The endearment penetrated the cloudy haze of Rosina's mind. One hand left off from the vain effort to afford comfort to the wrenching at her womb, and came waveringly up to touch the face that hovered so close to her own.

'You came,' she whispered. 'Help me, Raith!'

'You may be sure I will.' He became aware again of her frozen limbs, and glanced swiftly about at the shock-ridden faces of the servants. 'Someone run to the village for the doctor! Prepare the bed—a hot brick! Something to drink. Anything to keep her warm. *Go!*'

They scattered as Raith stripped off his riding frock, and wrapped it about her.

'Come, Rosy. We must get you into the house.'

The pain had dulled again to an ache, and Rosina had drifted off into the half-swoon that had accompanied each bout of pain, and overtaken her efforts to find her way home.

'Rosina!'

The sharp tone jerked her back into consciousness. She glanced wildly round, and found his face again.

'Raith! Pray don't scold me.'

He drew her close again. 'No, sweetheart, no. Only tell me what has happened to you?'

Rosina groped for his hand, and it closed about hers. 'I scarce know. I came out—I know not why. F-flowers, Raith.'

'Flowers?' he echoed blankly, rendered stupid from fright. Then, with memory of the blood, the meaning of the slang term sank in.

'You mean the monthly flux?'

She clutched his hand. 'I was not expecting…it took me unawares.'

'It is that only?' he gasped out, the frantic tenor of his heart steadying a little. 'Thank God!'

'I could not—find my way. And there was…too much pain.' As she spoke of it, the griping agony took her again, and she cried out, her hand shifting out of his to press at her womb in a hopeless attempt at succour. 'Like this. I cannot move…'

'Hell and damnation!' Raith swore, and without more ado, set his arms under her, and lifted her from the ground.

She groaned as the change of position struck through her a flash of agony and, as of instinct, huddled into his chest, throwing her arms up and clinging with desperately clutching hands about his shoulders. She murmured his name, and he was brought near to weeping by the hint of a knowledge of deliverance that it contained.

'Raith…'

'I will have you safe in no time,' he promised her, and set off for the mansion as speedily as his burden would allow.

* * *

Rosina lay with eyes closed, but she was not asleep. The pain had dulled, due to a judicious dose of laudanum administered by Dr Barcliffe.

This worthy had arrived in haste, having been summoned from his little house in Ratley Grange village, somewhat flustered at being requested to attend Her Ladyship of Raith Manor. He was of too humble a station to be used to giving his services to any but the lesser gentry and the poorer folk hereabouts—most landowners in the area preferring to call upon his more affluent colleague in Kington.

Through the fogging effects of pain, Rosina had vaguely heard him speaking, in a nervous undertone, to Mrs Fawley, who had taken charge of her sickroom.

'I am unacquainted with His present Lordship, ma'am. I know him only by sight. Do you think he will wish to speak with me?'

'Undoubtedly,' had returned the housekeeper quietly. 'But for this present, I pray you be good enough to attend to Her Ladyship.'

'Of course, of course,' had come from the doctor hastily.

Next moment, Rosina had felt a cool hand on her brow, and had thrust her eyes open to find a bewigged and bespectacled face bent over her. It was of indeterminate years, but pleasant enough, if a trifle plump.

'It is not her head, doctor,' had protested Mrs Fawley impatiently.

In a daze, Rosina had heard the housekeeper explaining her predicament, and thought how grateful she had been this once for her new status. She had suffered from a girl, and had been caught out more than once—although never in thus compromising a situation. But not since Mama died had she had the luxury of giving herself over to the ministrations of others. Mrs Fawley and Joan had taken

care of her needs with sympathetic efficiency, and the
stained clothing, which she would have had to deal with
herself in the past, was mysteriously removed.

A hot brick wrapped in flannel had afforded considerable relief, and the application of two additional down
coverlets upon her bed—at, it transpired, Raith's orders—
had rapidly re-warmed her frozen blood.

She had been a trifle put out when Dr Barcliffe had
plagued her with a series of searching questions, which
she had answered with an increasing feeling of impatience.

How long had it been since her last experience? Why,
the usual length of time. Had she always this degree of
pain? Invariably. Was the blood loss any greater than
usual? She could not say. Had there been no warning?
No, none. Had there been any sickness before this? Not
sickness, no. Had she been moody at all? Yes, she must
say that she had.

And on, in much the same vein, until Rosina was ready
to scream. Then he had probed—with admitted gentleness—upon the swollen mound below her belly. Rosina
had endured this with difficulty, for the area was extraordinarily tender. Finally, she had been unable to help a flow
of tears at his intended words of comfort at the conclusion
of his examination.

'I cannot see any reason for Your Ladyship's immediate concern,' he said cheerfully. 'I think you will find that
these trials will end after you have successfully carried
His Lordship's child, and been brought to bed.'

He had coughed, apparently in embarrassment, as
Rosina began to weep. 'Pray do not upset yourself, Lady
Raith! I venture to prophesy that it will not be long before
these discomforts are a thing of the past.'

But the notion of bearing Raith's infant had pierced so
fiercely into the agony of mind that had been pushed aside

by the ills of her body, that Rosina had been unable to stop crying for some little time. He might have secured her safety—and used so tender a name for her that she wondered if it had been a product of her fevered imagination—but that did not mean that she was assured of a future that could include what must be done in order to get her with child.

'Dear, oh, dear!' had fussed the doctor over her head. And Rosina had heard him whisper to Mrs Fawley, 'I think perhaps I had better give Her Ladyship something to induce calm, as well as help the pain.'

Rosina had swallowed the laudanum without protest, and had been glad to find herself alone at length, but for Joan's faithful attendance even to this moment.

She knew, by the whispers exchanged between her maid and Mrs Fawley, that they thought her to have dropped asleep. It was more comfortable to be allowed to lie quiet, for the passing of the greater agonies in her womb had left her thoroughly exhausted. She was past thinking, and wished merely to lie here—forever, if need be. Only as long as she was not expected to take up again the complicated threads of her life.

A change in the quality of the atmosphere penetrated her consciousness. She became aware of added warmth at her cheek, and the near presence of a held-in charge of raw emotion. Her eyelids fluttered open—and she looked straight up into Raith's mutilated face.

She gasped, and found the grey eyes upon her. There was a strength of feeling in their depths that repelled her. She stared up at him, mute, and became aware that the back of his hand was laid against her face.

'I did not mean to wake you,' he said, and she heard effort in his voice.

'I was not asleep.'

He removed his hand, and Rosina discovered that he

was sitting on the edge of the bed. He looked away from her, and the source of the disquieting feel in the room traced down to his other hand, clenched on his knee.

'Oh, what is it?' Rosina asked involuntarily, an instant flittering at her heart.

'What should there be?'

Raith turned his head, and produced a smile. It looked mechanical, she thought. Then she remembered. He had been to see Forteviot. Her heart shrivelled, and she shrank into her pillows. She was not well enough to deal with this. Not at this moment.

'Pray leave me be now,' she uttered faintly.

He rose from the bed at once, and moved across to one of the wide windows. He ought to leave her be. It was shameful of him to be here at all—with these thoughts in his head. She was not fit for it.

But the distress of what had been suggested to him would not permit of his walking out of the bedchamber. His heart was so heavy, he wanted to lay his head upon her breast and weep out the hideous torments of doubt that had taken hold of his mind. But Rosina was ill with the cause of it, and he was no monster to lay his own burden upon her in this weakened state.

His continued presence in the room, however, began to prey upon Rosina's nerves. The dull ache of her womb flashed back into life, and she groaned without awareness.

Raith turned quickly. She had paled, biting her lip. Blood and thunder! 'Have you a resurgence of pain? Do you wish for more laudanum?'

She shook her head feebly, and brought one hand from under the covers to lay across her eyes. She did not want him to see how the intensity of his mood was affecting her. She could read him so well! Another jabbing pain made her gasp. Oh, it was too bad of him! She could not endure it.

'Raith—say what you have to and get it over,' she pleaded, a throb in her voice. 'Or else, go away entirely. You are radiating ill humour, and I am in no condition to deal with it.'

He came quickly across to the bed, and dropped down beside her, taking the hand from her eyes and holding it fast. 'Rosy, don't upset yourself! I don't want to say anything to you now. I will go, if you wish it. Only I am so riven! I can't bear to leave you—and yet I cannot...'

His voice died, as he saw the wetness on her cheeks. The fingers in his were trembling, and he held them to his lips and pressed a kiss upon them.

'Forteviot!' she got out. 'I knew he would do this.'

'No!' Raith said forcefully. 'He tried, but I would not believe him. I promise you, Rosy, I kept faith with you.'

'Then, *why*?' she cried desperately. 'What has occurred?'

'It was the doctor!' he burst out. And instantly regretted it. He gripped her fingers tighter. 'Hell and damnation, I did not mean to say that! The man is ignorant. He knows nothing of—' He checked himself.

Freeing her fingers, he leaped to his feet. 'Forgive me! I should never have begun this. I should not have come in here in this state.'

'It is too late now,' Rosina told him wearily. 'You had as well tell me. I will only lie here in a worse condition for wondering.'

Raith cursed again, and flung over to the window where the dull day had begun to darken. Without turning round, he let it out. Flat, and leaden.

'Dr Barcliffe told me that he believes you may have been pregnant—and have this day miscarried.'

For a long moment, he waited. No sound came from behind him. Not a sob, not a breath, not a word. At length,

unable any longer to endure her lack of response, Raith
turned to look at her.

Rosina had not moved. She was lying very still, and
she was watching him. He went with heavy tread to within
a few feet of the bed. The coal-black eyes met his. Never
had Raith seen so bleak an expression in them. A pulse
started up in his veins, and a horrible sensation of dread
enveloped him.

'Rosina?'

She did not answer. Only continued to look at him in
the same dead fashion. Panic overcame him.

'Deny it!' he begged. 'Are you not going to deny it?'

For a moment longer, Rosina continued to stare at him.
Then she drew the faintest of breaths, and turned her eyes
upon the tester above. Her voice was devoid of expression.

'I may be abed for a day or two. I shall be obliged if
you will not enter this room again.'

Raith drove his phaeton and pair with a slack rein, so
that the vehicle made but dilatory progress along the
eight-mile trip to Banbury. He was not keen to arrive at
journey's end.

Ottery had arrived back on Saturday, and sent to him
immediately. But Rosina had been still abed—or had kept
to her room, at least—and Raith had cherished hope.
Ottery had written again on Tuesday, yet it was Thursday
before Raith reluctantly forced himself to make the journey. Whatever the outcome of his lawyer's enquiries with
Herbert Cambois, it would make little difference. He had
offended beyond forgiveness. What mattered it whether
his wife's story received corroboration?

Had his informant been any other than a medical man,
he would never have given credence to the supposition.

The doctor had been apologetic, and diffident to a marked degree.

'My lord, I am most uncomfortable with Her Ladyship's condition.'

'How so?' Raith had demanded, in quick alarm.

'Oh, there is nothing to concern you, sir. She will be well again readily enough.'

Apprehension had made him impatient. 'Then what in thunder do you mean?'

The doctor had coughed, and brought out that damning theory. 'I fear, sir, that Her Ladyship has been so unfortunate as to lose a child.' He had evidently read Raith's reaction in his face, for his own had become suffused with colour. 'It is often so, with the first attempt, my lord. I believe you have been only a short time married.' He had coughed again. 'You need not fear, my lord, that I gave Her Ladyship any intimation of my findings. However, I sense that perhaps she guessed it for herself. She was uncommonly distressed by my attempt to convey a trifle of comfort.'

'What are you talking about?' Raith had asked, confused. The impact of the hideous news had made him stupid.

'I am afraid Her Ladyship wept bitterly, my lord, when I ventured to suggest that her troubles would end with a pregnancy brought to term.'

Raith had stared at the man, unable to comprehend anything more than the bare fact. But Rosina had been in tears! She was in pain. She was overwrought—that must be all. Was he supposed to think that it lent colour to this notion? It could not be true!

'Are you certain of this?' he rapped out.

Dr Barcliffe had shrugged eloquently. 'As certain as one can be, without an examination of the matter expelled.' He had seemed to feel that this answer was un-

welcome, for he had added with a haste that only served
to heighten the likelihood of his earlier assertions, 'But I
may be entirely wrong, my lord. Some females do experience quite shocking disorder upon these occasions.'

He had said enough. Raith had been once again upon
the rack. Almost he had been ready to demand of his
servants the evidence that might already have been removed from her garments, for all he knew. Or lost in the
woodlands. It had been torture to be flung back into that
acute distress of mind of which he had only that morning
been relieved.

The timing of it had been ill, and that was the end of
it. Coming so pat, immediately after the contradictions of
Forteviot's version of events against Rosina's, he had
fallen all too easily into the fatal trap of jealousy.

Truth to tell, Raith no longer knew whether he cared if
his doubts had any foundation. This last week had been
the most melancholy of his life. Rosina had withheld herself utterly. He had perforce obeyed her behest to remain
aloof from her bedchamber, but the days since had been
yet worse.

He could not blame her. The fault, he knew, was his
own—had been so from start to finish. He had made no
attempt to effect a reconciliation, for her withdrawal had
been chilling. He had driven her beyond any hope of pardon.

There was still the matter of Forteviot and this fellow
Cambois to be settled. He had heard nothing from the
former. It surprised him to think that the man had been
sufficiently intimidated by his threats. It might be that he
was biding his time. Or perhaps he had another scheme
afoot. Raith cared little. Nothing seemed to matter beside
the appalling loss of Rosina's esteem and regard.

When she had finally emerged from her room, her wan
looks and haggard eyes, blue-shadowed with strain, had

given fresh impetus to the overriding sensations of guilt and remorse. If, on the instant that he saw her when she entered the saloon before the dinner hour, he could have wiped out the whole of his conduct throughout the short period of their marriage, he would have done it without hesitation.

More poignantly, she was clad in the grey gown she had worn for their wedding. He did not think she had worn it to taunt him. But the message of its resumption—for she had latterly been dressed only in the new-purchased gowns—was clear enough. She wanted no part of her life as Lady Raith. She was once again Rosina Charlton—and beyond his reach.

Through dinner, she had spoken only as necessary, and she had eaten little. Only once had Raith ventured to suggest that even if her appetite was lacking, she ought to try at least to swallow something for the sake of her health. She had turned the black eyes upon him, frowning in that way of narrowing her eyes, as if she had the headache.

'I am not hungry. And my health is my own concern.'

Raith had said not a word more. The consciousness of Ottery's letter in his pocket had irked him. Yet he had delayed his response, beset by a vague hope that Rosina might soften. Ottery had purposely invited him to come to Banbury, so that Raith might hear the tidings he had to tell outside his own home. The implication of this was clear enough. On Wednesday night, Raith felt impelled to inform his wife of his purpose. He hardly knew why, unless it was with a half-formed wish of threshing the matter out.

'I am going into Banbury tomorrow,' he had begun, once they were seated at dinner. He had got no further.

'Your movements have nothing to do with me, my lord,' Rosina had said flatly.

For one seething instant, Raith's hot temper had flared. But he had controlled it, and once again closed his lips upon any further utterance. It was not merely disheartening. It was damning. Rosina had turned into a model of the wife of convenience that he had originally negotiated.

He was entering the outskirts of Banbury, and was obliged to give his attention to his cattle. It did not take him many minutes to make his way to Ottery's offices. He divested himself of his outer garments, and was ushered immediately into his lawyer's inner sanctum. A hearty handshake greeted him, together with his friend's penetrating gaze.

'You look deathly, my lord!' Ottery said frankly.

'I feel it.'

'What in the world has been happening?'

'Don't even ask!' Raith passed a hand through his hair, worn untied and ragged, and sighed. 'I will tell you presently, Ottery—that you may know why I come so late.'

His lawyer eyed him with no little concern, as Raith flung himself into a chair at the small desk, and sank his head into his hands. Ottery closed the little wooden doors to the shelf opening on the wall which gave access to the judas painting within the other room, and crossed to a small table in the window embrasure, on which was placed a tray with a decanter and glasses.

'May I offer you wine, my lord? It is good claret.'

Raith dragged himself up. 'I thank you, no. I must keep a clear head.' He saw the troubled frown in the other's eyes, and attempted a smile. 'You found Cambois?'

'Indeed I did, my lord.' Ottery's features registered distaste. 'An ill specimen, I fear. I did not take to him.'

'That does not altogether surprise me.' Raith set his jaw. 'I am a little better acquainted now with the type of man he is. But let me hear your findings first.'

The lawyer had laid down the decanter, without pouring, and came across to take his own seat opposite. 'Mr Cambois was inebriated for much of the time, which is why it took so long to extract information from him. What I gleaned, I fear, is unlikely to be either to your taste, or your satisfaction.'

Despite all, Raith could not prevent a quickening of interest. And a resurgence of revulsion. He must not forget that this monstrous individual had been guilty of attempting to violate a young girl given expressly into his care. That much even Forteviot's testimony had agreed.

'Go on, Ottery.'

'I will be brief, sir. From what I could understand, Herbert Cambois sought to recoup his losses at the table by a sale of Miss Charlton's person to Lord Forteviot. He further stated that he had discovered Miss Charlton to be…' he hesitated, and Raith held his breath '…I shall say, unvirtuous.' Ottery's voice was entirely without intonation, flat and unemotional, as if he were reading an indictment in court. 'As a result, so he believed, of an illicit association with one of the male servants. The contract was broken, and he turned Miss Charlton out of doors.'

Raith's jaw was set. He could barely get the question out. 'Was she alleged to have been with child?'

Ottery's quick frown of puzzlement threw him into disorder, and he looked away.

'What makes you ask that, my dear sir?'

He clenched his fist. 'Answer, I pray you!'

'It was not even hinted at, my lord. Why—'

Raith threw out a hand. 'A moment!'

He felt choked by his own inward shaking, torn by a measure of relief and fears not wholly allayed. Cambois might not have known that part. He had expected the rest, but that made the hearing no less painful. He had thought that the tearing disquiet was buried under the loss of

Rosina's regard. He had been mistaken. Tortured by uncertainty, it was equally unendurable—to live with her, or without. Which was the more plausible: that Forteviot and Cambois were in a string, and Dr Barcliffe mistaken—or that Rosina had lied to him?

'My lord!'

He became aware that Ottery was calling him. The lawyer was holding out a ruby-filled glass.

'Drink this!'

Raith took it dumbly, and tossed off the wine. As he laid down the glass, his head began to clear. He glanced up.

'Ottery, you must release me from this marriage!'

His lawyer stared at him. 'Have you run mad, Lord Raith?'

Raith buried his head in his hands. 'I have not. But I shall undoubtedly do so if I do not extricate myself from this abominable farce.'

But Ottery was not of a mind to accommodate him. 'My lord, I do most earnestly beg of you to consider well what you are saying!'

Raith leaped from the chair, and paced up and down the restricted space to one side of the desk, reminding his lawyer of a caged animal. 'You do not know the circumstances.'

He gave Ottery a curt account of Rosina's given story, and of his dealings with Forteviot, ending with a brief summary of the diagnosis of Dr Barcliffe.

'I cannot rid myself of the suspicion that she sought the marriage because she saw a means whereby she might hide her condition.'

'And pass off this fictitious infant upon you? Fie, my lord!'

Raith eyed him wearily. 'It is possible, Ottery.'

'And you profess to love her? Think shame to yourself!' uttered the lawyer angrily, rising from his seat. 'Even I would take an oath to know Her Ladyship better than that.'

'Love, Ottery, has a way—for it matters so desperately!—of increasing suspicion and doubt.'

'Then rely on my judgement, my lord, for I have no doubts. If I must place Lady Raith's word against the evidence of two persons whose stories agree in every particular, I prefer to believe in your wife. You look at me with amazement, but think, my lord. Two witnesses—two different pairs of eyes—there must always be variance.'

Raith shook his head painfully. 'I don't understand you.'

'It smacks of collusion, sir.'

'And what of the doctor's evidence?'

'He said himself that he could be wrong,' Ottery pointed out. 'I had far rather trust Lady Raith.'

Raith heaved a sigh, in which desolation sounded. 'So had I, Ottery. Which is exactly why I am unable to do so. I would never be free of the notion that I had deceived myself.'

The lawyer was eyeing him with a trifle of suspicion. 'My lord, I hesitate to say this, but I do not believe this is all your reason.'

'How well you know me.' Despair engulfed Raith, and he sank back against the table. 'She will not even speak to me! What is the use of continuing? She wants to be released as much as I, for she cannot endure the sight of me.'

Ottery laid a hand upon his shoulder, saying in a more moderate tone, 'My lord, you are making assumptions based upon nothing more than your observation of her distress.'

This reminder only served to make Raith writhe the more. 'If you had only seen her! I can never forgive myself—why should she? There is no point in discussing the matter. We must separate!'

'You say so only because you think there is no hope, sir.' His lawyer looked upset. 'You are making a grave error, I am convinced of it.'

Raith shook his head. 'There is more of my brother in me than I knew. Just as his obsession of jealousy ruined my life, so will mine affect Rosina's. I am not fit to be the keeper of so delicate a soul.'

Ottery sighed. 'You do yourself an injustice, my lord. I venture to think that Lady Raith might take a different view.'

'You are mistaken,' Raith said dully.

'Besides which,' pursued the lawyer, ignoring the interjection, 'there is a deal of difficulty about the whole matter. If you were looking to divorce, you must know how problematic is that path. And if you intend only to separate, you will be tied.' He waved a dismissive hand. 'But this is nothing to the purpose.' Abruptly, he seized Raith by the shoulders. 'I cannot approve this course, my lord! Do not, I counsel you, put yourself out of the way of a future which may well prove your salvation.'

Raith took the hands from his shoulders, holding them hard. 'You are a true and loyal friend, Ottery. If I could take your advice, I would do so.'

'But—?' queried the other.

Raith let him go, and smiled, unaware how his features twisted, nor of the husky quality in his voice. 'But Rosina does not want me. I do not blame her for that, but it is beyond my endurance. I had rather live without her.'

Chapter Ten

Rosina stood quiescent while Joan unlaced the bodice of her chintz gown, and dipped her arms back for its removal. As if she had been used all her life to being waited upon, she shifted her limbs as required, almost without thought.

Thought was too painful a luxury. Better this deadness of mind wherein no stray memory was permitted to stir the fringes of that well of sensation that hungered deep within her heart. She had schooled herself to suppress every vestige of feeling. Or she had tried to. Particularly in his presence, when each nuance of expression was a livelier goad than any amount of concentrated imagery.

Memory was an intrusive thing. A dangerous indulgence. But it could be controlled. Reality—in which Raith's charged passion smouldered, reaching out to her despite the shelled protection of her heart—was more potentially explosive. Rosina could only be thankful that her spouse had avoided her as assiduously as she avoided him.

She lifted her arms so that Joan could slip her nightgown over her head, wondering why she was still here, being dressed for her bed. She had expected every day that Mr Ottery would have come to instruct her to pack her belongings in preparation for her journey to Withibrooke. It was not possible that her guardian had not supplied fuel to add to the flame of unappeasable envy that had poisoned her husband's mind against her. Rosina knew her case to be hopeless, and had spent these several days in a mood of dull acceptance of the inevitable.

'Will Your Ladyship sit for me to brush your hair?'

Rosina sat. The feel of the bristles stroking over her head was soothing. She closed her eyes. It was almost like being once again a little girl, with the caress of the brush in Mama's gentle hand, and the crooning voice lulling her closer to sleep. It was how Gatty had comforted her, too, the night she had finally arrived at the cottage—and collapsed into a sobbing heap. Her chest hollowed out. How would Gatty manage this time? There was no comfort that could soothe the void which was opening up before her.

Abruptly, she leaned forward, dropping her face into her hands, catching at her breath as the agonizing sobs fought to be free of her iron restraint.

Two hands grasped at her shoulders. 'M'lady? Oh, m'lady, I do wish as how something might be done for you.'

Rosina pulled upright, thrusting down on the betraying emotion. 'I am quite all right, Joan.'

The maid laid down the brush, and bobbed a curtsy. 'Begging your pardon, m'lady, but I know as you're not. Nor His Lordship ain't neither!'

'Joan, you forget yourself!'

'I know, m'lady, but I'm your personal maid, and if I don't say something, no one won't,' uttered the maid with determination.

Rosina eyed her in the mirror. She should have known that the servants were well informed. Why should they not be, especially with this skeleton staff? But the last thing she wanted was to discuss the intricacies of her marriage with her maid. She had, it appeared, little choice.

'I wouldn't have said nothing, only Mr Kirkham is that troubled over His Lordship, and—'

'Why is Kirkham troubled?' interrupted Rosina, an instant tattoo starting up in her pulse.

Lord knows she was aware of the turmoil of Raith's mind! She had been relieved by his absence from dinner tonight. She had kept her room more than four days, even to the near finish of her troublous monthly time, but she could hardly stay cooped up there. On emergence, the unavoidable encounters at dinner had stretched her nerves to the utmost. She had studiously evaded either Raith's gaze or his conversation. She could not trust herself to look at him, and had to steel herself to withstand the moody emanations of his volatile temperament.

'Mr Kirkham says His Lordship has spent half the night in his library these few days,' disclosed the maid, adding significantly, 'with the brandy decanter. Mr Kirkham is afraid he will drink himself to death, like our late lord!'

Dread rose up in Rosina's breast. 'His Lordship's brother?' But, no—Raith had hated his brother. He would not follow his example.'

'Yes, m'lady,' said Joan, adding darkly, 'and His Lordship come home from Mr Ottery's not a half hour since, looking like a death's head on a mopstick, so Mr Paulersbury says.'

A jolt smote Rosina's chest, and she put up a hand to her mouth. She stared at the maid's apple-cheeked features without seeing her. Ottery was then back! What had her guardian said? What had Raith been told? Despite all her resolution to accept the fate she had assumed to be coming, the prospect of its imminence threw her into instant apprehension. An irregular flutter started up in her pulse, and her mouth went dry.

'M'lady?'

She blinked, and realised that Joan was staring at her. Rosina pulled herself together, and rose from the dressing stool. 'That will be all, I thank you.'

The maid followed her into her bedchamber, and placed a candle by the bed. She waited while Rosina climbed between sheets, and tucked her in.

'Good night, m'lady.' She hesitated, and then dropped a curtsy. 'Mayhap His Lordship is safe in his bed, m'lady. He rung for Mr Paulersbury not a moment before you rung for me.'

This intelligence did nothing to ease the ferment of Rosina's mind. The knowledge that at night Raith was but four doors away had been a species of torture to her. She had lain in her bed, desperately trying not to indulge an idiotic wish that he might come to her. How should he do so—even did he wish to!—when she had withdrawn herself so sternly?

But that he had today seen Ottery, and come home looking—what had Joan said? An expression that gave her a hideous image! It could only mean the worst. This must be the finish. Tomorrow, he would summon her to the saloon, and inform her that their marriage was to be dissolved.

Such an intense shaft of distress shot through her at this thought that she was for several moments incapable of getting her breath. When she did, she blew out the candle, and thrust herself down into the covers, burrowing so that the sound of her bursting sobs might not penetrate through the intervening walls to the ears of the man for whom she grieved.

There was no question of sleep. When her tears abated, she lay in the darkness, listening, against all reason, for the impossible sound of a footstep. She tossed and turned, fighting a growing pressure that urged her to get up and go to him—to know for certain what he intended.

Why question it? She knew what must happen. There could be but one outcome. She had heard nothing from Forteviot, but that did not mean that the evil wretch had not contacted Raith. Now she knew that Ottery was come with information from Herbert Cambois, she could hope for no succour. Had there been a favourable outcome, would Raith not have come to her instantly? He was gently disposed towards her, and would not have kept her unnecessarily in suspense.

At length, Rosina could endure it no longer. She sat up in bed, and groped in the darkness for the tinderbox that was kept on her table. When she tried to strike the flint for a light, she discovered that her hands were shaking. It took some time, but at last she managed to relight her candle.

She got up and shrugged on her wrapper, and in short order had reached the antechamber, where her nerves stayed her from knocking upon Raith's dressing-room door.

For a moment or two, she toyed with the idea of going back to bed. But she would not sleep. And the longer she lay awake, the more her anxiety would grow. It was better to beard Raith now—and find out the worst. After all, if he meant to set her aside, she had a right to know of it.

Screwing up her courage, she returned to the door, and listened for a moment. Suppose he was asleep? She drew a determined breath. If he was, then she must wake him. With the thought, she lifted her hand and rapped smartly on the door. No sound came from within. Rosina bit her lip, and grasped the handle.

It was the first time she had been inside Raith's dressing-room. It resembled her own, and she could see little in the dim light from her candle, but for an apparent overflow of garments. Rosina hurried through to the bedchamber door, and once again halted to listen. She could hear nothing. If he was there, he was certainly asleep.

She did not knock this time, but stealthily opened the door. The curtains were not drawn, and the bed was empty. Rosina swept her candle about, but no movement disturbed the shadows. Rosina did not know whether she was relieved or disappointed. Slowly she advanced towards the door that led to the corridor, recalling what Joan had told her. A frisson went through her at the remembrance of Kirkham's expressed fears.

Moving with a swiftness born of other than her wish to find out her fate, Rosina trod softly down the stairs, and across the hall to a door leading to the rear of the mansion. She had been shown the library but once, by Mrs Fawley, but she remembered the way.

As she approached the door, Rosina could see a glimmer of light beneath it, and knew that her husband was in there. Her heart skittered madly, as the thought of her mission came back to her mind. She hesitated outside the door, fighting an impulse to withdraw again. But it would not do. She gathered her courage, and seized the brass handle.

She did not immediately see him, and for an instant was conscious of disappointment. But a pool of light caught the centre of the room, and Rosina followed it. She saw his arm, hanging slackly over the side of a chair, his fingers just above an overturned glass which must have fallen from his hand.

Rosina came around the chair, and her heart melted. Raith sat slumped, tousled hair ragged about his shoulders, his bed gown open and awry over a long nightshirt. He was asleep, or nearly so, breathing in that stertorous way that Rosina instantly recognised. Her spouse was drunk!

Rosina sought for the bottle. She had seen this often enough at Nun Eaton, and could judge of the level of Raith's inebriation. She found a wine bottle tucked on the floor by one leg of the chair. It was a quarter full. Rosina sniffed the contents. Not brandy, thank the Lord! Then he was probably not more than semi-drunk. She would likely be able to get him to bed.

Any thought of discovering his intentions had gone out of her head. All was forgotten but for his present plight. Her maid's words came back to her. If this was how he had been spending each night—! Small wonder Kirkham was worried.

She placed her candlestick alongside his own on the mantel, and leaned down, taking hold of his shoulder, and shaking him. 'Raith! Raith, wake up!'

She was obliged to call him several more times before any response was forthcoming. But at length he stirred, opening bleary eyes and gazing up at her in apparent recognition.

'Rosy? What are you…?'

He blinked, and Rosina shook him again. 'Raith, you must get up! Come, I will help you to bed.'

The wickedest gleam came into his eyes, and he grinned up at her. 'That, wife, is decidedly inviting.'

A tinge of colour crept into Rosina's cheek. His speech was only slightly slurred, but she was quite aware that it was the wine speaking. He would not otherwise have greeted her in this fashion. Doubtless he thought her a figment of his overheated imagination!

'Come, Raith,' she said again, and pulled at his arm.

'Give me a moment—I will certainly come.'

He sat up with an air of determination, but it was only with Rosina's help that he was able to get to his feet. She snuffed his candle, and then slipped her shoulder under his.

'Lean on me.'

'Too close for comfort,' he muttered. Before she knew what he would be at, he had turned her head to him and planted a quick kiss on her lips.

Rosina's balance gave slightly, and they both staggered. Raith was laughing, and she was obliged to speak sharply to pull him into awareness.

'For the Lord's sake, take care!'

'Don't s-s-scold, wife,' he uttered in an injured tone. 'I am doing my best.'

'No, you are not, Raith. Stand still a moment.'

He obediently halted, swaying a trifle. Rosina shifted her position so that she took a little more of his weight, and then reached to the mantel for her candle.

'A very juggling act, Rosy,' he commented, amused.

'Do you think you can remain on your feet?' she asked anxiously, feeling him sway again.

Raith chuckled. His potations had rendered him pleasantly foxed, but he was not incapacitated. 'I won't fall down.'

'Are you sure? Shall I wake Paulersbury?'

He brought his free hand to the small one that was clutching at his waist, and covered it. 'I had much rather have you. Paulersbury is not nearly s-s-so pretty.'

Rosina was betrayed into a giggle. 'Raith, will you have done?'

'I am yours to command,' he said. 'Lead on.'

It was with difficulty that the two of them negotiated the passage, and at the stairs, Rosina had to withdraw her support.

'I cannot manage with the candle as well. Take the banisters, Raith.'

He grasped them, and she slipped out from under his shoulder. She urged him onward, but Raith did not speak as he dragged himself up the stairs. He was beginning to

sober, and the delight of this adventure was slipping away
from him. He was not yet capable of working out why
Rosina had come to find him. Nor why she should be thus
amicable. A hazy idea of the depression of spirit that had
driven him to seek solace in wine floated at the back of
his mind, but its portent escaped him. He knew only that
Rosina's presence was heart-warming. He did not wish to
lose that.

Rosina kept close behind him as he climbed the stairs,
afraid that he might lose balance and fall. The moment he
reached the top, she slipped quickly back into her previous
position. She felt his arm come about her, and divined a
change. It was rather Raith holding her to him, than she
providing support.

Her heart fluttered, and her breath shortened a thread.
She could no longer speak, and they entered his bedchamber in silence. Raith dropped to the bed, staring up at her.
Rosina avoided his gaze, and laying the candle down,
pulled the covers open. Then she came back to him, and
her hands reached to push the bed gown over his shoulders.

Raith's fingers came up and caught at hers. Rosina
stilled, and her gaze returned to his face, and met the grey
eyes full. Her heart missed a beat.

'Stay with me, Rosy!'

Her fingers quivered, and her eyes filled. 'In your bed?'

Raith nodded. 'I am a trifle foxed.'

A smile glimmered on her lips. 'I see that.'

'But I know what I want.' He released her hands, and
slipped his arms about her, pulling her to him. 'Stay—
this once. Let the devil take tomorrow. I need you tonight.' He laid his scarred cheek against her bosom.

Rosina's heart was in tatters. She could no more have
resisted him than she could have flown to the moon.
Without a thought, she took hold of his face with both

hands, and shifted in his grasp. Raith's head came up, and the next instant he was drawing her down. Their lips met.

It was a blissful dance. His mouth gentled hers, a probing caress that sent heat flittering down her veins. It lasted but a moment, and she felt his indrawn breath. Then her mouth was seized, and she was falling.

Raith brought her to the bed, and rolled so that she lay upon the opened covers. His lips pressured for entry at her mouth, and his hand ran strongly down her waist and hips.

Rosina moaned as the warmth spread through her body. Her lips parted at his insistence, and the velvet touch within threw her into uncontrollable reflex. Her hands clutched about his back, and her mouth answered the demands of his with frenzied need.

He groaned aloud as his lips left hers. 'Oh, Rosy, how I have yearned for this!'

'I, also,' she gasped, and heard his indrawn breath of desire just as his lips closed once more with hers.

His hand slid over her breast, causing a tingling at her loins, and her limbs, seeming as if they had a will of their own, began to twine with his. The kisses intensified, and for several moments, Rosina was lost in the deep well of Raith's passion. But presently, a tugging at her nightgown stirred vaguely at the tortured memory, and she stiffened a touch.

Raith felt it. He came away from her mouth, his breath hoarse, and looked down into the black of her eyes. No! This was not how he had meant to take her. Releasing her, he struggled to his knees, and drew her up also. His fingers caressed her face.

'You are afraid.'

'Yes,' she said, and caught at his hand. 'But I am more afraid of losing you tonight...'

In the glow of the candle, he saw the waif who had

captured his heart, and drew her fingers to his lips. 'Rosy, if you come into my bed, we will both be lost.'

Her breath caught on a sob. 'Then lose me in a memory that I may cherish.'

Raith's heart contracted. He pulled her to him, kissing her with tenderness. Her wrapper slid from her shoulders, and he drew off her nightgown. The candlelight played upon the contours of her slim form, and Raith tugged at his breath.

'You are adorable.'

Rosina blushed. She was acutely self-conscious, and she trembled, not with fear, but with a rise of anticipation that quickened in her veins as she watched Raith remove his own garments and toss them aside. The sight of his unclothed state both shocked and thrilled her. But she saw him only momentarily, for Raith brought her quickly under the covers, and slid down into the bed, bringing her nakedness to rest against his own.

The touch of his skin was warm and dry, but the rough hardness of his limbs made her gasp. Heat engulfed her as his hands pressed her to him, playing over the softness of her buttocks and thighs. She opened her eyes to find his face close to hers upon the pillow. He was lying on his right side, and the ridged cut was hidden from her. But as he raised his head to kiss her, she saw it full and a wave of compassion made her close her body tightly into his—and cling.

Raith groaned, and the demand of his lips increased. Rosina answered him strongly. His hands caressed her limbs, and his fingers rode her inner thigh, seeking her hollows. Rosina gasped, clutching at the tough skin, unknowing where her hands travelled, conscious only of the swelling intensity of her need and the demanding pressure of his mouth on hers.

She was ablaze, breathless as the fever tingled in her

veins. She knew that Raith spoke, but heard him only as a distant murmur, unaware of the meaning of his words.

'Sweetheart, love me! I need you to love me. Give me that at least.'

Even had she understood him, she could answer him only with little moans that escaped her lips. The power of the tempest he was arousing was making her delirious. She gave him her lips, freely, with intent, a vague wisp afloat at the back of her consciousness that this would give him what he wanted.

Raith took the offering, and the wine of her sweetness drove him to mastery—despite that she had not offered him her heart. He covered her, and readied her limbs. Her eyes opened, and he leaned quickly down to kiss her, a resurgence in him of an apprehension of her fears. Then he entered her.

The shock of the invasion made Rosina cry out. It was a small sound, but at once she felt Raith's lips on hers, gentling and murmuring endearments.

'Softly, sweetheart—my lovely rose—hush now.'

He pursued it, and Rosina whimpered. He encountered resistance, but it was not of her making. His heart soared, and he held back, his lips caressing her cheeks, her eyes, her throat. Then he found her mouth and gave a whispered warning against her lips.

'Courage, my sweet, for I may hurt you now.'

He thrust. Rosina uttered a little cry, gripping involuntarily with her thighs, as her fingers clutched at his shoulders. But the piercing was gently made, and his kisses gave her courage to endure it.

Then he lay still for a space and presently the warmth returned, overtaking the ache. It was stronger than before, and her hands slid from his shoulders to caress his back, as her breath hissed. He moved but slightly, and Rosina gasped as the fire intensified. A throbbing at her loins drove her to seek his lips of her own accord, demanding in her turn.

Ardently then, Raith took her, giving her kiss for kiss, until the urgent frenzy of his own need threw him momentarily out of control. Rosina felt the increase of his passion with a soaring flight of ferment, and all thought was gone as she gave herself wholly to his will. There was some sort of explosion in her head, and then she heard only the heave of her husband's breath, and became aware of the spent weight of his body.

Presently he rolled, pulling her with him, but holding her strongly so that they remained entwined.

'*My wife,*' he murmured, in a tone of intense satisfaction, and kissed her.

Rosina hugged as much of him as she could, and wished for this moment never to end.

'Oh, Anton,' she whispered involuntarily.

'Rosy, my sweet,' he breathed, holding her closer.

A few moments later, his clasp about her slackened, and the more even tenor of his breath told her that he slept.

Rosina awoke to find herself tucked into her spouse's body, which followed behind her the contours of her own. One arm was thrown across her and his hand lay slackly over hers, in the place where he had held it as he fell asleep. She recalled that they had woken in the night, and Raith had taken her again, with yet greater passion.

There had been less pain, and she recognised that the ministrations of his hands and lips had been designed to prepare her for his mastery, for she had been awash with desire before ever he covered her body with his own.

Afterwards, he had cuddled her close, and Rosina remembered turning in his arms, half-asleep. She had felt him pull her to him, his lips soft on her shoulder and neck, and his fingers had imprisoned her hand.

Rosina was almost sure that he had said, at a murmured whisper of the night, that he loved her. She did not know whether she had emptied to him the strength of her own feelings. If she had not, it could only be because she could not speak under the violence of passion he had aroused in her to match his own. How ardent had been his love-making. If it could but remain so!

She slid carefully from him, and out of the bed, hunting about for her discarded garments. The grey light filtering through the closed drapes at the window showed her the scattered clothing—Raith's and hers—which had fallen to the floor. She found her nightgown, which was cold to the touch, and put it on. She shivered a little as she shrugged into the wrapper, for it was early and no fires had yet been lit.

But she did not wish to be discovered here—especially by Raith himself. He had been drunk last night. Rosina knew how drink had a way of wreathing men's brains with a sort of madness, so that they became no longer masters of their actions. She could not bear it if, upon waking and finding that he had broken his own resolve, Raith's volatile temper would flare. In one of his moods, he was capable of saying the most wounding things. After last night's tender mouthings, it would be altogether agonizing.

She returned to the bed, and watched him sleeping for a moment. Raith's ruined cheek was exposed, his hair falling away from his face. Stealthily, Rosina drew near and reached out. But she dared not touch it, for fear of waking him. Her fingers hovered over it as she traced the line, as if she might imprint the shape of it in her mind's eye, that it would stay with her in memory. It was so much a part of him—of Anton, whom she loved—that she found it endearing. It was odd to think of him as Anton, but it had been easy to call him by his name last night.

'I love you, Anton,' she whispered. And then quickly and quietly crept away to her own apartments.

In her bedchamber, she found the fire already burning. Perhaps it was not so early, after all. A dreadful thought struck her. Had the kitchen wench, whose duty it was to light the fires, come in and found them together in Raith's bed? Fearing to wake them, she must have sneaked away. Lord, the news of their coupling would be all over the house!

On a sudden thought, she went into her dressing-room and felt the jug that stood in the basin. It was warm. Oh, she was undone indeed! Joan had already been into her room and found her missing.

For a moment, Rosina was embarrassed. Then it struck her that she need not go back to bed and dissemble. She returned to her bedchamber and tugged at the bell-pull.

Her maid's demeanour was perfectly respectful. But Rosina caught a knowing glance or two cast her way when Joan thought she was not looking. Yet the maid brought tidings that effectively drove away her consciousness, instead filling her with dismay.

'Begging Your Ladyship's pardon, but there's a gentleman downstairs. Mr Kirkham would have denied him, but he swears as he'll not go until he sees either yourself or His Lordship.'

The pearl of Rosina's happiness shredded away. She had never a hope that it could last. But could she not have been permitted to treasure it for just a little longer? Was it her guardian, come to plague her? Dear Lord, but was there to be no end?

'Who is it, Joan? Did he give his name?'

The maid was apologetic. 'It's Lord Forteviot, m'lady.'

The entirety of her heart's triumph of the night van-

ished at a stroke. The dead weight of inevitability struck
at her once more. Had she dared to imagine that the fact
of Raith having claimed her could change her ill fortune?
She ought to be accustomed to the cruel blows of fate.

'Help me to dress.'

A desperate calm descended upon her as she performed
her ablutions, and allowed Joan to clothe her. She chose
the old gown of blue kerseymere, perhaps with an unconscious wish of appearing before Forteviot in as unattrac-
tive a guise as she could find. She placed one of her close
caps on her head, and then left the bedchamber, unable to
overcome a slight quaking at her breast.

She gripped the banisters hard as she came downstairs,
recalling last night's perilous journey with her husband,
in the opposite direction. But she must not think of Raith!
That were to destroy her composure—and she had need
of it.

Entering the saloon, Rosina stood in the doorway for a
moment, surveying Lord Forteviot. He was standing by
the window, and he looked round at her approach. He was
dressed with his usual flamboyance, sporting a striped
waistcoat under a blue cloth coat and black breeches. He
bowed with a mocking flourish, all his habitual urbanity
in his voice.

'My dear Lady Raith, how do you do?'

Rosina shut the door, and moved into the room. She
wasted no time in pleasantries. 'What do you want?'

He leaned back a little, surveying her. 'You look pale,
my dear Rosina. Have you been unwell?'

She eyed him with resentment. 'I do not wish to discuss
my health with you, sir. Why are you here?'

Forteviot spread his hands. 'But why do you suppose?
I had hoped to see Raith, but I dare say you will do.'

Rosina's pulses stirred, and she walked across to the
fireplace and gripped the mantel. She must not let him

succeed in what she knew to be a deliberate intent to unsettle her. She turned to look at him again.

'Pray, what is it you want, sir?'

The sneer became pronounced. 'My poor innocent, did you imagine, because you have heard nothing from me for a week and more, that I had abandoned my purpose? I regret that I must disappoint you. I have been revisiting the scene of our first meetings, Rosina.'

A shiver shook her. 'You mean that you have been to see Herbert Cambois?'

He nodded. 'It was necessary. The man is unreliable, to say the least. Do you know, the fool had done almost nothing to find you? I rather regretted having left the matter in his hands when I saw the announcement of your marriage.'

Had she not known that it would be her undoing? But a creeping sensation of dismay began to invade her as she recognised the implication of his words. Had he spoken with her guardian before he came here?

'At first I thought he had played me false, perhaps received a higher price for you from Raith—unlikely as that seems, I admit,' he continued. 'Happily, as we discovered, it was but a fortuitous accident.'

'Fortuitous?' She bit her lip, a riot of conjecture in her head. 'How so? How do you know anything of it?'

He smiled in that smug fashion. 'The trail was most interesting. One of the housemaids was able to point the way.'

'Aggie! You fiend, what did you do to her?'

Forteviot laughed. 'Nothing very much. Threats were sufficient, I assure you. The rest was easy. I had primed my good friend before I left. Armed with new knowledge, I came straight on here.'

The whole hideous plot unravelled as if Rosina read it

in a book. They had planned this! Forteviot and her guardian together.

'You will appreciate how important it was that Cambois held to the facts I had outlined—hence the need to visit him. But my anxiety was relieved. He has not failed of his part.'

'You relieve my mind,' Rosina said.

'Oh, bravo, Rosina!' uttered her tormentor. 'Your sarcasm is almost worthy of my own. But I fear it is an empty triumph. You will no doubt know that Cambois has sustained a visit from your husband's lawyer.'

Rosina had known it, and guessed that Ottery had given her spouse an unfavourable account. What else from her erstwhile guardian's lips? But she had not then thought it had been a concerted plan between the two of them.

'You will thus be scarce surprised to hear that your tale is told,' he pursued, in that feline manner that set her teeth on edge. 'Anton was already shaken by my testimony. Though I must say that his efforts to retain his faith in you were quite touching—and of better use than I had supposed.'

A frown creased Rosina's brow. What was he at now? 'I do not understand you.'

The smile grew, and Forteviot moved a little closer, purring. 'How should you? Your naïvety could never appreciate my cunning. There was always the possibility that I might lose the game, for he could choose to set you aside.'

'How do you know he will not?'

'I don't,' he admitted, with no diminution of that smugness that so much disgusted her. 'If he does, I can always use you as I first intended.'

The hot words left her lips without intent, spoken from the heart. 'Over Raith's dead body!'

Forteviot laughed gently, and she instantly regretted her

outburst. 'Precisely. Anton Raith's mawkish sentimentality is likely to induce him to keep you, whether or no he believed me. Which means, my dear, that I shall have my money from him, or raise a scandal about his ears.'

Rosina heard him with a dawning sense of horror. The remembrance of Raith's murmured words rose up painfully in her mind. 'We will both be lost.' Only now did she see what he had meant. That he had given in to his need of her must mean that he would feel himself committed to the marriage, no matter what. And Forteviot would profit by it! Cambois also?

'How did you enlist my guardian's help? Is he to receive a cut of the proceeds for his pains?'

'How clever of you to guess,' sneered the other.

'You vile creature! You intended all along to convince Raith of my guilt,' she accused, her tone vibrant and low. 'You knew he must be hurt by the story becoming known. You knew of his past sufferings at his brother's hands, and now you will play upon his chivalry to undo him. You are despicable!'

Forteviot's thin smile creased his lips, and sarcasm was in his voice. 'Am I? How dreadful! The reflection, I am happy to say, is unlikely to deprive me of sleep.'

She wanted to slap his smug face. But she must deny herself that pleasure. The resolve was forming even as she spoke. Cost what it might, she would not allow this creature to harm Raith.

'Rest assured that my husband will be informed,' she said flatly. 'Now go, if you please.'

Forteviot's smile broadened. 'By all means. I have done what I came to do. Tell Raith that I will come tomorrow— to collect his note of hand.'

The first thing Raith became aware of was the too-bright light. He groaned and closed his eyes again, putting a hand to the dull ache that made itself felt at his brow. He was conscious next of thirst. There was a familiarity about his symptoms, and their meaning crept into awareness.

Hell and damnation! Had he been drinking too deeply again? The sound of drapes being drawn, and a soft footfall indicated the presence of his valet.

'Paulersbury—water!'

'Very good, m'lord.'

Raith cautiously opened his eyes again. The room was a trifle less bright. Paulersbury had evidently divined his condition, for he had half-drawn the drapes once more across the windows. It must have been the opening of them that had woken Raith. He made an effort to raise himself upon the pillows—and made the discovery that he was unclothed.

Blood and thunder! Had he been so far gone that he had been unable to put on his nightgear? No—for Paulersbury had readied him for bed last night as usual. Then—

His thoughts checked on an impossible notion. Rosina! The vague image of tangled limbs and tempestuous kisses erupted into a full-blown remembrance. Raith hissed in a breath on the intense rapture of it. Was it remembrance? Had he dreamed again? His heart twisted. Could he have imagined the sweet abandon of his wife's surrender? An echo of her voice came back to him. *Give me a memory that I may cherish.* Oh, Rosy!

He threw himself up, and was obliged to clutch at his head at the instant protest therein. Through narrowed eyes, he took in the rumple of the bedclothes. She had been with him! An impulse of memory made him throw the covers back. He stared at the spots of red upon the sheets. His eyes pricked.

'Your water, m'lord.'

Instinct made Raith fling the bedclothes over the evidence. A second later he realised that his valet would have discovered it in any event. But nothing, he thought thankfully, need be said. The sheets would be discreetly changed. He took the glass and emptied its contents.

And then he saw the note.

It was lying on the pillow near where her head must have lain. An instant premonition of disaster struck him. No! Rosy, sweetheart, no—*not now.*

He barely had courage to reach out for the folded sheet. A dull thudding started up in his chest. With fingers that shook slightly, he spread it open.

'My lord—' Could she so address him still, after last night? 'My enemy has been here this day.' Forteviot! What in thunder had the villain said to her? A scandal—but he had threatened it before. And it was not news that his hints had been deliberate. Had he not been persuaded of the scoundrel's intent to blacken Rosina's name to him? So it was a plot between Forteviot and her guardian. Ottery had been right.

But as he read the final sentences penned by the waif whom he had hounded, he had no thought of Forteviot or Cambois.

'I tell you this because I would not wish you to be in mystery as to why I am gone. I cannot bear to bring you these distresses. Pray, Anton, let me go. It is better that we part. Mr Ottery will know what to do to make it right. I will remember always—Rosy.'

Remember? Did she imagine that he could forget? Let her go! Rosina, were you mad? Rather than lose her, he would endure ten thousand scandals! But where was she now? How long had she been gone? Perhaps she had not already left.

Urgency threw him out of bed, and he staggered. Leaping to his aid, the valet caught him.

'Take care, m'lord!'

Raith steadied himself, driven by necessity, and shook
the man off. 'I am all right. Fetch me a bucket of water
so that I may dip my head in it!'

Shifting away, he drew on the robe that Paulersbury
was holding out, and made unsteadily for his wife's bedchamber, throwing open the four doors that lay in his way.
The room was empty. But a cursory glance about the
dressing-room showed him that a hasty departure had
been made. Drawers and closet doors were open, their
contents poking forth, a clutter of garments upon the floor.

Raith strode through to the bedchamber and tugged on
the bell-pull, his eyes raking the room. The bed was made,
and there were no further signs in here. The ache at his
head intensified, and he was obliged to hold to one of the
bedposts as he attempted to make his way back to the
dressing-room.

He was engaged in sifting through her closet, trying to
reckon up which gowns Rosina might have taken, when
he was disturbed by the maid Joan.

'M'lord!' she gasped, bobbing a curtsy from the doorway to the bedchamber.

'When did Her Ladyship leave?' he demanded without
preamble.

Joan looked blank. 'I—I don't rightly know, m'lord.'

'Don't lie to me!' barked Raith.

'But I don't know, m'lord,' pleaded the girl. 'Last I
saw she went down to see that there Lord Forteviot,
and—'

'You have not seen her since?'

'No, m'lord.'

Raith's heart sank. He moved away from the closet and
waved at the maid. 'Are any gowns missing? Quickly,
girl!'

Thus adjured, Joan hurried to the closet. Presently she

was able to report that only one had been removed, besides that which Rosina had been wearing. Hope lit in Raith's breast. Perhaps she had not gone with the intention of remaining away for long. But in that case, why had she written as if she meant to leave him? He had supposed at first that she must have gone to her nurse at Withibrooke. But she could not have been safe there. How could Mrs Hoswick protect her?

Blood and thunder, *where was she*?

'Go down and tell Kirkham to come to my bedchamber—immediately!' he ordered tersely, and swept through to his own apartments.

Paulersbury had brought a jug of cold water which he was tipping into the basin. Thankfully, Raith splashed his face. Then he tore off his bed gown and threw the icy liquid over himself in handfuls that wreaked havoc upon the floor of his dressing-room. Ignoring his valet's protests, he performed hasty ablutions, and was in the act of donning his rust-coloured frock-coat and waistcoat, over buckskin breeches, when a discreet knocking heralded the arrival of his butler.

'Kirkham, what an age you have been! For God's sake, where is Her Ladyship? Did you see her leave the house?'

'I did not, m'lord,' admitted the elderly retainer, 'but I have made enquiries, and I understand from Parton that the chaise left not half an hour since.'

'Then Parton knows where she has gone?'

'It appears that Her Ladyship desired Catterline to drive her to Banbury.'

'Banbury?' Of course! Relief swept through Raith, as a line from Rosina's note came back to him. She had gone to consult with Ottery. Consult? Or was it a refuge—from her husband?

Chapter Eleven

Rosina regarded the lawyer seated on the other side of the desk with some anxiety. 'Can you not arrange it, Mr Ottery?'

Under the grey wig, the kindly features creased with concern. 'I can oblige you, ma'am, if you wish for it. But I am loath to do so—without talking to His Lordship. My dear Lady Raith, have you considered the consequences?'

'I need only consider the alternative,' said Rosina desperately, pulling at her fingertips. 'I will not have my husband face the shame and disgrace of hearing my name—no, *his* name, for that is the one I bear—abused.' She looked at the lawyer, all her heart in her eyes. 'You best know how much he has already suffered, Mr Ottery. I will not be the means of bringing to him further cause for bitterness.'

The lawyer rose from his chair, and moved a trifle restlessly about his own office. Rosina watched him, puzzled by his attitude. He seemed deeply troubled. What ailed him? Surely he must see the rightness of her demand?

'What is the matter, Mr Ottery?'

He paused by the desk, looking down at her with an expression hard to interpret. 'Lady Raith, you have put me in a quandary. I saw His Lordship only yesterday, when he came to me here to be given certain information.'

Rosina coloured, looking away. 'I know what it was. Lord Forteviot informed me that my guardian had given you a similar tale to his own.'

'Not similar, Lady Raith. Exactly the same.'

Something in his voice made her look back at him, a wild hope in her breast. 'Can it be…' She swallowed, and tried again. 'Mr Ottery, did you believe him?'

The lawyer shook his head. 'I told His Lordship that I was inclined rather to believe in you, for I felt certain that a collusion had been formed between these two gentlemen.'

Rosina felt a bursting at her heart. Tears welled at her eyes, but she dashed them away. She bit her lip, and turned her eyes away from the intent concern in the lawyer's face.

'But *he* did not accept it, did he?' she uttered huskily.

Ottery did not answer, and Rosina forced herself to look at him. She was right, then. Raith had chosen rather to believe in the falsehood. He had not been drunk last night from elation! Hurt gripped her, and it was some moments before she was able to speak.

'How much do you know, Mr Ottery?' she asked, giving him look for look. 'Why could he not trust me? Was it the doctor's evidence?'

The lawyer compressed his lips, and Rosina found herself burning with resentment. As if impelled, she rose from her chair, leaving in it the cloak that had slipped from her shoulders. She took a hasty turn about the room. His silence was driving her mad!

'Must you be so discreet, Mr Ottery?' she cried, facing him. 'I am sure you know it all. Pray, why must I be left in ignorance? I thought you approved me. I thought—'

'Don't, ma'am!' he interrupted. A sigh left his lips, and

he came up to her. 'Won't you sit down again? Believe me, Lady Raith, I am on your side.'

'As is my husband,' she replied tightly. 'He will not set me aside, no matter what he believes.'

The lawyer's eyes regarded her keenly. 'Are you certain?'

Rosina looked him full in the face. 'He has given me reason enough to be so.' A faint flush stained her cheek. 'That is not to say that he has not thought of separation. But he will not now be willing to part from me. That is why—'

'That is why you are proposing to sacrifice yourself,' put in the lawyer gently.

'I am relying on you, Mr Ottery. Pray help me.'

He took one of her unquiet hands in his. 'Lady Raith, you cannot possibly expect me to aid you to leave him. Especially in the light of what you have said.'

Rosina regarded him with suspicion in her face. 'You would do so, had the request come from him.'

The lawyer looked altogether upset, but before he could respond, they were interrupted by a disturbance outside the office door. There was the sound of a slam, and a raised voice—one all too readily recognisable. Rosina jumped, and her heart began to hammer in her breast. Two other voices answered, and a second later the door flew open, and Raith entered the room.

He stood in the aperture, stripping off his gloves, dangerous under the broad-brimmed hat, the greatcoat emphasising his height. He was pale, and his features were set, the scar standing out white.

His eyes found Rosina. 'I thought so,' he said grimly, and threw aside his gloves on a chair by the door. The hat joined them.

Rosina's pulses were rioting, but she faced him squarely. 'It—it is of no use to t-try to s-stop me, Raith.'

'Rosy, I can't let you do this!' He took a few hasty paces towards her, but checked as Rosina backed away. Hurt entered his eyes. 'What, has nothing changed? Rosina!'

'One moment, my lord,' interrupted the lawyer, moving quickly to the door.

Raith swung round. He had left the door open behind him. He threw a hand to his aching head, and shifted to one of the windows. Rosina had come up against a bookcase, and she stood with her back to it, her hands grasping at its edge.

That Raith had come after her both warmed her heart, and filled her with dismay. That he would fight her going she could not doubt. Lord knew it was difficult enough without that! The very sight of him brought back such a strong recollection of his passion of the previous night that her loins stirred—adding nothing to her comfort, and thoroughly undermining her determination.

Ottery spoke a word of dismissal to the clerks within the other room, and then closed the outer door. He went across to Raith, addressing him with all his habitual calm.

'Allow me to take your coat, my lord.'

With impatience, Raith turned and allowed Ottery to help him out of the enveloping greatcoat, his eyes on Rosina. The lawyer laid aside the garment on a convenient side table, and returned to his desk.

'Lady Raith has asked me to arrange to release her from this marriage, my lord.'

Raith's heart jarred painfully, and he saw the flooding consciousness enter his wife's face. His voice was barely steady. 'So I had guessed. Did you agree?'

'How could I, sir, without knowing your mind?'

A long sigh left Raith's lips. 'You might be pardoned for supposing it to be other than it is.' He looked again at Rosina, and found his waif in residence. Hell and damnation, but this demanded privacy!

He crossed to the inner door, and opened it. 'You will permit us to make use of your room?'

Ottery bowed. 'Lady Raith, will you not go apart with His Lordship?'

Rosina stood her ground, her eyes upon her husband, her voice a trifle shaky. 'No, Mr Ottery, I will n-not. You know so m-much that there can be nothing said between us that you may not hear.'

She saw Raith wince, and was obliged to damp down upon a rise of distress. The lawyer's eyes went from one to the other. He coughed.

'I believe matters ought better to be resolved between you, ma'am, without a witness.'

'No!'

'Rosy!'

With pain, Raith saw his wife fling away to the position he had just vacated by the window. Unable to help himself, he let go the door handle, and came towards her. She threw up her hands, and the dark orbs showed panic.

'No, you must not. Don't come near me!'

He stopped, but his eyes were despairing. 'Not come near you? You cannot be afraid of me, Rosy—not now.'

'It—it is not that.' Rosina looked down at her unquiet fingers. 'You have—too much p-power to affect me. My resolution will f-fail, Raith, if I am alone with you.'

His heart melted, and he moved to her, cupping her cheek. 'I want it to fail, Rosy. I cannot let you go!'

She looked up at him. 'I knew you would say that.'

He released her. 'Yet you took clothes from your closet. You meant to escape me! What, was Ottery to conceal you somewhere? Surely you know that he would not aid you.'

Rosina glanced across at the lawyer. 'No, but he would

do it for you, if I can convince him of the rightness of my request.'

'I beg to differ, ma'am,' came from Ottery himself, bringing Raith's head round. 'His Lordship best knows how much I am against separation.'

Rosina wrenched away from her spouse's hold. 'Then you did mean to set me aside!' She paced away from him, pulling at her fingers. 'Oh, I knew it. Last night—when I came to find you—that is why you had been drinking.'

'Rosina—'

'No, don't say it!' she cried, turning on him. 'You have no need to excuse yourself. I had guessed it, in any event. It was why I had looked for you—to ask you—so that I might know my fate for certain. Only my maid told me that Kirkham had been troubled about you, and in my anxiety I forgot it.'

Raith was very pale. He made no attempt to approach her. His voice was low, but a thread of vibrant passion ran through it. 'You have a right to be wounded, Rosina. But you do not know the whole. There were reasons—'

'I know them,' she interrupted, a break in her voice. 'Why do you suppose I am here? Do not imagine that I blame you, Raith.'

'You may not blame me, but you are wounded none the less.'

Rosina could not deny it, but nor could she say it—and add to Raith's distresses. 'It is immaterial. No one else will believe, any more than you did, that Forteviot and my guardian were lying.'

'Do you think I care any longer?' he uttered. 'Whatever may have been my feelings yesterday—'

'But I care, Raith.'

He was silenced. So wrapped up had he been in his own pride that he had not considered Rosina's emotions. She was right. People would believe what they wished to, and the least hint of the circumstances alone would be enough to damn her. He looked across at Ottery.

'I cannot have her pilloried. We have to stop him!'

'Undoubtedly,' agreed the lawyer, but his glance was on Rosina. Raith looked back at his wife, and found her eyes huge in the white face.

'Raith, I don't care for that.'

'Don't you?'

'I could bear it for myself, but I will not have you condemned for a chivalrous impulse.'

'It has nothing to do with chivalry,' he said hastily. 'If I must care, it can only be on your behalf, Rosina. My concerns were purely selfish, I admit that. I have no interest in what the world may say.'

Rosina eyed him wistfully. 'Could you ignore it—when there is not a soul who will receive your wife? The true facts of our marriage are bad enough, Raith. Lady Doddinghurst was quick to find flaws in Mr Ottery's story.'

'It was poor at best,' admitted the lawyer.

'But it is better than the slightest whisper of what Lord Forteviot proposes to tell the world,' Rosina pointed out. 'Raith, you think you may withstand it, but I know your temperament. I cannot stay with you only to poison your life.'

A constriction lodged in Raith's chest. 'Do you imagine that people will talk any the less for your leaving me?'

Rosina looked away. 'For a while, perhaps. But if I am not there to—'

'If you are not there,' he uttered painfully, 'I had as well cut my own throat now! Rosy, this is pointless.' He crossed to the desk, throwing a wild hand at his lawyer. 'Ottery, for God's sake, help me!'

The lawyer rose up from his desk and came to lay a calming hand upon Raith's shoulder. 'You are too impatient, my lord. Allow Lady Raith at least the opportunity to give rein to the sensations that are driving her.' He gripped the shoulder he held. 'I think you do not understand that her whole design is to spare you, sir. She has no thought of herself.'

Raith let go an uneven breath, and dropped to perch upon the desk. His eyes went to Rosina's. 'Then it makes even less sense that she should wish to end our marriage.'

The bleak look in his face tore at Rosina's heart. 'But I don't *wish* for it!'

'Then—'

'My lord, leave it!' cut in the lawyer sharply.

Raith compressed his lips, and wrenched his eyes away from Rosina's expressive countenance. Blood and thunder, but Ottery was right! Small wonder she would not go apart with him, if he could not let her edge in a word without some forceful interruption. What had she said? That he had too much power over her? He glanced at her again, rueful now.

'Am I ever this overbearing?'

Her tiny smile gleamed on Rosina's lips. 'You are not easy to withstand, my lord.'

'But you have held out against me—several times.'

The smile disappeared, to be replaced by a look of determination. 'I must this time.'

Raith felt the protest welling up, and had to fight to suppress himself from utterance. He looked at his lawyer. 'What am I to do?'

Ottery gave him a grim smile. 'Hold your tongue, sir.' Then he looked across at Rosina. 'I will engage to keep His Lordship in check for the moment, ma'am.'

Raith watched her begin to pace, her fingers busy in that fidgeting way she had when upset or anxiety gripped her. He found himself moved more by her distress than

his own selfish need. As the portent of her words began
to penetrate, he was affected almost beyond endurance.

'You must not think I blame you, Raith. It is all my
fault. I should never have taken this step. If Gatty had not
suggested it, I should not have thought of answering that
advertisement. I was trying to obtain a post. Any post—
though housekeeping was all I knew how to do. I should
have done just that. Forteviot could less easily have found
me were I occupied as a servant. Even had he done so, it
could not have involved anyone else.' She paused, glancing round at her spouse. 'You, Raith. I cheated you from
the first. I used you—trying for a security that was impossible to achieve. And this is what has come of it!'

Raith would have spoken then, but Ottery forestalled
him. 'My dear Lady Raith, you must not reproach yourself
for that. You were as much used.'

'As much cheated!' put in Raith violently.

'Wait, my lord!' Ottery laid a hand on his arm. 'Had
you any more to say, ma'am?'

'Any more?' Rosina threw her hands to her face. 'Oh,
so much! If I had only known—had I an inkling of who
he was.' She wafted vague fingers and looked at her husband. 'I don't mean your identity. But *who* you are. What
has been made of you by—by the bludgeoning of fate…'
Her voice began to fail, and she had to swallow on the
rising tears. 'Had you been any other man—one less affected by… I might have borne to be the means of bringing this trouble upon you.'

The tears escaped, trickling down her cheeks, and
Raith's eyes riveted upon them, his heart too full even for
thoughts, let alone words or deeds.

'Even could you find a way to stop Forteviot—how can
I stay? I could not hope to assuage the torment that lives
within you. It is too strong—too deeply set. And for the

origin of that wound which you take such pains to shield—'

She stopped, her hand flying to her mouth, as if she would push back the words. But nothing came either from her husband, or the lawyer, and the quivering fingers shifted.

'You see? I cannot even speak of it, for fear of awakening that bitterness with which you scourge yourself—with which you distance me unbearably.'

'Not any more!' burst from Raith abruptly.

'My lord!'

'Ottery, I can be silent no longer!' He was up, moving swiftly across the room towards her. 'Rosina, if you are to leave me because of that—! Don't you know how your presence in my life has changed me?' He took her by the shoulders. 'By thunder, I know how ill I have used you on that account! But only because I was afraid that you could not favour me.'

'You assumed it!' Rosina accused him, wrenching away. 'You would not let me near you.'

'Do not forget your own reluctance!' he returned, stung. 'If common decency led me to refrain from forcing you to endure this repulsive countenance of mine—'

'Raith, it has never been repulsive to me,' Rosina cried despairingly. 'That is what I am trying to make you understand.' She caught sight of the lawyer's face, and shifted towards him. 'Mr Ottery, I appeal to you.'

'I have always believed His Lordship to be over-sensitive,' agreed Ottery, looking at Raith.

Rosina turned. 'There! And you need not imagine that I do not know why it is so. You had not been nearly as aware of it had it not been inflicted by your brother Piers!'

There was a silence. Raith went white, and shot an accusatory look at his lawyer. Ottery shrugged.

'This does not come from my lips, my lord.'

His eyes shifted to Rosina's face. 'How did you know? Unless—was it Kirkham or my housekeeper who told you?'

Rosina sank into the chair before the desk, sighing deeply. 'Release me, Mr Ottery, I beg of you!' Her eyes filled and she looked up at the lawyer, her voice quivering. 'See h-how useless it is? He supposes me to be so g-great a fool that I c-cannot guess at it.'

Raith caught himself up, abruptly recognising how his defences had gone up. 'Oh, God, Rosina! I didn't mean it.'

'No, you never do,' she uttered, clasping her hands tightly together in her lap. 'That is the tragedy.' She saw that Mr Ottery was frowning down at her. 'Pray don't look upon me thus severely, Mr Ottery.'

The lawyer's face cleared. 'Nothing of the sort, ma'am. I was merely trying to decide how best to acquaint you with His Lordship's history.'

'Ottery!'

'My lord, you gain nothing by your silence. Her Ladyship has a right to know. And—if you will be advised by me—the more she knows, the easier it will be for you to communicate upon the subject.'

Raith crossed to the window. It was not a pretty story, and the very mention of it brought to mind the memory of his brother's vicious act. The whistling lash—the distorted witness faces—the shocking violence of the pain—and the welling blood. Behind him, he heard Rosina's voice, the tremble of it a stronger reproach than what she said.

'He n-need not tell me, if he does not w-wish to. Rather let me speak, Mr Ottery. You do not want to hear this, Raith, but I will s-say it now.'

He did not turn, and Rosina continued, husky and low. 'When the first shock had died, I was consumed not with repulsion—but with curiosity. I wanted to touch your face, to know how it felt.' She saw him flinch, and caught the lawyer's eye. Mr Ottery was looking grim, but he said nothing. Rosina was emboldened to pursue her course. 'I was ashamed of myself, and so I did not know how to respond to you, when you spoke of it so bitterly. At last, when you allowed me to touch it, in one of your vile moods—'

'Don't remind me!'

It was a muttered outburst, but Raith remained with his back to the room, staring unseeingly out of the window.

'When you allowed me to touch it,' Rosina resumed, 'the sensation under my finger did not offend me. It was even pleasurable, so that I did not dare to speak of it. For you had told me of that other creature, and—'

'*Enough!*' Raith swung round. His eyes were afire, and Rosina winced. 'Oh, don't look so afraid! If I am angry, it is not with you—but with my brother. He follows me even into my marriage!' A mirthless laugh broke from him. 'Why would he not? It was to prevent me finding a wife that he slashed at my face—with his whip.'

Rosina gasped, her fingers flying to her mouth. 'Dear Lord, but he must have been insane!'

Raith shrugged. 'That—or merely vengeful.'

It was Ottery who took up the tale. 'I must bear part of the blame. I had foolishly told His late Lordship of the inheritance, which, as you know, Lady Raith, was dependent upon matrimony.'

'It was money left to me by my maternal grandfather,' Raith put in.

'But why should the fact of the inheritance affect Piers?' asked Rosina, quite appalled.

Raith looked at Ottery. 'You tell her.'

'Sheer malice, ma'am, for it gave him independence, which prevented the late Lord Raith from giving vent to his lunatic envy. Mr Raith—as your husband was then styled—desired to take up a commission in the army,' explained the lawyer. 'Provision had been left by his father, but his brother refused to honour it. Since it was not in the will, I had no power, even as executor, to force him.'

'I took him up on it, and we quarrelled,' Raith said. 'Piers had guests. Gambling cronies—Forteviot among them.'

'Oh, dear Lord!' uttered Rosina, her countenance paling. 'Then that is why…'

Raith set his teeth. 'Yes, that is why. I imagine it must have been grist to his mill to discover that it was I who had married you.'

'He saw it all?'

'He was witness to my humiliation, yes. We were in the hall, I remember, and the altercation became public.' His jaw tightened, and the scar stood out white. 'Piers snatched up his weapon too suddenly for me to know what he would be at.' His eyes burned at the memory. 'The blow felled me.'

'Oh, Raith!'

'It was viciously done, but I felt more rage than pain. I scrambled up and closed with Piers. I know I managed to get the whip out of his hand, but I was overcome. By the servants, or his friends—I don't know.'

There was fury in Rosina's voice. 'If I had only known this when that vile man came to the house!'

'The next thing I knew, I was sprawling on the ground outside the mansion.' Raith's glance met and held Rosina's. 'That is when Piers chose to jeer at me, bidding me try now to find myself a wife.'

Rosina was harrowed for him. 'What happened to you? How did you manage?'

'He had the sense to come to me,' Ottery cut in.

'Kirkham helped me to a horse, and I rode to Banbury.' He came across the room and placed his arm about his lawyer's shoulder. 'You see now why this fellow can never be sufficiently repaid. Ottery not only took me in, but nursed me until the wound was healed. Finally, he furnished me with the means to obtain a commission—'

'It was, I need hardly say, a loan, which has long since been repaid,' put in Ottery. 'And as for the rest—'

'—and then he packed me off to the Army.'

'—it is only what anyone would have done,' finished the lawyer in the same breath.

'No friend could have done more!' Raith removed his arm, and took a step towards his wife. 'It does not end there, Rosina. He has done more to help me through the exigencies of our marriage than you can ever imagine. If you needs must run away from me, you could not have chosen better.'

Hastily, Rosina rose up from her chair, whisking away. 'I don't know what to do. I wish you had not told me this—no, I don't mean that. I am glad you have told me.' She turned to face both men. 'But I am doubly determined that Forteviot shall not harm you. Pray, Raith, if the only way it can be prevented is for us to part—'

'Here is a change of tune,' he said quickly, coming up to her and seizing her hands. 'Rosy, stay with me, my dearest love! Let us fight him together. Ottery will find a way. And if he cannot, I shall know how to do. That scoundrel will not dishonour your name!'

But Rosina hardly heard him. Her attention had caught on that precious endearment, and her pulse had begun to beat rather rapidly. If only his feeling for her truly went so deep! She did not know how faint was her voice.

'What did you call me?'

The coal-black eyes gazed up at him with so much

wistfulness in them that Raith's heart turned over. 'If you look at me like that, I can't recall anything I said.'

'You said—' She found herself unable to repeat it. She swallowed. 'Never mind it. What can Mr Ottery do?'

'A great deal,' came from the lawyer behind them. 'Better, I feel sure, than what I suspect to be your intended solution, my lord.'

Rosina pulled away, and turned quickly to face him. 'What do you mean, sir?'

But it was Raith who answered—through his teeth. 'He means that, left to myself, I will slaughter the villain!'

'You mean to call him out?' Rosina blenched. 'But he may as readily kill you, Raith—and I should die then!'

Raith's chest hollowed out, and he groped for her hand, his voice pitched low. 'If you care so much, how could you leave me?'

She looked round at him, equally fervid. 'If you care for me, how can you put yourself in danger?'

The lawyer intervened. 'My dear sir, there is no need for any such foolishness. I have the matter well covered.'

Raith released her fingers. 'Then, if it will change her mind, for God's sake, tell her what you may do!'

Ottery retired behind his desk, and sat down. 'The most obvious thing would be to go to Mr Cambois and extract a written statement of the true version of events.'

'You may rely on me for that!' promised Raith threateningly, flexing his fist and moving across to the desk. 'What else?'

'If you will hand into my safekeeping all the pertinent correspondence, I will face Lord Forteviot with the intelligence that I am in possession of sufficient evidence to have him up on a charge of attempted blackmail.'

'Will that suffice?'

'Oh, I think so, my lord. He cannot raise a scandal without involving himself in a public exposure of villainy.

If Her Ladyship is pilloried, we will have enough counter-evidence to support an attack upon his own reputation. I doubt Lord Forteviot will take the risk for a paltry twenty thousand pounds. Men of his stamp drop that much in one night's play.'

'By thunder, you're right, Ottery! There will be no point in it. And I will see to it that Cambois keeps mum.'

Rosina heard it all with a leap of the heart. She had not thought it possible that there might be a solution—other than the one she had sought. Her veins were rioting, and it was with a burgeoning of hope that she saw Raith turn to her again.

'Rosy—what do you say now?'

She glanced at the lawyer. 'May we—can we speak alone?'

Raith's face lit in triumph. 'At last!'

He seized her wrist, and led her hastily to the inner door. 'With your leave, Ottery.'

'You are my guest, my lord,' smiled the lawyer.

A moment later, Rosina found herself in a little chamber behind the lawyer's office, with the door closed, and her husband leaning against it. She moved into the room, pausing by the desk and turning to face him.

'Well?' he demanded.

She bit her lip. 'Raith, after last night—'

'Oh, by thunder, last night!' he breathed.

Rosina flushed, and looked away. 'You—you had not the intention to take me, I know that.'

'Does that rankle?' he asked painfully, coming away from the door. 'Rosy, believe me—though I asked Ottery yesterday to free me, it was not for lack of faith.'

'How can I blame you?' she said, her gaze returning to his. 'After what that doctor said.'

'It is true that I did waver,' he told her frankly. 'I was seduced into the idea that you had married me—'

'To conceal my condition? Oh, Raith.'

'Don't look at me like that, Rosina. I am all too ashamed. If you had heard how Ottery berated me! But he knew it was not truly that which drove me.'

That wistfulness crept into the coal-black eyes. 'How could it be otherwise?'

Raith's heart thrummed unevenly. 'You went away from me—in spirit, I mean. I thought I had lost you altogether, and I swear to you, Rosy, that was more to me than if you had been less than pure.'

Rosina stared at him blankly. 'It is not possible.'

'You may ask Ottery. I thought you hated me, and I could not live with you—knowing that, believing it.'

'I hate you?' Her fingers crept to her bosom. 'Raith, how could you suppose it? You won my heart long since.'

'Rosy!' He came up to her, and caught her wavering fingers to his lips. 'I own I hoped—after last night—that you had some feeling for me.'

'And you for me,' she returned, gripping his hand. 'I thought I heard you say that you loved me, but—'

'Thought!' He dragged her into his arms, and kissed her. 'I am so desperately in love with you that I think I am going mad! I have been so from the very beginning.'

Rosina's heart thumped wildly. 'Raith, that cannot be true.'

'Can it not?' he uttered grimly. Shifting, he turned her to the wall, and went quickly to open the cupboard doors that concealed the aperture through which the dark shadow of Ottery's portrait could be seen. 'Look at this!'

Rosina looked at him in puzzlement, and moved to examine it, but the significance escaped her for the moment.

'Look closely.'

She did so, and gave a cry as she came upon the view, through a slight veil, of Ottery's office. It was obvious that anyone sitting beyond the desk must be visible. The place was empty. Had the lawyer had tact to leave, knowing that he must overhear anything that was said in this room? A surge of emotion rose up in her breast. She turned, unable to find words, merely gazing at her spouse.

He had retreated to the other side of the room, and his look was rueful. 'Yes, I deceived you from the first. I saw and heard all.'

'I felt it,' she said unexpectedly. 'All the while, I felt I was being watched. I thought it had been a trick of those horrid eyes in that portrait. But it was you!'

His hands went up in a gesture of despair. 'What can I say? From the first instant that I saw you—looking quite as you do now, with just such a cap—I was lost. Every moment that you sat in that chair, every word you said, only served to attract me the more. I was too afraid that I would lose you, if you had a sight of my face.' He sighed deeply. 'And then, after we married, and I was so close to you—I was locked in a situation which put me into a state well-nigh akin to madness.'

'Then when you cut at me,' she said slowly, 'and threw your bitterness in my face—'

'I could not tolerate any mention of my disfigurement. Only because I wanted you so badly, and I could not believe that you might begin to reciprocate my affection.'

'But I did so in spite of it—perhaps because of it,' she told him. 'Your very touchiness made me privy to your deepest feelings, Anton.'

'Yet I hated myself for what I was doing to you.'

He dared at last to approach her again, but he did not touch her. Rather his eyes, deeply agonized, searched hers.

'Rosy, I loved you at sight, and time—knowing you, discovering the magical wonder that you are—has only served to strengthen that feeling. If you had left me—had

I tried indeed to put you aside—I could not have endured it! I would not have been able to rest until I had you back.'

At that, her elusive smile played upon Rosina's lips. 'I had every expectation that you might command my return, my dear, imperious lord.'

'Which was why you flew to Ottery for protection,' he said, his features softening.

But Rosina's coal-black eyes looked up at him in some distress. 'But though you might love me enough to waive the matter, I wish I could have a way to prove myself, for how can you ever be sure—'

'Rosy, you little fool!' Her naïvety touched him, and he cupped her face, saying gently, 'My darling, don't you know that last night gave me incontrovertible proof of your innocence?'

Rosina stared. How was it possible? Vaguely she recalled something Mama had said. Only it was so long ago, and the subject had never again been of relevance.

'Do you mean that you knew by—by—'

'By making love to you, yes.'

Her gaze widened. 'Then, if you had done so at the outset, we need never have been through all this agony.'

Raith shook his head. 'I don't think it could have been avoided, sweetheart. In one way or another—and that is my blame.'

'No, it is your brother's,' Rosina said fiercely. On impulse, she reached up and drew his face down to hers, pressing a kiss to the scar. He stiffened, but he made no attempt to draw away. 'There. That is what I think of your countenance, Anton Raith.'

A slow smile crept across his face. 'I own I had rather you kissed it than struck at it.'

Consternation seized Rosina. 'Don't speak of that! I have suffered agonies of remorse. Oh, Raith, forgive me!'

She threw herself into his arms, muffling her face in his shoulder. Raith clutched her to him, pressing her close.

'Don't, Rosy. You have so much more for which to forgive me that I am glad of that morsel of punishment.'

'Don't say so,' she begged, lifting drowned eyes to his. 'I thought you would beat me in revenge.'

'Have you run mad?' He grinned. 'You must have seen that my bark is far worse than my bite. I could never touch you, sweetheart. Except for *this*.'

His lips came down on hers, and his kiss drove away the tears, melting her bones. She sagged into him, and he drew her tighter, crushing her to his chest. His mouth left hers, but only to murmur against her lips.

'Rosy, I adore you.'

'And I love you, Anton.'

He seized her lips again, and the exchange became intense. For quite some time Rosina had no opportunity for speech, but at length, her husband was induced to release her mouth, but only so that he might give out a heated groan.

'God, I cannot wait to get you home again!'

Rosina blushed. 'But it is the middle of the day, Raith. You cannot possibly—I mean, how can we—?'

His arms cradled her, and his lips traced a path about her forehead, cheeks and eyes. 'Very easily.'

'But the servants!'

'There are locks to the doors, are there not?'

'Yes, but—'

Raith raised his head suddenly. 'By thunder, how right you were about the stupid formality of that arrangement of our bedchambers. Shall we choose another—together?'

A shy smile settled upon Rosina's lips. 'But then we could not make assignations in the antechamber. We might choose whether you are to visit me, or I am to come to you.'

Her spouse laughed. 'That, wife, is a most romantic notion.'

'Yes, and only think,' pursued Rosina, becoming momently more enamoured of the idea, 'the servants will never know where to find us in the morning.'

'That will certainly keep them on their toes.'

'Besides which,' she ventured, with a flash cast up at him from those coal-black eyes, 'when you are horrid, which is bound to happen now and then, and lose your temper with me—'

'You may lock the door against me?' enquired Raith politely. 'I dare say you would prefer not to face the consequences of that.'

Rosina giggled. 'Why, would you break the door open?'

'I should not need to. You would have to come out sooner or later. I will bide my time.'

'The day you bide your time, Raith, I will look to see pigs take wing!'

Her spouse grinned. 'Then you will not be surprised at my present impatience for an assignation—and I will not wait until tonight.'

The black eyes flirted up at him. 'I am rather afraid that I may be too exhausted from last night's exertions—'

'Rosy!'

'But if you so command me, my lord,' continued his wife demurely, 'I must obey.'

Raith drew a breath, and sighed it out with intense satisfaction. 'How excellent a thing is the marriage vow.'

And Rosina, as his lips claimed hers in tacit promise of a furtherance of those ecstasies she had enjoyed last night, could not but reciprocate with the deepest approbation of her conjugal duty.

* * * * *

Lady Jane's Physician
by
Anne Ashley

Anne Ashley was born and educated in Leicester. She lived for a time in Scotland, but now lives in the West Country with two cats, her two sons and a husband, who has a wonderful and very necessary sense of humour. When not pounding away at her keyboard, she likes to relax in her garden, which she has opened to the public on more than one occasion in aid of the village church funds.

Chapter One

1819

Having been instructed from a very young age in the correct behaviour expected of a person of quality, Lady Jane Beresford didn't betray her feelings by uttering a shriek of delight as her eyes caught sight of the milestone informing her she was nearing her journey's end, but contented herself with a faint, well-bred smile of satisfaction.

Most members of her social class would have applauded such restraint. Any forceful displays of emotion were considered vulgar in the extreme: behaviour all too often seen in those belonging to the lower orders. And how Jane envied them that at least! The lives of the poor might be hard and cheerless for the most part, but they were free to give full rein to their feelings whenever they chose, whereas…

She couldn't prevent the tiny sigh of discontentment from passing her lips. She would have been the first to admit that, being a daughter of the Earl of Eastbury, she had been spoilt and indulged from birth, given everything money could buy. Fine dresses and jewels had always been hers for the asking, so why did she feel so utterly dissatisfied with her lot? Why had she been experiencing, with increasing frequency, the need to break away from her highly privileged existence, and to loosen those constricting ties which bound her to certain members of a family whose sole ambition for the past four years had been to parade her on the *Marriage Mart* in the hope of finding her a suitable husband?

Lost in her far from pleasant reflections, she gave an almost imperceptible shake of her head. She didn't know what lay at the root of her seemingly ever-increasing dissatisfaction. All she did know was that there must be more to the life ahead of her than being married to some eligible gentleman, running his house efficiently and bearing his children. If there was not, then the future stretched out before her as desolate as a barren waste.

At least, she mused, trying desperately to take heart, by flatly refusing to accompany her father and mother on their trip to Italy, she had taken that first and so very important step down the road to blessed self-determination. Next month, when she attained her majority, she would be financially independent—free to live where and with whom she chose. She had made no definite plans as yet, but she felt little desire to remain in Kent. Large though the ancestral home was, there were times when it seemed grossly over-crowded, especially on those occasions when her only brother and his wife made one of their frequent and extended visits, or when any one of her married sisters descended on the family home, bringing spouse and progeny with her.

Coming out of her reverie, as the post-boys slowed down the team of horses to negotiate the gap between two massive stone pillars, Jane turned to her sole companion who had sat silently staring out of the window for most of the journey. 'February is hardly the best time of year to go travelling any great distance, but I am so pleased I took your advice, Latimer, and accepted my cousin's invitation to stay at Knightley Hall.'

'You seemed so disinclined to remain in Kent or stay with any of your sisters, my lady,' the abigail responded, casting her mistress an almost furtive glance. 'You always speak so fondly of Lady Knightley. It seemed the obvious solution to your problem of where to stay whilst your parents were on the Continent.'

'Yes, but remember we'll be in Hampshire a few weeks only. Then we'll be off on our travels again to stay with my aunt, Lady Templehurst, in Bath.'

There was no response.

'I hope you do not find travelling too wearisome, Latimer?'

'Not at all, my lady.'

And that was it, Jane thought, no more nor less, the barest minimum of conversation as usual. With that one exception, when Latimer had suggested accepting Sir Richard and Lady Knightley's invitation to stay in Hampshire, they seemed never to exchange more than a dozen words at any one time. How she missed dear old Fenwick! One could at least hold a decent conversation with her. She cast the maid a thoughtful look. No, Latimer most certainly wouldn't have been her first choice for a personal maid, but, she reminded herself, she had been given little say in the matter.

When her former maid had been forced to retire through ill health, Jane would have been quite content to have had one of the young servants employed in her father's ancestral home to look after her, but her mother would have none of it. Standards needed to be maintained and, without consulting her daughter, the Countess had taken it upon herself to find a replacement for Fenwick.

Jane's fine almond-shaped eyes narrowed as she studied her maid's attractive profile. Although Rose Latimer had been her personal maid for a little over two months, and had proved extremely efficient in her work, Jane, for some inexplicable reason, had been unable to attain anywhere near the same rapport with her as she had enjoyed with her former maid. She couldn't quite put her finger on what it was about Latimer that she didn't like, for the woman had most certainly never been found wanting in any way and had come, according to the Countess, with a glowing reference from Lady Fairfax, for whom Latimer had worked for more than ten years. But there was certainly an air of reserve about the attractive young abigail that seemed almost to border on—yes—resentment.

'Here at last!' Jane remarked, as the hired vehicle came to a halt at the front entrance of a very imposing stone-built mansion.

Without waiting for a response, which she doubted she would have attained anyway, Jane stepped down from the carriage. After casting a cursory glance across the front aspect of the attractive Georgian building, she walked briskly towards the front door, which was opened before she had reached it by a very efficient young footman, resplendent in smart black and silver livery.

No sooner had she handed her fur-lined cloak to the manservant than Lady Knightley emerged from one of the rooms and came tripping lightly across the hall to embrace her warmly.

No one observing them together could have failed to notice the resemblance between the two young women—hair, eyes and build all ample testament to their kinship. No one could have failed to appreciate the depth of their mutual regard either, which was most strange in the circumstances. Although they had seen each other occasionally as children, when large gatherings of the Beresford family had been organised, it had been only during the past three years that they had met with any degree of frequency, and had swiftly become firm friends.

Jane had not infrequently pondered over this undeniable fact. Yet she would have been the first to admit that they had little in common. Her cousin's life revolved around her husband, their two small children and their niece, whereas she spent nearly all her time in society, engulfed in the social whirl, where she rubbed shoulders continuously with the cream of British aristocracy.

Holding her very welcome guest at arm's length, Lady Knightley cast an admiring glance over the very fashionable carriage outfit. 'Green becomes you exceedingly well, my dear, but then you always did know precisely what suited you.'

Jane's immediate response was to cast her very fine eyes over her relative's stylish appearance, thinking as she did so that Elizabeth had regained her trim figure remarkably quickly considering that she had less than three months before presented her husband with a second pledge of her affection, a son this time, who was destined to inherit this much admired country residence and the lion's share of his father's wealth.

'By your sublime air of contentment, Elizabeth, I must assume that both Louisa and baby Stephen are well, and that your darling niece, Juliet, is in fine fettle, too?'

Jane could never mention Juliet's name without remembering that dreadful morning, nearly four years before, when she had read an account in the newspaper of the tragic deaths of Sir Charles Knightley, his wife and their young son in a carriage accident. Blessedly, Juliet, little more than a babe, had been staying with relations at the time, and since the loss of her parents had been brought up by her uncle. Richard had never coveted the title, but had proved himself more than capable of stepping into his brother's shoes. He was a devoted guardian, and Jane knew that both he and Elizabeth looked upon little Juliet as their own child.

At mention of the children Lady Knightley's expression grew more serene. 'Yes, they are all hale and hearty—thank goodness! You'll get numerous opportunities to visit the nursery during your stay, so I shall resist the temptation to behave like a proud mother by parading my offspring before you now.'

'She'll take a chill and become too ill to visit anyone if you leave her standing in this draughty hall for very much longer,' a faintly sarcastic, but very attractive, deep masculine voice unexpectedly remarked, and Jane turned to see her cousin's very personable husband framed in a doorway.

Sir Richard Knightley was one of the few gentlemen with whom Jane had always felt completely at ease. Without the least hesitation she moved smilingly towards him and found herself enveloped in a pair of strong, muscular arms.

From the very first time they had met, a few months after his marriage to Elizabeth had taken place, she had liked him and had taken little notice of the wicked stories circulating at the time about his hurried marriage being a complete failure. One glance at the couple had been sufficient to convince her, if not those malicious Society tabbies whose chief object in life was to circulate spiteful untruths, that Sir Richard Knightley was very much in love with his pretty young wife, and she had glimpsed nothing during the intervening years to make her doubt her first impressions and change her mind.

As Sir Richard disengaged his welcoming hold, she looked up at his smiling face. He was undoubtedly a very attractive man, handsome enough to send any young girl's heart a'fluttering, but it was his intelligence and easy charm of manner which had, and still did, attract Jane. His being married, of course, placed him outside that category which she termed 'The Predatory Male', a species which she continued to keep at a discreet distance. Three highly successful Seasons, where she had been courted and flattered by dozens of eligible bachelors, and some not so eligible, had not turned her head, as might well have been the case with a less sensible young woman. Instead, her success had had the opposite effect. She had become, perhaps, a trifle too cynical, and most certainly never accepted any stranger at face value.

Unfortunately the air of cool reserve she tended to adopt whenever in the company of strangers, most especially those of the male gender, had earned her something of an undeserved reputation. Certain sections of Society considered her a trifle aloof, haughty, even, but Sir Richard knew this was far from the truth. As far as he was concerned she was the most convivial member of his wife's family—a warm and very caring young woman, whose manners were unimpeachable.

Entwining her arm through his, he took welcome charge of their guest by escorting her to a chair placed near the fire in the comfortable and very elegantly furnished drawing-room. 'I trust there was no last-minute hitch before your parents set off on their trip to Italy?' he enquired, handing her a glass of Madeira before seating himself beside his wife on a nearby sofa. 'I must confess I was more than just a little surprised when we received your letter accepting our invitation. Elizabeth and I were firmly convinced that you would want to sample the delights of Venice and Rome.'

'What a shallow, frivolous creature you must think me! Just goes to show how wrong one can be,' Jane quipped, before she suddenly became aware of the Knightleys' rather elegant attire. 'I must say you both look as fine as fivepence! I do not imagine for a moment that you put on all your finery in my honour. Expecting other guests, are we?'

'Yes, you impertinent little wretch!' Richard responded good-humouredly.

'A small dinner-party, that is all. Nothing grand, I

assure you,' Elizabeth put in, before her cousin and husband could indulge in one of their light-hearted bantering exchanges. 'I arranged it before I knew you would be staying with us, Jane. It will be my first social event since giving birth to Stephen, and I'm rather looking forward to it. But you mustn't feel obliged to join us if you feel disinclined or tired after your journey. Richard and I will quite understand.'

'Dear me! Do you think me such a poor creature as to be overset by a few hours' journey in a carriage? Of course I shall join you!'

'I'm so glad!' Elizabeth exclaimed with evident pleasure. 'You see, I've invited Lord Pentecost and his mother. It would be difficult to exclude them, their being such close neighbours,' she went on, raising her voice slightly in a valiant attempt to drown her husband's derisive snort. 'Lady Pentecost is not well liked, as you know, Jane. And I'm afraid poor Perry has become very withdrawn since his father's demise. I was wondering if you'd mind very much if I placed him next to you at the table? You always did get along so well together.'

Jane stared down into the contents of her glass, seeing images from the past when she and Lord Pentecost had been children and had indulged in some mischievous prank. 'I haven't seen dear Perry since he came into the title. I shall enjoy catching up on all his news.'

She cast a surreptitious glance in Richard's direction, and could only assume by his dour expression that he wasn't experiencing much delight at the prospect of having the new Lord Pentecost and the Dowager as his guests. 'You both know, of course, that the Dowager Lady Pentecost is a friend of my mother's, and Perry was a frequent visitor to our home when he was a boy. What you are not perhaps aware of is that at one time my darling mama seriously considered the prospect of marriage between us.'

Richard's dark brows rose, ample confirmation that he, like Jane herself, considered the mere idea as ludicrous in the extreme. They simply would not suit.

'Mama is not always very wise, Richard,' she remarked with a faint half-smile. 'But there was never the remotest chance of a union between our families. Not only would I never consider the idea, even though I like Perry very well, but my father would never countenance such a match.'

She sighed, and there was an unmistakable flicker of sadness in her lovely grey-green eyes. 'Papa, like so many other misguided souls, considers poor Perry half-witted. To call him so is to do him a gross injustice, believe me. He's immensely shy, has little self-confidence, and will do almost anything to avoid a quarrel, but he's certainly no fool, and is a completely different person when away from that odious mother of his.' She looked across at her interested listeners steadily. 'Believe me, there are very few I would rather have placed next to me at the dinner-table.'

On learning that the party had been arranged for early in the evening, Lady Knightley being one to keep strictly to country hours when residing in Hampshire, Jane didn't delay in going up to the charming bedchamber allocated to her for the duration of her stay, and, within a relatively short space of time, dressed in a very stylish evening gown of dark green velvet, she rejoined her host and hostess.

As Jane had been drilled from a ridiculously young age in the gentle art of polite drawing-room conversation, neither Richard nor Elizabeth experienced the least qualms in leaving her to her own devices when their guests began to arrive. It wasn't very long before the drawing-room was humming with voices raised in cheerful discourse, and Elizabeth was on the point of abandoning her position near the door when a tall, loose-limbed man, with over-long and slightly waving light brown hair, came striding purposefully into the room, and checked her intention of rejoining her husband by taking her roughly into his arms and planting a smacking kiss on her cheek.

Completely unruffled by the unpolished greeting, Elizabeth gazed up at the late arrival with an unmistakable depth of affection in her eyes. 'Well, well, well! Wonders will never cease. I cannot in all honesty say that I was expecting you to grace our rather informal little gathering with your august presence, Dr Carrington,' she teased him.

'Little baggage! You know full well that I never refuse an invitation to dine here without a very good reason,' he responded with all the blunt informality of a long-standing friendship.

He turned his head, and Elizabeth watched those clear, alert grey eyes of his scan the room. She had known Dr Thomas Carrington for many years and looked upon him as a dear and much loved surrogate brother, but, being a young woman of sense, this did not mean she was blind to his faults. Tom had always possessed a rather brusque manner which, it couldn't be denied, occasionally bordered on the downright rude, and he had an acid tongue which he never made the least attempt to sweeten when in the presence of the fair sex. In fact, more often than not, it was the ladies who succeeded in rousing his somewhat peppery temperament, especially those who were forever making far too much of trifling ailments.

His blunt manners certainly did little to endear him to many members of her sex, but those females who called upon his services with good reason were without exception extremely satisfied with his undeniable abilities, and many would not hear a word said against the man who was universally acknowledged as being a very fine physician.

He had lived in the area almost as long as she had herself and, therefore, was acquainted very well with nearly everyone present. So she knew, by the sudden frown which creased his high, intelligent forehead, the instant his keen gaze had fallen upon the stranger in their midst.

'Who is that over there talking with the Pentecosts?' Although Elizabeth had not infrequently twitted him over his seeming indifference to the ladies, there was little that escaped his notice and, like any other red-blooded male, he certainly admired a pretty face and trim figure. 'A relative of yours?' he added, instantly perceiving the resemblance.

'Yes, my cousin, Lady Jane Beresford. Don't you recall my telling you that we were expecting her to stay with us for a short while?'

'No, can't say I do remember.' He tut-tutted. 'Another aristo, eh? I think the French had the right idea, there, trying to cleanse their land of the scourge. Still,' he went on, ignoring the fulminating glance he received, 'one must be fair and keep an open mind. After all, you and Sir Richard are quite acceptable.'

Elizabeth's expression turned to one of combined

affection and exasperation. She had heard his derogatory views on her social class too many times in the past to be offended by anything he might say and, truth to tell, in many ways she agreed with him. But what would her well-bred cousin make of him? she wondered. There was no denying that Lady Jane Beresford was the epitome of a lady of quality, accustomed to every attention and courtesy, whereas Tom was not precisely renowned for playing the chivalrous gallant, and had never been known to put a guard on his tongue, no matter how refined the company might be.

She was spared the unnerving task of making the introductions quite so early in the evening by the sudden appearance of her very efficient butler, who announced that dinner was served, and she promptly secured the offices of the good doctor to escort her into the dining-room. Unfortunately, there was little she could do to prevent her casual-mannered friend, who had never been one to stand on ceremony, from indulging in a slight breach of etiquette by nodding his head in acknowledgement as Jane, on the arm of her childhood friend Lord Peregrine Pentecost, passed his chair. He received what could best be described as a frosty stare in response, and followed her progress down the length of the table with a decidedly disapproving frown.

'Haughty little madam!' he muttered as he seated himself on his hostess's right. 'There may be a certain similarity between you in looks, Lizzie, my love, but that's about all. That little minx needs taking down a peg or two and taught a few basic manners.'

Elizabeth almost choked. 'I hardly think you're in a position to criticise, Dr Carrington,' she remarked, coming immediately to her cousin's defence. 'You're not precisely overburdened with a surfeit of good manners yourself.'

His shapely brows rose in exaggerated surprise. 'And when have you ever heard me being deliberately rude to anyone without good reason, may I ask?'

'Frequently!' she responded without preamble. 'Whereas my cousin is extremely polite as a rule, most especially to those less fortunate than herself. I have never heard her talk down to anyone, not even the lowliest servant.'

'Well, that's something, I suppose,' Tom responded fair-mindedly and, under the pretext of reaching for his glass of wine, leaned forward and cast a smiling glance at his friend's cousin who, at that precise moment, happened to be gazing absently at the simple, but very effective, flower arrangements adorning the table. Their eyes met and held briefly, before Jane turned away, her finely arched brows almost meeting in a severe frown above the bridge of her decidedly aristocratic little nose.

Although Dr Carrington wasn't to know it, her far from approving expression had nothing whatsoever to do with his actions, which, had he but known it, would have amused rather than annoyed her. She had not noticed his nod of acknowledgement when she had entered the dining-room. Truth to tell, she was only vaguely aware of his existence, for her thoughts were centred on her childhood friend and the drastic changes she had perceived in him.

Elizabeth had most certainly not exaggerated when she had remarked on the fact that Lord Peregrine Pentecost had altered during the past year. He had come into the title upon the death of his father almost

twelve months ago. He had just attained the age of
three-and-twenty at that time, and one might have
supposed that this new status would have boosted his
self-esteem. Sadly, though, this had not proved to be
the case. In fact, during the short time Jane had been
conversing with him, she thought that he seemed
more withdrawn than ever, almost in an enclosed
world of his own.

'Perry, what's wrong?' she asked gently, and was
dismayed to see him start so violently that he almost
dropped his fork. 'Is there something troubling you?'

He seemed to debate within himself, but if he did,
just for one moment, consider confiding in her he certainly thought better of it, for he merely said, 'No,
I'm fine.' But the smile which accompanied the assurance nowhere near reached his kindly blue eyes.
'And delighted to see you again after such a long
time. I didn't realise you intended visiting Hampshire.'

'For a few weeks only, Perry. I could, of course,
have stayed with one of my sisters whilst the Earl and
Countess are abroad, or remained with my brother
and his wife, who have once again installed themselves in the ancestral home, but I find the over-
protective attitude of my family a little trying at times,
as you know.'

This drew a spontaneous chuckle from him which
was a relief to hear. 'Yes, I recall clearly that when
you were a little girl your family always tended to
treat you like some fragile doll, which was quite foolish when one comes to consider it. You were such an
intrepid little thing, always game for any lark. I suppose, though, it's only natural for them to concern
themselves about you, your being so much younger

than the rest of them. I certainly wish I had brothers and sisters.'

'I thought you looked upon me as a sister, Perry?'

He appeared to consider this. 'Yes, I suppose I do in a way... Certainly as a dear and trusted friend. You're one of the few people I feel completely at ease with, Janie. You're always so open and honest, and say precisely what you think, at least to me, but I can never recall your saying anything deliberately hurtful. Hetta's rather like that too.'

'I think we've known each other for far too long not to be completely truthful with each other.' She cast him a thoughtful glance. 'Who, by the way, is Hetta?'

Realising instantly, by the sudden guarded look which took possession of his fine, aristocratic features, that on this occasion, at least, she had been a little too inquisitive, Jane prudently changed the subject, and within a relatively short space of time had her friend conversing easily again.

Elizabeth wasn't slow to perceive how relaxed the young baron appeared in her cousin's company, and as soon as the ladies had returned to the drawing-room, leaving the gentlemen to enjoy their port and brandy, she didn't hesitate to take Jane to one side and thank her for putting a guest, whose introversion could be a little trying at times, at his ease.

Jane waved one slender white hand in a dismissive gesture. 'As I've mentioned before, Perry's fine when he's out of reach of his mother's pernicious influence.' She frowned slightly as she cast a surreptitious glance in the formidable Lady Pentecost's direction. Even as a child she had never liked the woman, and failed to understand how her mother could look upon such a scheming, tattle-mongering harridan as a friend.

She then cast a sweeping glance over the other ladies present, most of whom were completely unknown to her. 'Is there a lady here by the name of Hetta?' she asked, focusing her attention briefly on a slender girl of about seventeen, whose bright golden ringlets danced about her very pretty face each time she moved her head, and whose china-blue eyes always fell shyly before any continued scrutiny.

'No, my dear. There's no one here with that name. In fact, the only Hetta I know is Miss Henrietta Dilbey, the local squire's niece. She came to live with him several months ago after her mother died.'

Jane regarded her cousin steadily. 'Why haven't they been invited here tonight? Not up to snuff?'

Elizabeth couldn't help chuckling at this blunt enquiry. Although Lady Jane's manners were faultless in public, as Lord Peregrine had remarked, she did not mince words with those whom she knew well. 'No such thing! The squire is well respected in these parts, and his niece is a charming young woman. Unfortunately the poor man is suffering from the gout at the moment, and Hetta sent me a very prettily worded letter declining the invitation. And now that I have satisfied your curiosity, Cousin, you can do something for me, and entertain the ladies on the pianoforte while we await the arrival of the tea things.'

Jane complied, if not with enthusiasm precisely, then with a complacency born of vast experience at being asked to display her undoubted talents.

From the tender age of ten, when she had first shown signs of superior musical gifts, the Countess of Eastbury had encouraged her youngest offspring to entertain the other members of the family for short periods during the evenings. It certainly had been a far from rare occurrence for Jane to display her skill on more formal occasions, when high-ranking personages had been staying at the ancestral home, and it had been quite the norm for her to play a selection of country dances when the younger members of the Beresford household had wanted to enjoy an impromptu romp.

Consequently, after the tea trolley had been removed, it never occurred to her to demur when a unanimous request for her to play again was raised. Seating herself once again before the very fine instrument placed in the corner of the room, she entertained the ladies by playing a popular tune of the day, and then acquiesced further by agreeing to accompany Elizabeth in a duet.

It was while the cousins, each acknowledged as having been blessed with a well above average singing voice, were halfway through performing a hauntingly lovely ballad that Sir Richard led the gentlemen back into the room. He, of course, had been privileged to hear Elizabeth and Jane perform together quite frequently, but Dr Carrington, trailing in the rear, had not been so fortunate and was instantly captivated by the flawless performance.

Tom would have been the first to admit that he had not infrequently passed rather uncomplimentary remarks about what he stigmatised as insipid after-dinner entertainment. Listening to what Society considered to be an accomplished young lady displaying a modicum of skill on the pianoforte or harp did not rate highly in his assessment of an enjoyable evening. Generally he avoided such gatherings like the plague, but found himself now, quite surprisingly, unable to draw his attention away from the charming vista in the corner of the comfortable drawing-room.

He had always considered Elizabeth, with her well-proportioned figure and finely boned face, a fine specimen of womanhood, but it was the female whose fingers moved with undeniable skill over the instrument's keys who captured his attention.

At first glance, the resemblance between the cousins appeared quite marked, but, after closer inspection, he could perceive several very discernible differences: Lady Jane's hair was, he decided, rather more liberally streaked with auburn tints, her large almond-shaped eyes were a little greener than her cousin's, the shapely mouth a little fuller; and there was most definitely a more distinctive aristocratic line to the nose. There was no denying that both had been blessed with delicate high cheekbones, and there was certainly a similarity in those softly rounded chins, but it would have been quite wrong, he decided finally, to suggest that they were alike as two peas in a pod.

When the rendition came to an end both ladies, refusing all entreaties to perform again, moved away from the instrument to permit another of the female guests to display her musical talents. Elizabeth was on the point of steering her cousin in the direction of a footman, who was bearing several glasses of wine on a silver tray, when she noticed her good friend the doctor heading in their direction.

At any other time it might have occurred to Elizabeth to wonder why her friend, who could never be described as a sociable animal, should actively seek an introduction to an aristocratic young lady with whom, on the surface at least, he couldn't possibly have anything in common. He had seemed quite indifferent to the several young ladies she had brought to his notice during the past three years, in the hope that one might capture his interest and persuade him to venture down the matrimonial path, and all her well-meaning efforts had been in vain.

She had come to the conclusion that Dr Carrington belonged to that group of unfathomable males who from birth were destined to remain confirmed bachelors, and she only hoped, after making the introductions and moving away to mingle with her other guests, that for once in his life Tom could manage to control the provocative side of his nature and behave like a perfect gentleman. But she didn't hold out much hope.

Unaware of the slight concern her relative was experiencing on her behalf, Jane withdrew her hand from fingers that were strong and yet surprisingly gentle, and found herself being closely scrutinised by a pair of thickly lashed and rather penetrating grey eyes.

Somewhere in the recesses of her mind memory stirred, and she vaguely recalled being told about a doctor for whom Elizabeth had a warm regard. 'Am I right in thinking that you and my cousin have known each other for some considerable time, Dr Carrington?' she asked, in an attempt to break the uncomfortable silence which followed their hostess's departure.

'Yes, we have, ma'am,' he responded in the most attractive deep, throaty voice. 'We lived together in Bristol for several years before she married Richard.'

Jane blinked up at him, wondering if he realised

just what might have been inferred from that admission. She knew enough about her cousin's upbringing to be certain that nothing untoward had occurred between Elizabeth and this young doctor, and only innate good breeding prevented her from bursting out laughing at such a verbal blunder.

'Er—yes. I recall now that my cousin went to live with her maternal grandmother shortly after her father died. I assume, Dr Carrington, that you must have resided there also?'

Tom regarded her much as he might have done some half-witted child. 'Didn't I just say so?' he remarked, in a voice betraying slight impatience, and Jane, unaccustomed to being spoken to in such a fashion, experienced a rare spasm of irritation.

'No, sir. You did not. In fact, you almost made it sound as if you and my cousin—' Only just managing to check herself in time, she didn't know whether to feel amused or piqued at the ease with which she had nearly been led into uttering something so indecorous. 'Yes, yes, of course you did,' she finished in some confusion, not knowing quite what to think of her cousin's friend.

In this, at least, they were in perfect accord, for Tom most certainly didn't know what to make of her. She was undeniably strikingly lovely, but that, he very much feared, was all she had to commend her. There had been a great deal of inbreeding over the years in these old aristocratic families, which had led to the inevitable, tragic consequences. It was common knowledge that many mansions dotted about the land possessed a secret, well-locked room where a family member was hidden away from prying eyes. He wouldn't suggest for a moment that Lady Jane might end her days by being kept firmly under restraint, but from their short conversation so far he suspected that there wasn't very much in her upper works.

'How long do you intend staying here with the Knightleys?' he asked, deciding it might be wise to keep their conversation, brief though he intended it to be, on simple topics.

'Until mid-March. Then I shall be journeying on to Bath.' Jane was of a similar mind—much better to converse only on mundane subjects. 'I do enjoy travelling about this land of ours, don't you, sir?'

'I can take it or leave it,' he returned dampeningly. 'But I hardly think this season, when the weather can be so confoundedly unpredictable, is the best time to go careering about the country, ma'am. Damned foolish if you ask me!'

It was as much as Jane could do to stop herself from gasping at such impudence! How dared this person presume to censure her actions? Never before could she recall experiencing such a surge of animosity towards a virtual stranger, and almost felt a sense of relief when she noticed the Dowager Lady Pentecost crossing the room in their direction.

'Ah! So you are becoming acquainted with the good doctor, Jane, my dear,' remarked the Dowager, whose reputation as a vicious tabby had been well earned. 'He has made something of a name for himself in these parts.'

As an ill-mannered bore, no doubt, Jane thought nastily. But years of being schooled in polite behaviour could not be so easily forgotten, and she satisfied herself by responding with honeyed sweetness, 'And, no doubt, it is well deserved.'

Tom's eyes narrowed fractionally, but the Dowager

detected nothing amiss and her thin-lipped mouth twisted into that falsely ingratiating smile which had always managed to set Jane's small white teeth on edge.

'I assure you, dearest Jane, that one hears nothing but excellent reports about him wherever one visits in the locale.'

'You exaggerate, ma'am,' Tom countered, his tone making it abundantly obvious, to one of his listeners, at least, that either he was bored with the topic of conversation, or far from enamoured with the company in which he now found himself.

'If it wasn't for the fact that Clarence Fieldhouse, another very worthy physician in the area, has been our family doctor for many years,' Lady Pentecost went on, just as though he hadn't spoken, 'I would have no hesitation in calling upon Dr Carrington's services.' Once again the tight-lipped mouth curled into its unpleasant smile. 'However, unlike many others you see here tonight, Jane, I believe in remaining loyal to those who have served my family well.'

'I applaud your sentiments, ma'am,' Tom took the opportunity to say as she paused for breath. 'Loyalty is always to be commended. So long as it is not mistaken for bigoted idolatry.' And with that, and the briefest of nods, he swung round on his heels, leaving the Dowager almost quivering with indignation, and the Earl of Eastbury's youngest daughter still not knowing quite what to make of him.

For a few moments Jane studied his elegant, long-striding gait as he headed across the room in their host's direction, and was unable to suppress a grudging half-smile of admiration. Dr Carrington might be abrupt to the point of rudeness, but one couldn't help admiring someone with sufficient pluck not to balk at indulging in a verbal battle with the formidable Lady Pentecost—and, furthermore, coming out the clear victor after one rapier-tongued gibe. Yes, he had certainly risen in her estimation, she was forced to admit, although whether or not that was sufficient reason for her even to consider liking him a little was quite another matter.

Chapter Two

'How wonderful to see you up and about so early, Jane,' was Lady Knightley's pleasant greeting as her cousin, bright-eyed and impeccably groomed as always, entered the breakfast parlour the following morning. 'I trust you slept well, and have fully recovered from the rigours of yesterday? Both Richard and I thought you were utterly splendid remaining downstairs with us throughout the entire evening.'

Slanting a faintly mocking glance at her cousin, Jane seated herself opposite, wondering as she did so whether living for such long periods in the country might not be having some adverse effect on her cousin's mental powers.

'My dear Elizabeth, a day's journey by carriage and attending a party which ended just after midnight is hardly likely to overtax such a hardened socialite as myself who, I might remind you, is quite accustomed to retiring as late as four in the morning.'

Elizabeth couldn't help smiling at this. 'Yes, I do tend to forget that your lifestyle is vastly different from my own,' she admitted wryly. 'I really don't know where you get your energy from, my dear. I find a fortnight in the capital more than enough, and cannot wait to return to the peace and quiet of the country to recuperate.'

Reaching for the coffee-pot, Elizabeth poured her cousin a cup of the freshly made brew. She had been granted little opportunity for private conversation the previous evening, her duties as hostess having kept her fully occupied, and, although she was very well aware that Jane had absolutely no difficulty in mixing with strangers, she could not help wondering how her impeccably mannered cousin had coped with one or two of the guests.

Curiosity got the better of her and she found herself saying, 'I'm certain you must have found some of those present last night rather peculiar characters, to say the least, Dr Carrington to name but one. He's a particular friend of ours, but I know his manner can be—well—a little odd at times.'

Years of practice held her in good stead, and Jane succeeded without much difficulty in suppressing a rather wicked smile before refreshing herself from the contents of her cup. Odd was hardly how she would have described him. Downright rude was much nearer the mark! But in view of the fact that the doctor was a close friend of the family's she refrained from speaking her mind, and merely made some vague response, before tactfully changing the subject by politely requesting the loan of a mount in order to explore the estate.

The morning looked set to remain dry and the unfamiliar countryside beckoned. Nevertheless, knowing that Elizabeth was eager to display the youngest members of the Knightley family, Jane paid the first of what was destined to be many visits to the nursery during her stay. Consequently, quite some time had elapsed before she returned to her bedchamber in order to change into her riding-habit so that she might indulge in her favourite form of exercise.

As she had no intention of riding beyond the estate, Jane dispensed with the services of a groom and set off across the park in the direction of the home wood. Although it was cold, with a biting wind sweeping the country from the east, the sky was virtually cloudless and the weak February sun was doing its best to brighten the landscape. There was no denying, though, that parks, no matter how grand, never looked their best at this time of year, and Sir Richard's acres were no exception. Trees still bare of their greenery could hardly be described as an awe-inspiring sight, and the few evergreens doing their best to add splashes of colour didn't improve the woodland setting enough to increase her desire to explore the area in any great depth.

She had just encouraged Elizabeth's mare to cross a shallow brook, choked with twigs and decaying leaves, and was on the point of turning onto a track which would eventually lead, she hoped, to a different part of the estate, when she distinctly heard a trill of feminine laughter, quickly followed by a deeper masculine rumble.

Apparently she wasn't the only one out exploring the woods that morning, she mused. In all probability it was nothing more sinister than a pair of innocent locals taking advantage of a short-cut across Sir Richard's land. Many of the country folk living in the village near her father's estate did precisely the same thing, and they never did any harm. Her father certainly didn't object to his lands being used for such a purpose and she doubted very much that Richard, kind-hearted soul that he was, would object either.

In any event, she had absolutely no intention of playing the informant, and was about to be on her way, when she distinctly heard a very familiar voice exclaim, 'Oh, Hetta! You do say the drollest things!'

The next instant Lord Pentecost, accompanied by a lady whose slender form was swathed in a voluminous grey cloak, appeared from behind a dense clump of pine trees. Leading their mounts, and deep in conversation, they seemed oblivious to Jane's presence, and for a few moments she was able to observe them undetected. She was a little too far away to see their expressions clearly, but any fool could tell by the bursts of spontaneous laughter that floated across in the air that they were very much at ease in each other's company.

Feeling suddenly intrusive, and yet knowing that she couldn't possibly go on her way without being observed, Jane decided to delay no longer in making her presence known. Digging her heel into the mare's flank, she rode slowly towards the happy couple, eventually attracting her childhood friend's attention.

'Why, Janie! What a delightful surprise!'

Lord Pentecost certainly sounded genuinely pleased to see her, but Jane experienced the uneasy feeling that he would have been far happier if their paths had not crossed. She had no wish to force her company on her friend and his companion if they preferred to be alone, but at the same time felt that it would appear abominably rude if she went on her way again without exchanging a few pleasantries first. So, kicking her foot free of the stirrup, she slipped to the ground and covered the last few yards on foot, noticing as she did so that her friend was scanning the area of wood behind her rather keenly, as though he was expecting to see someone lurking behind a tree.

'Out and about on your own, Janie?' At her nod of confirmation, he seemed to relax slightly and did not delay in introducing her to his companion, Miss Henrietta Dilbey.

Jane found herself being regarded very warmly by a pair of soft brown eyes before a tiny hand reached out to capture hers. 'Perry mentioned earlier that you were staying with the Knightleys. He has talked of you so often that I was hoping we should meet during your visit.' The greeting, spoken in a soft and pleasantly mellow voice, sounded sincerely meant, and Jane found herself instantly drawn to Lord Pentecost's charming companion. 'The one thing he didn't tell me, though,' she went on, releasing her gentle clasp, 'was how very pretty you are.'

Jane could quite easily have returned the compliment. A dainty creature of below average height, Miss Dilbey possessed the most delicately featured elfin face, framed with a riot of bouncy chestnut curls. At first glance she appeared little more than a child, but the directness of her gaze and her dignified, self-assured air gave Jane every reason to suppose that they were quite possibly much the same age.

'Hetta came to live in the area several months ago,' Lord Pentecost remarked, drawing Jane's attention to his fine aristocratic features and bright golden locks.

No two people could have complemented each other more, she decided. Perry, lean and of moderate height, possessed a shoulder perfectly situated for the diminutive Miss Dilbey to rest her head, should the notion ever take her.

'Yes, I recall my cousin remarking on it yesterday evening, Perry,' Jane responded, turning her attention once again to his companion. 'You reside, I understand, with your uncle, Miss Dilbey?'

'Yes. He very kindly invited me to live with him after my mother passed away last year...' her sweet, bow-shaped mouth curled into a tender little smile '...although insisted would be more accurate, I suppose. He decided that I had endured sufficient hardship because of what he termed my father's folly and my mother's stubborn pride, and would not hear of me finding a position as a governess or paid companion.'

'Papa was a dear man, my lady,' she went on to explain as they began to walk slowly onwards, leading their mounts, 'but was not very wise when it came to business matters. Mama was a proud woman and refused all offers of help after Papa died. She sold our lovely home in order to pay off outstanding debts and we were forced to take rented accommodation. We could no longer afford the luxury of servants, and it was only by exercising the strictest economy that we managed to get by.'

'I think you are quite remarkable to remain so cheerful after all that has happened to you,' Perry announced, regarding Miss Dilbey with evident respect, but the lady would have none of it.

'Nonsense, Perry! I have been more fortunate than most. Many gently bred females are forced to find some genteel occupation in order to live, but I have been blessed with a kindly uncle. He spoils me quite dreadfully, and I'm ashamed to say I like it very much.'

Jane experienced more than a twinge of admiration

for the down-to-earth Miss Dilbey, too, and couldn't help wondering whether she would have remained quite so cheerfully resigned to her fate if she had suddenly found herself in a similar situation.

No, she didn't think so, she decided, after giving the matter a moment's consideration, and feeling more than just a little ashamed of herself. Through no fault of her own, Henrietta Dilbey's circumstances had been much reduced after her father's demise, and yet she had, it appeared, remained cheerful, accepting her lot with good grace—whereas she, Lady Jane Beresford, the daughter of a wealthy peer of the realm, having always been able to demand every comfort and luxury, had been for some considerable time completely dissatisfied with her life.

Really, it wasn't shame she ought to be feeling, but disgust, she thought, trying desperately to shake off her sudden feeling of despondency. What on earth was the matter with her? She had everything money could buy, so why was she experiencing, increasingly, these moods of utter discontentment? What was it that she wanted, expected from life that she didn't already have?

Successfully suppressing a heartfelt sigh, she forced herself back to the present, and began to notice how completely relaxed her childhood friend appeared. She couldn't ever recall hearing Perry converse with quite so much confidence. All at once he seemed an entirely different person—quite the self-assured gentleman and blissfully contented with life. But she swiftly came to realise that it was merely a façade.

'I'm afraid this is where I must leave you both,' he said as they emerged from the wood onto a narrow road. 'I promised Mama that I would escort her on a visit to a neighbour, so I had better not be late, otherwise I'll only receive one of her scolds. I would very much appreciate it, Janie,' he went on, turning to look directly at her, 'if you wouldn't mention meeting with me this morning. Mama would be sure to hear about it, and then I would be subjected to an inquisition each time I wished to go out, with her demanding to know where I was going and whom I intended to see.' He sighed. 'I have few pleasures in life, and should like to retain the ones I have for as long as possible, you see.'

Jane most definitely did not see—not at all; but she gave him her assurances, none the less, before he mounted his horse and rode away in the direction of his estate.

'You look slightly disapproving,' Henrietta remarked, smiling faintly. 'And if it's the sight of Perry, a fine horseman by anyone's standards, mounted on that deplorable slug, I cannot say I'm surprised. If I had my way that would be the first of many changes I would make, and encourage him to purchase a mount more worthy of his capabilities.'

Jane, in fact, hadn't noticed his mount, but now that her attention had been drawn to the beast she couldn't help but agree. 'But the unsuitability of his mount was not what was perplexing me, Miss Dilbey,' she freely admitted. 'It was why Perry should imagine that his mother could dictate how he should go on.'

There was a moment's silence before Henrietta said, 'I should have thought that you, having been acquainted with the family for many years, would have been in a better position to answer that than I, my lady. I have lived in the area not much above six months, and have met Lady Pentecost on very few occasions, but even I have come to the conclusion that she is a most unpleasant and domineering woman.'

'Well, yes. She's always been that,' Jane responded with a dismissive wave of her hand. 'But Perry's no longer a child. He's all but reached the age of four-and-twenty…master in his own home, surely?'

'Is he, my lady?'

There was something in Miss Dilbey's suddenly hard, almost disgusted expression that sent a shiver of apprehension feathering its way down the length of Jane's spine, so when her companion suggested that they ride for a while she didn't hesitate for a moment. Evidently Henrietta was privy to certain information concerning the young Lord Pentecost, and Jane was still sufficiently interested in the welfare of her childhood friend to try to discover just precisely what was causing him so much disquiet. She wasn't left in ignorance for long.

'I never met Perry's father,' Henrietta began. 'He died a few months before I came to live with my uncle, but common report would have me believe that he was very like his son, shy and retiring, preferring the solitude of his library to paying calls on friends and neighbours, although he was, by all accounts, a frequent visitor to my uncle's home. According to Uncle Silas, the late Lord Pentecost played an excellent game of chess. Perry is like him in that way, too.' She paused for a moment to stare straight ahead, before surprising Jane by asking how much she knew about the Pentecost family's history.

'Not very much, I'm afraid. Perry's father married

quite late in life. He'd turned forty. Lady Pentecost was not precisely just out of the schoolroom, either, but she did, by all accounts, come to the marriage with a substantial dowry, which went some way, I suppose, to compensate for her unfortunately domineering nature.'

Miss Dilbey betrayed her rather mischievous sense of humour by chuckling at this wicked observation, but then became serious again. 'Have you ever heard mention of insanity in Perry's family? Am I correct in thinking that the late Lord Pentecost's brother died a lunatic?'

'Perry's father did have a brother, certainly,' Jane concurred, but with a mild look of surprise. 'I do know that he died young, but I cannot recall ever hearing that he was insane.' She cast Miss Dilbey a searching glance. 'Who told you such a thing?'

'Perry himself. But I'm not certain who told him,' Henrietta admitted. 'And, of course, it is the great fear that he may succumb to madness himself that is causing him such mental anguish. Today he was in a rare cheerful mood, my lady, but I have seen him in such despair that he can hardly bring himself to utter a single word.'

For several moments Jane was too stunned even to speak, her mind a whirl of discordant thoughts. 'But Perry isn't mad, merely shy—unsure of himself.'

Henrietta nodded in agreement. 'And it is hardly surprising in the circumstances,' she remarked, the light of battle suddenly flashing in the depths of her attractive brown eyes. 'How could one expect the poor man to be self-assured and decisive when throughout his life he has been under the influence of his mother, a dictatorial creature who, I do not doubt, has continuously ridiculed his every action and criticised his every word? And his father has done little to improve his son's lot. What on earth possessed him to make such a ridiculous will?'

Jane had been staring straight ahead down the unfamiliar lane, digesting everything that was being said, but the reference to the late Lord Pentecost, who, she was very well aware, had been very fond of his sole offspring, drew her head round.

'I cannot believe he disinherited Perry. Besides, the estate must have been entailed.'

'Oh, yes. The land and title are Perry's, right enough, but he is unable to touch so much as a penny of his father's private wealth until he attains his thirtieth birthday, or in the event that he marries.' Miss Dilbey's expression clearly betrayed her deep concern. 'From what Perry tells me, I understand that his choice of wife will not be his alone. He must marry a female of good birth, and then only with his mother's full approval, in order to attain his inheritance.'

A sigh escaped her. 'One must suppose, in view of the fact that he was very fond of his son, that the late Lord Pentecost acted out of the purest of motives, but he certainly did his son no favours by insisting that Lady Pentecost must give her consent to any marriage.'

'No, indeed,' Jane agreed, clearly seeing now her childhood friend's unfortunate predicament, and cast a thoughtful glance in her companion's direction. 'You show a deal of concern for Perry's welfare, Miss Dilbey. You are obviously very fond of him.'

'Yes, I am,' she freely admitted, 'but I'm trying

desperately to be sensible and not to allow my regard to deepen.'

Jane had already come to the conclusion that Henrietta, for all her diminutive size, was not one to boggle at plain speaking, and therefore didn't hesitate to say, 'Because you believe Perry's choice would not find favour in his mother's eyes?'

Henrietta's spontaneous gurgle of laughter was answer enough, even before she said, 'As I've already mentioned, Lady Pentecost and I have found ourselves in each other's company on very few occasions, but already we have had—how shall I phrase it?—differences of opinion. The Dilbey family is an old and respected one, but even if I were an heiress I still do not believe I would find favour in her eyes, simply because I am not a cowering female whom she could dominate.'

Although she didn't doubt Henrietta's sincerity for a moment, Jane found the latter observation rather perplexing. After all, a marriage between Perry and herself had once been fervently hoped for, and Jane would hardly have described her own disposition as pliant—although, she supposed, she would have more than met Lady Pentecost's high ideals in every other respect.

Her eyes narrowed as she tried to recall that occasion, nearly two years ago, when her mother, during a quiet evening at the ancestral home, had suggested a union between the two families. After Jane's blunt refusal ever to consider such a thing, the subject had never once been raised again.

She didn't doubt for a moment that the Countess had passed on her daughter's sentiments. But, surely, if Lady Pentecost had truly desired the match, she wouldn't have accepted defeat so easily? Now that she came to consider the matter, something about the whole business just didn't ring true. Perhaps it had not been Lady Pentecost who had desired the match, but her husband, in failing health, who had wished to see his son suitably married.

'So, you believe Lady Pentecost hopes for a daughter-in-law whom she could dominate, as she does her son?'

'There are times, certainly, when I think just that, but then at others…' Henrietta shook her head, looking and sounding genuinely perplexed. 'There is a very wealthy family by the name of Boddington living not far from here whose eldest daughter, Louisa, is both pretty and biddable—admirably suitable for Perry's wife, you might think, and yet I cannot in all honesty say that I have witnessed or heard anything to suggest that Lady Pentecost is desirous of a match between them. In fact, I have been present on two occasions when she has said something intentionally derogatory, it seemed to me, about her son, which only succeeded in showing Perry in a very poor light.

'Truth to tell, I don't know how that scheming woman's mind works. I wouldn't be in the least surprised, though, to discover that she doesn't wish her son ever to marry. After all, she rules the roost at Pentecost Grange. And as long as Perry remains a bachelor she will continue to enjoy her comfortable existence.'

She gave a sudden whoop of laughter. 'Oh, dear, would you listen to me? I'm getting as bad as Perry with all my suspicions. He's certain the servants at the Grange spy on him. I don't know whether this is true or not, but I do know that Lady Pentecost pensioned off many of the older servants shortly after her husband's demise, and had the audacity to replace them with persons of entirely her own choosing.'

Knowing only too well how autocratic the Dowager Lady Pentecost could be, Jane was not in the least surprised by this snippet of information. 'Oh, she did, did she?'

'I'm afraid so. And from what Perry tells me they are completely loyal to her. It must be dreadful living in that house, fearing that your every movement is being watched. It is little wonder he asked you not to mention seeing him. He must cherish his moments of freedom away from the place, and those ever watchful eyes.'

'But that is just it, Miss Dilbey—he isn't ever free. He's shackled to his mother by the will his father made and by his own dark fears.... Yet shackles, Miss Dilbey, can be broken.'

Jane was silent for several thoughtful moments before she enquired, 'Has Perry discussed his concerns over his health with anyone else? With his doctor, perhaps?'

'I'm not certain, but he may well have done so. Unfortunately, Dr Fieldhouse is a particular friend of his mother's. So, if Perry did consult him, I would imagine that the Dowager is very well aware of the fact.' Henrietta's sigh was clearly one of exasperation. 'I do wish Perry would seek Dr Carrington's services. Unlike Dr Fieldhouse, Thomas Carrington is highly respected in these parts.'

'So I have been led to infer,' Jane responded, with such a decided lack of interest that Henrietta, always sensitive to a person's sudden change in mood, looked at the Earl's daughter sharply.

'Was the good doctor amongst those at Lady Knightley's dinner-party yesterday evening, by any chance?'

Jane's far from approving look spoke volumes, and Henrietta frankly laughed. 'Oh, dear. Evidently he didn't make a very favourable impression. He's my uncle's physician, so I have come into contact with him on several occasions. His manner can be a little curt at times, but I don't dislike that. He's a plain-spoken man, but a trustworthy one, and a very fine doctor.'

'That, too, I have been led to infer,' Jane responded with a grudging half-smile as she focused her attention on the road ahead. Then, returning to their former topic of conversation, she said, 'As a rule I'm not one to interfere in matters that do not directly concern me, but Perry's a friend of mine, and I couldn't with a clear conscience turn my back on him when he's quite obviously in need of support. And you've certainly told me enough to make me feel decidedly uneasy about several matters concerning him.

'I think the first thing to be done is to try to discover more about Cedric Pentecost. Although Perry must be certain that his uncle was insane, I'm not convinced at all, for I feel sure I would have learned about it. I don't expect it will be an easy task uncovering the truth. Cedric Pentecost has been dead for a number of years, but there are surely some people still living in the district who must remember him?'

Henrietta nodded in agreement. 'I thought of doing precisely the same thing, only I decided it would appear rather odd if a virtual stranger started asking questions about someone who had been dead for more than a quarter of a century. Besides which, Perry told me all that he did in the strictest confidence. The last thing in the world I want is to start spreading rumours. The poor man has enough to contend with without people gossiping about him behind his back.'

'Well, quite! Be assured, though, that I shall be discretion itself,' Jane pledged. 'However, if you've no objection, it might be wise to take the Knightleys into our confidence. My cousin Elizabeth is no fool, and she has a fondness for Perry.' She didn't add that Sir Richard did not think quite so highly of the young baron, but even he, she felt certain, could be persuaded to discover what he could about Perry's uncle.

They had by this time ridden some considerable distance. Richard's wood had been left far behind, and they were surrounded by open fields. Henrietta, drawing her mount to a halt as they arrived at a crossroads, turned to Jane with an apologetic smile.

'This, I'm afraid, is where we must part company. I'm sorry I've taken up so much of your time this morning. You must think it most odd that a complete stranger should confide in you in such a way, but I've been at my wits' end, just not knowing what to do for the best. It really was a godsend your coming here.'

'Do not build up your hopes, Miss Dilbey. I'm not certain that there is very much I can do to help, though I shall certainly pay a call at the Grange, and try if I can to have some private conversation with Perry.' She glanced about her at the unfamiliar countryside. 'You, however, are in a position to help me by disclosing the quickest way back to Knightley Hall. Needless to say, I haven't a clue where I am.'

Henrietta obliged, and soon afterwards they parted company, with Jane setting off in the opposite direction. She had ridden no more than a couple of hundred yards when she became aware of her mount's slight limp. Kicking her foot free of the stirrup, she slipped to the ground. The shoe appeared to be intact, but it was clear that something was wrong. So she decided to make things more comfortable for the animal by leading the mare across a field which, if Miss Dilbey's directions turned out to be accurate, ought to bring her out on the road leading to Knightley Hall's main gateway.

Keeping half an eye on the mare, to ensure that the discomfort was not worsening, she set off across the pasture, her mind dwelling on the unenviable situation in which her friend Perry now found himself. So deep in thought did she become that she failed to notice that the middle of the field was absolutely peppered with rabbit holes, until the inevitable happened and she suddenly found herself in an inelegant heap on the damp grass.

It was only when, cursing her clumsiness, she tried to rise to her feet again that she realised she had not come through the unfortunate episode unscathed. Her right ankle began to throb painfully, and by the time she had reached the road on the far side of the field she was finding each step an excruciating effort.

A milestone set in the grass verge made a convenient resting-place while she considered her plight. Knightley Hall's main entrance couldn't be that far away, she felt certain, but it was pointless shying away from the fact that it wouldn't be an easy task getting there. She was just debating whether to press on, regardless of the pain, or stay precisely where she was in the vain hope that Richard, who had gone out early that morning to the small market town nearby, might come bowling along the lane in the very near future, when she detected the distinctive sound of hoof-beats.

Horse and rider were a little too far away for her to see them clearly, but she felt sure that, although it was most certainly a tall and powerfully built man, it wasn't Richard, who, according to Elizabeth, had gone out in his curricle. It certainly wasn't advisable to accost complete strangers in isolated spots, yet there were occasions when the strict rules of conduct governing the behaviour of young, unmarried females were best ignored. And this was definitely one of them, she decided, as the traveller drew steadily nearer, and she realised with a feeling of relief that the gentleman astride the sturdy cob was not a complete stranger after all.

'Good morning, Dr Carrington,' she said hurriedly as he doffed his hat in acknowledgement, and she experienced the dreadful suspicion that he had every intention of simply riding by and leaving her to her own devices. 'I'm afraid I've been rather foolish, and am in need of your help.'

Drawing the gelding to a halt, he at last dismounted and regarded her healthy complexion in silence for several moments. 'What seems to be the trouble, ma'am?' he enquired, with such a marked lack of interest that it was on the tip of her tongue to tell him not to bother to concern himself and be on his way, but sense prevailed.

'I've hurt my right ankle. I'm certain it's only sprained, but it is rather painful,' she explained, managing to control her rising ire at his continued, impassive regard. 'Elizabeth's mare developed a limp, and so I decided to walk her across the field back to the Hall. Unfortunately my foot managed to find its way into a rabbit hole.'

With a decidedly unsympathetic air, he knelt down in front of her and began to loosen the laces of her right boot. 'It would appear that you and Elizabeth's mount are well matched.' He tutted. 'A pair of right clumsy fillies!'

Totally unaccustomed to receiving even the mildest insult, Jane was momentarily lost for words, and by the time she had formulated something cutting to say in response to the far from accurate observation the doctor's attention was fully occupied in trying to remove her calf-boot. So, she merely contented herself with casting him a frosty glare which went completely unnoticed. However, she was forced to concede that, although Dr Carrington's manners were acerbic in the extreme, his touch could not have been gentler as he examined the injured ankle.

'Yes, it's only sprained,' he confirmed, 'but you're going to need to rest it as much as possible for the next couple of days.' He did take the trouble to glance up at her then, and could easily detect the glint of disapproval in the lovely grey-green eyes, and assumed this stemmed from pique at being forced to remain housebound.

For some perverse reason, for he certainly didn't consider himself a vindictive person, Tom gained a deal of wicked satisfaction from the knowledge that her freedom would be drastically curtailed, if only for a short period. Like most members of her social class, she was undoubtedly accustomed to doing precisely as she chose, when she chose, and he didn't consider that it would do her a mite of harm to learn that she could not have everything her own way all the time.

If nothing else, it would teach the pampered little madam to look where she was putting her feet from now on, he mused, successfully suppressing a smug grin as he turned his attention to her mount.

'Like yourself, she's not badly injured,' he remarked, after raising the mare's foreleg to examine the hoof. 'There's a stone wedged in there. Unfortunately I've nothing about me to prise it out—' his impatient sigh was quite audible '—so it looks as if I'll be put to the trouble of escorting you back to the Hall myself.'

Put to the trouble…? Jane could hardly believe she had heard correctly. Why, it was tantamount to telling her that she was nothing more than a confounded nuisance!

She felt her hackles rise, a rare experience for her, and couldn't resist saying, in retaliation, 'Please do not put yourself out on my account, Dr Carrington. I'm certain I shall manage to hobble back… eventually.'

'I dare say you could,' he agreed, with infuriating calm, 'but it would show a marked lack of good sense, not to mention a sad want of conduct, for you to make the attempt, in view of the fact that I've been kind enough to offer my services, don't you agree?'

In rapidly mounting frustration, Jane allowed him to help her to her feet, and was in the process of deciding whether he was being deliberately provoking, or was merely too dull-witted to recognise sarcasm, when he further confounded her by lifting her effortlessly high in the air. She experienced a fleeting moment of sheer helplessness before being settled on the cob's back, and was astonished to discover that she didn't dislike the sensation in the least.

'For heaven's sake relax, girl!' Tom admonished in his usual forthright manner as he eased himself into the saddle behind her, and slid one arm about her trim waist in order to grip the reins, while stretching out with the other to grasp those of Elizabeth's mare. 'You're perfectly safe. I'll not let you fall.'

The assurance did little to ease those strangely disturbing sensations rippling through her. Thomas Carrington might well be a pillar of the community and a much respected physician, but Jane found it impossible to see him in that comforting light when his strong, muscular leg was resting against her thigh and his broad expanse of chest was pressed so firmly against her slender back that she was almost too frightened to breathe lest he detect the loud thudding of her heart. There was no doubt about it—he certainly belonged to that most intriguing of species: the dangerously attractive, all-powerful male—domineering, menacing and most definitely best avoided.

Although Jane's pulse remained annoyingly erratic throughout the mercifully short ride back to the Hall, at least the embarrassed hue had faded from her cheeks, and she accepted with real gratitude the doctor's supporting arm as she limped towards the house.

'Is your mistress at home, Medway?' Tom enquired when they finally stepped into the front hall.

'Yes, sir. She's in the nursery,' the butler responded, casting the Earl's daughter a look of sympathy.

'In that case be good enough to lead the way to Lady Jane's bedchamber, and then go along and inform your mistress that her cousin has met with a slight accident.'

Evidently believing her incapable of walking further, and allowing her no say in the matter, anyway, Tom swept her into his arms and went striding up the stairs in the butler's wake. Although Jane was slender, with little or no superfluous fat on her anywhere, the feat could not have been an easy one, and yet she noticed that he wasn't even breathing particularly heavily when he entered the bedchamber and placed her down on the very comfortable bed.

She refrained from comment when he calmly deposited himself down beside her, and once again eased her foot gently out of the calf-boot, but when, without so much as a by-your-leave, he raised her skirts and attempted to roll down her stocking she decided his liberty-taking had gone quite far enough.

'Don't be ridiculous, girl!' he admonished, slapping her restraining hand away none too gently. 'I'm a physician, and quite accustomed to seeing bared limbs every day of the week.'

'Be that as it may, Dr Carrington, but I really think my maid or Elizabeth ought to be present while you carry out your examination,' she argued, in a vain attempt to bring to his attention the gross impropriety of the situation.

'I don't doubt one or the other will be here presently,' he responded, secretly amused by this becoming display of maidenly modesty, even though it was completely wasted on him. 'In the meantime let me assure you that your virtue is quite safe. I'm not in the habit of ravishing innocent young damsels—at least, not in the forenoon, or when I'm carrying out my duties as a practitioner, that is.'

By the flashing look of annoyance she cast him, it was evident that she was unaccustomed to being teased, but whatever response she might have made was held in check by the sudden appearance of the lady of the house, who swept into the room demanding to know what had occurred.

'Thank heavens you happened along, Tom!' Elizabeth remarked with real gratitude when she had been regaled with the short list of her cousin's misfortunes. 'The poor girl might have been stranded there for hours. It isn't a particularly well-used road.'

This timely reminder that she hadn't even been gracious enough to offer her own thanks pricked Jane's conscience. She was on the point of rectifying this sad lapse in good manners when her rescuer succeeded in destroying any feelings of gratitude she might have felt.

'Yes, most opportune!' he said. 'But is the chit appreciative…? No, not a whit! I was forced to endure a stony silence throughout the entire ride back here, and since our arrival she's been glowering at me like an infuriated kitten. There's ingratitude for you! Why, it's enough to destroy the good Samaritan in any upstanding citizen.'

Succeeding yet again in curbing a smile at the fulminating glance he received, Tom rose from the bed. 'Have a cold compress put on that ankle, Elizabeth. It isn't a particularly bad sprain, but she'll need to rest it for a couple of days. Besides,' he added, as his parting shot, 'a couple of days in bed will do her the world of good. Give her the opportunity to study a book on civility.'

Jane had been hard-pressed to contain her temper since first meeting up with him, and never more so than now. 'Well, really!' she exclaimed the instant he had left the room. 'He has the cursed impudence to suggest that I need to read a book on etiquette!'

Never before could she recall feeling so exasperated with anyone, and for the first time ever did not attempt to conceal her feelings of ill-usage. 'He may be a friend of yours, Elizabeth, but I shall take leave to inform you that he is the most ill-mannered creature it has ever been my misfortune to encounter!' she announced, giving full rein to her temper, and was then further incensed when her cousin's only response was to dissolve into whoops of laughter.

Chapter Three

Tom contemplated the flickering shadows on the low ceiling of the bedchamber before transferring his gaze to the woman lying silently beside him. Her glossy dark brown locks, framing her face, were in some disorder, and her eyes were closed, but he sensed that she wasn't asleep.

After their pleasurable activities between the sheets, the bedcovers, not surprisingly, had become entangled and seemed to have knotted themselves around the swell of her hips. She made no attempt to cover herself, but then, why should she? She had nothing of which to be ashamed. She was a fine figure of a woman by any standards: full-bosomed and curvaceous. She had bared her charms for him on too many occasions during the past couple of years or so for her to feel the least self-conscious of her nakedness in his presence. There was no denying that she had made an excellent mistress, both passionate and loyal, but after what she had disclosed this night there was no way that their mutually satisfying liaison could continue.

A sigh escaped him. Poor Margaret, a young

widow with a son to raise, certainly hadn't enjoyed an easy life, though she had, he supposed, been more fortunate than many of her class. Squire Dilbey, a good-hearted man with rigid principles, had not evicted her from this cottage when her husband had died, as many other members of the landed gentry would undoubtedly have done, but had allowed her to remain, and at a reduced rent.

Tom recollected clearly that it had been in his capacity as a physician that he had first come into contact with the very attractive young widow. Margaret had been left very low after a particularly virulent bout of influenza and her young son, Ben, naturally anxious over his mother's weakened state, had walked the four miles to Melcham to seek the doctor's help, a luxury they could ill afford. Ben had paid off the debt by doing odd jobs at Tom's rented house. Even at the young age of eleven, Ben had proved himself a good little worker, and Tom had continued to employ him ever since to help around the house and tend the small garden.

That, too, he supposed, would cease in the very near future, if Margaret went ahead and married the blacksmith. It would certainly benefit her son if she did. The blacksmith, a widower with two young daughters, certainly needed a woman about the place. Ben would benefit from learning a good trade, and his mother would no longer be forced to work those long hours, sewing by the light of a candle in order to put some food on the table.

Tom looked down at her again with a touch of regret in his eyes. Margaret Ryan was certainly no whore, but he supposed he had treated her as such during these past years, visiting this cottage whenever the mood had taken him, and paying for his pleasures by depositing some coins on the dresser before he had left each time. Fond of her though he was, as far as he was concerned their long association had been little more than a business transaction, and there was no denying that she had been grateful for the extra money. Perhaps he had been selfish to use her in such a way, but nothing, he told himself, could be changed by suffering pangs of conscience now.

Swinging his feet to the floor, he quickly scrambled into his discarded clothes and went almost silently over to the door. Force of habit sent his hand into his coat pocket to draw out his purse, but then he checked himself, remembering clearly her request.

'This time just for love,' she had said, before pressing her full, rounded breasts against his chest and drawing him down onto the bed. He doubted very much that the passionate interlude which had followed had very much to do with that emotion—not on his side, at least—but he would not insult whatever feeling she might have experienced by paying for his pleasures this time, and quietly he left her, knowing instinctively that she wanted no words of farewell.

Wrapping his cloak more tightly about him against the frosty evening air, he collected his mount from the small stable, and took one final glance back at the cottage as he made slowly for home.

There was no doubt in his mind that he would miss Margaret Ryan, but if it was the security of marriage she now felt she needed, then he wouldn't selfishly try to stand in her way. After all, there could never be any question of a marriage between them. Without doubt she had the power to satisfy him physically, though certainly not mentally, or in any deeply emotional way. But then, he reminded himself, no female had ever ignited that elusive, loving tenderness in his breast, not even Elizabeth whom he had always cared for above any other woman.

He arrived at the road leading to Knightley Hall, and instinctively drew his mount to a halt, recalling clearly the chance encounter with Elizabeth's cousin that morning. How he had ruffled that aristocratic little madam's feathers! That dagger-look she had cast him before he had left the bedchamber still had the power to amuse him even now. Unless he mistook the matter, there was a great deal of fire beneath that ice-cool reserve of hers—a great deal more to that young woman than mere physical beauty, he decided, with a complete turnabout of his former opinion. She, he didn't doubt for a moment, could certainly stimulate him mentally.

Although he had been careful not to show it, the prickly little darling already attracted him physically, but he was sensible enough to realise that there would be little point in getting to know her better. She was as far above his touch as…as he was above Margaret's.

God, how he hated this class distinction! It placed insurmountable barriers between people, but there was little point in trying to pretend that it didn't exist. Lady Jane Beresford belonged to the cream of aristocracy, whereas he, in her eyes, was no doubt nothing more than a struggling country practitioner, worthy of a polite exchange of pleasantries, but little more. No, there was no future in trying to get to know the lovely Lady Jane better. And it might prove dangerous for his peace of mind, he decided, urging his mount homewards, for him to try to do so.

* * *

The following day Jane was relieved when Dr Carrington did not pay a return visit to the Hall and see how her injury was progressing. The ankle remained badly swollen, and Elizabeth was all for summoning her friend back, but Jane wouldn't hear of it, declaring that it would be a waste of the doctor's time, and that the swelling would subside if she rested.

Perversely, though, during her second day in bed, she began to feel piqued that Dr Carrington hadn't been sufficiently interested in her well-being even to send a note to inquire how she went on, but put these feelings of irritation down to the fact that she was already heartily sick of the forced confinement.

Thankfully, by the third day she deemed her ankle sufficiently recovered to risk a venture out of doors. Her two days of inactivity had given her ample opportunity to dwell on that very enlightening conversation with Miss Dilbey, and, although she didn't doubt for a moment Henrietta's sincerity and genuine concern, Jane still felt the need to talk to Perry first, before committing herself to doing anything on his behalf. Not that she thought there was very much she could do by herself, but for the time being, at least, she decided it would be wisest to keep her own counsel, and not to confess her feelings of unease to others.

Consequently, Jane left the Hall without informing either her host or hostess where she was bound. Evidently Richard held her in no way responsible for the slight injury to his wife's mare, deeming it an unfortunate occurrence that could have happened to any rider, and raised not the smallest objection to her borrowing one of his prized geldings. He did, however, insist that this time she took the sensible precaution of being accompanied by a groom. This was an edict that proved very beneficial, for the young stable-lad had been born and bred in the area, and was able to escort her to her destination in very good time.

Since Perry had usually visited them, it had been eight years since Jane had accompanied her mother on her one and only short visit to Pentecost Grange. In truth, she had no very clear recollections of her stay, but had to own as she entered the grounds that the moderately sized Restoration mansion, set in its acres of open parkland, was very pleasing to the eye. Any woman would be more than content to be mistress of such a fine house. If Lady Pentecost was, indeed, very reluctant to relinquish her position to another, then no one could blame her for that—providing, of course, that she didn't resort to underhanded stratagems to retain her position which would be detrimental to her son.

Still doing her level best to keep an open mind, Jane approached the front entrance and was admitted by a small, shifty-eyed individual in a suit of black cloth, who she presumed was the butler. If he turned out to be one of those servants recently employed by Lady Pentecost, Jane could quite understand Perry's unease, for on first impressions she wouldn't trust the man an inch.

'Is your master at home?' she enquired, taking a moment to gaze about her before looking back at the servant to discover a most disrespectful expression on his thin, sharp-featured face.

'And which master would that be, miss?' was his eventual surly response.

All Jane's proud aristocratic breeding came to the fore and she cast her eyes over him in a glance of such icy contempt that he visibly blanched. 'You would do well to keep a civil tongue in your head when you address me, my good man. Now, inform Lord Pentecost at once that Lady Jane Beresford is here to see him!'

'The young master is not at home at present,' he responded, sickeningly obsequious now, 'but the mistress is receiving in the drawing-room.'

Jane hardly gave him time to announce her before she swept regally past into the room. She took a moment to cast a quick glance at the gentleman sprawled at his ease in the chair by the hearth, for all the world as though he owned the place, before turning her attention to the formidable matron seated on the sofa.

'Why, my dear! What an unexpected pleasure!'

'Unexpected, ma'am?' Jane quizzed, very much on her guard. 'You must surely realise that Mama would not be best pleased if I was not courteous enough to pay one of her oldest friends a visit whilst I was residing so close by.'

Lady Pentecost appeared highly delighted by the explanation, so it was perhaps just as well that she didn't realise that Jane considered her mother somewhat unwise when it came to her choice of friends. Jane's expression, however, gave nothing away, nor did she betray her utter contempt for Sir Willoughby Wentworth when at last he managed to ease his massive bulk out of the chair in order to take her hand in an over-familiar grasp.

'You know my brother, of course. He's staying with us for a short while.'

'Yes, we've met before on several occasions, ma'am,' Jane responded, successfully withdrawing her hand from the obese baronet's podgy-fingered grasp before accepting the invitation to sit on the sofa.

'And we have another guest staying with us for a few days,' Lady Pentecost informed her, with an infuriatingly self-satisfied smile. 'The Honourable Simon Fairfax called unexpectedly yesterday to offer his belated condolences on my husband's sad demise. He was journeying to Bristol to stay with friends, but I managed to persuade him to remain with us for a few days. And he's promised to return to us next month to attend my spring ball. I do trust that you will still be here, dear Jane. I should be most disappointed if you were to return to Kent and not honour us with your presence. My little spring gathering is considered quite an event hereabouts.'

'I'm not returning to Kent, but shall be journeying on to Bath to stay with my aunt, Lady Templehurst, for a while. I shall be delighted to attend.' Whether she gained much pleasure from the event remained to be seen, but she realised that it was to her advantage to see as much of Perry as possible in order to gain a clear idea of what kind of life he was leading here at the Grange. 'And shall you be remaining here for your sister's party, Sir Willoughby?'

'Oh, aye, aye! Must lend my support. Play the host, don't you see?'

'No, sir. I'm afraid I do not see.' Jane raised her finely arched brows in exaggerated surprise. 'Surely, as master of this house, that role falls to Perry?'

'Well, ordinarily, of course it would.' Lady Pentecost hurriedly intervened. 'But I'm afraid dear Perry hasn't been himself of late, almost permanently locked in a world of his own. Surely you observed that at the Knightleys' dinner-party the other evening?

It would be quite heartless of me to expect him to host such a large party, when his uncle has very kindly offered his services.'

So, Henrietta had certainly not been fanciful when she had suggested that all was not as it should be here at the Grange. How very cunning the odious Lady Pentecost was to feign consideration for her son as her reason for not wishing him to take his rightful place at her side during the forthcoming event. Whereas, if the truth be known, the real reason was possibly an attempt to undermine further his position as master of this house. After all, it would show Perry in a very poor light if he were to appear unequal to the task of playing host at his own spring ball. And hadn't Henrietta suggested that Lady Pentecost seemed to revel in making her son appear inadequate in front of others?

Jane's eyes narrowed speculatively as she glanced in the formidable Dowager's direction. Perhaps it just might be possible to persuade Lady Pentecost that she wouldn't be precisely basking in approval, either, if it was seen that her son's role had been taken by another. Social position was all-important to her, and this, Jane realised with lightning clarity, might just prove to be the chink in the formidable lady's armour.

'I certainly did perceive a difference in him, ma'am. But—' she shrugged '—it was only to be expected in the circumstances. Some people take longer to get over a bereavement than others. His father's death was a great loss to him, as you above anyone else should know.'

'Indeed, yes,' Lady Pentecost agreed, if a touch warily. 'And it is simply because he is not himself that I feel it would be grossly unfair to expect him to host my spring ball.'

The possessive *my* did not go unnoticed, but Jane wisely chose to ignore it. 'Your consideration does you great credit, ma'am, and it is only natural that you should wish to protect your son.' She took a significant moment to glance at the wall behind Lady Pentecost at a very fine portrait by Sir Joshua Reynolds of a former mistress of the Grange. 'Unfortunately there are those in Society who would not view your actions in that very commendable light.'

'I'm afraid I do not perfectly understand you,' Lady Pentecost responded, visibly bristling. 'I think you must explain precisely what you mean.'

'Oh, come, ma'am! You must recall, surely, the way the Dowager Lady Merrivale insisted that her son host her ball the year before last. The Viscount, like Perry, is not fond of large social gatherings. But at least Perry does not stammer! It cannot be denied that the young Viscount's speech impediment caused some merriment during the proceedings, but the general consensus of opinion was that the Dowager was quite right in persuading her son to do his duty. And that was far more of an ordeal for the young Viscount than Perry shall be forced to endure. Lady Merrivale's ball was, after all, held during the height of the Season with five hundred guests present, not a small country affair where one is surrounded by friends and neighbours.'

She waited a moment for Lady Pentecost to digest fully what had been said, before adding, 'Nevertheless, knowing Perry as I do, I doubt he will relish the prospect, but better that he make the attempt than relinquish the role to another, and have malicious rumours circulating that you were too selfish a mother to offer him your support.'

It was quite evident by Lady Pentecost's suddenly thoughtful expression that she had not considered this possibility, but Jane was sensible enough to realise that it would be unwise to expound on the topic further and thereby risk arousing suspicions in that far-from-obtuse lady's mind. She was, therefore, heartily thankful when an interruption occurred, and she turned her head to see Perry, accompanied by the strikingly handsome Simon Fairfax, enter the room.

'Hello, Janie. How nice to see you again!'

'I thought it time I paid a visit to the Grange. And I did have a particular reason for wishing to see you, Perry.'

She rose from the sofa and, without enlightening him further, offered her hand to the blond-haired, blue-eyed Adonis standing beside him. Many considered Mr Fairfax the most handsome man on the social scene by far, and there was no denying that he was well favoured in both face and form. His address was polished and his appearance was always faultless, but for some obscure reason that Jane herself had never been able to understand she had never quite liked him. Nevertheless, her innate good manners came to the fore and she betrayed none of her slight reservations about him as she politely enquired after his parents.

'They are both quite well, my lady, although I did suspect that my father was about to succumb to one of his frequent bouts of gout.' His teeth flashed in a sportive smile. 'Consequently, I decided to make myself scarce by paying a visit to some friends of mine residing near Bristol. My father is not at his best at such times.'

'And I am so glad you decided to visit us here,' Lady Pentecost put in, looking remarkably well pleased at having such a handsome gentleman residing with them, if only for a few days.

'I could not pass so close by without enquiring how you go on, ma'am, and offering my belated personal condolences on your loss.'

Although Lady Pentecost appeared to find nothing amiss in these disclosures, Jane most certainly did. Perry's father had died almost a year ago. Wasn't it leaving it rather late to express one's sympathy now? Added to which, the Fairfax estate was situated in Berkshire, and the main post road from London to the west of the country was more than twenty miles' distance from Pentecost Grange. Simon Fairfax had hardly been passing close by if his intention had been to visit Bristol.

'Did you say you wished to see me?' Perry asked, breaking into Jane's puzzled thoughts.

'Oh, yes, I did.' She cast him a bright, wickedly impish smile. 'Sir Richard happened to mention over breakfast this morning that he might be selling one of his hacks, and I instantly thought of you and wondered whether you might be interested?'

'It isn't the grey, is it, Janie?' he asked, with all the excited interest of a schoolboy.

'Yes, it is, as it happens.'

'Oh, by Jove! He's a prime un!'

'Very likely,' his mother put in with a decidedly disapproving sniff. 'Sir Richard, as we all know, is quite renowned for the horseflesh he keeps. But I hardly think you are in need of a further mount.'

Jane didn't know which irritated her more—Lady Pentecost's lofty assumption that her word was law, or Perry's submissive attitude to his mother's every whim. By his crestfallen expression it was plain that he wouldn't even attempt to force the issue, but Jane was made of sterner stuff.

'What a pity! You would have looked as fine as fivepence on that grey, Perry. Although…' she paused to affect a puzzled expression '…Sir Richard did seem disinclined to offer the animal to you.'

The grossly false admission had the desired effect and Lady Pentecost's chin rose sharply. 'And why, pray, did he seem reluctant?'

'Well, ma'am, for some obscure reason he didn't seem to think Perry was up to handling the gelding.'

'What!' Sir Willoughby, looking positively indignant, eased his large bulk upright in the chair. 'You may tell Sir Richard from me that if he thinks that about the boy then he's far out. My nephew has his faults, plenty of 'em. But I'll give the lad his due— he's got a fine seat on a horse.' He turned his disapproving gaze in his sister's direction. 'This is what comes, Sophia, of keeping rubbishing job horses in your stable. You could at least see the boy was decently mounted!'

'It wouldn't hurt, surely, just to take a look at the grey?' Mr Fairfax remarked suavely, breaking the silence which followed the baronet's unexpected outburst. 'I certainly wouldn't object to casting my eyes over Sir Richard's cattle.'

Lady Pentecost, admitting defeat with bad grace, announced pettishly that Peregrine might do as he liked, and Jane would have felt extremely grateful to Simon Fairfax for his support if she hadn't gained the distinct impression by the look he cast her that he, at least, was perfectly well aware of what she had been about.

'That's settled, then!' Unable to hold that penetrating, blue-eyed gaze, she turned to her friend. 'It is time I was on my way, Perry. I'll tell Sir Richard to expect you in the morning.'

Delaying only for the time it took to make her farewells and to secure Perry's escort to the stables, Jane left the uncomfortable atmosphere of the drawing-room, almost sighing with relief as she stepped outside the house.

'I don't think you were being perfectly truthful back there, Janie, were you?'

'About what, Perry?' she enquired, all wide-eyed innocence.

'About Sir Richard. You see, he let me try that grey of his a few months back, when we met up by chance along one of the lanes. He told me I handled the horse very well.'

'No, I wasn't being truthful,' she admitted at last. 'But it turned the trick, did it not?'

'Oh, aye! That's why I never said anything at the time. Thought it might work. You see, Mama doesn't care what she says about me herself, but she doesn't like it when she discovers that others have been saying unflattering things about the family.'

Jane cast him a look of approval. No, there really wasn't much wrong with his understanding. She then changed the subject by remarking on his mother's evident delight at having Mr Fairfax under their roof.

Perry's sudden frown betrayed his feelings clearly enough, even before he said, 'Don't like the fellow very much, Janie. Although I've been acquainted with him for several years, he's never been what I'd call a particular friend.' He shook his head. 'Dashed odd the way he turned up that way. Suppose he must have had his reasons for visiting, but I don't believe for a moment that it was because he wished to offer his condolences over my father's death. Dashed smoky, if you ask me! Wish Mama hadn't asked him to stay.'

No, Perry certainly wasn't the fool many people took him for. It was just a pity that he didn't exert his authority a little more, Jane decided, and echoed her thoughts aloud.

'Not much point in doing so really,' was his rather lethargic response, and she experienced more than just a twinge of annoyance of his apathy.

'Oh, for heaven's sake, Perry! You are master of this fine estate, and it's high time you accepted the responsibility. You're more than capable of running this place, and making your own decisions. You know you are.'

'Yes, I do know. Trouble is, though, I might start to enjoy it too much, and then when the time came for me to give it up…'

As his soft voice trailed away, Jane looked at him closely and reached out her hand to touch his arm as she quickly discerned the look of helpless desolation in his kindly eyes. She realised she would be betraying the fact that Henrietta had confided in her, but felt she had little choice, and said, 'Perry, you surely don't truly believe there is something wrong with you mentally, do you? Why, it's preposterous!'

'Is it, Janie? I suspect you certainly thought so at one time, otherwise why did you flatly refuse to entertain the notion of a marriage between us?' There was a decidedly quizzical lift to his left brow. 'Oh, yes, I heard all about it. Mama told me.'

Jane realised that little would be gained by trying to deny it and, quickly deciding that attack was her best form of defence, gave him back look for look. 'Well, don't try to pretend that you were not mighty pleased that I did quash the idea. You've admitted yourself that you look upon me as the closest thing you've ever had to a sister. Why, we virtually grew up together. How on earth could I possibly view you in the light of a prospective husband? I never have, and I never shall. But that does not mean that I have ever suspected that there is something wrong with you mentally. I can only wonder at your mother putting such a ridiculous notion into your head!'

'It wasn't Mama… It was my father.'

'Your—your father?' Jane was stunned. 'When did he tell you? What did he tell you?'

'It was a few days before he died,' Perry answered, his eyes firmly fixed on his acres of rolling parkland. 'He said he was very concerned about me because I reminded him so much of his brother. I'd never heard him talk about Uncle Cedric before, so it came as a very great shock to me. He said that it was a blessing that he died when he did, because he feared he would have had to be placed in an asylum.'

'But, Perry, that doesn't mean that your father considered you might end the same way,' Jane rushed to assure him. 'Remember your father was very ill when he told you this and, maybe, was a little confused himself.' She searched wildly for something else to say—anything which might put his mind at rest. 'Have you discussed this with anyone else?'

'I told Hetta, of course. It was she who told you, wasn't it?'

Jane nodded, not attempting to deny the fact.

'Mama confirmed it was true, but said I wasn't to worry…said that she would always look after me.'

Yes, I just bet she did! Jane thought angrily, certain now that Henrietta's suspicion that the Dowager was taking advantage of the situation was well founded.

'I spoke to Dr Fieldhouse, too, some months ago,' Perry added.

'And what did he say?'

'He told me that I had been a weak child who had suffered from convulsions—and an overheated brain.'

'Well, and what of it? Many small children are similarly afflicted. It doesn't presuppose that they will go mad in later years.'

'Perhaps not,' he conceded. 'But you cannot deny, Janie, if you're honest, that I'm not perfectly normal. Mama is forever telling me so. I never feel easy in the company of strangers. I become ridiculously tongue-tied and always manage to say the wrong things.'

Jane couldn't forbear from smiling at this. 'Believe me, Perry, you are certainly not unique in that. Practice at small talk is all that is required to overcome that particular difficulty. And you know yourself that you behave completely differently when in the company of friends. There is no trying to get away from the fact that you are, basically, a very reserved person, but that doesn't mean there is anything seriously amiss with you mentally.'

Jane did her best to reassure him further as they continued their stroll towards the stables, but this was no easy task when a seed of doubt had been sown in her own mind. Had it been Lady Pentecost who had initially enlightened him about his uncle, Jane would certainly have suspected some ulterior motive and dismissed the revelation out of hand. However, the late Lord Pentecost was an entirely different matter. He had been touchingly fond of his sole offspring, and would never have said or done anything deliberately to hurt him.

It might well be, as she had suggested, that Perry's father had been confused in his mind during his final days. Nevertheless, as she had told Henrietta Dilbey, she knew little of the Pentecost family history, and was even more ignorant on the complex subject of insanity. But for the sake of her friend she was determined to discover all that she could about both!

Chapter Four

For a few seconds Tom ignored the rapping on the door and continued to study the notes on his desk. Then he remembered that his housekeeper had stepped out to take a few provisions to a sick old lady living nearby, and hadn't returned as yet.

There were times when the door-knocker was never still, but he would far rather not have a moment to himself, seeing an endless stream of patients, than sit idly twiddling his thumbs, his skills as a physician wasted simply because the vast majority couldn't afford a doctor's fees. He had made it a policy never to press for payment and this custom had certainly been beneficial to the poor folk of Melcham and those living in the surrounding area who were, now, not afraid to call on his services. It was true that payments were not always prompt, nor were they always paid in the coin of the realm; it was not uncommon for him to discover the odd rabbit or game bird, or even a sack of vegetables, on his doorstep.

Wondering who, or what, might be awaiting him this time, he opened the door, and instantly recognised, by the lustrous russet-coloured curls peeking be-

neath the rim of the elegant beaver hat, precisely who
had surprisingly called, even before she drew her attention away from the busy main street and turned to
face him.

'Why, Lady Jane! This is an unexpected pleasure!'
He moved to one side, allowing her to enter the narrow passageway, and noticed at once the slight limp
as she made her way into his consulting-room. 'Your
ankle is still giving you some trouble, I see.'

'What…? Oh, no, not really. I suppose I've exercised it rather more than I should today. No, that isn't
why I'm here,' she explained, seating herself on the
chair placed by the desk. 'Although it does remind
me that I owe you payment for your services, Dr Carrington.'

He sat down behind his desk and regarded her in
silence for a long moment, suddenly wondering why
it was that he found it virtually impossible to view
her in the light of a patient. There was no denying
the fact that she was an exceptionally lovely young
woman, but he had treated scores of pretty females
during his professional career, and had never found
the least difficulty in viewing any one of them as just
another being in need of his professional help. So
what was it about this young woman that set her quite
apart from all the rest?

'I believe I mentioned that I experienced the whim
to play the good Samaritan that morning. There will
be no charge.'

'Very generous of you, Dr Carrington. However,
unlike so many, I can afford to pay and would prefer
to do so,' she responded, wondering why he was regarding her in that peculiar and most disconcerting
way—his gaze so intense, it seemed as though he was

continually assessing her. It was impossible to know precisely what he was thinking, but she guessed by the slight narrowing of his penetrating grey eyes that her last remark had not pleased him overmuch.

'You see, I find I'm in need of your help again, Doctor, and it would be quite wrong of me to expect all your services to be free of charge,' she continued, in an attempt to placate him. Whether she had succeeded in her aim was difficult to judge, so she decided it might be wise to come straight to the point of her visit. 'How knowledgeable are you on the subject of insanity? Have you come across many cases during your professional career?'

She couldn't have astounded him more if she had just confessed to being a man. It crossed his mind to wonder whether she might not be indulging in some mischievous prank in retribution for his rather uncalled-for remarks the other day, but he doubted whether such a refined, aristocratic young lady would demean herself by resorting to such tactics. Besides which, those lovely eyes of hers, never wavering for a second, gazed across the desk at him in all seriousness, betraying, if anything, only a deep-seated concern.

'During my training in London I did undertake to visit one or two asylums housing the mentally unbalanced, certainly. I have come across the rare case during my professional career, and have seen many examples of the natural deterioration of the brain in the elderly, but I have no specialised knowledge on the subject of mental illness, save that I could recognise certain, very obvious symptoms.'

The deeply worried look did not diminish, and he experienced the most overwhelming desire to comfort her, to reassure her that she had nothing whatsoever to fear, but without knowing specifically what was troubling her his well-meaning intentions might do more harm than good.

'What, precisely, is concerning you, my lady? Have you been suffering from severe headaches of late? Have you, perhaps, suddenly found yourself in a place and had no notion how you got there? Do you hear voices, or see strange visions?'

For a few moments Jane was too stunned to speak and it took a monumental effort to stop herself from gaping across the desk at him. The implication of his impertinent questions was abundantly clear: he had the temerity to suppose that she was here on her own account. Never before had she been so insulted, and only her genuine concern for Perry prevented her from informing the presumptuous individual seated opposite precisely what she thought about him.

'We appear to be at cross purposes, Dr Carrington,' she told him with careful restraint. 'My unease of mind, if I may phrase it so, is not on my own account. Perhaps it might save further misunderstandings if I asked the questions.'

Amused by the all too evident resentment at what he considered his quite natural assumption, and experiencing a grudging regard for her praiseworthy self-control, he decided that the more he saw of Lady Jane Beresford, the more he liked her. He suspected that deep down she was a very restful young woman, who would be as happy sitting quietly by a fireside, plying her needle or reading a book, as she would be attending the grandest ball. He suspected, too, that she possessed hidden depths, hitherto untouched, and experienced a strangely powerful desire to be the one to peel away all those layers of highly polished aristocratic reserve and reveal to the world the real essence of the woman beneath.

Leaning back against the chair, he gave her his full attention, more than willing to satisfy her curiosity by answering any questions she might pose, but before she could even open that delectable mouth of hers to commence her inquisition there was a thunderous pounding, as though someone was trying to kick down his front door.

Jane, understandably startled, watched in some concern as the doctor stalked from the room. She could only assume that the perpetrator of the clamorous interruption was either inebriated, or in desperate need of help. A hurried exchange of voices filtered down the passageway, before Dr Carrington came striding back into the room, followed by a huge giant of a man, who must have stood easily six feet six in his stockinged feet, holding an injured youth in his massive arms.

Her presence having been forgotten completely, Jane rose from the chair, uncertain what to do. In the circumstances it wasn't likely that the doctor would be free to give her his attention for some time, and she wondered whether she ought not to slip quietly away, yet hesitated in doing so if there was a chance she could be of some help.

Calling over his shoulder, Tom requested a basin of water and some clean towels. He had addressed himself to the burly individual, who had removed his misshapen hat and now stood twisting it nervously round and round in his large, work-roughened hands. However, one look at the man's sickly pallor was sufficient to inform Jane, at least, that for all his great strength his constitution was weak when it came to the sight of blood.

'Why not take a seat?' she urged him, indicating the chair she herself had just vacated, and he cast her a look of real gratitude. 'You sit there whilst I get the basin. No doubt Dr Carrington will wish to ask you some questions.'

Having no idea of the layout of the house, Jane took a minute or two to locate the spacious kitchen. She managed to find the items she needed without any difficulty, and as luck would have it there was a clean apron lying over the back of one of the chairs. Remaining only for the time it took to remove her hat and jacket and roll up the sleeves of her silk blouse, she slipped the apron over her head, and then quickly returned to the consulting-room.

'Where did you find him, Sam?' she was in time to hear Dr Carrington ask.

'On the Pentecost estate. I were out there in the cart delivering some work I'd finished doing for 'em. Young Ben 'ere had been lying in the woods there all night, seemingly. It were lucky he managed to crawl as far as the road, otherwise I'd never 'ave seen 'im.'

'You young fool!' Tom growled, addressing himself to the boy whose face was contorted in agony after the removal of his boot. 'You're damned lucky it was Sam who found you and not the gamekeeper.'

Placing the bowl and the clean towels down on the table by the doctor's elbow, Jane looked down at the badly torn flesh on the boy's right leg, and knew without being told what device must have caused the injury. Her father was very much against the use of mantraps. He would not entertain the employment of such evil devices anywhere on his land, and, now that Jane was seeing for the first time the results of re-sorting to such inhuman poaching deterrents, she could well understand her father's staunch opposition.

'You're lucky, young Ben, that the trap was faulty and didn't spring fully closed!' Tom announced, after he had washed away some of the blood, and could see better the extent of the injuries. 'Otherwise your ankle would have been crushed. As it is, it's still a damnable mess!'

Jane felt sorry for the boy, who could not, she guessed, have been much above thirteen. He was re-ceiving scant sympathy from the good doctor, and perhaps he really didn't deserve very much. There was little doubt in her mind that Ben had foolishly been breaking the law during the night, even though the dreaded word 'poaching' had been avoided being mentioned thus far.

'Is there no one who ought to be informed about what has occurred?' she asked, and received a strange look from Tom, who seemed suddenly to be aware of her continued presence, before he glanced briefly over his shoulder.

'Yes, I suppose Margaret had best be told without delay. Would you see to that, Sam? Try not to alarm her. The ankle isn't broken, but I'd like to keep him here for a few days to keep an eye on it.'

'Aye, I'll do that, Dr Carrington.' The huge man eased his large bulk up from the chair and went across to the door. 'I've a mind to take m' belt to the young varmint for the needless worry he'll cause 'is dear ma.'

'Loath though I am to deny you, my friend, that pleasure I intend shall be mine!' Tom announced, casting the boy a look which boded ill for him once his injuries had healed.

'It—it's the fust time I ever done it, Dr Carrington,' was Ben's nervous response as Sam's heavy footsteps could be heard retreating down the passageway. 'And I only went along for a lark.'

'I'll fetch some fresh water.' Jane hurriedly picked up the bowl and tactfully left the room before Tom gave vent to the wrath all too obviously bubbling up inside him. By the time she returned poor Ben looked decidedly chastened, and she could only guess at the peal which had been rung over him. 'Is there anything else you need?'

'There are some rolled-up bandages in that drawer over there,' Tom responded, nodding in the direction of a tall cabinet. 'You'll find some laudanum in the cupboard, and will you also bring me that bottle on the far right on the bottom shelf?'

Once the injury had been cleaned, and the leg bandaged up, Tom carried the boy out of the room. Jane could hear the sound of his footsteps above as she tidied the consulting-room and returned the bowl and soiled towels to the kitchen. She had just rolled down her sleeves and was about to put on her jacket when Tom came striding into the kitchen, his face as black and forbidding as a thundercloud.

'Now you've seen, firsthand, the needless suffering your class seem to delight in causing, Lady Jane Beresford! That boy was damned lucky not to lose part of his leg. I've been forced to amputate more than once before.' He ran impatient fingers through his thick, slightly waving hair, while his eyes, hardened by biting resentment, swept over her in a look of undisguised contempt. 'It might so easily have been yet another young life ruined, and for what…? Stealing some paltry rabbit or pheasant. I hope you feel damned proud of yourself and your rapacious kind!'

Never before had Jane met with such open hostility. It seemed almost as if he hated the very ground she walked upon, but she knew this couldn't possibly be true. What harm had she ever done him, after all? His wrath over the boy's injury was understandable, but why was he venting his anger on her? She desperately wanted to defend herself, to try to explain that not all people of her social class were insensitive to the suffering of those less fortunate than themselves, but her throat was suddenly numb and the words refused to come.

Whatever else he might have hurled at her, unjustified or not, was destined to remain unspoken, for the door-knocker could be heard again, and he swung round on his heels, leaving her prey to a maelstrom of conflicting emotions, not least of which were anger and a deep feeling of hurt.

With hands that were far from steady, she reached for her hat and went out into the passageway in time to see him wrapped in an attractive woman's arms. He was doing his best to comfort her with reassuring words, spoken in a voice totally at variance with the one he had used only moments before. Jane guessed that the woman was the injured boy's mother, and her evident distress was only natural, but she sensed a familiarity between them, an almost lover-like intimacy.

They passed by her without a word, and mounted the stairs, but Jane had no intention of awaiting the doctor's return and let herself quietly out of the house. Hurt and anger still gnawed deep inside her, but these feelings were overshadowed by the sudden surge of a quite different emotion, one she had never experienced before and one which she feared to name.

By the time Jane was dressing for dinner that evening she had managed to place the unfortunate events of the morning into perspective. She still felt profoundly hurt by Dr Carrington's verbal assault, but, being a young woman blessed with a great presence of mind, she refused to dwell on the unwarranted abuse, and had been able to concentrate her thoughts on the far more pressing problem of how best to help her friend Perry. There was no doubt in her mind at all now, after her visit to the Grange, that he was in dire need of someone's help.

'Yes, that will do very nicely, thank you, Latimer,' she remarked, after the last curl had been pinned into place. She studied her reflection for a moment, and then rose from the stool in order to collect her shawl.

'Oh, by the by, I had the unexpected pleasure of coming face to face with the son of your former employer. Apparently he's staying with the Pentecosts for a few days and should be riding over with Lord Pentecost tomorrow morning to look over one of Sir Richard's horses.'

As it was a rare feat, indeed, to raise any sort of response from the taciturn maid, Jane was rather surprised when Latimer immediately enquired, 'Tomorrow morning, did you say?'

'Yes, that's right.' Jane glanced across the room at her then, but rather too late to glimpse the sparkle which, for one unguarded moment, flickered in the maid's dark eyes, a strange mixture of euphoria and anticipation. 'Why? Were you hoping to see him?'

'Of course not, my lady.' Latimer looked flustered for a second or two, but quickly regained her composure. 'I—I cannot deny I was fond of him. Master Simon was always kind to me. He—he's such a thoughtful gentleman.'

'So I have been led to infer. I must confess, though, Latimer, this benevolent side to his character comes as a complete surprise to me. I've met him on numerous occasions in the past and had always considered him a young gentleman too busy in the pursuit of his own pleasures to give his fellow man more than a passing thought.'

A decidedly furtive glance was cast in her direction, but as Jane was busy arranging the shawl about her shoulders she missed this, too. 'Tidy up here, Latimer. I shan't need you again today.'

As her parents were highly social creatures, it was rare for Jane to sit down to dinner with less than a dozen people present. It made a pleasant change, therefore, to dine with just her host and hostess for company. The meal was delicious and Jane was tempted into sampling nearly all the varying dishes, but the conversation for the most part went over her head, with her answering any questions directed at her in monosyllables. Elizabeth exchanged a meaningful look with her husband, and because Richard was fond of his wife's young relative he didn't linger over the port, but joined the ladies in the drawing-room to take tea.

'Have you something on your mind, Jane?' he asked, coming straight to the point. 'You seemed in a world of your own during dinner.'

She smiled as she watched him take the seat opposite, touched by his genuine concern. 'Yes, I have,

Richard, and you may be able to help,' she told him, and at once had his full attention. 'What do you know about Perry's family? Were you well acquainted with his father?'

'Was anyone?' It seemed a glib response, yet there was nothing in his demeanour as he settled himself more comfortably in the chair to suggest that he was anything other than serious. 'He was a man who preferred his own company. He was amiable enough whenever our paths happened to cross, but he certainly wasn't a man for socialising very much. He always struck me as someone who would have been perfectly content to be a recluse.'

He had told her no more than she already knew herself, so Jane didn't dwell on his response, but went straight on to ask what he could tell her about the late Lord Pentecost's brother.

'Not very much, I'm afraid. He died young. I was still in short-coats at the time.' Richard frowned in an effort to remember. 'I believe he fell from his horse while riding over the estate. Don't think he ever regained consciousness.'

Jane didn't attempt to hide her astonishment. 'His death was a direct result of a riding accident?'

'Yes… Yes, I'm certain I'm right, but I don't recall all the details.' He regarded her keenly. 'Why the sudden interest, Jane?'

'Because Perry has been led to believe that his uncle died a lunatic, Richard. And he has this morbid fear that he, too, will succumb to madness.'

'Good gad!' Richard couldn't have looked more astonished. 'Well, it's the first I've heard of it. Although, if there was madness in one's family, one would certainly refrain from advertising the fact.'

'Well, quite!' Elizabeth agreed, before frowning heavily. 'But Perry isn't mad, merely very shy.'

'That is precisely what I think, Cousin. But if a person is told often enough that he isn't normal, it isn't inconceivable that he may one day come to believe it himself.'

Jane then went on to relate the disturbing conversation she had had with Perry that morning. 'Now, had it been Lady Pentecost who had told him about his uncle I would be inclined to dismiss the whole thing, but it wasn't. And I have a dreadful suspicion that she is playing on poor Perry's fears.'

'In what way?' Richard asked, pausing in the act of taking a pinch of snuff.

'Oh, I don't know,' Jane responded, feeling suddenly weary after the unpleasant events of the day. 'Perhaps I'm merely being fanciful because I don't like the woman and wouldn't trust her an inch. But I hadn't been at the Grange more than five minutes before she made a point of saying that Perry had been behaving rather strangely of late.'

'Now you mention it,' Elizabeth remarked, her frown returning, 'she said something very similar to me the other week when we came upon each other in Melcham.'

'From what I can gather she has remarked on her son's state of mind to several persons hereabouts. But that isn't all. That great barrel of blubber Sir Willoughby Wentworth is at present staying at the Grange. And looking for all the world as though he owns the place! But what really made me fume,' she went on, when her listeners had managed to control their mirth at her unflattering description of the baronet, 'was the way that odious woman had the sheer effrontery to suppose that she could forbid Perry from purchasing that grey of yours.

'Which reminds me, Richard. I owe you an apology,' she added, having the grace to look shamefaced. 'I'm afraid I intimated that you considered Perry unequal to handling the gelding—which was sufficient, of course, to force Lady Pentecost to do an abrupt about-face. Dear Perry, though, saw through my little stratagem at once.'

'Then he certainly isn't the slow-top most people take him for. But it really is up to him to be more assertive in his own home.'

'I know, Richard.' She sighed. 'Perry is by nature very easygoing. That doesn't mean I think him incapable of making decisions. On the contrary, I'm certain he could quite easily make a success of running that estate of his—it's whether or not he'll make the attempt. I very much fear that, while he has this dark cloud hanging over him concerning his late uncle's mental state, he's going to continue leaving everything in his mother's hands.'

'As Elizabeth will no doubt tell you, I never concern myself over other people's troubles,' Richard announced, after a moment's intense thought. 'But what I am prepared to do is talk to some of our older neighbours who might remember Perry's uncle. In the meantime, if you are determined to help your friend, you could do no better than consult Thomas Carrington. He, I don't doubt, will be able to answer any questions on the subject of mental health.'

'I had already considered that,' Jane confessed, looking and sounding decidedly nettled. 'I paid a call on him this morning, as it happens. Unfortunately my visit was not well timed and his attention was required elsewhere.'

She decided against enlightening them as to the events which had taken place at the doctor's house. Poaching was, after all, a serious crime, and she had no intention of spreading the story abroad and risk bringing more trouble to young Ben.

'I must say that I do not think your doctor friend improves on further acquaintance,' she remarked drily, forcing both Elizabeth and Richard to suppress smiles. 'However, for the sake of my friend, I suppose it behoves me to beard the lion in his den just one more time.'

Chapter Five

Although Jane had made it abundantly clear that she was far from enthusiastic at the prospect of making a return visit to the doctor's premises in Melcham, she was determined to do so, and directly after breakfast the following morning, with the same trusty young groom to accompany her, she set off in the direction of the small market town.

February was rapidly drawing to a close and the damp, depressing days which had plagued most of the month seemed to be a thing of the past. There had been a noticeable rise in temperature, too, during the latter half of the week, and, although Jane wouldn't have said that it was precisely mild for the time of year, the flora seemed to have responded to the degrees of extra warmth and wild primroses abounded everywhere.

From a very young age she had always taken a keen interest in her surroundings, and invariably discovered something whilst out and about to capture her notice, no matter where she happened to be, and today's venture abroad proved no exception. As they reached the outskirts of Melcham her attention was quickly drawn to a moderately sized house, which she had failed completely to observe the day before, her mind having still been dwelling on that most unpleasant interlude with Dr Carrington.

Drawing her mount to a halt, she peered through the high black railings that partially shielded the pleasant grounds from the busy street, and studied the charming dwelling that was constructed in the same warm, creamy-coloured stone as the Knightleys' Georgian mansion. It nowhere near approached the grandeur of Knightley Hall, but it was just the kind of house that would suit her very well.

She had been for some months seriously considering the possibility of setting up her own establishment. It wasn't that she didn't love her family dearly, because she most definitely did, but she couldn't deny the fact that she had little in common with her mother, whom she considered on occasions quite light-minded, and who never seemed completely happy unless she was presiding over a house full of guests—and the mere thought of making her home with one of her sisters was enough to send her into a decline. As the youngest member of the family, she was still looked upon as a child, and she found her sisters' over-protective attitude claustrophobic and their well-meaning but unsought advice faintly irritating.

In less than a month she would have attained her majority, and would be financially independent. She was very much looking forward to the freedom her substantial inheritance would give her, and a house like this one, large enough to invite guests to stay, but not so large as to make most of the rooms superfluous, would suit her admirably.

The curtains drawn across the ground-floor windows led her to suppose that the house was not occupied at the present time. She was just debating who might possibly own the charming property—a successful lawyer or prosperous merchant?—when out of the corner of her eye she glimpsed a tall figure striding along the road in her direction, and was astounded to discover that her heart, for some inexplicable reason, seemed to be trying to pound its way out of her chest.

'Why, Lady Jane!' Tom doffed his black beaver hat with all the practised ease of a Bond Street beau. 'It must have been fate that decreed we should meet up unexpectedly this way.'

Jane looked down from her horse at his ruggedly handsome and smiling countenance in some confusion. Really, he was a most disconcerting man! The last time he had spoken to her it had been with something akin to loathing in his voice, and yet here he was, not twenty-four hours later, looking and sounding genuinely delighted to see her. What an enigma the infuriating creature was, to be sure!

'Well, it so happens, Dr Carrington, that I was on my way to see you,' she told him, seeing no reason to deny the fact.

'Life is full of coincidence, is it not? I myself had every intention of paying you a visit today,' he further confounded her by confessing. 'And as the weather, too, appears to be favouring us, shall we make the most of it by enjoying a short stroll?'

As Jane could think of no earthly reason to refuse, she allowed him to assist her to the ground, and then watched as he turned to her groom who, for some reason best known to himself, was taking an active interest in the proceedings.

'Be good enough to take Lady Jane's mount to my home. I'm sure my housekeeper will be only too happy to furnish you with a tankard of ale and a slice of her delicious apple tart whilst you await our return.'

Thus dispensing with the groom's undesirable presence, Tom returned his attention to Jane, who was regarding him with a mixture of curiosity and suspicion. 'Yes, very well done of me, wasn't it? Now you can safely ring a peal over my head for the disgraceful way I behaved towards you yesterday, without anyone else listening.'

Jane was completely taken aback. It had certainly occurred to her that he must have a specific reason for desiring privacy, but never in her wildest imaginings had she supposed that his actions had stemmed from such unselfish motives. Evidently he had suffered pangs of conscience over his outburst and wished to make amends. She would not have supposed for a moment that this rudely abrupt individual, who had seemed from their very first meeting to delight in being deliberately provoking, was capable of such gallantry. Life was full of surprises!

Rapidly increasing confusion had an adverse effect on her natural poise. Falteringly, she made a less than lucid attempt to try to assure him that it had never for an instant crossed her mind to allude to that particular incident and that she harboured no ill will, but he cut in abruptly.

'Then you are being far more gracious than I have any right to deserve, ma'am!' His anger was all too evidently directed at himself. 'I was completely out of order! My boorish behaviour was totally inexcusable and I can only beg your forgiveness.'

This generous apology, spoken with such sincerity, touched her deeply. She had not infrequently bridled at his curt manner and less than gentlemanly behaviour, but for some inexplicable reason she attained no satisfaction whatsoever at seeing him standing before her, if not precisely humbled, then clearly betraying a disgust of himself.

'On the contrary, Dr Carrington, there was some excuse for your outburst,' she surprised even herself by responding. 'You were naturally concerned about that boy, who had been quite cruelly and needlessly injured. And over that, at least, we are in complete accord. I, like my father, abhor the use of mantraps and believe their use should be outlawed. But that does not mean I approve of poaching. The persons involved in such activities have scant regard for their victims. In most instances the animals suffer a protracted and painful death. And there are those who would say that the boy suffered no more than he deserved.'

'You, unless I much mistake the matter, are not amongst their number?'

He was looking at her so intently that she would have found it impossible to lie, even had she wished to do so. 'No,' she admitted, hardly aware that he was slipping her arm through his as they commenced their stroll. 'I am not.'

A sigh escaped her. 'Heaven knows, we've had our fair share of bad harvests already this century, Dr Carrington, and I for one could not blame a man for breaking the law in order to put some food in his children's bellies. Sadly, though, this frequently isn't the case. Throughout the length and breadth of the land organised gangs of poachers steal vast amounts of game, and not in order to feed their families, but merely for gain. Even so, I consider the penalties for such activities far too high, yet I can also sympathise with the many landowners who regularly have their stocks depleted.'

'Against all the odds, my lady, I am beginning to think that you and I have more in common than I would ever have believed possible.'

Jane was frankly startled by the softly spoken admission, and more so when she suddenly realised that they were strolling arm in arm, for all the world like a pair of lovers, along the private drive of the house she had been admiring a little earlier.

'Oh!' she muttered, growing quite pink with embarrassment as she quickly extricated herself from his gentle hold. Then, perversely female, promptly wished she had not done so, for there had been something highly comforting in the feel of the latent strength beneath the sleeve of that loose-fitting jacket. Never before could she recall being so acutely aware of the powerful aura a gentleman, well favoured in both face and figure, could exude, and felt attracted whilst at the same time faintly intimidated by it.

'Why are we here, Dr Carrington?' she asked, trying desperately to quell the strange sensation in the pit of her stomach which threatened to ripple its way through every part of her. 'You should have said that you were making a professional call, and I would willingly have awaited your return at your house.'

'Rest easy, ma'am. I am not here in any professional capacity, merely keeping an eye on the place in the absence of its owner, a friend of mine,' he explained, extracting a key from his pocket to unlock the front door. 'His mother had been ill for some time and passed away several months ago. Since her death, John has been travelling extensively throughout Europe. In his last letter he informed me that, although he intends returning to England in the spring, he has no intention of living here, as he owns a house in London, and wondered whether I would consider purchasing this property. He knows I've always liked the place.'

'Really?' Jane's ears pricked up at this. 'And are you going to buy it, Dr Carrington?'

'I cannot deny that I'm very tempted, and yet I keep asking myself whether I really need a house of this size, charming though it is. Come and take a look around,' he invited, throwing wide the door to allow her to step into a far from spacious but adequately sized hall. 'And whilst I take you on a guided tour you can tell me why you wished to see me today.'

Although it was hardly considered correct behaviour to enter an unoccupied abode with a gentleman who was a virtual stranger, it never entered Jane's head for a moment to demur. Not only did it grant her the chance to discuss her concerns with the doctor without fear of interruption, but it offered the golden opportunity to inspect a dwelling that she herself might well consider purchasing.

'I wished to continue the discussion we were having yesterday, before your time was taken up by more pressing matters.' She waited until he had thrown back the curtains to enable her to see the front parlour more clearly, before asking, 'How is the young lawbreaker who was responsible for bringing our conversation to an end yesterday progressing?'

'In some discomfort—which is no more than the damnable young fool deserves!' he growled, making not the least attempt to put a guard on his tongue in her presence. 'I still don't think he realises just how lucky he's been. If it hadn't been for Sam finding him, he might well have been dragged before the local magistrate by now with a prison sentence looming. I've been trying to drill into him that it wouldn't have mattered a whit to the authorities that he hadn't been actively poaching. Just his being there would have been sufficient to condemn him.'

He was still experiencing a deal of anger over Ben's escapade, but at least today he had his feelings well under control. Raising his eyes, he watched Jane move with all the fluid grace of a born dancer about the room, and was reminded yet again how grossly unfair he had been to vent his ill humour on her.

She had unselfishly done everything humanly possibly to help when Ben had been carried into the house, yet something inside him had snapped when he had walked back downstairs to the kitchen, and had seen her standing there, rolling down the sleeves of that expensive silk blouse before slipping her arms into the jacket of her stylish riding-habit. Why, that outfit alone would have kept a poor family adequately nourished for several weeks!

There was no denying the fact that Lady Jane Beresford epitomised everything he considered most unjust in society. She belonged to the class that had altogether too much of everything; she belonged to the class that unfairly governed this land, passing laws to protect their privileged positions to the detriment of the majority; she belonged to the selfish class that kept the poor downtrodden, forcing them to toil long and hard in order to eke out a meagre existence.

He wasn't so prejudiced that he wouldn't accept

that there were many just and caring members of the aristocracy, who wished for change and to see a fairer distribution of wealth—Richard, to name but one— but these, sadly, were definitely in the minority. A ruthless determination to retain their way of life at any cost was all that mattered to most of Lady Jane's kind. So why was it, he wondered, that he felt strangely drawn to this young woman? Was it merely a strong physical attraction he felt, or something far more profound?

Thrusting these rather disturbing thoughts aside, he tried to recall the gist of their conversation the previous day. 'If my memory serves me correctly you were experiencing some concern over the mental state of…a relative of yours, perhaps?'

'No, not a relative, Dr Carrington.' She hovered for a moment, uncertain, then decided only complete honesty would serve. 'I'm worried about a friend of mine, Lord Pentecost.'

She saw his dark brows suddenly snap together before he turned and led the way out of the room, and couldn't forbear to smile. 'I'm tolerably certain that Lord Pentecost is not precisely basking in the sunshine of your approval at the moment, but—'

'That's putting it mildly,' he interrupted, opening the door to a spacious drawing-room. 'Hardly surprising in view of what occurred yesterday.'

'Indeed, no. But I doubt Perry was responsible for having those inhuman contraptions placed on his land,' Jane responded, in defence of her friend, and without further ado went on to disclose Lord Peregrine's fears. 'And because he has been told that he is very like this uncle he is now convinced that he will end the same way.'

'If his uncle's condition was an isolated case, then I should say that was most unlikely.' As her concern for the young baron was abundantly obvious, he would dearly have liked to terminate the discussion on that optimistic note, but knew it would be an insult to her intelligence to do so. 'However, if there had been other instances in past generations, then I'm afraid there may be some cause for concern. Do you happen to know for a fact that any of his ancestors suffered a similar condition?'

'No, I'm afraid I don't know, and unfortunately I'm not really in a position to find out, either. I certainly wouldn't dream of asking his mother,' she confided, looking and sounding decidedly hostile. 'I have the dreadful suspicion, you see, that she's taking advantage of Perry's fears.'

'No, I'm afraid I don't see,' he returned with that innate bluntness which so characterised him. 'In what way is she taking advantage?'

'Because he's convinced himself that he hasn't any kind of a future, he leaves the running of his estate to his mother. I also believe that he considers marriage out of the question—which, of course, ensures that the Dowager remains mistress at the Grange.'

She regarded him solemnly, much as an enquiring child might who was eager for knowledge, but who was a little afraid of learning some unpalatable truth. 'You must have come into contact with Lord Pentecost from time to time, Dr Carrington. Have you ever suspected there might be something more seriously wrong with him than extreme diffidence?'

'No, I have not,' he replied, and the prompt assurance instantly erased much of the concern in her eyes, but he could see that she was still not completely reassured. 'Why doesn't Lord Peregrine have a talk with Dr Fieldhouse? He, I understand, has been the family's physician for years. He might know a little of their history and would be in a position to allay any fears.'

By her sudden frown he knew that this suggestion, for some reason, didn't meet with her approval. He had scant regard for Dr Fieldhouse himself, considering him a bigoted fool for refusing to employ more modern methods of treatment, and a disgrace to their profession for offering his services only to those who were in a position to grease his palm with shining gold coins.

'Or he could, of course, pay me a visit. I would be more than happy to see him, and if I considered there were grounds for concern I could furnish him with the name of a colleague of mine in London who is more of an expert in this particular branch of medicine.'

'Would you do that, Dr Carrington?' She regarded him with real gratitude. 'I should feel so much easier if you were to speak with him.'

It quite amazed him to discover that he was more than just a little willing to comply, if not to alleviate the young baron's concerns, then certainly to restore this young woman's peace of mind.

'I shall be happy to do so,' he assured her, feeling highly gratified by the warm look of approval she cast him. 'But you must remember that he is to all intents and purposes Dr Fieldhouse's patient and it would be quite unethical for me to call at Pentecost Grange merely at your behest. However, it is quite another matter if Lord Peregrine, himself, should decide to consult me.'

'Of course, yes…yes, I'll have a talk with him.' She didn't attempt to disguise the immense feeling of relief she was experiencing. No matter what her personal opinion of Thomas Carrington might be—and she was still far from certain whether she liked him or not—she felt, like so many others, that one could put complete faith in him as a physician.

She was about to express her sincere thanks for his invaluable help in the matter, when for the first time she became embarrassingly aware of precisely where they were standing. So engrossed had she become in their conversation that, apart from the first couple of rooms they had entered, she had taken precious little interest in her surroundings, and had been blissfully unaware that at some point they had re-entered the hall and had climbed the carved wooden staircase to the upper floor.

'Oh, dear,' she muttered, staring in some alarm at the bedchamber's most prominent feature. 'I really don't think it is at all the thing for us to be alone in here, Dr Carrington.' His immediate response to this gross understatement was to roar with laughter which, quite naturally, only succeeded in adding to her discomfiture.

'My dear young woman, if seduction had been on my mind I would have made use of the large sofa in the drawing-room, and not waited to ravish you in the comfort of a four-poster bed!'

Then suddenly it wasn't amusing any more. There she stood, an exceptionally lovely and infinitely desirable young woman, a matter of a few feet away. It would be a simple matter to reach out for her and begin to satisfy that ever increasing desire in his loins, but iron control kept his arms firmly by his sides and stilled his eyes from wandering over the delectable virginal body just begging to be awakened to the untold joys of lovemaking.

Had it been any other young woman standing there perhaps he might not have attempted to retain such a rigid hold on his baser instincts. But this was no ordinary young woman, and no man possessed of any degree of honour should consider soiling innocence and, furthermore, innocence of such high quality.

No, the Lady Jane Beresfords of the world were not for the likes of him. Much safer to consort only with those females of his own class, or those like Margaret Ryan who knew the rules. Lady Jane was well above his touch and destined for some wealthy aristocrat, who would sample the sweet reward of his patience on their wedding night, and not before. The truth was a bitter pill to swallow, but better to begin treatment now before the undesirable and highly threatening condition which he preferred not to name could take a firm hold.

'Forgive me, ma'am. In my professional capacity I see a great many females in just such surroundings, which, of course, is quite in order, but my doctor's mantle, never left off for very long, makes me tend to forget the social niceties at times.'

Feeling suddenly extremely foolish for making such an issue of it, Jane led the way out of the room and down the stairs to the hall. As he had quite rightly pointed out, he was a doctor and, as such, would adhere to the rigid codes of conduct when dealing with members of her sex. The trouble was, though, that for some inexplicable reason she was finding it increasingly difficult to view him in the light of a practitioner and, unless she was very much mistaken, just for one unguarded moment, his view of her had been far removed from that of a patient.

'This is a fine house, Dr Carrington,' she remarked, in an attempt to break the uncomfortable silence which was threatening to lengthen between them. 'If you should decide not to acquire it, I think the owner will have little difficulty in getting it off his hands.'

'That's true enough,' he agreed, gazing almost wistfully about the charming hall. 'I cannot help asking myself, though, what the deuce I would need six bedrooms for?'

She chuckled. 'Well, at the moment you don't, of course. But I should think it highly likely that you'll marry one day, and when you've a wife and a growing family you might be glad of the extra space.'

The instant she had spoken she sensed a change in him, even before she turned to see his eyes glinting like chips of ice, sharp and dangerous. 'We had best not tarry here longer, ma'am,' he announced, his tone as coolly unfriendly as his expression.

She followed him outside, wondering what on earth she had said or done now to put him so suddenly out of temper. He really was the most unfathomable creature!

When Jane arrived back at Knightley Hall it was to discover that Lord Pentecost had called, but had ridden back out again almost immediately with the master of the house, and that her cousin was at present in the drawing-room.

Deciding to change out of her habit before joining Elizabeth, Jane smiled to herself as she headed across the hall towards the staircase. She was delighted that Perry had made the effort to view the grey. It proved

that he had far from lost complete interest in every
aspect of his life; more importantly, it offered her the
opportunity to speak with him again, and confess
what she had taken it upon herself to do on his behalf.

She had almost reached the head of the stairs when
she chanced to turn her head and saw her personal
maid hurrying across the hall in the direction of the
kitchen area. Even from this distance she could see
that Latimer appeared far from her usually composed
self: her face looked decidedly flushed and she was
twitching at the folds of her gown as though she felt
she was in some slight disorder.

A few moments later she caught sight of a tall figure emerging from the front parlour. Blond head bent,
as though immersed in his own thoughts, he didn't
notice her, and Jane followed his progress across the
chequered floor of the hall. Unless she was very much
mistaken, Latimer had been coming from that direction, too. If this did turn out to be the case then it
seemed more than likely that she had been ensconced
in that sunny little room with Simon Fairfax. How
very odd! she mused. What on earth could Simon
have wished to impart to a former employee that he
could not have said in front of Elizabeth in the drawing-room?

Once in her bedchamber she didn't delay in summoning her maid, and whilst being assisted into one
of her very fashionable morning gowns, an elegant
but practical creation in dark blue velvet, she asked
in a light, conversational way how long Sir Richard
and Lady Knightley had been entertaining their morning callers.

'I didn't know they had any, my lady. I've been

fully occupied since you rode out earlier with pressing several of your gowns in the laundry.'

The response came easily enough, and Jane might not have given the matter any more thought if she hadn't chanced to glimpse a smugly satisfied smile, quickly suppressed, reflected clearly in the tall mirror standing in the corner of the room.

Now, what possible motive could there be for telling such a deliberate lie? she wondered, collecting her fringed blue shawl before leaving her room. Was she such a dragon of a mistress that her maid feared to mention that she had passed a few innocent pleasantries above stairs with the son of her former employer? By her own admission, Latimer had been happy working for the Fairfax family, and if she did still harbour a secret *tendre* for the handsome son—well, what of it? She wouldn't be the first attractive young woman in service to indulge in foolish fantasies. But that didn't alter the fact that her maid had been far from truthful, and Jane had to admit that she resented this.

If and when she did set up an establishment of her own, she felt she would need people about her whom she could trust implicitly, and she had to own that there had always been a certain something about Latimer that she had never quite liked. There was no denying, though, that it would be totally unjust to use this morning's insignificant occurrence as a means of being rid of her. Quite contemptible, in fact! No, she wouldn't make up her mind just yet whether to keep Latimer or not; she would wait until they returned to Kent before finally making a decision. Then, if she still felt she would be happier with a new personal maid, she would grant Latimer plenty of time in which to find a new position.

She entered the drawing-room to discover that Sir Richard and Perry had returned, and to find the handsome Mr Fairfax, now seated beside her cousin on one of the elegant sofas, doing a sterling job of entertaining his host and hostess with a lively résumé of the latest town gossip.

Jane was delighted to hear that Perry had made up his mind to have the grey, and was even more pleased to learn that he had accepted Sir Richard's kind invitation to spend a quiet evening at the Hall playing chess some time. It was precisely this sort of thing that might help him to acquire an interest in life once more, which hopefully might lead to his taking a more active part in the running of his estate. However, she didn't envisage any significant changes taking place until he was freed from that burdensome mantle of fear that permanently shrouded him.

She was naturally eager to tell him of the conversation she had had with Thomas Carrington earlier, but was forced to wait until both gentlemen had taken their leave of the Knightleys and she accompanied them out to the stable yard. Her opportunity came when Mr Fairfax, who evidently had not done so on their arrival, began to inspect Sir Richard's fine string of horses, but Perry's reaction to her disclosures was far from enthusiastic.

'I don't see what good it would do talking to him, Janie. Like most people round here, he probably thinks I belong in a sanatorium already.'

'People don't think that, Perry. At least Sir Richard and Elizabeth most certainly do not, and neither does Dr Carrington. He gave me every reason to believe that if your uncle's case was an isolated one, then you have nothing to worry about. Do you happen to know if any of your ancestors were similarly afflicted?'

He shook his head. 'Father never spoke about his family very much. I could always ask Mama, I suppose. Perhaps she might know.'

'No, don't do that,' she responded a little too urgently, and he looked at her sharply.

'Why ever not?'

Jane swiftly sought some plausible reason for his not doing so. 'Well, because it might upset her if she discovered just how concerned you were. It would be much better if you tried to discover the truth yourself.'

He seemed to accept this, and after a few moments said, 'Well, I don't suppose it could do any harm to have a talk with Dr Carrington, and I shan't mention anything to my mother. She wouldn't like it, you see. She hasn't a good word to say about him.'

Jane resisted the temptation to retort that the Dowager Lady Pentecost rarely uttered a good word about anyone, but prompted by rising frustration and anger couldn't prevent herself from saying, 'It's high time, Perry, that you began to take control of your own life. How on earth do you imagine your neighbours…your servants…anyone will ever respect you when you continually kowtow to your mother's every whim? For heaven's sake, learn to stand on your own two feet!'

With that she stalked back towards the house, already bitterly regretting her harshly spoken words, but knowing they had needed to be said. Sir Richard had been so right: Perry must learn to assert himself. There was little she or anyone else could do to help if he wasn't prepared to do something to help himself.

Chapter Six

'Now,' Jane remarked as she took her seat opposite the Knightleys in their well-sprung travelling carriage, 'Caroline Westbridge is that charming lady you introduced me to at your dinner-party. If my memory serves me correctly, she is your nearest neighbour, a widow and, I believe, has one son who is at present up at Oxford.'

'What a memory you have!' Elizabeth was genuinely impressed. 'I must have introduced you to a dozen or more strangers that night. How on earth can you remember such details?'

'Practice, Cousin.' Jane's lips curled into a wry smile. 'I was instructed from an early age, and had an excellent teacher in my darling mama. She instilled in me how very important it is to remember the smallest details about a person, so that one has something to fall back on if the conversation should ever flag. Added to which, there are those who, on first encountering, always make a favourable impression.' She didn't add that there were also those who most certainly did not, her mind's eye conjuring up a clear image of a ruggedly handsome face, with its square determined jaw, almost hawk-like nose and clear, intelligent grey eyes.

She hadn't seen Dr Carrington since their meeting in Melcham the week before, but that hadn't prevented him from intruding into her thoughts rather too frequently for her peace of mind. She had repeatedly told herself that this simply stemmed from her concerns over Perry, whom she had also thought about often, and whose hurt expression after her ill-tempered outburst had continued to prick her conscience.

Something certainly had needed to be said by someone, that was for sure. Perry simply couldn't possibly go on as he had been doing, living from day to day and allowing others to make his decisions for him. But was she in any better case herself? Hadn't she always been guilty of precisely the same thing: kowtowing to the wishes of her family and living an undeniably pleasant but, none the less, meaningless existence, where the pursuit of personal pleasure was the only thing that mattered? Even now, when she had seriously considered the possibility of setting up her own establishment, she still remained far from certain that it was what she truly wanted—was far from sure that she would be any happier being her own mistress than she was now.

Really, she was hardly in a position to criticise poor Perry, she inwardly chastised herself. At least he had some excuse for behaving the way he did, with the dreadful prospect of insanity looming on his life's horizon. What excuses could she make for being miserably discontented, for being gripped by this ever increasing lethargy? She owed Perry an abject apology for ripping up at him that way. No doubt he would be amongst those at Caroline Westbridge's dinner-party this evening, and with any luck she would be able to have a few minutes' private conversation with him.

Unfortunately she was denied the opportunity to make her peace. On arriving at Mrs Westbridge's charming Tudor manor house she was informed by Caroline that, because Lady Pentecost was a little out of sorts, the family would not be attending. Jane was naturally disappointed to learn this, but brightened almost at once when she saw that Henrietta Dilbey was amongst the guests.

She seated herself without invitation beside Henrietta on the sofa, and, after exchanging a few pleasantries with Miss Dilbey's uncle, whom she found a very likeable and jovial man, she turned to Henrietta. Without further ado, she explained what she had been doing on Perry's behalf since their encounter in the wood.

'Strangely enough I'm rather relieved to hear you say that you feel all is not as it should be up at the Grange,' Henrietta admitted. 'Although I have never for one moment suspected that there might be anything seriously wrong with Perry mentally, I must confess there have been occasions when I've thought him slightly neurotic over certain things—this obsession he has that people are spying on him, to name but one.'

'Over that, I think he has every reason to be concerned,' Jane didn't hesitate to inform her. 'The butler at the Grange is a most unpleasant fellow and, I understand, is one of those servants recently employed by Lady Pentecost. He's a surly, shifty-eyed little rodent, and I wouldn't trust him an inch. That doesn't alter the fact, though, that Perry should be master in his own home.' She studied the delicately painted figures on her exquisite pearl-encrusted fan. 'And I'm afraid I told him so in no uncertain terms.'

Henrietta smiled. 'Yes, I know. He rode over to the house the other day to show us the grey. That is most definitely a step in the right direction. It was so good seeing him suitably mounted!'

Jane's sombre expression remained, and Henrietta sensed the reason behind it. 'You were perfectly right, you know, to say what you did,' she assured her gently. 'Perry must stand on his own two feet. I must confess there have been numerous occasions when I have wanted to scold him for precisely the same reason. We can only hope that he possesses the good sense to listen to your advice, and also makes the effort to visit Dr Carrington.'

Jane looked at her sharply. 'Do you suspect there's a good chance he might not?'

'I'm not sure,' she was honest enough to admit. 'Maybe he's afraid of having his worst fears confirmed. He was certainly in a very subdued frame of mind when last I spoke with him, I know that. It's such a pity he has decided to absent himself from this gathering tonight.'

A sudden commotion by the door drew her attention and she glanced across the room, her eyes widening in astonishment. 'Oh, but surprise, surprise! Dr Carrington has not done so. And he's looking as fine as fivepence, too! What on earth has come over him? I know Mrs Westbridge is a particular friend, but it's most unusual for him to accept a dinner invitation. It seems only your cousin is able to prise him away from his work and persuade him to enjoy an occasional evening out.'

Miss Dilbey was not the only one to raise a brow as Dr Carrington, whose unsociability was renowned, strode across the large drawing-room in his hostess's direction, but Jane was oblivious to the many startled expressions bent in his direction. She returned her attention to her fan and put it to good use on her suddenly glowing cheeks, deciding that she must be ailing for something to have suddenly grown overheated this way. After all, it wasn't as though she was unused to seeing a fine physique displayed to perfection in a pair of tight-fitting pantaloons, which covered well-muscled limbs without so much as a hairline crease, and a masterpiece of tailoring expertly encasing a pair of superior shoulders.

Sir Richard was one of the few whose expression remained impassive. It was not completely unknown for Tom to enjoy an evening in genteel company, but it was certainly not a common occurrence. Caroline Westbridge was a charming and well-liked person, and Tom had struck up a friendship with her and her son soon after moving into the district, so he didn't give the young doctor's arrival a second thought until later, when, seated at the dinner-table, he happened to catch a pair of penetrating grey eyes, giving little away, it had to be said, steadily regarding a certain lady. If she was aware of the attention she was receiving she certainly betrayed no sign of it. In fact, she seemed in a strangely subdued frame of mind.

'You're very quiet this evening, Jane. Something troubling you?'

If the truth be known she was unhappy over several things, not least her foolishly immature reaction at Dr

Carrington's unexpected appearance, but she had no intention of admitting that.

'I was hoping to see Perry here this evening, Richard,' she responding, gaining some comfort from the fact that it wasn't a lie. 'I'm afraid I'm suffering from a surfeit of remorse. I was rather sharp with him when he came over to the Hall to purchase your grey.'

'He looked in fine trim to me when I came across him exercising his new acquisition yesterday. The lad's got an excellent seat on a horse, I'll give him that.'

'Was he out on his own?'

'Yes. I understand their guest has at last moved on, but is expected back next week for the ball.' He reached for his wine glass and fortified himself from its contents before saying, 'Loath though I am to indulge in vulgar gossip, am I right in thinking that Lord Fairfax is struggling to keep the creditors from his door?'

'It's certainly a rumour going about, and it wouldn't surprise me if it turned out to be true. He's an inveterate gambler and a notorious womaniser.' She kept her voice low, but there was no mistaking the censure it contained. 'You might have supposed that a man who won't see his sixtieth birthday again would have preferred the quiet comfort of his own fireside, rather than…than expending what little energy he still possesses in the pursuit of frivolous and ruinous pleasures that he can ill afford.'

Richard much admired the delicate restraint. Evidently she would have liked to be far more unreserved and scathing. 'Perhaps he is looking to his son to restore their fortunes. There's no denying that Simon Fairfax is a handsome devil.' He cast her a surreptitious glance, remembering clearly the way Simon had looked in her direction when he had paid that visit with Perry to the Hall. Unlike Tom's prolonged but benign scrutiny, Simon's unguarded look had been penetratingly hard and calculating. Richard hadn't liked it at all, and it had left him with an acute feeling of disquiet—foreboding, almost.

'No doubt he's on the lookout for an heiress, Jane.'

She found herself instantly responding to the thread of warning in his deeply resonant voice. 'Well, it certainly won't be me, Richard. I have found myself in his company on numerous occasions during the past three London Seasons. There's no denying that he's extremely pleasing on the eye, but I find his elegant charm rather too studied for my taste. Added to which, there are all the signs, inadequately concealed to a person who can lay claim to any depth of perception, that he'll turn out to be as debauched as his father.'

Richard couldn't help smiling at this ruthless dissection of the man's rather imperfect character. She could, he didn't doubt, have said a great deal more to the Honourable Simon Fairfax's discredit, but she had said sufficient to make her estimation of him quite plain, and to allay the slight fear he had been harbouring that she might be susceptible to a handsome face.

No, Elizabeth's young cousin was certainly no fool, he mused. She didn't accept people at face value, which was no bad thing. However, he couldn't help wondering whether the imperfections she so easily perceived in members of his sex might not be, in part, the reason why such a lovely young woman, favourably blessed in face and form, had chosen thus far not to marry.

If she were waiting for *Mr Perfection* himself to cross her path before she would even consider taking the matrimonial plunge, then he feared she was destined to end her days an old maiden aunt. But, no— Jane had far too much common sense to believe that such a paragon of all the virtues existed. He suspected, though, that she was certainly looking for something in a prospective husband that she had thus far failed to find in any one of those many dashing young sprigs who had paraded before her during her Seasons in London.

Without conscious thought, he fixed his gaze on an immaculately attired form seated a little further down the table, and a notion occurred to him—so novel that he almost dismissed it as ludicrous, but not quite. Reaching for his glass, he took a further fortifying swallow. It was high time he invited his good friend the doctor to a quiet family dinner again, with perhaps a hand or two of cards afterwards. Yes, he mused, the evening might prove most enlightening.

The following evening Jane was in her bedchamber studying her reflection in the tall pier-glass, wondering why she was taking so much trouble over her appearance. After changing her mind three times, she had finally selected to wear the green velvet gown she had donned for the dinner-party on the evening she had arrived at the Hall. The dress suited her very well, its rich dark colour emphasising the green in her eyes and the glorious rich red highlights in her russet locks. On any other occasion her appearance would have satisfied her, but it certainly didn't now.

Really, she must be quite mad to take such pains over her appearance, she reflected, simply because that odious Dr Thomas Carrington might, just might, condescend to come to dinner. She couldn't understand why Elizabeth and Richard, a most discerning couple, thought so highly of him. He was abominably rude! Why, he'd barely taken the trouble to speak to her at Caroline's dinner-party, and the few words he had forced himself to utter could hardly have been described as flattering.

She had been conversing again with Henrietta, who had just disclosed her uncle's plans to take her to London for a few weeks in the spring, when Richard had brought his friend across to the sofa on which she had been sitting.

'Add your entreaties to mine, Jane, my dear,' he had said. 'I'm trying to persuade Tom to join us for dinner tomorrow evening and, later, make up a foursome at whist.'

'Oh, yes, do, Dr Carrington,' she had responded, a completely unforced and quite dazzling smile curving her lips. 'It would be such a pleasant, relaxing evening.'

'I'm sure it would, ma'am,' he had responded, if not slightingly, then certainly with a distinct lack of enthusiasm. 'But even the prospect of enjoying an evening in your distinguished and charming company could not induce me to neglect my patients, should there be any in need of my services.'

Odious man! she thought angrily, more vexed with herself, if the truth be known, for still feeling unaccountably hurt by his far from gallant response. He was so confoundedly rude most of the time that she couldn't understand why she should have imagined, on the morning he had shown her round that pleasant house in Melcham, that she quite liked him. Foolish beyond measure! She most definitely didn't like the infuriating creature... No, not a whit!

Annoyance added an extra sparkle to her eyes and a becoming flush to her cheeks, both of which intensified as she swept into the drawing-room to discover the person whom she was desperately trying to convince herself that she never wished to see again sprawled at his ease in one of Sir Richard's comfortable chairs. He had reverted to his casual form of attire: loose-fitting jacket, a clean but abysmally tied cravat, slightly creased unmentionables and, of all things, top boots, which she took, for some inexplicable reason, as a deliberate insult to herself.

Tom, more amused than irritated by her ill-concealed look of staunch disapproval at his far from appropriate attire, rose to his feet. 'I must ask you to excuse my appearance, ma'am. I received an urgent summons from one of my patients late in the afternoon, and rather than run the risk of arriving late for dinner I didn't return to my house to change, but came straight here.'

She raised one slender white shoulder in a nonchalant shrug. 'So long as my cousin does not object... No doubt, though, she is far too gratified that you have condescended to accept her dinner invitation to dwell unduly on any social niceties—or lack of them.'

Elizabeth was astonished. Never before had she heard her cousin speak in such a haughty, ill-natured fashion to anyone. She didn't for a moment suppose that Tom's casual appearance had instigated such blatant hostility, and could only assume that he had, at some point in the not too distant past, said or done something to offend Jane—which, knowing him as she did, wouldn't have surprised her in the least.

She cast a pleading glance in her husband's direction, hoping for support, but all he did in response was to stroll across the room in the direction of the decanters. Men were simply useless at times! Unless someone could restore Jane's normally sunny humour, the evening promised to be an unmitigated disaster.

'Come and sit by me, Jane,' she invited, patting that portion of sofa beside her. 'I haven't seen you since your visit to the Dilbeys this afternoon. Did you have an enjoyable time?'

'Yes, very.' And her completely unforced smile went some way to lessen her cousin's fears of impending doom. 'I like Hetta very much,' she admitted, betraying the fact that she and Miss Dilbey were now on familiar, first-name terms. 'She's a charming person.'

'I couldn't agree more,' Richard said, handing her a glass of Madeira. 'She's a level-headed young woman who, as you quite rightly pointed out, has an abundance of charm, and would make any man a good wife.'

'Had you anyone particularly in mind?' Jane quizzed him.

'No, my dear. It has always been my policy never, I repeat never, to meddle in other people's private affairs—unless, of course, they concern me in some way. In fact, only one person has ever induced me to disregard this excellent maxim.'

Even Tom betrayed mild surprise at this admission. 'Good Lord, Richard! Who on earth possesses the strength of character to steer you off the straight and narrow?'

'The fair Lady Jane, no less.'

'Me?' Jane experienced a deal of pleasurable satisfaction at learning this and, ignoring Dr Carrington's tut-tut of disapproval, asked, 'And how, pray, did I induce you to do that?'

'Your deep concerns over a certain someone's well-being, m'dear.' He smiled at her instant expression of understanding. 'I rode over to see General Sir George Lansdowne this morning. He's a crusty old rogue who'll talk endlessly about his years in the army if you give him half a chance. He's well into his eighties, and has lived in Lansdowne House, which is less than a mile from the Grange, all his life. I thought if anyone could tell me about the Pentecost family, then he could.'

'And did you discover something of interest?' his wife prompted, when he paused to sip his wine.

'Not a great deal, I'm afraid. It was as I told you, Jane. Perry's uncle died as a direct result of a riding accident.'

She frowned slightly. 'So we still don't know whether he was mentally deranged at the time.'

'As I've mentioned before, I've never heard tell of it, although Lansdowne did seem to think that Cedric had been unwell for several weeks, and that was why the late Lord Pentecost had brought him back from Oxford. He couldn't, however, recall any of the details.' Finishing off his wine, he placed the empty glass on the mantelshelf behind him. 'If Perry wishes to learn more, then it's really up to him to make his own enquiries.'

'I expect he'll do just that,' Tom announced unexpectedly, drawing all eyes to him. 'He came to see me this morning,' he went on to explain, 'and we had a long talk. He has given me every reason to suppose that from now on he intends to call upon my services, should the need arise, and, therefore, I'm not prepared to betray a doctor-patient confidentiality by discussing the matter further…except to say that it is my considered opinion he has little to worry about.'

Jane felt all her pent-up animosity towards him ebbing away. Dr Carrington hadn't needed to say anything, and she suspected the only reason for disclosing as much as he had was purely and simply for her benefit, to ease her burden of worry.

'That ought to prove most interesting,' Elizabeth remarked, with an impish smile, 'if you are ever called upon to visit the Grange.'

Tom didn't pretend to misunderstand. He had made no secret of the fact that he had scant regard for Lady Pentecost. 'If I am summoned by Lord Pentecost, then of course I shall go.'

'I wonder if you'll now receive an invitation to their spring ball?'

'Highly unlikely, Elizabeth, if the Dowager has any say in the matter, and I certainly shan't lose any sleep over once again being deliberately excluded. Besides which, it's immaterial anyway. I'm intending to travel into Wiltshire next week to spend some time with the eminent surgeon William Dent, who, you may recall, was rewarded with a knighthood for his services during the Peninsular War.'

'Oh, dear. We shall be thin of enjoyable company in the near future. Jane intends to leave us then, too.' Elizabeth turned to her cousin with a look of entreaty. 'Are you sure you cannot postpone your departure another week? It seems you've been with us no time at all.'

'I should love to,' Jane responded, touched by her cousin's genuine affection. 'But I'm afraid it's impossible. I promised Lady Templehurst that I would be with her on my birthday.'

'In that case, of course you must go. I know how very fond you are of our aunt Augusta.'

Elizabeth fell into a reminiscent mood. 'I haven't set eyes on her for years, not since the day of my father's funeral. I recall being terrified of her as a child, but I suspect that beneath that crusty exterior beats the heart of a very kindly soul. She never forgets to send me a little something on my birthday. I really must make the effort to visit her or, perhaps, invite her here. Do you think she would come, Jane?'

'I'm certain she would. She's well into her sixties now, but apart from a little rheumatism she's healthy enough, and is quite able to travel long distances, though it's rare these days that she does so. And she's always had a soft spot for you. She frequently asks after you, and I know for a fact that she always preferred your father to mine.'

Elizabeth was shocked. 'Never tell me she said so to your face?'

'Aunt Augusta, as you very well know, has never been one to hide her teeth. Nearly every member of the family is somewhat in awe of her, even my father. Heaven knows why!' She cast a fleeting glance in Tom's direction. 'The only way to deal with ill-tempered people is to stand up to them, do you not agree, Dr Carrington?'

He hadn't missed the wickedly provocative glint in her eyes, and was very well aware that the veiled gibe was directed at him. 'In most cases, yes,' he responded, successfully suppressing a smile. 'But it is not always advisable to instigate wrath in the elderly. I can offer you a case in point. Not long after I had set up my practice in Bristol, I had a patient who was renowned for his innate bad temper. You remember him, Elizabeth, I'm sure—that cross-grained old curmudgeon, Josiah Peacemore. A most inappropriate name! Well, to cut a long story short, he worked himself up into a passion and suffered an apoplexy which took him off.'

'Really, Dr Carrington?' Jane was all wide-eyed innocence. 'This didn't possibly happen directly after he had sustained a visit from you, by any chance?'

'Little baggage!' he muttered, sending both Jane and Elizabeth into such paroxysms of mirth that neither saw the tender look which accompanied his far from polite response. But Richard most certainly noticed it. It told him much of what he wanted to know, and made him feel faintly uneasy.

Chapter Seven

Sir Richard's light travelling carriage was a master-piece of the coach-maker's art. The generously padded interior cocooned its occupants in velvet luxury as, hardly so much as swaying, it bowled along the narrow, twisting lanes.

It was quite dark by now, so Jane didn't try to pierce the gloom in a vain attempt to take one of her last chances to view this delightful part of England. How she would dearly love to see it in late spring and summer when the countryside was at its most glorious! How she wished, now, that her visit had not been quite so short! Elizabeth and Richard could not possibly have made her feel more welcome, and she had no desire to bring her pleasant stay with them to an end, but she knew she must. A promise was a promise, and she was a female who believed in keeping her word, so she must leave for Lady Temple-hurst's house in Bath the day after tomorrow.

It was rather a pity, though, that she had been denied their company on her penultimate evening in Hampshire, but it couldn't be helped. Elizabeth, having succumbed to a slight chill, had spent the past two days closeted in her private apartments in an attempt not to pass on the infection. The children, as far as Jane was aware, were thankfully betraying no symptoms, but poor Richard most certainly was.

He had woken that morning with a sore throat and a blinding headache. Ever the considerate gentleman, though, he had still been more than willing to escort her to the Pentecosts' ball, but she wouldn't hear of it. The sensible place for him was by his own fireside. Besides which, there had been no real need of his added protection. With the highly competent head groom tooling the equipage, the trusty young stable-lad who had accompanied her on her many exploratory rides sitting beside him on the box, and with her maid to bear her company, she was safe enough.

'When, precisely, do you intend commencing your journey to Bath, my lady?' Latimer asked, breaking the silence which had ensued since taking their seats in the carriage.

'I've arranged for the post-chaise to be at Knightley Hall directly after breakfast the day after tomorrow. I wish to arrive in Bath in good time for dinner.'

Even though she still remained far from certain that she would retain Latimer's services for very much longer, she had no intention of making what might well turn out to be the maid's last few weeks in her employ uncomfortable by behaving coolly towards her, and so enquired pleasantly, 'Are you looking forward to embarking on the second stage of our travels, Latimer?'

'Yes, my lady, I am,' the maid responded, betraying for the first time ever a modicum of enthusiasm to continue conversing.

As Jane was destined to discover to her cost, this

ought to have made her suspicious, but she didn't give the rare display of animation a second thought, except to say, 'I hope you haven't been too bored during our time here in Hampshire?'

'Not at all, my lady. I have found sufficient work to occupy me.' Latimer's attractive dark eyes flickered with something akin to regret as she stared levelly across the carriage at the Earl of Eastbury's daughter. 'No one could ever accuse you of being an exacting mistress and I enjoyed the several walks I was able to take across the estate. But I must confess that I'm more than ready, now, for a change.'

They had by this time joined the line of carriages waiting to deposit their passengers at Pentecost Grange's impressive colonnaded front entrance. When it came to their turn to alight, Jane parted company with her maid in the spacious hall—she to make her way to the large salon where the ball was being held, Latimer to join the other abigails in a room on the upper floor, where they would no doubt pass their time indulging in idle gossip, if not called upon to make lightning repairs to accidental tears in their mistresses' expensive gowns.

As Jane drew near the entrance to the large salon she saw Perry standing beside his mother near the door. Appropriately attired in full evening garb, a long-tailed black coat and black satin knee-smalls, he looked remarkably composed in the circumstances. Like his father, he had no great fondness for the large occasion and was most certainly not overburdened with a surfeit of small talk either, so Jane was rather surprised, not to say relieved, when he managed to extract a chortle of amusement from the lady at the head of the small queue of guests waiting in line to greet the host and hostess.

'You look to be bearing up remarkably well,' she quizzed him, when at last she reached the head of the queue.

'I wouldn't go as far as to say that, Janie,' he returned, with a smile of such real warmth that she was certain he felt no animosity towards her for her scathing remarks at their last meeting. 'I understood that Uncle Willoughby was to lend Mama his support, but then it was insisted upon that I perform my duties.'

'I'm afraid, Perry, that my influence might be to blame for that,' she admitted, drawing him aside a little so that his mother could not overhear. 'If I'm not very careful I stand in the gravest danger of turning into an interfering old harridan. But I simply couldn't bear the thought of Sir Willougby usurping your position.'

'Oh, so it's you I've to thank for this, is it?' But his look of mock severity didn't fool her for a moment. 'I'll have a thing or two to say to you later, my girl. And don't forget to save me a dance.'

How wonderful it was to see her childhood friend coping, if not superbly then at least adequately enough, with what for him must surely be a considerable ordeal, Jane mused as she wandered into the large salon, which was already quite crowded with what she supposed must represent the cream of Hampshire society. It was no use supposing that Perry's disposition would ever change to that extent and, in truth, she wasn't so very certain that she wished to see any great transformation in him. However, there could be no doubt that a weighty burden had been lifted from his mind and she would always be grateful to a certain doctor for bringing this about.

Her thoughts were echoed by Miss Dilbey, who, having been looking out for Jane's arrival, had meandered her way round the groups of elegantly attired and chattering guests towards her quarry.

'Although he's considerably easier in his mind now that he's spoken to Dr Carrington,' Henrietta confirmed as they made themselves comfortable on two vacant chairs placed by the wall, 'he's still determined to visit the specialist in London when he goes there in the spring.'

How very interesting! Was Perry's real motive for journeying to the capital merely to attain a second opinion about his mental health, or was the underlying reason, perhaps, a desire not to be parted from his good friend Miss Dilbey? What a pity, Jane mused, that she herself had more or less decided to forgo the Season this year. It might have proved most interesting to see how things progressed between the two of them, now that Perry's mental health was no longer a bar to a closer relationship developing.

She cast Hetta a quick appraising glance. She was still in half-mourning and wearing the same pearl-grey gown that she had donned for Caroline Westbridge's party the previous week. The colour suited her well enough, but Jane sincerely hoped she hadn't inherited her mother's stubborn pride, and would permit her uncle to buy her some new dresses when she went to London in the spring. Her uncle was certainly no pauper, and it would be nice to see Hetta dressed in more vibrant colours once her period of mourning came to an end.

'And how has the Dowager Lady Pentecost taken

this evident change we perceive in her son? Does she know he intends to go to London?'

'Oh, yes. He's told her that, but hasn't explained the reason why.' Hetta grinned wickedly. 'She was not best pleased to hear that he had consulted Dr Carrington, though. And Perry was far from happy to discover that she had somehow managed to find out about the visit, and promptly insisted on sending his new practitioner a belated invitation, which, as you can imagine, didn't go down too well with his darling mama.'

Jane raised one white shoulder in a dismissive shrug. 'She ought to be mighty well pleased, then, that he didn't accept.'

'Oh, but he did!'

Jane didn't attempt to hide her astonishment as she gazed about the room in vain for a glimpse of Tom's tall figure. 'But he told me he was travelling into Wiltshire.'

'Be that as it may, he's here. He came with Mrs Westbridge's party. I thought I saw him accompanying her into the room set out for cards a little earlier.'

A delicious feeling of euphoria washed over Jane. Their leave-taking after that most enjoyable dinner at Knightley Hall a few evenings before had been swift and slightly formal, considering the camaraderie which had rapidly grown between them after the initial frosty start. At Richard's behest, Tom had called to examine Elizabeth the previous day, but Jane had been out enjoying her daily ride and had missed seeing him—a circumstance that had caused her more disappointment than she cared to admit.

A tall figure suddenly appearing before her sent her

pulse rate soaring, but a feeling of acute disappointment swiftly followed to restore her to normality
when she raised her eyes to those of Simon Fairfax.

'Good evening, Lady Jane. Will you do me the
singular honour of partnering me in the next set of
country dances which is now forming?'

How polished the address! What an abundance of
elegant charm this tall, blond-haired Adonis oozed!
Surely she must be the envy of nearly every young
female in the room. So why was it, Jane wondered,
placing her fingers on the immaculate sleeve of his
long-tailed coat as he guided her to the area desig-
nated for dancing, that he, and all those dashing
young blades like him, never caused the least fluttering in her young breast? Why was it that she would
much rather be in the company of a certain gentleman
whose manners were more often than not less than
perfect, and whose frequent acerbic remarks would
most certainly never find favour in any polite drawing-room?

'You are leaving the area soon, so I understand,
Lady Jane,' Mr Fairfax remarked as they came together in the set.

That he should be aware of this fact did not occur
to her for a moment as strange. 'Yes, I leave the day
after tomorrow,' she managed to respond before they
separated again.

'But you are not returning to Kent, if my memory
serves me correctly, but are journeying on to Bath.'

Now, this knowledge of her intended movements
did strike her as odd, until she suddenly recalled that
she had divulged her intention to visit Bath to Lady
Pentecost on the morning she had paid a visit to the
Grange. Evidently the Dowager must have passed on

this information. How else could Simon Fairfax have known?

'Yes, I'm paying a short visit to my aunt, Lady Templehurst, and shall be returning to Kent some time in April.'

'Does that mean that you are intending to deprive us of your unrivalled presence during the forthcoming Season, my lady?'

'My plans are uncertain, sir, but it seems highly unlikely that I shall visit the capital this spring.'

'All the young blades will be desolated by your absence. You have been one of the brightest lights for the past three Seasons.'

My money is the glittering attraction, you mean, Jane countered silently—the Simon Fairfaxes of this world not fooling her for an instant. How shallow they all were! How insipid their polite but meaningless utterances! She would far sooner endure Dr Carrington's hard-eyed disapproval and provocative remarks any day. Infuriatingly rude creature he might be on occasion, but at least he was honest!

The set came to an end and Jane was thankful for it, but her relief was destined not to last very long. She was afterwards partnered by a string of elegant young gentlemen, all equally proficient in making polite but faintly insipid small talk, and all equally well versed in passing the pretty compliment designed to raise a blush in a young maiden's cheeks, but not in hers; she had been on the receiving end of just such banal flattery too frequently in the past for it to have the least effect on her. The only one of her partners who didn't bore her to tears was Perry, who was a surprisingly graceful dancer, and someone who never attempted to make unwelcome overtures.

After he had returned her to her seat by the wall, he solicited Hetta's hand and Jane, pleased to hear Hetta accept at least this one request for her to dance, followed their progress down the large room for a few moments before transferring her gaze to the ample figure of their hostess, who was standing on the opposite side of the room, close to the long French windows. Lady Pentecost was conversing with a middle-aged matron who looked suspiciously as though she was made in a similar mould to the formidable Dowager. They had their heads together and their eyes were focused on the swirling dancers, but precisely who was the object of their no doubt spiteful remarks was difficult to judge.

Jane could only hope that it was neither Perry nor Hetta—could only hope, too, that Perry's new-found confidence didn't lead him into foolish indiscretion. For the time being, at least, it might be wise for them to keep their ever deepening friendship secret. Although Jane didn't doubt Hetta's ability to stand up to the Dowager, neither did she underestimate Lady Pentecost. Perry's darling mama could, and no doubt would, make things very uncomfortable for Hetta if she considered for a moment that there was the remotest possibility that Miss Dilbey, the niece of a person whom the Dowager no doubt considered an insignificant country squire, might one day become her successor.

'And what can possibly be causing you such concern, I wonder?' a deep voice unexpectedly remarked, making Jane start visibly.

'You could do a body a mischief, Dr Carrington, creeping up that way!' she snapped, which hid quite beautifully her underlying delight at seeing him, and which dispelled the growing suspicion she had been harbouring that he fully intended to ignore her as much as possible, just as he had done on the occasion of Caroline Westbridge's party, by remaining in the card room throughout the entire evening.

Without waiting for an invitation, he plumped himself down on the vacant chair beside her and astonished her further by asking, 'Is it, perhaps, because you fear that a certain twosome might foolishly betray their feelings?'

Dear Lord, but wasn't he astute! Jane thought, smiling in spite of herself. His total refusal to dissemble was so very refreshing after the sickening string of platitudes and innuendoes she had been forced to endure since her arrival.

'Yes,' she admitted with equal frankness. 'But I must confess I'm rather surprised Perry chose to confide in you so soon over that particular area of his life.'

'He didn't,' he returned blandly. 'But I've seen them together often enough when I've been called out to Squire Dilbey. One would have to be a simpleton not to have perceived the blossoming friendship.'

'As yet, I think friendship is all it is,' Jane confessed. 'But I have high hopes, providing of course a certain someone doesn't succeed in throwing a rub in their way.'

Tom's eyes moved fleetingly in the Dowager's direction, before his attention returned to the far more pleasing aspect of the delicately featured face beside him, with its straight aristocratic little nose and its softly rounded chin, which had the tendency to lift on occasions, clearly betraying displeasure. The muscles in his abdomen seemed to knot suddenly. Why did this occasionally haughty little madam have the power to affect him so?

'Yes, I can quite understand why that harridan might give cause for concern,' he remarked, regaining control of himself with an effort. 'Just as Richard's apparent absence tonight is causing me no little unease.' He looked at her sharply, his disapproval all too apparent. 'Never tell me you came here by yourself?'

'No, my maid accompanied me.'

'Of course. How very foolish of me! A lady's maid—a most excellent deterrent to any would-be attacker!' He raised his eyes ceilingwards. 'I don't know what Richard was about, allowing you to come unescorted!'

'He wished to accompany me, but I wouldn't hear of it,' she responded in defence of a gentleman she much admired. 'Poor dear, he was feeling quite under the weather. He's taken Elizabeth's chill. Besides which, the head groom and a stable-boy, well armed, I might add, offered ample protection.'

The explanation did not satisfy him, and he remained at his most dictatorial. 'You should consider yourself fortunate that I have no say in your behaviour, young woman, because I tell you plainly I would never permit you to go gallivanting about in such a feather-brained fashion. It's high time you had your wings clipped!'

It occurred to Jane, then, that she might well have bridled had he adopted such a high-handed tone with her even a few days before. Now, however, only a warm feeling of satisfaction glowed deep within her because he liked her well enough to be concerned over her safety, but she had no intention of admitting it.

'Tell me, Dr Carrington, did you prise yourself away from the card room and seek my company merely for the pleasure of pinching at me? If so, it might be best, all things considered, if you returned to your game forthwith,' she advised in clipped tones, and he might have believed her genuinely piqued had his eyes, ever alert, not detected the slight betraying twitch at one corner of that delectable mouth of hers.

'No, I did not, you provoking little witch,' he returned, making the far from flattering epithet sound more like an endearment. 'I sought you out for the sole purpose of asking you to stand up with me. And, unless I'm very much mistaken, they are about to play a waltz.'

Jane couldn't prevent a smile as he led her onto the floor. Not for an instant would it have occurred to him that she might not have been granted permission to perform this particular dance. Although he had, for reasons best known to himself, been less than pleased to discover that she had travelled here without a male escort, he would no doubt consider many of the other rules governing young ladies' behaviour ludicrous in the extreme and not worthy of consideration.

What a complex creature he was, to be sure! she mused, taking a brief surreptitious glance up at him through her long, curling lashes as he began to swirl her quite expertly about the floor. She couldn't recall any other gentleman of her acquaintance who had the ability to affect her mood so easily, one moment annoying her unbearably, the next making her blissfully content. Although there was no denying he could be confoundly rude, it was, perversely, his no-nonsense attitude which attracted her. After all, what else could it possibly be? she wondered, trying desperately to ignore the gentle pressure of that shapely, long-fingered hand resting lightly on her waist while she continued the attempt to assess him dispassionately.

There was no denying that he possessed a fine physique, which was certainly displayed to advantage to-night in that same elegant evening attire he had donned for Caroline Westbridge's party the previous week, but his appearance, she suspected, would never be of any real importance to him. His cravat, though well starched, was plainly arranged; his shirt points were so low as not to be worth a mention, and his plain, cream-coloured waistcoat would no doubt be stigmatised as downright unimaginative by the fash-ion-conscious element in Society. There was nothing remotely ostentatious in his dress, yet she rather thought she preferred his elegant sobriety to the flam-boyant styles affected by most of the dashing young blades in London.

Yes, all in all, he was a most attractive man, rug-gedly good looking rather than handsome, she de-cided, and couldn't understand why, having all but attained the age of thirty, he had remained a bachelor.

A wicked possibility suddenly occurred to her and it took a monumental effort to suppress a chuckle. Outwardly appealing he most definitely was, but his peppery temperament would certainly be a little off-putting to those faint-hearted members of her sex. She doubted, however, that this was the main reason for his continued single state. No, it was much more likely that, totally dedicated to his profession, he hardly gave matrimony a single thought.

It would have astounded Jane, therefore, had she known just how frequently the subject of marriage and, more especially, thoughts of being married to her, had been occupying Dr Carrington's mind of late.

Tom would have been the first to admit that women had played only a very small part in his life thus far. Selfishly, he supposed, he had used them merely as a means to assuage his bodily needs, and had never been in the least danger of mistaking a natural masculine desire for anything deeper. Only Elizabeth and her grandmother, his kindly benefactress, had ever retained a place in his affections. Why, he had almost come to believe that he possessed a natural immunity to the more tender emotions, until the fateful evening, just three short weeks ago, when he had taken it into his head to attend that dinner-party hosted by his good friends, the Knightleys.

He had tried desperately to convince himself that the resemblance to his dear friend Elizabeth was what had attracted him to Lady Jane Beresford, but he hadn't been able to delude himself for long. The more he had come into contact with her, the more he had felt drawn to this aristocratic young woman who, against all the odds, had turned out to be something of a kindred spirit.

The muscles in his abdomen decided to twist themselves into yet another of those self-torturing knots. Ye gods! Hadn't he tried everything humanly possible to stem this ever increasing yearning to be near her? It was sheer madness to suppose that there could ever be any future for them. How could there be when they belonged in different worlds? The sooner they went their separate ways, the sooner his life would return to a semblance of normality, he knew, and yet he had felt he couldn't leave for Wiltshire without seeing her just one more time.

The mere thought that their paths were unlikely to cross again in the foreseeable future was sufficient to have an adverse effect on his concentration and he came perilously close to missing a step. 'I must apologise,' he said, after very nearly treading on her toes. 'I'm afraid I do not dance very often and am a little clumsy.'

'On the contrary, sir, for a tall man you dance with remarkable grace,' she countered, relieved that he had spoken at last, for the awful suspicion that he intended to conduct the whole dance in stony silence had certainly crossed her mind. 'It comes as no surprise to learn that you do not allow yourself the luxury of practising too often, and I can only wonder at what prompted you to come here tonight. I clearly recall your saying you would be journeying into Wiltshire.'

He hesitated a moment only, before responding with, 'My dear young woman, my nature being what it is, how on earth could I resist the temptation of seeing our esteemed hostess's reaction when I unexpectedly appeared before her? Believe me, I was very well aware that my belated invitation was not written in her fair hand.'

Jane frankly laughed at this piece of devilment, causing several pairs of interested eyes to turn in their direction. 'I hope you were not disappointed?'

'On the contrary. Her expression of astonished outrage was a deliciously mouth-watering moment that I shall savour for some weeks to come. Her one consolation, of course, was that should she have choked on the words of greeting she was forced to utter, then she would have had the very person at hand to administer to her needs.'

His incorrigibility continued, keeping Jane in a high state of amusement as he cast aspersions on several other pillars of the community who were present that evening, and who didn't rate very highly in his estimation, and the dance, for her at least, came to an end all too quickly.

As he returned her to the chair beside Hetta's, Jane felt more than just mildly disappointed that he didn't ask her to stand up with him a second time. She followed his progress across the room, her disappointment swiftly turning into a far more unpalatable emotion, and one that she had experienced before in the not too distant past, as she watched him lead a very pretty girl, dressed very becomingly in a gown of lavender silk, onto the dance-floor.

More than a little bewildered by the resentment she was experiencing at seeing him dancing with another young lady, Jane took the opportunity, while Hetta was conveniently being held in conversation by two neighbours, to move quietly away. She felt the sudden need to be alone for a while, to try, if she could, to make some sense out of this sudden surge of jealousy gnawing painfully inside, and made a beeline for one of the tall French windows which had been left slightly ajar to counteract the heat given off by the hundreds of candles.

Her expensive silk shawl offered little protection against the coolness of the March evening, but she was not deterred. Making her way across the deserted terrace, she went down a series of stone steps to the garden. Gaily coloured lanterns illuminated that part of the path near the house for those guests wishing to

enjoy a breath of air. Not that there would be too
many willing to forgo the warm comfort of the salon—none except those, perhaps, troubled like herself, who preferred to be alone.

She had walked no more than a dozen yards away
from the house when she thought she detected the
sound of footsteps further along the path and took
immediate action by concealing herself behind a
sturdy tree. She hadn't even begun to unravel the tangled mass of conflicting thoughts whirling about in
her head, and was unwilling to relinquish her solitude
until she had. So she waited, expecting to see someone pass by, but surprisingly no one did.

Then she heard a further sound behind her and
slightly to her right, quickly followed by an urgently
whispered, 'Are you sure you know precisely what to
do and where to go?'

The voice was undoubtedly masculine, and the
softly spoken 'yes' in response most definitely feminine and, furthermore, vaguely familiar.

'Then we're almost home and dry, my little love.
Just be patient for a while longer, and then we'll be
together. Our problems will soon be at an end. By
this time next week we'll be safe across the Channel,
enjoying all the delights Paris has to offer.'

Heavens above! Had she inadvertently stumbled
upon a lovers' tryst? The planning of an elopement,
perhaps? Her own concerns thrust aside for a moment,
Jane suddenly felt very intrusive, but dared not move
for fear of disturbing the evidently star-crossed pair.
More murmured exchanges followed, none of which
she could clearly hear, before there was the distinct
rustling of clothing and low moans of pleasure floated
across in the air.

Jane's upbringing might have been sheltered, but she was not so naive as not to have a fair notion of what was taking place a mere few yards from where she stood. The gentleman, obviously unable to retain control over his passion, had decided to take advantage of what he imagined to be an isolated spot, and the woman, evidently only too willing to oblige him, was uttering seductive words of encouragement.

With an embarrassed hue already flaming her cheeks, Jane couldn't bear the added mortification of being discovered now, and took the opportunity to tiptoe quietly away whilst the lovers were otherwise engaged. She had almost reached the house when her hopes of an unobserved return to the salon were dashed by a tall figure towering above her on the terrace.

For a few moments it was as much as she could do to stare up at him, then she managed to regain a modicum of self-possession and walked slowly up the stone steps. 'Why, Dr Carrington! What on earth are you doing out here?'

'I might ask you the same question.' His alert eyes scanned the darkened garden for a moment before turning to her upturned face. 'Are you feeling unwell? You appear a little flushed.'

Drat the man! He never missed a blessed thing! 'As a matter of fact I was feeling a little warm earlier,' she responded, quickly turning the lingering evidence of her acute embarrassment to her advantage. 'That is why I stepped outside for a breath of air.'

'You stepped rather further than just outside,' he returned, regarding her much as an irate guardian might an erring ward. 'This propensity you have for wandering about on your own really ought to have been curbed long ago.'

'And what, pray, could possibly have befallen me by taking a short stroll in a private garden?'

Her airy response might have fooled most people, but certainly not him. Taking her chin in his warm fingers, he turned her face up to his. 'I'm not sure... But something most certainly did.'

All at once she didn't know or care particularly whether the amorous couple were still in the garden, perhaps now observing them. She was aware only of him; of those ever alert, but far from cold grey eyes holding her as securely captive as the strong fingers grasping her chin. She watched, almost mesmerised, as he transferred his gaze to her mouth, and closed her eyes in eager anticipation of what must surely follow, but fate had decreed that she was destined not to experience those perfectly sculptured and sensual lips on hers. The French windows were suddenly thrown wide and Hetta stepped out onto the terrace in time to see them, like a pair of guilty lovers, step hastily apart.

'Ah! So, you've found her, Dr Carrington. I thought I saw her go outside.'

'Did you come in search of me for any particular reason?' Jane asked him, in a voice that sounded remarkably composed in the circumstances.

'Yes, I came to ask if you'd permit me to escort you in to supper,' he explained, sounding equally unruffled, 'and of course to partner me in the supper dance...'

'Which is just about to begin,' Hetta informed them, leading the way back inside.

Evidently, in his typically arrogant fashion, he took

her silence for acquiescence. Not that Jane minded particularly, for if the truth be known she was far too bemused by her totally uncharacteristic, almost wanton behaviour to concern herself about much else.

She really couldn't understand what had come over her. It most certainly wasn't the first time she had found herself alone with a member of the opposite sex who wasn't a close relative. On several occasions during the past three Seasons she had foolishly allowed herself to be inveigled into a compromising situation by some eager young gentleman, and others not quite so young, wishing to subject her to a display of masculine passion. A frosty glare had usually sufficed in dampening their ardour, but if that had failed she had never hesitated to administer a sound box to the ears or a sharp kick on the ankle, and her honour had remained intact.

Yet this time she had felt completely different. The most peculiar sensation, a strange combination of longing and apprehension, rippled through her, and she was forced to admit that she might have been in the gravest danger of losing that well-preserved virtue of hers had she found herself in a more secluded setting with Dr Thomas Carrington. She had experienced not the least desire to repulse any advances; in fact, the opposite was true. She had desperately wanted to feel those strong arms about her—had been eager to experience the pressure of those wholly masculine lips on hers. Would she have been satisfied with one embrace only or, like the woman in the garden, would she have been only too eager to encourage further intimacies?

With a supreme effort she tried to control the diverse emotions warring within her, and Tom, aware of it or not, did much to restore her composure by behaving like the perfect gentleman.

Throughout their dance together he kept up a flow of small talk, and when they went in to supper, joining Perry and Hetta at their table, he proved himself such an entertaining raconteur that even Perry, appearing completely relaxed, had his share of the conversation.

Tom didn't attempt to leave her side throughout the remainder of the evening, a circumstance noted by several of those present, and he even went so far as to escort her outside to Richard's waiting carriage when the time came for her to leave.

It might have been her imagination but she thought she could detect his hands shaking slightly as he reached for the fur-lined rug and placed it over her knees. There was definitely a slight tremor in his deep, attractive voice as he made his farewells, wishing her a safe journey to Bath and declaring the hope that they would meet again some time in the future if she should decide to pay another visit to Hampshire.

Strangely, though, he seemed disinclined to prolong their leave-taking, and gave her no time at all in which to respond. Closing the carriage door abruptly, he disappeared back inside the house, leaving her prey to such a wretched feeling of desolation that for the first time ever she was thankful for her maid's taciturn disposition, for she suddenly discovered that she could not have uttered a single word even had she wished to do so.

Chapter Eight

It was a commonly held belief that travel improved the mind. But Jane, making excellent progress on her journey to Bath, failed to see how this particular trip could improve the state of hers. Each mile that took her further away from Hampshire only succeeded in adding to her unhappy state. Even the excellently prepared luncheon which she had forced herself to eat at that very superior posting-house had failed completely to lift her spirits. There was no getting away from it—her despondency had reached an all-time low!

For almost a month she had been allowed to do more or less as she had pleased. Staying at the Hall had been like sampling blessed freedom after years of confinement. The Knightleys couldn't possibly have done more to make her feel welcome—which, to be fair, was no more than her sisters always did, but, unlike them, Elizabeth and Richard had taken excellent care of her without undue and suffocating attention. Was it any wonder, then, that she was very reluctant to leave a place where she had sampled the sweet taste of liberty?

A low moan succeeded in piercing through the ever increasing layers of gloom that were wrapping themselves around her, and Jane turned her head to look at her maid. 'What is it, Latimer? Are you feeling unwell?'

'I do feel a little peculiar, my lady,' she responded faintly. 'I think it must have been something I ate back at the posting-house.'

They had partaken of the same fare in the inn's private parlour, and Jane certainly wasn't experiencing any ill effects. 'I should think that highly unlikely. I feel perfectly well, and we both sampled the same food.'

'Except the game pie, my lady,' the maid reminded her. 'You didn't have any of that.'

Jane watched, concern rapidly mounting, as Latimer slipped a hand beneath the serviceable cloak and placed her fingers gingerly against her stomach. Her colour was still good, but it appeared that she was in no little discomfort.

'Would you like me to stop the carriage? A few minutes in the fresh air might set you to rights.'

As though it was an effort even to move, Latimer eased herself slowly forward in the seat and peered through the window. 'I believe I know where we are. I travelled this route several times when I was employed by Lady Fairfax. Her carriage met with a slight accident on one occasion and we were forced to seek shelter at an inn not far from here—just off the main road, it was. I hate to be a nuisance, my lady, but do you think we could stop there for a short while?'

Jane didn't even take a moment to consider the matter. Pulling down the window, she called out. The carriage came to a halt and one of the post-boys appeared before her on the road.

'It be only a few miles to Calne, my lady. It might be best if we made straight for there,' he advised, after listening to her request to pull off the main road at the next turning and find the inn.

'Oh, my lady, I really do not think I could remain in the carriage until Calne.' Latimer placed a suddenly trembling hand to her temple. 'I'm beginning to feel a trifle faint.'

That settled the matter as far as Jane was concerned. There were few things more unpleasant than being forced to sit in a closed carriage for any distance when one's head was spinning and one's stomach threatened to expel its contents at any moment. Nevertheless, after travelling down a narrow and twisting country lane, only wide enough for one carriage, for what seemed a very long time, without seeing so much as an isolated barn, Jane began to regret her hasty decision.

'Are you sure there is an inn along this road, Latimer?' she asked, leaning out of the window in a fruitless attempt to catch sight of any habitation. 'There appears to be only fields as far as the eye can see.'

'I—I'm certain it's this way, my lady,' the maid confirmed, peering out of the other window. 'Oh, look! There is a house just up ahead. Perhaps we could stop and ask directions there?'

Against her better judgement, for she was now firmly convinced that there was no hostelry hereabouts, Jane complied. The red-brick dwelling, set a little way back from the road, was surrounded by farmland, but there was sufficient room in front of the few dilapidated outbuildings to enable the post-boys to turn the carriage and, from the smoke billowing from one of the chimneys, the place appeared to be occupied. If nothing else, at least she might be able to procure a glass of water for her maid, she thought, stepping down from the carriage.

Just as though they had been expected, the front door opened suddenly and a gaunt middle-aged woman came scurrying down the path like an excited child. 'I heard the carriage and thought it were my master returning,' she announced, with a forced smile which put Jane in mind of the Dowager Lady Pentecost. 'We don't get many people travelling this way.'

Hardly surprising as the road didn't appear to lead anywhere, Jane mused, subjecting the stranger to a swift appraisal. Judging by her attire, the woman was undoubtedly a high-ranking servant, possibly a housekeeper, but not a particularly conscientious one if the soiled apron was anything to go by. Nor did the house, on closer inspection, appear particularly well maintained. The paintwork on the doors and windows was cracked and peeling, and the small front garden was in urgent need of attention. The dwelling's isolation gave one to suppose that its owner was something of a recluse, who was, moreover, unwilling, or perhaps unable, to effect necessary repairs.

'Can you tell me if there is a hostelry nearby where we could seek shelter for a while? My maid is feeling unwell.'

'The nearest be a few miles further on, but it ain't the sort of place for the likes of you, my lady. It's nothing but a hedge tavern.' The woman peered into the carriage and let out an exclamation of dismay.

'Oh, you poor dear! Come along with me and lie down for a while. You look right poorly!'

Jane, on the other hand, thought Latimer, rosy-cheeked and bright-eyed, looked positively blooming in the circumstances, but looks, she knew, could be deceptive. Added to which, the maid had always been conscientious, not once neglecting her duties because of some trifling ailment during the whole time she had been employed by the Beresford family, so it would be unjust, not to say downright heartless, Jane thought, to deny her the time to recover sufficiently to continue the journey.

After instructing the post-boys to turn the carriage and await further orders, Jane entered the house to discover a thick-set man of middle age and average height awaiting her in the small, dimly lit hall. His large, work-roughened hands gave her every reason to suppose that he was not just employed in the house, but was expected to undertake a wide variety of du-ties, which in itself was not an uncommon practice. What did surprise her, however, was that the owner of such a neglected house could afford the luxury of employing two servants, given the fact that little or no money had been spent on the property for, she guessed, some considerable time.

'The missus 'as taken the young lady upstairs for a rest,' he informed her, closing the door and showing her into a small parlour which smelt stale and unused, even though a good fire was burning in the grate. 'Sit yerself down and mek yerself comfortable,' he invited politely enough, but eyeing her in a way that made her feel uneasy. 'The missus oughtn't to be long,' he added, casting her one last furtive glance before leav-ing the room.

Jane was hardly given time to take stock of her shabby surroundings before the door opened again and the woman who she assumed was the house-keeper entered.

'How is my maid feeling now?'

'Still a mite poorly. Said it was something she ate.' She moved across to the window and gave the faded drapes a twitch, sending a cloud of dust rising in the air. 'Think we ought to do something about your carriage, though, ma'am. Can't expect the post-boys to stand twiddling their thumbs until you can be on your way again. Unfortunately there isn't room in the stable for the horses. Perhaps it would be best if the carriage awaited you at the posting-house in Calne. My master should be home soon. He's a kind-hearted gentleman who would be only too willing to convey you to The Bell in his own carriage once your maid's fit enough to travel.'

'That's most kind, but I really don't think I can impose—'

'Not at all!' the housekeeper interrupted, her thin-lipped mouth curling into yet another of those un-trustworthy smiles. 'The master will be glad of your company, and, if it should turn out that your maid isn't fit to travel to Bath until tomorrow, I'm certain you'll get a room at The Bell.'

Jane had no desire to remain in this house, but couldn't bring herself selfishly to desert Latimer unless she had no option but to do so. It wouldn't hurt to grant her maid an hour or so in which to recover, but if it became necessary she would seriously have to consider continuing the journey alone, leaving Latimer with sufficient funds to travel to Bath when she was able.

A sudden thought occurred to her, and she looked at the housekeeper sharply. 'How did you know our eventual destination?'

Only for an instant did the woman seem slightly discomposed. 'Your maid must have told me, Lady Jane.'

Latimer had evidently been in a rare talkative mood, for it seemed that she had also revealed her mistress's identity, Jane mused, deciding it might be wise in the circumstances to see her maid before she made any decision regarding the removal of the carriage to the inn at Calne.

Without the least hesitation the housekeeper acquiesced to Jane's request to be taken to her maid, and led the way out of the room and up the narrow staircase which, covered in a film of dust, was further proof that the servant was not overfond of work.

'In here, my lady,' she said, opening the door at the very end of the narrow passageway.

Jane was granted only sufficient time to register that the room was unoccupied when she received a violent push, the force of which almost sent her sprawling to the floor. Before she could regain her balance someone grasped her from behind, a smaller hand relieved her of her fashionable bonnet and a gag was securely tied over her mouth, effectively stifling the terrified cry that rose in her throat. Then both her hands and feet were bound with a merciless disregard for her delicate skin, before she was finally picked up and virtually tossed down on the bed.

The speed with which the assault upon her had taken place left Jane breathless, and it was as much as she could do to raise her head a little. However, it wasn't the smugly satisfied expressions on the faces of the housekeeper and her husband that made her blood run cold, but the sight of Latimer, appearing completely unruffled as always, framed in the doorway.

'Well, we've done our part, Rosie, old girl. Now all we need do is await the master's arrival.'

'Not quite, Mrs Talbot,' Latimer countered, her steady gaze never wavering from the recumbent figure on the bed. 'There's still the post-boys to deal with. You had better attend to that, Ralph.' She waited until both husband and wife had left and then, just as though she was unable to break the habits of a lifetime, she bent to retrieve the discarded bonnet, and the reticule which had been dropped in the struggle, and carried them from the room without uttering another word.

Jane heard the key turn in the lock and listened to Latimer's retreating footsteps. A few minutes later she clearly detected the sound of a carriage moving off and realised, with a sinking feeling in the pit of her stomach, that the post-boys were leaving, and with them any hope of an immediate escape.

Still unable to comprehend fully just what had happened, or why, she tried to ease herself into a sitting position. It took some time, but eventually she succeeded in her objective, and stared about the makeshift prison. Like the downstairs parlour, it was shabbily furnished and in urgent need of a clean, though the bedcovers at least appeared to have been recently laundered, no doubt in readiness for her visit.

There wasn't a doubt about it; her kidnapping had been well planned. But whose was the brain behind the abduction? Jane wondered. Certainly not Latimer's, although she was forced to concede that the wickedly deceitful creature had played her part well. Not until the housekeeper had foolishly mentioned Bath had it occurred to Jane that all was not as it should be, and even then she hadn't for a moment suspected that their arrival at this place had been anything other than a quirk of fate. What a fool she had been!

For several minutes she was forced to do battle with rising anger and a passionate desire to be avenged, but eventually she was able to regain control of her turbulent thoughts and began to wonder what lay behind her abduction. Monetary gain was the most obvious motive, of course, but why had her kidnappers put their plan into effect now? After all, it would have made more sense to carry out the abduction while her father could be easily approached with the ransom demand. Why wait until the Earl was out of the country? Her captors might need to keep her hidden away for several weeks before they received their ill-gotten gains. No, it just didn't make sense. More was wanted than mere money… But what?

She wasn't left wondering for long. The sound of a light carriage, a phaeton or curricle, she guessed, pulling up outside reached her ears. Then there came the sound of voices below, quickly followed by footsteps mounting the stairs. A few moments later the key was fitted back into the lock, the door swung open, and several things that had puzzled Jane during her sojourn in Hampshire suddenly became crystal-clear.

'Oh, my dear girl! My servants have been unnecessarily rough with you. Allow me to make you a little more comfortable.'

With one judicious tug the offending gag was removed and Jane might have felt at least a modicum of gratitude if it hadn't been for the smug satisfaction she easily perceived on the handsome face looming above her. Anger threatened to return with a vengeance, but she succeeded in containing it and even managed to affect one of Lady Pentecost's fallacious smiles.

'The not so honourable Mr Simon Fairfax... I should have known!'

'Now, now, my darling. You mustn't be rude to your future husband.'

His glib response confirmed her worst fears. The instant she had seen him, she had guessed what he had planned for her. Marriage, of course, would secure her entire fortune, and safe in the knowledge that her family would accept the forced alliance, rather than face a monumental scandal, he could continue to go into Society with his reputation intact. But first of all he would need to get her to the altar, and if he thought she would acquiesce willingly he had underrated his quarry.

Seating himself on the bed, he placed one perfectly manicured hand on either side of her and stared with evident appreciation at her far from friendly countenance. 'God! You're even captivatingly lovely when somewhat dishevelled. I chose well when I decided upon you for my bride.'

Refusing to be intimidated by his nearness, Jane made no attempt to press herself further back against the mound of pillows, even though he was so close she could almost feel the heat his body exuded. 'You may have chosen, Mr Fairfax, but what on earth makes you suppose that I'll agree to be your wife?'

His self-satisfied smile did nothing to stem the ever

mounting animosity she was feeling towards him. 'My dear, a little time for calm reflection will force you to accept that you have little choice.'

He then turned his attention to the cord binding her ankles and was silent for a moment while he dealt with a particularly stubborn knot. 'I'm sure you'll be sensible and not make a bolt for the door,' he continued in the same infuriatingly confident tone. 'It would be futile to make the attempt, believe me. I would catch you before you had reached the stairs. I'm also sure that you'll soon see sense, and agree to my proposal. The only alternative, of course, is social ruin once it becomes known that you have spent several days…and nights…in my company.'

'And you, of course, would ensure that it did become common knowledge,' she responded, wondering how long she would be able to resist the temptation to raise one of her recently released feet and place a well-aimed kick on some part of his immaculate attired person.

'You do me an injustice, my lady. I should never stoop so low as to sully a fair lady's name. I cannot, however, vouch for the discretion of my servants.'

Jane regarded him for a few moments in silence. Handsome though he was, he had never rated highly in her estimation, and he had now plummeted to an all-time low. He was quite simply despicable.

'And Latimer, I do not doubt, numbers amongst this small group of devotees,' she couldn't resist remarking in a voice of thinly veiled contempt.

'Of course.'

'In that case you are in my father's debt, sir. He has been paying your servant's wages these past three months.'

'I'm certain that such an upstanding gentleman will not press for payment, in view of the fact that I'm shortly to be joined by marriage to his noble family.'

'I wish,' she responded, turning slightly to enable him to untie her hands, 'you would rid your mind of this erroneous belief you harbour that I should consider marriage to you preferable to social ruin.'

'And I sincerely hope you rapidly come to accept the fact that you really have no choice.' His clipped tone betrayed clearly enough that her finely honed dart of derision had succeeded in piercing the veneer of unruffled reserve, but Jane's feeling of immense satisfaction was destined not to last very long.

'I have with me a special licence. Tomorrow you attain your majority and therefore can legally marry without your father's consent. You have until then to accept your fate with a good grace.'

Rising, he moved over to the window. As he remained standing with his back towards her, Jane could only assume that, with his customary confidence, he retained no fears that she would escape. No doubt he had one of his degenerate servants posted in the hall in the event that she should be foolish enough to make the attempt, but she had no intention of doing so, at least not yet—not until she considered there would be a better than even chance of success.

'You shall not find me an unreasonable husband,' he continued, and she forced herself to listen. 'I shall make no unnecessary demands, but I do intend that ours will be a marriage in every sense. I should never wish to force myself upon you and am prepared to be patient—providing, that is, you do not compel me to use those very means in order to persuade you to agree to the union in the first place.'

His meaning, although delicately phrased, was all too sickeningly clear. 'So, you would even be loathsome enough to stoop to rape to attain your ends,' Jane murmured, successfully concealing her rising fear, but not the utter contempt she felt.

'Not through choice, no, my dear.' And for the first time there was an element of regret in his voice. 'But needs must, as they say.'

He came back across to the bed and stared down at her, but she could not now bring herself to look at him, although that was precisely what she would be forced to do for the rest of her life, unless she could somehow manage to extricate herself from this trap which, through a dogged resolve to achieve independence, she had helped set for herself.

If only she had listened to her brother and had agreed to make use of one of the family's carriages, and to be accompanied by their loyal and trusted servants! If only she had accepted Richard's kind offer of his escort to Bath... But no, she had been foolishly determined to prove to all the members of her family, to everyone, that she was infinitely capable of making her own arrangements and more than able to look after herself. And just look where her stubborn pride had brought her!

She gave herself an inward shake. This was not the time to indulge in bitter self-recriminations. She had until tomorrow to find a way out of this mess, but certainly not longer. She didn't doubt for a moment that if she continued to refuse to acquiesce willingly he would ensure that she had no choice. So it might be wise in the circumstances to lull him into a false sense of security, by allowing him to believe that she was at least beginning to accept her fate.

It was an effort, but she forced herself to look at
him again. 'It would seem, sir, that you hold all the
cards, but you cannot expect me to be enthusiastic
over what life has in store for me. It is hardly flattering to know that you are coveted for your wealth
alone.'

'You underrate yourself, my dear. There are a number of heiresses brightening the *Marriage Mart* these
days. One or two even more lovely than you, some
might say. But you have always possessed a special
something that sets you quite apart as far as I am
concerned—grace, poise, charm—call it what you
will. I have admired you for some little time, though
I do realise, of course, that you have scant regard for
me.'

The knowledge didn't appear to trouble him to any
great extent, as his next words proved. 'I shan't lose
any sleep over that, however, for it is my considered
opinion that you have scant regard for most members
of my sex. In all the years I've known you, I have
never once seen you betray a preference for any particular gentleman's society.'

A ruggedly handsome and frowning countenance,
with penetrating grey eyes, suddenly appeared before
her mind's eye, and the memory of a deep, attractive
but disapproving voice commenting on her folly instantly erased those taut lines about her mouth. How
she wished, now, that she had taken heed of Dr
Thomas Carrington's sage advice about the sheer stu-
pidity of travelling about on her own!

Simon Fairfax was not slow to perceive the wistful
expression that just for one unguarded moment flickered across her features. 'Obviously I am in error—
there is someone. Dear me,' he remarked, with a flash

of wry humour. 'Am I likely to have some star-crossed gallant after my blood when the wedding has taken place?'

'No, you are not.' She rose from the bed, and he made no attempt to stop her taking up his former stance at the window. 'Would you be kind enough to leave me alone now, Mr Fairfax? As you perhaps can appreciate, I need to come to terms with what has befallen me.'

'Of course, my dear. But first I must ask you to write a letter informing those concerned that you have no further need of a hired carriage. I shall then go to Calne to collect your trunks and deal with the necessary payments.'

Knowing that it would avail her nothing to object, Jane seated herself at the small table upon which writing materials had been placed, and dutifully penned the letter he dictated.

'Thank you, my dear. I am so glad you have decided to be sensible. It makes everything so much pleasanter, don't you agree?' He read the missive through before slipping it into the pocket of his fashionable jacket. 'I regret having to leave you in this deplorable house,' he added, turning back at the door. 'It isn't what you're used to, I know, but it's only for a couple of days. I inherited the place some months ago from a distant relative and installed the Talbots here when I thought up this little scheme. Mrs Talbot is very lax in carrying out many of her duties, but she is a fair cook. We'll dine when I return.' And with that promised 'treat' in store he went out, leaving her to chafe once again at what had befallen her.

She went across to the window, and it came as no great surprise to discover that it had been firmly nailed shut, no doubt in readiness for her confinement. The room was situated at the rear of the building. Below was a neglected garden, choked with weeds, with one or two ill-pruned fruit trees. Beyond the rickety garden fence were open fields stretching as far as the eye could see, with just the occasional small copse dotted here and there to break the monotony of the flat landscape.

More importantly, however, a small lean-to had been constructed along part of the back wall. It certainly couldn't be reached from here, even if it were possible to open the window, but there was every chance that access might be gained from the room next to this one. If she could manage to climb onto that sloping roof, then surely it would be a simple matter to reach the ground?

The sound of the key being fitted into the lock yet again interrupted her hopeful deliberations and she turned, unable to prevent a spark of hostility from brightening her eyes when the door swung open to reveal her visitor.

Oh, yes, she had been duped right royally! She had walked into the trap like a naive little fool, even though she had sensed from the beginning that there was something untrustworthy about Rose Latimer. Why, oh, why hadn't she acted upon instinct and been rid of the conniving wretch weeks ago? Well, that was yet something else to chalk up to experience, she supposed. And she would certainly make a point of choosing her own servants from now on, too!

'Mr Simon said I was to bring you this. It will be some time before you dine together and he thought you might like a little something to tide you over.'

Latimer put the tray bearing the bowl of steaming

broth down on the table beside the writing materials, and then turned, but didn't find it easy to meet her former mistress's unwavering and far from friendly gaze. She no longer considered herself a servant, but had agreed to continue acting the part until they arrived in Paris and she was rewarded for her part in Simon's scheme to acquire a rich bride. Then a totally different life beckoned, and one where she fully intended to issue the orders.

'Mr Simon has already left for Calne to collect your belongings. You'll no doubt wish to change for dinner. I'll help you, of course, should you require assistance.'

Jane couldn't prevent a grudging smile at this. The woman certainly had an abundance of brass-faced nerve. 'You may be sure I'll not require your services again, Latimer. You are, as one might say, relieved of all your duties. But just tell me one thing before you go,' she went on, arresting the woman's progress to the door. 'Did I prove such a difficult mistress? Did I treat you so unkindly that you felt the need to exact this kind of revenge?'

Rose lowered her eyes and stared blindly at a spot on the threadbare carpet. Not for the first time did she experience deep regrets over her part in Simon Fairfax's scheme to entrap the Earl's daughter, but what would the future have held for her if she'd refused to help him?

At the age of sixteen, when she had first given herself to him, she had believed he truly loved her, but she was older and wiser now and had come to accept that there could never be any lasting future for her with him. The Simon Fairfaxes of this world did not marry servant girls; they chose, when the time came, from their own social class. Lord Fairfax's excesses had brought the family to the brink of financial ruin, and Rose really couldn't blame Simon for taking measures, unsavoury though they were, to secure his own future. After all, by aiding him in this cause, she had done no less herself. She had been offered the opportunity to be freed from a life of dismal servitude and had jumped at the chance.

To ensure a bright future she had been expected to do little more than keep Simon informed of Lady Jane's movements, so that when the right opportunity arose he could put his plan into action. She had suffered no real pangs of conscience over this. Lady Jane Beresford was a very lovely young woman, and she didn't doubt for a moment that Simon genuinely desired her. Added to which, it stood to reason that the Earl of Eastbury's daughter would marry one day, and she could do a lot worse than wed the Honourable Simon Fairfax. He was both handsome and charming, and although it was unlikely he would make a faithful husband Rose didn't suppose for a moment that he would make an unkind one.

This belief and the conviction she had retained that she wasn't doing the Earl's daughter any real harm had, up until the night of the Pentecosts' ball, continued to salve her conscience. Even when, under the cover of darkness, she had slipped out of the house to meet with Simon in the garden and, after their passionate interlude, had agreed to follow his instructions to the letter, she still hadn't experienced any feelings of guilt at the part she must play in the kidnapping. It was only later, when she and her young mistress were about to return to Knightley Hall, that everything had changed, in a matter of a few moments, and she had begun to experience tormenting pangs of guilt.

Lady Jane Beresford, unless Latimer was very much mistaken, was a young woman on the brink of falling deeply in love, though she probably wasn't aware of it herself yet. There had been that message in her eyes when she had watched the young doctor walk back into Pentecost Grange, a look that had shouted clearly enough, Don't go! Don't leave me! And that selfsame look had been mirrored in Dr Carrington's eyes, too.

But what hope was there for them? Lady Jane was every inch the refined and elegant aristocratic lady. She would be expected to choose a husband from the highest in the land, not some obscure country practitioner, who might not be precisely purse-pinched, but who certainly couldn't compete with her wealth. Why, they stood as much chance of making a suitable match as she and Simon Fairfax! She had done Lady Jane a great favour by ensuring that her path and Dr Carrington's wouldn't cross again in the foreseeable future... Or had she?

'No one, my lady, could ever accuse you of being less than a very considerate mistress,' she said at last, and sincerely meant every word. She couldn't bring herself to add that she had made a determined effort not to become attached to her, and in part she had succeeded in this aim. Yet it had been impossible not to like and admire this warm-hearted young woman, who possessed that rare gift of being able to talk to those less fortunate than herself without making them feel in any way inferior.

'But I have always wished to better myself—had always hoped one day to be able to use my small skills for my own benefit. Simon offered me the chance of making my dream of becoming a milliner come true.'

With my money, Jane thought bitterly, whilst experiencing at the same time a grudging admiration. If it hadn't been to her own detriment she would have genuinely wished Latimer well in her endeavours. 'And where precisely do you propose to undertake this venture?'

'After…after the ceremony has taken place, Simon wishes me to accompany you to Paris. He suggested I make a fresh start there. He says the French lead the field when it comes to fashion.'

What deep game was that wretch Simon Fairfax playing? Jane wondered. It was quite evident that his relationship with this woman was rather more than that of master and servant. It was quite evident, too, by the way she spoke his name as though it were a benediction, that poor Latimer was quite foolishly devoted to him, but whether he returned her regard was open to question. He must know that there was little chance of her making a success of her venture in Paris, so Jane could only assume that Latimer had made a very satisfying mistress and that Simon had no intention of dispensing with her services quite yet. Her eyes narrowed speculatively. Might now be the right moment to sow a seed of doubt in her former maid's mind?

'What he tells you is quite true. The French are very chic. But they have little affection for the people of this country. They welcome us with open arms when we visit their towns and cities, and are more than willing to encourage us to part with our money. Whether or not they would conveniently forget the

many years our two countries were at war and pa-
tronise an establishment owned by an Englishwoman
is quite a different matter, especially in view of the
fact that they have superb modistes of their own. Believe me, Latimer, Mr Fairfax would be doing you no
favour by helping you to set up a business venture in
Paris. You would stand a far greater chance of making
a success if you established yourself in one of our
own rapidly growing cities in the Midlands or the
north.'

Latimer digested this sage advice in silence for several thoughtful moments, and then asked, unexpectedly, 'You really don't like Mr Simon at all, do you,
my lady?'

Jane knew little would be gained by lying. 'In view
of what he plans for me, it's hardly surprising, is it?'
There was an unmistakable thread of sarcasm in her
voice, but not a trace of bitterness now. 'I vowed that
I would never marry a man I could never love nor
respect, but fate has decreed otherwise, it would seem.
No, I do not care for him in the least, and in view of
his recent actions I could never bring myself to trust
him. And you would be extremely foolish to do so
either. If you take my advice, you'll not let him out
of your sight until he has rewarded you in full for
your invaluable help. He could never have carried out
his despicable plot without you, now, could he?'

'No, he could not,' Latimer agreed, with a hint of
regret. 'You must hate the very ground I walk on. I
just hope that one day you can find it in your heart
to forgive me.'

Jane resisted the temptation to wound with a pithy
response, for strangely enough she couldn't find it
within herself to despise this woman. She didn't even

blame her for wishing to better herself. She just resented being the means by which her former maid hoped to attain her ends.

'I don't hate you, Rose,' she admitted, calling her by her given name for the first time. 'I just wish…I just wish we could have known each other better. I had already decided that it would be to our mutual advantage if you found yourself a new position. I'd sensed a deep resentment in you from the first.'

'But not against you,' Latimer hurriedly assured her.

'I'm glad of that, at least.' It seemed to have become a time for confessions and Jane didn't have the least reticence in adding, 'Had I been aware of your ambitions, I might have been in a position to help you embark on your new career, but I'll not insult your intelligence by pretending there's the remotest chance I would consider doing so now, at least not willingly. That doesn't mean, however, that I wish you ill-fortune in your endeavours. But you can hardly expect me to be overjoyed, knowing that your hopes for the future were made possible by the total annihilation of my own.'

For several moments Latimer stood staring silently at some distant spot, and then, without uttering another word, left the room, leaving Jane to focus her thoughts once more on trying to find a means of escape.

Waiting for nightfall presented itself as the most sensible course of action. But could she afford to wait that long? Time certainly wasn't on her side. Furthermore, would the cover of darkness be of any real benefit? Reaching a sizeable habitation, where she could attain help, must be her goal, but, being totally unfamiliar with this part of the country, she might well find herself walking round in circles and run the risk of recapture.

It was all rather academic, anyway, she reminded herself, unless she could first escape from this room. The window, of course, was a non-starter, so the only way…

She moved slowly across to the door, silently blessing Simon Fairfax's relative for spending little money on the upkeep of the house. The door and its surround were excessively worm-eaten, which gave her every reason to hope that the wood might be easily gouged out to enable her to force the lock—if, of course, she could get her hands on something, a knife perhaps, to aid her. Dinner would offer an opportunity to purloin some useful implement, and then afterwards, when everyone had retired for the night, she could attempt to chisel away at the wood. It was a slim chance, perhaps, but likely to be her only one.

Examining the area around the lock more closely, in order to see what was involved, Jane placed her hand on the door-handle. Then the totally unbelievable happened: the door opened effortlessly. For several moments she was too stunned to think, let alone take advantage of her great good fortune.

Her eyes narrowed. Maybe luck had had precious little to do with it. Had Latimer inadvertently forgotten to lock the door behind her? Or had she quite deliberately given her former mistress a chance to escape? Jane wasn't certain, but she didn't intend wasting precious minutes pondering over the conundrum now.

Galvanised, she peered along the passageway. It was deserted, but that didn't mean that there was no one posted somewhere, possibly in the hall, vigilantly on guard. So, carefully closing the door, she tiptoed into the next room. It was much larger than the one she had been allocated and she suspected, from the fashionable male attire laid out neatly on the bed, that it was being used by Simon Fairfax, a circumstance which prompted her not to linger.

The window opened easily and, thankfully, with only the faintest protesting creak. As Jane had suspected, it offered easy access to the sloping roof below. Scrambling out and stepping down onto the slates proved no hardship. Unfortunately there was nothing near or leaning against the structure, not even a water butt, to aid her further descent. As luck would have it, though, it was no more than an eight-foot drop from the lowest point of the roof, although her recently injured ankle protested as she made the courageous leap down to the edge of what at one time must have been a lawn, but now could be best described as a weed-infested wilderness.

By the time she had scrambled over the rickety fence at the bottom of the garden she had forgotten her niggling hurts. Keeping close to the sides of the fields, in the hope that the hedgerows would conceal her flight, she put as much distance as she could between herself and her former captors. Only when she had reached the copse, three fields from the house, did she feel safe enough to rest for a while, but even then could not resist frequent glances over her shoulder just to ensure that there was no one following in hot pursuit.

Not a soul to be seen, thank goodness! So she could only assume that no one had yet returned to her room in order to collect her untouched broth. But it

wouldn't be too much longer, surely, before her flight
was discovered? It would take Simon little more than
an hour to reach Calne and return with her belongings, and she guessed he couldn't be that far away
from the house now. She might be granted a further
thirty minutes before the search for her began, but
certainly not longer.

Simon, she felt certain, would begin by scouring
the lanes about the house. After all, he could hardly
take his carriage across the fields. Which was some
comfort, she supposed, but not very much. Who was
to say that he hadn't one or two riding horses installed
in that run-down stable? And how many male servants had he with him to offer assistance? She had
seen only one man, Ralph Talbot, but she would be
foolish to assume that he was the only one.

She still considered her best plan of action was to
keep well away from any roads as far as she was able,
and if she remained moving more or less in the same
direction sooner or later, with any luck, she would
come upon a village or hamlet where she could seek
help. Simon could have no idea in which direction
she was heading. He would realise, of course, that,
on foot, she couldn't have got that far away, which
was sufficient inducement for her not to tarry.

Leaving the relative concealment of the small
clump of trees, she pressed onwards, doing her best
to ignore the threatening clouds building up from the
west, but unable to stop herself from dwelling on
what recapture would mean. Simon Fairfax, yielding
to what gentlemanly instincts he possessed, had not
resorted to undue force, but she doubted very much
that he would continue to behave in the same vein if
he got her in his clutches again.

She would no doubt find herself severely re-strained, making any further attempts at escape impossible. Not only that, she didn't doubt for a moment that he would resort to those vile extremes whereby she had no choice but to marry him. Surprisingly, the thought of being violated didn't induce a fit of the vapours, as it no doubt would have done in those faint-hearted members of her sex, but instilled in her a determination to outwit the villainous wretch.

Pausing to take a well-earned rest, she took a moment to look about her. Just how far she had walked she had no way of knowing, but she could perceive definite changes in the landscape: the flat arable land surrounding the house had given way to rolling pastureland, where sheep made the most of the fading light by grazing hungrily, barely giving her a cursory glance, and denser areas of woodland were now appearing on the horizon.

But for how much longer could she keep up this relentless pace? There was little point in trying to deny the fact that she was already experiencing the unpleasant results of the unaccustomed and lengthy exercise. Furthermore, unless she wished to add to her discomfort by spending the night in the open air, which certainly wouldn't be her first choice, then she would need to risk walking along a road in order to find some shelter.

She had already been forced to cross several by-roads, but these had been little more than deeply rutted tracks, no doubt used by farmers to gain access to their various fields. She had experienced little fear in walking for a short while along any of these until she had found a gateway or a gap in the hedge wide enough to scramble through. But had she put sufficient distance between herself and that house for her to risk trying to reach habitation by keeping to a highway? Might Simon Fairfax have abandoned any search he may have undertaken by now?

Climbing through a gap in the hedge, she found herself standing on the even surface of a road. It was wider than any of those she had travelled along to Simon's house, and must surely ultimately lead to her goal: a town or village. But which way to go, left or right?

She was still debating over this when she distinctly heard the sound of hoof-beats. It wasn't a carriage, but a lone rider, she felt certain, but even so caution prevailed and she took immediate action by retreating to the gap in the hedge. There was always the possibility that it might be Simon or his servant, Ralph Talbot, and even if not, dared she chance begging assistance?

She risked a second glance along the road and, watching the lone traveller appear round the bend, could hardly believe the evidence of her own eyes. It couldn't be…

Tears of joy blurring her vision, she scrambled from her hiding place, waving and calling frantically and almost stumbling in her eagerness to reach the blessed protection of that gentleman's side.

Chapter Nine

It was market day and the town of Devizes was buzzing with life, its busy main streets rapidly filling to capacity with a variety of carriages and farm carts, with beast of varying kinds, and with people buying or selling, or merely watching the spectacle.

Tom, woken early by the first of the farmers herding his stock to market, quickly abandoned the idea of trying to go back to sleep, and for a while leaned out of his bedchamber window, watching the street below quickly become a hive of activity.

Market days were vastly important to the people of the town and surrounding area: occasions when they hoped to attain some financial reward for their hard labours, as well as times for festivity, when folk who hadn't seen one another for several weeks, maybe months, got together to exchange stories and gossip generally.

Shops and taverns did a roaring trade. Long before Tom had finished eating his breakfast, the inn where he was putting up was becoming crowded with the menfolk, many of whom had been up since daybreak, wishing to quench their thirst.

Tom spent the day exploring the town and viewing
the wares for sale on the many stalls. There was much
to see and a great deal to capture his interest, but from
time to time he would catch sight of something—a
girl with reddish hair, or a more affluent young
woman decked out in her finery—that would revive
a poignant memory. Unfortunately it had happened
rather too often, each occasion leaving him slightly
more depressed, so that by the time he was ready to
leave to dine with Sir William Dent he wasn't looking
forward to the evening ahead with any great enthusiasm.

'The horse be saddled and awaiting you, sir,' the
innkeeper's very obliging wife informed him as he
descended the stairs into the coffee-room.

'Thank you, Mrs Pegg. I'm unable to say what time
I'm likely to return, but I hope it won't be too late.
You and your husband have already had a long and
very busy day.'

'Don't you concern yourself none over that, Dr
Carrington. We always stay open till late on market
days. There's always some who don't know when to
stop celebrating. Mind, those with any sense won't
leave it late before they start for home. The weather's
changed for the worst during the past hour. The rain's
keeping off for now, but I reckon it'll come afore the
day's out, so if you decide to stay at Sir William's
for the night I'll understand.'

Although Sir William Dent's fine country residence
was situated some five miles from Devizes, he was a
well-known figure in the town. His hospitality was
famed, and as he had three unmarried daughters, all
as plain as pikestaffs, still residing under his roof Mrs
Pegg couldn't see the eminent surgeon wishing to lose

the company of such a personable young gentleman
as Dr Carrington too soon.

'And don't be afraid I'll let the room if you've not
returned by the following day, neither.'

Assuring her that this was highly unlikely, Tom
went to collect the hired mount from the stable yard
and, following directions given by the innkeeper, left
the town heading in an easterly direction.

The main road was still quite busy with people
making their way home, their arms filled with their
purchases, and with their pockets and purses notice-
ably lighter, no doubt. By the time Tom turned onto
the slightly narrower road which, according to Pegg's
directions, would eventually lead him right past Sir
William's door he had the highway virtually to himself, and his mind, as it too often did, began to dwell
once again on Elizabeth Knightley's cousin.

How he had tried to fight that ever increasing attraction to her, but for all the good it had done he
might as well have saved himself the effort. His mind
might continue to assure him that he had been sensible in not trying to see her again before he had left
Hampshire on the morning after the Pentecosts' ball,
but his heart had continued to proclaim quite otherwise. He could ignore the all-too-painful truth no
longer—he had for the first time in his life fallen
deeply in love.

If the knowledge hadn't been so agonising he
would have laughed at the absurdity of it all. The
level-headed and conscientious Dr Thomas Carrington, whose dedication and no-nonsense manner had
won the respect of the Hampshire community he
served, had fallen victim to Cupid's arrow. Oh, yes,
Venus's mischievous son had pinked him nicely; the

potent dart was firmly embedded, and it would be some time, Tom felt sure, before the wound began to heal—if it ever did completely.

But life must go on and in the meantime he must throw himself into his work with renewed vigour. Yes—that was the best cure. Feeling sorry for himself and yearning for something far above his touch was no way to deal with the painful ache which rarely left him. It would be foolish to imagine that he would always successfully blot out the image of those beautiful, laughing eyes set in a finely boned countenance from his mind, so he must face the fact that for some time to come he would see something or someone that would ignite bitter-sweet memory.

As he rounded the bend in the road, it seemed as if fate, capricious wench, had decided to corroborate this conviction. A young woman, with reddish-brown hair cascading about her shoulders in some disarray, suddenly appeared from nowhere. He closed his eyes in an attempt to disperse the image, but a beloved and well-spoken voice calling his name forced them open again.

'Good God!' He stared down at her as she reached his side, still reluctant to believe the evidence of his own eyes. 'Am I dreaming, or is it really you?'

'Well, of course it is!' She raised her arm and he automatically obliged by helping her into the saddle before him.

Still somewhat shaken by the great love of his life's miraculous appearance, he managed to enquire, 'Would it be too much to ask what you're doing in this out-of-the-way place and…' he looked about him '…seemingly alone?'

'Would you believe it, Tom,' she said, using his

given name as though it were the most natural thing in the world, 'I was abducted? Such impudence!'

Having the most desirable of creatures virtually sitting on his lap did little to ease his mounting confusion, but eventually the rather unbelievable explanation managed to penetrate the delicious feeling of euphoria doing its best to numb his thought processes. 'Abducted? By whom, may I ask?'

'Simon Fairfax. Oh, do not let us tarry here!' she urged. 'For all I know the wretch might be out looking for me at this very moment.'

She had hardly finished speaking when they both heard the sound of a carriage. Moments later a curricule came bowling towards them, and there was no mistaking who was handling the ribbons.

'Oh, Tom, it is he! Quick, let us away over the field. He cannot possibly follow us there.'

'Damn it, no! I won't turn tail and run. I'll confront the black… Here, what are you about, girl?'

Jane, seeing no sense in spending time arguing, took matters into her own hands, or more accurately the reins, and urged their mount through the gap in the hedge. Once in the field, she headed for the large area of woodland at the opposite end. She heard a shot ring out, and caught Tom's sharp intake of breath, but was unaware that there was anything badly amiss until she slowed the horse down to a walk in order to steer a safe path through the dense area of trees.

'They certainly can't follow us now,' she remarked, experiencing a deal of satisfaction at the ease of their escape. Then, turning her head, she easily detected the lines of strain in Tom's face and a moment later noticed the blood oozing from the wound in his left thigh.

'Oh, good gracious! You're hurt!'

'I'm all right,' he lied. 'It's nothing but a scratch.' He ground his teeth, though whether this was in anger or pain Jane wasn't perfectly sure. 'If I ever get my hands on the villain who discharged that pistol, I'll...'

'Was it Simon?'

'No, the blackguard seated beside him.'

'That was his servant, Ralph Talbot.'

Jane watched him take a handkerchief from his pocket and knot it around his leg. By the ever increasing stained area on his breeches she knew the wound was not as slight as he would have her believe, but there was little she could do to help him now and she concentrated on keeping to as straight a line as possible. The wood seemed to go on for ever and beneath the canopy of dense branches it was quite dark and eerie. To add to their troubles rain began to fall, lightly at first and then with a vengeance. Then, if that were not sufficient ill luck, the horse decided to cast a shoe.

The gods, it appeared, were ranged against her, seemingly delighting in the endless string of misfortunes with which to plague a hapless damsel, but Jane steadfastly refused to become down-hearted. She had escaped Simon Fairfax's infamous clutches yet again and, most satisfying of all, she now had the comfort of this highly dependable man's protection.

Tom, experiencing none of her optimism, managed to assist her to alight, and watched in growing concern as she grasped the bridle and bravely led the horse onwards. It should have been he who eased the mount's burden by continuing on foot, but he was only too brutally aware that he would be foolish to make the attempt. He needed to conserve his strength in the event that they met up with Jane's abductors again, though just how much use he would be in any confrontation was open to debate. He was experiencing no feeling of dizziness as yet. But how much longer could he remain fully conscious if he continued to lose blood at the present rate? Experience told him not for very long.

At Jane's sudden exclamation of delight, he raised his eyes to see a large clearing a little way ahead and, more importantly, a cottage with several outbuildings. At least they could now shelter from the rain and, hopefully, find help.

When no one appeared at the front entrance in answer to Jane's summons, Tom gingerly eased himself down from the saddle, wincing slightly as he put his weight on his injured leg, and set up a shout, but still no one came. 'Try the door.'

Although she feared they might be mistaken for a pair of opportunist thieves, she was more concerned about Tom's condition and immediately obeyed the command by raising the latch. The door swung open effortlessly to reveal a large kitchen that was both warm and spotlessly clean. Tom took the initiative then and, brushing past her, was the first to enter the spacious room that appeared to function as the main living quarters. He noticed the table and benches placed against the far wall, but was more interested in getting the weight off his injured leg than taking stock of his surroundings, and made a beeline for the settle, which was invitingly placed close to the range.

He glanced across the room as Jane turned to close the door, and experienced a deal of regret at what he must ask of her, but knew he had little choice. 'I'm afraid I'm going to need your help to get my boots and breeches off.'

She hesitated, but only for a moment.

She saw him grimace as she pulled off his left boot, and he noticed her blush fiery red as she peeled away his breeches. A look of horrified fascination took possession of her features as her eyes became seemingly transfixed on a certain part of his anatomy. It was quite evident that she had never seen a man naked before, a fact that he found both infinitely gratifying and faintly amusing, but he resisted the temptation to tease her and succeeded in drawing her out of her entranced state by suggesting she fill a bowl with water.

Once most of the blood had been cleaned away, Tom was able to examine his injured thigh more closely. The wound in itself he didn't consider serious, but it was situated in such a position that he could not easily reach it to extract the lead shot. Without being told, Jane was very well aware of this fact too, and she went about the kitchen, opening the various cupboards and drawers, searching for what she would need to perform the unenviable task herself.

The extraction of the bullet was not easy or pleasant for either of them, but was achieved successfully and in quite a remarkably short space of time considering that Jane's slender hands were completely unskilled. The ordeal, not surprisingly, left Tom exhausted, and Jane didn't delay in completing her unpleasant task, binding the wound up deftly with strips torn from a linen sheet, and then helping Tom cross the kitchen and into the adjoining room which she had noticed earlier was a bedchamber.

Once she had coaxed him into giving her his slightly damp shirt and had him settled in the large and comfortable bed, she went back into the kitchen, returning a few minutes later with a glass containing a generous measure taken from the contents of a bottle she had found in the larder.

Tom disposed of the amber liquid in one large swallow. It wasn't very long before the brandy took effect, dulling the pain in his leg sufficiently for him to doze. He slept only fitfully at first, but then fell into a much deeper and more restful sleep. When eventually he awoke, it was to discover the room in darkness with only the faintest chink of light creeping beneath the door. It took a few moments for all his faculties to return, and with them a surge of panic.

Jane didn't delay in entering the bedchamber in response to his frantic shouts. 'So you're awake, are you?' she remarked, looking and sounding as though she hadn't a care in the world as she went about the room lighting the various candles. 'I was hoping you'd sleep through until morning.'

'You shouldn't have allowed me to sleep at all, you foolish chit!' he ground out, and she couldn't prevent a smile. Scolding was so much a part of his nature, after all. 'What would you have done if that black-guard Fairfax had found his way here, may I ask?'

'I would have been prepared,' she informed him with infuriating calm. 'But, as you have probably gathered by now, he didn't turn up. And neither, which is really disturbing, has anyone else.'

Uninvited, she seated herself on the edge of the bed, betraying clearly enough her unease of mind. 'I cannot help but feel that something must have happened to the owner of this place, Tom. I know it's not uncommon for country folk to go out leaving their doors unlocked, but not when they intend to be away for any length of time. I assume the man earns his living as a woodcutter, and he certainly wouldn't be working until this time of night. Why, it's almost ten o'clock! And where, I ask myself, is his wife?'

His brows rose at this. 'And what makes you suppose that there is a wife?'

She regarded him as though he had taken leave of his senses. 'Look about you, for heaven's sake! The place is spotless. I'm not suggesting for a moment that a man is incapable of keeping his home clean, but it would be a rare member of your sex who would concern himself with adding such touches as those,' she pointed out, drawing to his notice the vase of wild flowers on the bedside table.

'No, I suppose not,' he was forced to concede.

'I'm certain they meant to return long before now. No one who keeps chickens and ducks leaves them wandering about at night for the fox to get. And,' she went on, not offering him the opportunity to respond to this, 'soup had been prepared, no doubt in readiness for their supper—which reminds me, I'll fetch you a bowl. I've eaten my fill already. It's delicious.'

She returned, carrying the broth and a large chunk of crusty bread on a tray which she set down on his lap once he had managed to ease himself into a more upright position. He discovered he was very hungry and, after sending her for a second helping, demanded in his rather blunt way a detailed account of precisely what had happened to her that day since leaving Knightley Hall.

'And that is what comes of gadding about the country unprotected, my girl!' he announced when he had learned all, his forthright tone betraying clearly enough his staunch disapproval, but concealing quite beautifully his intense relief that nothing worse had befallen her. 'You are far too lovely to go careering about on your own!' Then, detracting from the compliment somewhat, he added, 'It's a thousand pities you weren't blessed with the same degree of brains as looks!'

He shook his head as though at some private thought. 'Thank the Lord that maid forgot to relock that door.'

'Well, now, I've been pondering over that,' she responded, not appearing unduly chastened by his scathing condemnation of her actions. 'I think she deliberately left it unlocked to give me a chance to escape. We indulged in perhaps the longest conversation we'd ever had. Something I said must have pricked her conscience. Or maybe I made her realise that Simon Fairfax is a selfish rogue and not to be trusted. She's certainly excessively fond of him, but I don't think she's foolishly blind to his faults.'

Tom was silent for a moment, digesting this, then remarked, 'It sounds to me as if Fairfax had been planning your abduction for quite some time.'

'Several months, I shouldn't wonder. His mother and mine have been friends for years, and ladies do tend to gossip. My mother must have informed Lady Fairfax that I would shortly be looking for a new abigail. No doubt Simon learned of this and told his mother to suggest Latimer for the post. Once she had been installed in our household, it was merely a case of waiting for the right opportunity to carry out his plans.'

'I assume that to avoid a scandal you won't inform

the authorities about what has befallen you…' Tom's
suddenly grim expression boded ill for Lord Fairfax's
son and heir '…but if I ever get my hands on him…'

'I must confess that it irks me to think he'll get off
scot-free,' she admitted, feeling no small desire to be
avenged herself, 'but there's little I can do. I don't
wish to cause embarrassment to my family by making
this day's escapade common knowledge. Besides,'
she sighed, 'as you quite rightly pointed out, I've only
myself to blame. If I had ensured that I had adequate
protection, instead of foolishly striving to attain a little independence by loosening those constricting ties
that have confined me since birth, none of this would
have happened. Being an heiress is not all joy, Dr
Carrington, believe me.'

Up until that moment he had assumed that the
highly privileged and pampered life she led, where,
no doubt, the most arduous task she undertook in any
one day was trying to find some pleasurable way to
keep herself amused, suited her admirably. He ought
to have known better.

During the short time he had known her she had
proved herself to be a warm-hearted and level-headed
young woman who cared deeply for her fellow man—
her concern for her friend Lord Pentecost and her
willingness to do all she could when young Ben had
been injured were ample testament to that.

Had he needed more proof of how deeply he had
misjudged her then he had been given it now. Most
young women, no matter what their social class,
would have succumbed to a fit of the vapours if they
had experienced half of what she had been forced to
endure this day. She was without doubt a rather exceptional young woman who, he now felt certain, pos-

sessed many hidden talents hitherto untouched and untried simply because of the many petty restrictions placed upon her by her highly privileged birth.

How frustrating it all must be to be forced to endure such a hidebound existence! He could quite understand, now, why she had striven to attain a little freedom, but knew it would be quite wrong of him to give voice to his thoughts and thereby possibly encourage her to take further risks in the future.

'Well, no real harm has come of it this time,' he remarked, turning his attention back to the delicious soup. 'But you're not, figuratively speaking, out of the woods yet. You may have escaped the fiendish Fairfax's clutches, but you're now in mine— A far worse fate, my dear, I assure you.'

The only effect his evil leer had upon her was to ignite a delicious gurgle of laughter. 'Oh, no, Dr Carrington, you cannot frighten me. I know I'm perfectly safe with you. Simon Fairfax possesses all the trappings of a man of honour, whilst he is anything but, whereas you…' she paused for a moment in order to choose her words carefully '…you would never attempt to affect the manners of a gentleman, though that is, fundamentally, precisely what you are.'

'I'm not gentleman enough to give up this bed to you for a start, my girl,' he countered.

'In the circumstances I wouldn't expect you to. I'm quite content to make shift with the comfortable chair in the kitchen.' She went about the room blowing out the various candles, leaving just the one on the bedside table for him to extinguish when he was ready. 'I'm rather tired, so I shall bid you goodnight, and shall see you in the morning, when I intend to have a good breakfast awaiting you.'

I don't doubt it for a moment, Tom thought, watching her leave. You have more than lived up to my expectations… I can only hope, my darling girl, that I possess the strength of character and am truly gentleman enough to live up to yours.

Chapter Ten

Tom awoke the following morning to the pleasant sound of melodious humming. He had forgotten what a lovely voice she had. But then, he reminded himself, everything about Lady Jane Beresford was quite above the norm. Even her ability to accept her present, unenviable situation with a kind of resigned optimism was much to her credit. What a remarkable young woman she was!

The delicious aroma of freshly baked bread suddenly assailed his nostrils, bringing a smile to his face and the inevitable pangs of hunger. Then he noticed his clothes, not only dried but pressed too, neatly folded over the back of the chair. He knew that his friend Elizabeth could, and often did, turn her hand to the most mundane tasks, but he had always considered her rather exceptional. Never had it occurred to him for a moment to suppose that there were other high-born ladies, having servants in abundance to pander to their every whim, who were capable of performing such basic tasks for themselves, let alone willing to do so. It appeared he had much to learn about the ways of the aristocracy, he mused, suffering only slight discomfort from his injured leg as he swung his feet to the floor and scrambled into his clothes.

The bedchamber door, kept well oiled, made only the faintest sound as he pushed it wide and stepped into the warmth of the kitchen to find Jane bent over the stove. From somewhere she had managed to lay her hands on an apron. She had the sleeves of her dress, businesslike, rolled up to her elbows, and those bared portions of slender arms were liberally splattered with flour. She looked so completely at home performing the task of preparing breakfast that it was difficult to believe that it was not a daily duty but a rare occurrence which, he supposed, by her continued cheerful humming, still retained the appeal of novelty.

She turned suddenly, as though sensing she was being watched, and that spontaneous smile which never failed to reach her eyes curled up the corners of her delectable mouth.

'Naturally I'm delighted to see you up and about, but do you think you are being altogether sensible to exercise that leg so soon and risk reopening the wound?'

'I've no intention of overtaxing myself, Jane. But if I remained idling in that bed, comfortable though it is, I would soon be like a bear with a sore head, growling and unapproachable.'

The puckish streak in her nature couldn't allow this to pass without comment, and, all wide-eyed innocence, she looked across the room at him. 'What…? More than usual, you mean?'

'Little baggage!' he muttered good-humouredly, appreciating the gentle sarcasm. 'Am I such a bad-tempered boor?'

'You have been known to be, yes,' she answered, with brutal frankness.

He couldn't help but admire her candour, even though it wasn't precisely to his credit. Yes, he had been grossly unjust to her on more than one occasion during their short but far from uneventful acquaintanceship, he was forced silently to admit. Perhaps it had been a defence mechanism triggered off by some innate masculine wisdom that had sensed from the first that this woman posed a real threat to his comfortable bachelor existence. If that was true, his armour had been woefully inadequate to cope with the onslaught of such formidable feminine weapons, for his defences against her were completely shattered now.

It would be grossly unfair, though, he reminded himself, to allow his feelings for her to surface. They were in a very precarious situation: together like this and completely alone. The last thing he wanted was to add to her mounting troubles by making her feel wary or remotely uncomfortable in his presence. She was in dire need of his support, and from the very complimentary remarks she had passed the previous evening it was quite evident that she trusted him implicitly. He was still far from certain whether he could live up to her expectations. After all, he was only flesh and blood and she, the gorgeous darling, was an exceedingly lovely young woman, totally feminine and infinitely desirable.

None the less, when she joined him at the table, bringing with her the fruits of her early morning labours, he managed, on this occasion at least, to control the strong urge to take her ruthlessly into his arms and subject her to a display of virile masculine passion. Instead, he encouraged her to tell him something of the life she had led at her ancestral home in Kent.

Conversation might have been the last thing on his mind, but he soon found himself absorbed in what she was saying. He had quite naturally assumed that, being a member of the privileged class, she had enjoyed a happy, carefree childhood, and to a certain extent his assumption had been correct. But as he listened to her recalling events in her past he gained the distinct impression that there had been numerous occasions when she had been a very lonely, somewhat isolated little girl, who had frequently sought the companionship of the servants below stairs. This, of course, went some way to explain her ability to converse so easily with people, no matter what their status, for he himself had noted on more than one occasion the gracious way she had always spoken to the Knightleys' servants.

'And your visits to the kitchen were certainly well worthwhile,' he remarked, helping himself to more eggs and a third delicious roll.

The compliment drew a gratified smile to her lips. 'Unfortunately we have a French chef now, who doesn't like sharing his domain with anyone. But years ago Mrs Blagdon reigned supreme in the kitchen. She was a dear soul, who was very indulgent and taught me a great deal about the art of cooking. I was never bored when I could escape from my governess and go down to the bowels of the house.'

'Am I right in thinking that your brother and sisters are much older than you?' he asked when she fell silent.

'Yes. My mother produced four children in as many years. Then waited a further ten before bringing me into the world. My sister Clarissa is the nearest to me in age.' Her smile was replaced by a slight frown. 'I love them all dearly, but…'

'But you resent the way they still continue to treat you as though you were a child,' he finished for her with quite remarkable perspicacity. 'You must find that quite irksome. I know I should.'

'Yes, I do,' she freely admitted, while at the same time fervently wishing that she hadn't allowed increasing resentment at her family's almost claustrophobic protective attitude to lead her into taking such a foolishly ill-conceived stand. Really she had only herself to blame for her present predicament.

Not that she minded so very much for herself: sheltering in this cottage and having to do everything for herself made a refreshing change, and if the truth be known she was enjoying the experience hugely, but she had been suffering pangs of conscience over Tom's involvement. Not only was she responsible for getting the poor man shot, but she had unwittingly forced him into taking on the role of protector. Strangely, though, she could think of no one she would sooner have to take care of her than this sometimes infuriating man.

The realisation hit her quite forcibly, and it certainly didn't help to lessen her confusion to discover him regarding her rather keenly, those intelligent and highly perceptive grey eyes of his seeming able to probe the depths of her mind and read her every thought with uncanny accuracy.

'Well, that's enough about me,' she announced, in a valiant attempt to give her bemused thoughts a new direction. 'Tell me something about yourself.' And although he obliged her readily enough she gained the

distinct impression from the quizzical smile that he
knew the precise reason for the swift change of subject.

She had learned something of his past, of course,
from her cousin. She was aware that he had lost both
his parents at a young age and that Elizabeth's grandmother, a lady for whom Tom had felt the utmost
fondness and respect, had brought him up. She
learned that his father had been an apothecary, and
that his mother, of good yeoman stock, had come to
the marriage with a dowry sufficiently large to enable
her young husband to purchase business premises in
the centre of Bristol.

When his mother had died Tom had continued to
see something of her family, and kept in touch even
now with his aunts and uncles and various cousins,
but of his father's family he said not a word. Jane
thought this rather strange and enquired whether his
father had been an only child.

'Yes, he was. Both my paternal grandparents died
before I was born.'

'And was your grandfather an apothecary, too?'

'No, a clergyman. He was fortunate enough to attain a living on a large estate in Norfolk for a while
before finding another, but far less lucrative one, in
Gloucestershire.' He regarded her for a moment in
meditative silence. 'I thought Elizabeth might have
enlightened you.'

'About what?'

'About my paternal grandparents.'

By her ill-concealed puzzlement it was evident that
she hadn't a clue what he was talking about, and he
should have realised that she was completely ignorant
of his family's history. Elizabeth was not a garrulous

person, while Jane was certainly far from an inquisitive one and had no penchant for scandal. His grandparents' lives, and ultimately that of his father, might have been so vastly different if it hadn't been for the bigoted and unforgiving attitude adopted by his great-grandfather. It was a subject he rarely alluded to, but for some inexplicable reason he felt the need to hear Jane's views on the happenings which had occurred more than half a century ago.

'My grandfather, Percival Carrington, came from the professional classes. He was an intelligent man who chose a career in the church. As I've already mentioned, he was offered a living on a vast estate in Norfolk. He fell deeply in love with his benefactor's eldest daughter, and they married, but against the wishes of her father. He disowned her completely, and even went so far as to take his petty revenge by giving my grandfather's living to another. My grandmother had no further contact with any member of her family. She died shortly after giving birth to my father in what for her, a young woman accustomed to every luxury, must have seemed abject poverty.'

Jane listened to this sorry tale in silence while she tried to bring to mind those amongst her many acquaintances who owned sizeable properties in the county of Norfolk. 'What was your grandmother's maiden name?'

His white teeth flashed in a sportive smile. 'Davenham.'

One finely arched brow rose so sharply that it seemed as if she were being manipulated by some invisible puppeteer. 'Well! I cannot say that I'm surprised you keep that connection very quiet. I'd not want it universally known, either, if I were related in

any way to the Marquis of Fencham. The present
holder of the title is the most self-opinionated, obnoxious little worm who ever drew breath, and his
wife isn't much better—touched in the upper works,
if you ask me, which tells you something of what
their offspring are like. You may be sure, Tom, that
I'll never breathe a word of the relationship between
you and that family, distant though it may be.'

That she had assumed that it was he who chose not
to recognise his noble relatives, and not the other way
round, left him totally nonplussed for several moments, and then he threw his head back and roared
with laughter. If he had ever experienced any bitterness over his aristocratic relatives' complete indifference to his existence, he certainly felt none whatsoever now.

'You quite astonish me at times!' he told her when
he was able.

'I'm sorry if I seemed rude, Tom,' she responded
with total sincerity, 'but I don't care for that family
at all.'

'Don't apologise, darling girl. You're like a breath
of fresh air.' Then, realising he was in the gravest
danger of losing that iron control he was exerting over
himself and reaching out and taking her in his arms,
he followed her example of minutes before by turning
his thoughts in a new direction and focusing his attention on the contents of their temporary dwelling-
place.

'I must say this is rather palatial for a woodcutter's
abode. There are not many hailing from the lower
orders who can afford a kitchen range, let alone such
an up-to-date one. And the furniture, although not

precisely Chippendale or Hepplewhite, is extremely
well made.'

'Ah, yes! I've been meaning to tell you about that,'
Jane responded, reaching for the coffee-pot and obligingly refilling his cup before seeing to her own. 'After
I had let the chickens and ducks out this morning, I
had a look around. There's a large outbuilding just
beyond the hen-coop, and it's filled with all manner
of things from cradles and toys to chairs, stools and
tables. You name it—it's in there. He's not a woodcutter but a woodcarver. And a very good one, too.
But just where he's hiding himself remains a mystery.'

Tom shrugged his broad shoulders. It wasn't that
he was indifferent, it was just that he had enough to
concern him without worrying unduly about errant
carpenters. 'He'll turn up sooner or later.'

'I hope you're right. I had a wander through the
woods early this morning to see if…'

'You…did…what?' he thundered, regarding her as
though she had taken leave of her senses. 'Of all the
feather-brained things to go and do! What would have
happened if you'd met up with Simon Fairfax, may I
ask?'

Betraying no outward signs of having taken offence
at his sudden slide into a belligerent mood, Jane
calmly took a sip of coffee before defending her actions by saying, 'I'm not such a widgeon as to go
abroad unarmed.'

She then gestured towards the Welsh dresser upon
which she had placed a dragoon's pistol. 'I would
imagine it's a souvenir from the war. Heaven only
knows how our host came by it. It's in perfect working order. I spent some time cleaning and reloading

it last night, as well as the rifle in the corner over there.'

His expression changed dramatically, and he regarded her now with a mixture of astonishment and grudging respect. 'Do you mean to tell me you're capable of handling such weapons?'

'Of course,' she answered with simple pride. 'You forget I enjoyed a misspent youth. My brother frequently took me out shooting with him—still does for that matter. My father's rather proud of the fact that he has at least one daughter who's not completely ignorant in the use of firearms.

'I'm sorry if that shocks you, Dr Carrington,' she went on to say, after fortifying herself again from the contents of her cup. 'I realise, of course, that you're in the business of saving lives. And, believe me, I wouldn't willingly shoot anyone, not even the infamous Simon Fairfax. But if I had come upon him in the woods this morning I wouldn't have hesitated in getting him into my sights. However, I never for one moment expected to run into him. He might be a loathsome, unprincipled wretch, but he's certainly no fool.' She shook her head. 'No, he's long since gone—with my money, all my clothes and my jewel box, I do not doubt. Which reminds me…'

Delving into the pocket of the borrowed apron, she drew out a small brooch, a dainty circlet of pearls set in a silver mounting, and placed it upon the table in front of him. 'I found that beside the settle this morning when I was sweeping the floor. It looks quite old to me and worth something, I shouldn't wonder. Further proof that our host and hostess are not precisely purse-pinched.'

'Well, actually, it's mine,' he surprised her by admitting. 'It belonged to my grandmother, a relic of her affluent past. Poor woman was forced to sell most of her jewels, but for some reason couldn't bring herself to part with this. Sometimes I wear it in my cravat if the mood takes me.' His teeth flashed in a roguish smile. 'I had a fancy to dazzle Sir William Dent yesterday with my finery.'

This reminder of his intended destination forced Jane once more to concentrate her thoughts on the best way to get them out of their present predicament. Although Tom had been determined not to remain in bed, it would be foolish to pretend he could walk very far, or ride any distance, without reopening his wound, so it would be left to her to find the nearest blacksmith in order to get the horse shod and then make her way to the nearest large town in order to hire a carriage.

Tom was very much against the idea of her going off on her own, but eventually she persuaded him to accept that there was no alternative, if they didn't wish to spend yet another night in the cottage.

All went well at first. The early spring sun, pleasantly warm, and cheering, shone down on her as she collected Tom's hired mount from the stable and walked along the narrow track which skirted the woods, and which eventually led to a narrow country lane. Fortune still favouring her, she soon came upon a local, walking in the opposite direction, who obligingly informed her that the nearest blacksmith's was in the village not two miles further along the road. Ill luck then decided to take its turn: upon arriving at the small habitation, she discovered that the blacksmith was out and wasn't expected home until lunchtime.

Accepting the set-back with a good grace, Jane left
the hired mount at the smithy, and strolled round the
village, passing the time of day with several inhabi-
tants and inspecting the small church. She returned to
the forge on the stroke of one, only to discover that
the blacksmith had still not returned. His wife, however, being a kind-hearted soul, took pity on the pretty
young stranger and promptly invited her to wait in
the comfort of the house.

Jane needed no second prompting. Nor was she too
proud to accept the kind offer of a bite to eat, and
during the nourishing meal of cheese and crusty
home-made bread, followed by a slice of delicious
apple tart, she was regaled with a humorous account
of life in the small Wiltshire village.

It transpired that the blacksmith's wife had lived in
the village all her life. She knew most everyone residing in the surrounding area, and was related in
some way to a great many of them.

'Then you are more than likely acquainted with the
people living in that charming thatched cottage by the
woods some two miles from here,' Jane remarked,
unable to let this golden opportunity of discovering
to whom she owed a debt of gratitude for her comfortable accommodation the previous night slip by.

'Oh, you must mean Percy and Alice Price's place
up by Bencham Wood!' the blacksmith's wife announced after a moment's thought. 'Yes, I know them
very well. He's a carpenter by trade. Very clever with
his hands, is old Percy. It's a nice little place, but I
shouldn't care to be stuck out there all by myself.
They seem contented, though. Lived there for years,
so they 'ave.'

'Strange that there was no one about when I called

this morning, don't you think?' The look Jane received in response to this, if not precisely suspicious, was certainly very thoughtful, and so, with scant regard for the truth, she hurriedly added, 'I'm staying with friends who reside some few miles from here. It was such a lovely morning that I decided to go out for a ride. It was in the woods that my horse decided to cast a shoe, so I called at that cottage to ask the whereabouts of the nearest blacksmith. But as I've already mentioned the place appeared to be deserted.'

The explanation seemed to satisfy the kindly woman. 'Oh, they were probably out in the woods somewhere themselves. Alice often goes along to help her husband find a suitable tree to cut down. Except when they journey to Devizes on market days, or visit their daughter, who has a farm near the town, they never venture very far.'

These snippets of information merely increased Jane's fears that something must have happened to the Prices. It was so difficult to know what to do for the best. She didn't wish to raise the alarm, and instigate a thorough search of the woods, only to discover that the errant couple had merely paid a visit to their daughter and for some reason had delayed their return.

She glanced at the grandfather clock, solemnly ticking away the passing of time, in the corner of the room. She really ought to have been in Devizes herself by now, arranging for the hire of a carriage, but there was little she could do until the blacksmith returned. She only hoped he wouldn't be too much longer, otherwise Tom wouldn't only be concerned over the whereabouts of the Prices, but would be frantic over her long absence, too.

* * *

It just so happened that Tom, having just satisfied his own hunger from the ample supplies in the larder, was not unduly worried as yet. He hadn't wanted her to go, it was true, but what choice had he but to capitulate? He was in no fit state to go himself, and wasn't foolish enough to suppose that the wound in his leg would have healed very much by tomorrow. None the less, if Jane was unable to hire a carriage, which was certainly a real possibility at this time of year when many more people were inclined to travel, then he would ride over to Devizes with her first thing in the morning, injured leg or no.

Every hour she was alone in his company compromised her further. If she didn't realise that, he most certainly did. He hadn't saved her from Fairfax's infamous clutches only to force her into a union with himself. So, the sooner she reached the safety of her aunt's house in Bath the better, even if it meant her continuing the journey on the common stage.

The thought that he would be parting from her soon was a far from pleasant one. He succeeded to a certain extent in forcing it from his mind as he took a leisurely stroll outside, examining the exterior of the cottage and its several outbuildings, but his injured leg began to protest after a while, giving him little choice but to return indoors and patiently await Jane's return.

Although he had recourse to his pocket-watch on numerous occasions, it wasn't until the afternoon was well advanced, and she still had failed to return, that he began to grow uneasy. Clouds, darkly threatening, had been gradually building up from the west, and by early evening it was raining quite hard, adding to his ever increasing disquiet. He had just decided that he could bear the waiting no longer and, foolish though it might have been, had made up his mind to go searching for her, when he detected the blessed sound of a horse's hooves.

A few minutes later the door opened, a bedraggled and sodden Jane stepped over the threshold, and Tom's anxiety found release in a thundering tirade.

Jane could not recall being scolded so comprehensively in her life before, and she might have been suitably chastened if it hadn't been for the fact that she was in a rare ill humour herself. 'Where the devil do you think I've been, you stupid creature?' she snapped back. 'I've spent the whole day waiting to get that dratted horse shod. I never even went to Devizes. And how dare you lecture me in such a fashion?'

'You deserve more than a telling-off, my girl,' he retorted, eyes glinting threateningly, but Jane refused to be cowed.

'If you dare say another word to me, Thomas Carrington, I'll…I'll throw something at you!'

She looked as if she meant it, too! Which, perversely, amused him, with the result that his own anger began to subside. He looked at her closely for the first time. Droplets of water running down the folds of the old borrowed cloak had already made a sizeable puddle about her sodden feet, and she was trembling, though whether this was from cold or temper he wasn't quite sure.

'Come and get yourself warm,' he coaxed, and she responded instantly to the much gentler tone, leaving clear footprints across the flagstone floor as she moved towards the range. He managed to persuade her to give him the cloak and her pelisse, and to remove her calf-boots, but when he asked her to step out of her dress she regarded him as though he had taken leave of his senses.

'I'm not standing here in just my petticoats, Dr Carrington!'

'Quite right, m'dear. I want everything. And please don't argue!' he ordered, when she opened her mouth to do just that. 'You're soaked to the skin, and I've enough to contend with without having you on my hands suffering a raging fever.'

His voice might have sounded quite matter-of-fact, faintly bored, even, but there could be no mistaking the determination in his eyes, and she realised that if she didn't do as she was told he wasn't above undressing her with his own hands. She waited until he had disappeared into the bedchamber before grappling with the hooks on her dress, and only just stepped out of its sodden folds when he came back into the kitchen, carrying a blanket.

'What? Not finished yet?' he remarked, with what she considered a tactless disregard for her acute embarrassment. 'Need any help?'

'No, I do not!' she snapped, only just managing to suppress the urge to box his ears soundly. 'And kindly turn your back. I've no intention of disrobing with you looking on.'

Tom cast her an impatient glance, but did as she asked. 'Might I remind you that I am a physician, and quite accustomed to seeing members of your sex in a state of undress.'

'I dare say,' she responded, hurriedly stepping out of her pantalets and wrapping herself in the blanket, which he had obligingly tossed on the settle behind her, before seating herself close to the range, 'but you are not my doctor. All right, you can turn round now.'

Smiling in spite of the fact that he found the whole maidenly performance faintly ludicrous, Tom bent to pick up the discarded garments. After placing them over a metal rail near the stove, he knelt carefully on the floor in front of her, so as not to put too much strain on his injured leg, and, ignoring her squeal of protest, placed her slender feet on his knee and began to rub the circulation back into her frozen limbs.

Jane dared not put up any kind of struggle for fear of losing her grasp on the blanket, and tried her best to ignore warm hands that might have been rubbing vigorously enough to remove a layer of skin, but were, none the less, having a disturbing effect on her pulse rate as they moved up and down her legs from slender thighs to trim ankles.

'Right,' he announced finally, rising again to his feet, but not before giving the top of her left leg an over-familiar and hearty smack. 'I'll get us something to eat, while you stay precisely where you are.'

The comfortable warmth of the kitchen was swiftly restoring her usual sunny humour, and his continuing authoritative tone no longer had the power to annoy her. She could even, now, smile at the fact that it wasn't precisely the way she had envisaged celebrating the attainment of her majority, and echoed her thoughts aloud.

'It's your birthday? Oh, yes! I recall your mentioning it when I last dined with the Knightleys. Why on earth didn't you remind me?'

'Surprisingly enough, the fact entirely slipped my mind until I was returning here in the pouring rain, feeling mighty sorry for myself,' she admitted, taking the bread and cheese he held out and refraining from remarking on the fact that it was precisely what she had eaten at luncheon. It would have sounded so pee-vish, so ungrateful. And ingratitude was the last thing she felt towards this man, she decided, watching him search through the well-stocked larder, before walk-ing back towards her with a bottle in his hand.

It wasn't precisely claret or burgundy, but Jane en-joyed the home-made wine all the same, and it did fortify her to a certain extent for his next very touch-ing gesture—one that she was to remember and cher-ish until the day she died.

Delving into his breeches pocket, he drew out the exquisite pearl brooch and, reaching forward, placed it into her hand. 'Happy birthday,' he said simply.

It was a moment or two before she could swallow the obstruction blocking her throat to enable her to say, 'Tom, I cannot accept this. It was your grand-mother's—the only keepsake you have to remind you of her.'

'I never knew her, Jane, so it holds little sentimen-tal value for me. Most of the time it lies in a drawer, forgotten. I'm certain my grandmother would whole-heartedly approve of seeing it in its proper place—adorning the gown of a lady of quality.

'Now, you've had a long day, so it would be sen-sible to retire early,' he went on, with an abrupt return to authoritative mode. 'We'll need to make an early start in the morning if we're to reach Devizes with a reasonable chance of securing a carriage to take you to Bath. You have the bed tonight. I'll be quite com-fortable here in this chair, with my feet resting on the stool.'

Jane didn't attempt to argue. She was feeling weary, and still more than a little overcome by the generosity of his lovely gift. Remaining only for the time it took to collect and light a candle, she went into the bedchamber, and didn't waste any time in getting into the comfortable bed. Which was perhaps just as well as Tom, without so much as a knock, came striding in a few moments later to ask if she required a nightgown.

Yet a further example of how thoughtful he could be. What an enigma the man was! 'I think I shall be warm enough, thank you.' She smiled a trifle ruefully. 'Besides, we've taken enough liberties without my making free with Mrs Price's night attire.'

'Price…? Is that their name?'

'Apparently so. The blacksmith's wife seemed to know everyone living in these parts.' Jane's frown clearly betrayed her continuing unease. 'Apart from the odd trip to Devizes, the Prices never go anywhere—which is rather worrying. I think we should inform the authorities tomorrow, don't you?'

'It certainly would be the very least we could do after making use of their home, but—' he shrugged '—I'm not unduly concerned, at least not now.'

She didn't perfectly understand this. 'Why? What do you mean?'

'Whilst you were out, I had a little look round the place,' he explained, seating himself on the edge of the bed without conscious thought. 'There are clear tracks—a cart's, I suspect—leading into and from that large stable. And there is evidence enough to suggest that they keep at least one horse. It was market day in Devizes yesterday, so I should imagine that is precisely where our errant benefactors were bound. The reason for their non-return, of course, remains a mystery.'

She made no response to this, and Tom, who had

been contemplating one ornately carved bedpost, wondering if it might not be an example of their host's fine workmanship, turned his attention back to her.

For several moments he stared into those beautifully coloured eyes, framed in lashes so long that they brushed against the delicate skin beneath, before transferring his gaze to the gorgeous russet-coloured locks, still slightly damp after her uncomfortable ride back to the cottage. Only a few feather-light tendrils caressed the unlined forehead, while the rest cascaded down to slender shoulders, perfect and white, rising above the bedcovers. Some detached part of his brain registered the tiny pulsating throb in the slender column of her neck, before he focused his attention on the gentle curve of her jaw and finally the perfect symmetry of a sweetly curved mouth.

He could feel his doctor's mantle slipping away and with it the iron control he had exerted over himself, allowing the virile male to surface and the raw, overwhelming desire he felt for this lovely young woman to take over. He lowered his head and his mouth captured hers, gently at first and then with a deepening hunger as he swiftly attained the response he needed to begin to satisfy this ever increasing longing for total fulfilment—which would be as new for him as it was for her, simply because it was engendered by love, not lust.

No thought of resistance had entered Jane's head. Her lips had parted instinctively and so willingly that she could no longer be deaf to the sweet message her young heart had been transmitting for days. She had fallen deeply in love. Now heart, mind and body were in such complete accord that when his lips left hers and began to explore the swell of her responsive breasts, and infinitely gentle fingers sought to caress and probe that softest of flesh between her thighs, she experienced no fear, only a desire for the increasingly pleasurable sensations rippling through her never to end, and an urgent need to caress and explore his body in return.

As her unpractised hands sought the lapels of his coat in a desperate attempt to ease it from him, he raised himself up and obliged her by shrugging his arms free and tossing the expertly tailored garment to the floor. His cravat and shirt quickly followed, offering her the unfettered view of magnificent shoulders and a broad and well-formed chest with its covering of dark, slightly curling hair.

Impatient to touch him, to feel that muscular strength beneath her fingertips, she reached out eagerly for the contact to begin, only to have her hand captured in a bone-crushing grip. His eyes, which only moments before had been devouring her every naked curve, were now fixed on the chest of drawers beside the bed. With his head slightly averted, she could no longer read the message their grey depths contained, but she sensed the drastic change in him, even before his every muscle seemed suddenly to grow taut.

Then, as though he could bear to touch her no longer, he thrust her hand aside, and rose from the bed. Quickly sweeping up his discarded garments, he stormed across to the door in three giant strides. 'Don't dare to leave this bedchamber tonight for any reason,' he rasped, before slamming the door closed behind him with a finality that left Jane devastated and with the wretched conviction that her eagerness to show her love had only succeeded in giving him a disgust of her.

Chapter Eleven

Jane woke to see a ray of bright morning sunshine filtering between the gap in the curtains. How she wished there were some way that warm shaft of light could melt the ice-cold misery encasing her heart, and penetrate the tangled, dark mass of conflicting thoughts in her brain! She might then be able to see, to understand what had wrought the sudden and drastic change in the man she loved, turning him in a matter of seconds from a gentle, considerate lover into a cold, unfeeling brute who seemed unable to look at her, let alone touch her.

It all seemed like some fiendish bad dream now, leaving her wondering whether she could any longer distinguish fact from fancy. Surely she had not misread the signs so badly? True—no words of love had passed his lips, but there had been such depth of feeling, such loving tenderness in his eyes before he had kissed her.

She shook her head, uncertain what to believe, but she refused to shy away from the very real possibility that whatever feelings he might have experienced were not strong enough to withstand the possible outcome of satisfying their mutual passion—were not sincere enough to prompt him to do the honourable thing and marry her... After all, what other possible explanation could there be?

The silent, bitter tears she had wept after he had left the room had in no way helped to ease the biting misery of total rejection, and she had no intention of giving way to such feminine weakness again. Thankfully, sleep, when it had eventually claimed her, had somehow managed to restore a modicum of self-esteem. She was Lady Beresford, the Earl of Eastbury's daughter, a young woman who had been taught from a young age to consider any display of forceful emotion as faintly vulgar, and for once in her life she appreciated this instilled doctrine. He had to be faced and, vastly humiliating though the prospect was, she fully intended to do it with dignity and with her head held high.

Without giving herself time to delay the inevitable a moment longer, she swung her feet to the floor, and noticed for the first time her clothes, placed neatly over the back of the chair. Just as she had done the previous morning, he had at some point slipped back into the room. She hadn't been aware of his presence, but then, perhaps, he had preferred it that way. No doubt he was looking forward to their next encounter with as little enthusiasm as she was herself.

She discovered him seated at the table when she entered the kitchen a few minutes later. The food on his plate appeared untouched, giving her every reason to suppose that either he had only just sat down, or his appetite had deserted him. There seemed to be a certain droop to his shoulders this morning, and, had she not been given a cruelly sharp lesson in the sheer folly of reading too much into a person's expression, she might have supposed that there was a look of complete desolation in those grey eyes of his. But she was wiser now.

He was possibly suffering from nothing more than lack of sleep because he had spent an uncomfortable night in the chair, she decided, joining him at the table, and not because he had been tormented with pangs of remorse over his behaviour. No, that wasn't fair, the voice of conscience told her. He wasn't an unfeeling care-for-nobody, and it would be grossly unjust to label him so. Of course he must regret what had taken place between them, must deplore his weakness in giving way to his baser instincts, but she refused to allow herself to indulge in the foolish hope that his air of despondency stemmed from anything more profound than that.

'Ah! Bread and cheese again,' she remarked when he just stared at her across the table, not making the least attempt to converse. 'I think when I've left this place I shan't choose to sample this particular fare again for some considerable time.'

This brought a faint twitching to one corner of his mouth. 'Yes, it certainly does become monotonous after a time, but I didn't wish to waste time cooking. It would be best if we made an early start.'

Which was tantamount to telling her, of course, that he wished to be rid of her company as quickly as possible, she thought miserably. Not only had he thrust the knife in, but he was cruelly twisting it, too!

Once again the proud blood of her noble ancestors coursing through her veins came to her aid and, refusing to betray just how deeply he had wounded her, she said, sounding sublimely unconcerned at the prospect of their parting, 'I'm in complete agreement with you. I must reach Bath today. Heaven only knows what my aunt must be thinking! Poor dear, she must be out of her mind with worry.'

He regarded her for a moment in subdued silence, his eyes holding hers as though by some hypnotic force. 'Janie, about last night—'

'I would prefer not to discuss what took place between us,' she interrupted and, reaching for the coffee-pot, was appalled to see her hand trembling slightly. 'It was most regrettable, and best forgotten.'

'Yes, perhaps... But—'

'No, Tom!' she cut in more sharply this time, trying desperately to control the rapidly mounting hysteria. Why must he torment her like this? Dear Lord! Was he so insensitive that he didn't realise just how much he had hurt and humiliated her? Surely he didn't imagine that she was some light-skirt who bedded any man who happened to take her fancy?

She wanted nothing more than to run from him, and might well have done so had she not suddenly detected a noise outside. Seemingly Tom heard it too, for he rose to his feet at once.

'It looks as if the owners have at last returned,' he said, reaching the window in time to see a lumbering cart come to a halt, and a middle-aged woman climbing down from the seat.

Jane wished the ground beneath her would open and swallow her up. She might have been spared the humiliation of having to discuss an incident she would far rather be allowed to forget, but now it seemed she was to suffer the embarrassment of trying to explain her presence in this cottage. Life could be mercilessly cruel at times!

Tom, easily discerning the look of entreaty in her eyes, responded instantly to the unspoken cry for help and limped over to the door. Jane heard him say clearly, 'Pray, madam, do not be alarmed,' before he introduced himself, though the exchanges which followed were just a series of muffled sounds.

It seemed an eternity before the door was thrown wide again, and much of Jane's acute discomfiture disappeared at the sight of the plump, middle-aged woman, whose gait could best be described as waddling, entering the spacious kitchen.

'Oh, Miss Carrington, you poor child! What a terrible thing to have happened to you! Set upon by such rogues, and your dear brother injured, too!'

Not only was the stranger, who she assumed was Mrs Price, a kindly soul, but very tactile, too. Jane rose from the table and instantly found herself encircled by a pair of fleshy arms for a few moments, which gave her just sufficient time to accept her surprising new identity. What else had her resourceful *brother* told them? Thank heavens he at least had his wits about him!

'Indeed, yes, ma'am. Vastly unpleasant! And I must thank you for your kind understanding at finding strangers making free with your charming home. But we had little choice, I'm afraid.'

'Don't you give it another thought, my pet. I'm very glad now I did forget to lock the door. Though I didn't realise I'd done so at the time, of course. We left for Devizes in such a hurry on market day.'

Jane cast a fleeting glance across at the aforementioned door, wishing fervently that Tom would return and offer some guidance as to the story he'd told. 'I did learn that you might have gone to Devizes,' she responded, feeling reasonably safe by continuing along this particular avenue. 'I called on a blacksmith in a small village not very far from here to get the horse shod, and the lady at the forge seemed to know you quite well. Your name is Price, I believe?'

'That's right, my dear.' She raised her eyes heavenwards. 'There isn't much the smithy's wife don't know. No doubt she kept you talking all day.'

Jane couldn't help smiling at this. Evidently the blacksmith's wife had earned herself something of a reputation for gossiping. 'I'm afraid she did, but that was because her husband didn't return until late. I was hoping to ride over to Devizes myself to hire a carriage, but I'm afraid I never made it that far.'

Mrs price gave Jane's arm a fond pat. 'Well, don't you worry your pretty head over that. My husband will take you and your brother over to town when you're ready to leave, if you don't mind travelling in the cart?'

'And is that not kind of them, Jane?' Tom remarked, thankfully not delaying his return a moment longer. Their eyes met across the room—Jane's with a look of comical dismay, Tom's sparkling with devilment and just for a moment there was a resurgence of that wonderful rapport which had existed between them.

'I've just been telling Mr Price, here,' he went on, gesturing to the man who was as lean as his wife was plump, 'how we lost one of our horses during the attack, but managed to make it here just on my hired mount.'

Jane merely smiled in response, deeming it safer to leave all explanations to her very inventive *brother's* fertile mind. They had at some point possessed a second horse… Now why was that? she wondered. She wasn't left in ignorance for long.

'I was escorting my sister to our aunt's house in Bath.' Tom addressed himself to Mrs price who was regarding him with patent approval. 'We spent the night in Devizes, and I suddenly took it into my head to pay a visit to an acquaintance of mine, Sir William Dent, but, as I mentioned outside, we fell foul of some ruffians, after my purse, I suppose, and never made it to our destination.'

Jane realised that he had evidently considered carefully before mentioning Sir William Dent, believing, no doubt, that the Prices, although perhaps not acquainted with him personally, must surely have heard of the famous surgeon. The gamble paid off, for the Prices seemed to require no further explanations, or assurances that the young couple were perfectly respectable.

'And, naturally, I shall reimburse you for the provisions we've consumed whilst we've been here, Mrs Price.'

'Pshaw!' She dismissed the idea with a wave of her plump hand. 'What's a few victuals? Besides, had it not been for you locking my chickens up at night, I swear the fox would have had most of 'em by now. That were the only thing that concerned me whilst we were away. But what could I do when our only daughter's first decides to come early?'

She had addressed her latter remarks to Jane, expecting a female to understand her dilemma perfectly, and she wasn't disappointed. Tom, however, fearing that the ensuing conversation on the joys of having grandchildren was likely to be a lengthy one, experienced no qualms in interrupting and reminding his *sister* that they really ought to be on their way.

Within a very short space of time Mrs Price, smiling broadly, stood outside, waving a last farewell to the delightful young couple, but as she went about her morning's work her round, normally cheerful face began increasingly to wear a very thoughtful expression. She grew impatient for her husband's return, and when he did eventually arrive home, in good time for his midday meal, she didn't waste a moment in asking whether the young couple were now safely on their way to Bath.

'I 'eard 'im ask about 'iring a carriage when we arrived at The Swan. And he 'as been putting up there 'cause the landlady knew 'im. Funny thing, though...' He scratched his grizzled mop of hair. 'She didn't seem to recognise the young lady.'

'I knew it!' Mrs Price clapped her hands together in triumph. 'Suspicioned as much right from the start!'

Her husband looked about the room in some alarm. 'Don't tell me they really were thieves, Alice! Dear Lord! What's missing?'

'Nothing, you old fool,' she responded lovingly. 'They weren't no thieves... But they weren't brother and sister, neither, if I'm any judge. I reckon they were a pair o' runaways.'

This pronouncement didn't appeal to the bewildered Mr Price any more than the idea that he might have been robbed. He tut-tutted. 'Right rum goings-on, I must say. And in our 'ome, too!'

'Now, Percy, I'm not suggesting for a moment that anything of that sort's been taking place. In fact, I don't think it 'as at all. When I went into t'other room to change the sheets, I noticed only one side of the bed 'ad been slept in. And there was a blanket folded up on the settle, so I reckon the young doctor slept in 'ere.'

He cast her a look of exasperation. 'What the devil are you talking about, then, woman?'

Mrs Price betrayed no outward sign of having taken offence at her husband's impatient tone. In fact, she looked as if she hadn't heard him at all. She just sat staring across the room, gazing at nothing in particular, for several thoughtful moments before saying, 'It was almost as if they were trying as hard as they could not to show their feelings…even to each other.' Her eyes suddenly brightened with a triumphant glow. 'But they didn't fool me. No, not for a moment! You'd need to be blind or just plain stupid not to see those two young people are deeply in love.'

The passage of time might have taken its toll on Lady Augusta Templehurst's eyesight, but certainly not on her intellect. Her thought processes were as razor-sharp as they had been in her youth. Consequently, when her niece finally arrived at Upper Camden Place late that afternoon, it didn't take her very long to come to the conclusion that the explanation offered for the belated arrival was far from the complete story. Nor did she suppose for a moment that the theft of belongings by a disloyal servant was responsible for her niece's very melancholy air. Wisely, though, she chose not to pry further, believing that in time she would be regaled with a full account of the happenings during the eventful journey to Bath.

During the following few days Lady Templehurst concentrated her efforts on replenishing part of the stolen wardrobe. She derived much enjoyment from accompanying Jane to the fashionable shops, and gained a great deal of satisfaction in finding her niece a new personal maid, whose creative fingers and sunny disposition could not fail to please.

She never tired of her favourite niece's company, and in the normal course of events would have found much pleasure in their daily visit to the Pump Room and the evenings spent at the Assembly Rooms and at private parties, but her satisfaction was marred by the fact that she knew Jane was not obtaining equal enjoyment from her stay.

Lady Augusta's reputation as a formidable matron had been well earned. Her abrasive wit and knife-edged tongue, an awesome combination, remained potent enough, even in her declining years, to cut any presumptuous character down to size, but no one could ever have accused her of being vindictive or heartlessly cruel. None the less, she would have been the first to admit that she was not blessed with any degree of patience, and, after almost two weeks of being subjected to her niece's alternating moods of forced gaiety and despondency, what tolerance she happened to possess rapidly began to wane.

Things came to a head one morning at breakfast. Lady Templehurst had just finished reading aloud a letter she had received from her brother's son and heir, and looked up to find her niece in one of her ever increasing moods of abstraction, gazing aimlessly out of the parlour window.

'Well?' she prompted.

'Yes, I'm glad George is well,' Jane responded vaguely. 'I hope Matilda is, too.'

Lady Templehurst raised her eyes ceilingwards. 'I

knew you hadn't been attending to a single word I said!'

The impatient tone had the desired effect, for Jane cast her aunt an enquiring glance. 'Evidently you find your brother's missives as tedious as I do myself, dear, so I shan't risk boring you further by asking you to read it for yourself, but shall enlighten you again as to its contents.'

After placing the letter down by her plate, she gazed fixedly across the table, just to ensure she still retained her niece's full attention. 'In his usual arrogant fashion my nephew has taken it upon himself to organise your life and include you in the small family party that intends travelling to Paris to meet up with your father who, it seems, has decided to leave Italy sooner than originally planned and remain for a short time in that gay city.

'George impertinently informs me that he is sending your father's carriage to collect you next week. In the normal course of events I would not have hesitated in ordering your father's coachman to tool the carriage, unoccupied, straight back to Kent, but in view of your present highly lethargic state I do not suppose for a moment that it is unduly important whether you are miserably discontent in Paris or Bath, or anywhere else for that matter.'

Jane was one of the few people who never took offence at any of her redoubtable relative's pithy utterances. And in this instance she had to own that the biting sarcasm had been fully justified. She had tried so very hard to feign pleasure in a visit that would normally have afforded tremendous enjoyment, but she had to face the fact that she simply wasn't adept enough in the gentle art of dissimulation. Her char-

acter was far too open for that. All her efforts had
been in vain. She had fooled no one, least of all the
wily Lady Templehurst.

She cast her aunt a look of apology. 'I've been
abysmal company, haven't I?'

'Yes, my dear, you have,' was the brutally honest
response.

'I'm so very sorry.'

'I do not doubt it for a moment, my love. Unfortunately, just an apology will not improve your present state of mind.' Her eyes never wavered from her
niece's lovely face. 'But a truthful account of what
precisely befell you during your journey from Hampshire just possibly might.'

Jane regarded her aunt with a mixture of gentle
affection and admiration. She might have guessed that
the explanation offered for her belated arrival in Bath
had been met with a certain amount of scepticism.

'What I told you before was not a complete pack
of lies, Aunt Augusta. My former maid did pretend
to be unwell, but we didn't stay overnight at an inn,
and I did not awake the following morning to find
both Latimer and my belongings gone. Nor did I remain a further day in order to inform the authorities
and instigate a search for her,' she freely admitted,
before going on to offer the truthful account.

'You showed great presence of mind, Jane,' Lady
Templehurst remarked with an appreciative gleam,
when her niece paused for a moment in her colourful
recitation.

'I would not have escaped so easily, Aunt, if Latimer had not left the door unlocked. And I truly believe that was no accident on her part.'

'Then it is much to her credit, and I can quite understand your reluctance to inform the authorities of her involvement. Though I must confess it grieves me to think Simon Fairfax will go unpunished. Like father like son, it would seem. I have always disliked Lord Fairfax intensely.'

'Unfortunately, Lady Fairfax is a friend of Mama's, so you can appreciate my dilemma.'

'Your mother has much to answer for, and not only in her choice of friends,' Lady Templehurst responded with unbridled censure. 'But, pray continue, my dear. We had reached the point where you had managed to escape from the house. What befell you next?'

All at once Lady Augusta perceived a change in her niece. She seemed suddenly to grow tense, her eyes clouding with that far-away, almost desolate look all too often seen since her arrival in Bath, but she continued her story in a clear, unwavering voice.

'And this friend of the Knightleys—you think he can be trusted not to betray the fact that you spent two nights in his company?' Lady Templehurst enquired when at last she had learned all.

The answer when it came was succinct and decisive. 'Yes.'

'You seem very certain of that, Jane.'

'I am. Dr Thomas Carrington is a man of honour.'

Lady Templehurst's lips curled into a knowing half-smile. 'A rare man, indeed.' There was a significant pause. 'But then, it would take a rare man to capture your heart, would it not, my dear Jane?'

The iron resolve finally crumpled. Lady Templehurst was out of the chair and beside her niece with quite remarkable speed for a woman of her advanced years. Gathering Jane into her arms, she allowed her to cry out her heartfelt misery unrestrainedly.

When at last the tears began to subside she said, with the honesty for which she was famed, 'I reserve the right to pronounce judgement when I have met this paragon of yours, Jane, and not before. Nevertheless, I shall not insult your intelligence by pretending that I am overjoyed with your choice of mate, although his station in life could hardly be described as contemptible. You may be certain of one thing, my child: if I do like him, and if I believe you would suit, then you shall marry your young doctor with my full blessing.' She was at her most imperious. 'And woe betide any member of the family who dares to prevent a union between you!'

Jane gazed up at her aunt with deep affection. 'I do not doubt for a moment that you would make the staunchest of allies, but the need for your support will not arise.' She couldn't prevent her lip from trembling, but managed to control the threat of more tears. 'The reason I shall never marry Dr Carrington isn't because I fear my family's opposition to the match, but simply because Tom doesn't care for me deeply enough to ask for my hand.'

Chapter Twelve

Tom reached for the quill and jotted a reminder in his diary to visit the rector's wife the following afternoon. Really, he was becoming quite forgetful of late. Important matters that once he would never have forgotten now seemed to slip his mind completely.

After sanding down the single entry in his bold, flowing hand, he was about to close the book, when his attention was drawn to the date printed at the top of the page, and he experienced yet again a resurgence of that distressing ache which, if the truth be known, never left him completely. Was it really just three short weeks since his return from Wiltshire? Dear God! It seemed like three years.

He released his breath in a sigh of doleful resignation. No man could have tried harder to put the past behind him and get on with life, but it was hopeless. Even his work, which he had thrown himself into with renewed vigour, had proved an insufficient remedy to heal a mind all too frequently tortured by images of a lovely aristocratic lady, whose indomitable spirit and ever lively sense of humour had captured his heart in a way that mere beauty never could.

The door opening intruded into his bitter-sweet reflections, and he looked up to see his housekeeper enter his consulting-room. 'A visitor for you, Dr Carrington,' she said, and a moment later Lady Knightley appeared before him.

Not even the sight of his dear friend could lift his spirits, but he did manage a semblance of a smile before inviting her to sit down. 'By your healthy bloom I can safely assume that you do not require my professional services.'

'Which is perhaps just as well,' she returned, if not precisely sharply, then certainly with an edge to her normally pleasant voice. 'I've a feeling I should need to be at death's door before you could bestir yourself to visit the Hall. You haven't called in to see us once since your return from Wiltshire.'

Tom glanced away from eyes that reminded him too painfully of someone else's, and under the pretext of placing his diary back into the top drawer of his desk he averted his face. Elizabeth knew him better, perhaps, than anyone else, and she was an extremely perceptive young woman. It wouldn't do to give her an inkling of what was torturing him during his every waking moment.

'As you can imagine I've been extremely busy. My young apothecary can deal with most things whilst I'm away, but there are certain cases he cannot handle.'

'I do know how hard you work, Tom. But you need to relax sometimes. You are becoming more and more antisocial. And I'm not the only person to remark upon it.'

'I'm sure the local gossipmongers are very well

aware that I was socialising only last Friday when I attended Margaret and Sam's wedding celebration.'

Elizabeth opened her mouth to respond to this, but then thought better of it, and merely watched in silence as he rose to his feet and began to clear the papers from his desk.

'There's only so much time a busy practitioner has to himself. So, if there's nothing else, perhaps you'll excuse me?'

Elizabeth received her congé without so much as a blink, but felt understandably hurt by this seeming indifference to her company. She knew Tom could be irascible at times and that his language was frequently blunt, but she had never known him to behave quite so uncivilly before, at least not to her. There was definitely something troubling him deeply.

She echoed her thoughts aloud when she rejoined her husband in his curricle a few minutes later. 'I suspected when I bumped into him last week that something was preying on his mind,' she went on to confess. 'I thought at the time it might have something to do with Margaret Ryan's wedding, but now I'm not so certain.'

She caught her husband's rather sheepish expression, and couldn't prevent a smile. 'Oh, come, Richard! Surely you do not suppose for a moment that I'm naïve enough to believe, simply because Tom isn't married, that he practises celibacy? He and Margaret Ryan have been much more than just friends for years. I do not doubt for a moment that he must have experienced some regret at losing such an obviously satisfying mistress, but I do not think it wholly responsible for his present subdued state.'

'A lady of your quality oughtn't to know about

such things, let alone discuss them.' Richard feigned shock before chuckling at the fulminating glance he received. 'Yes, I too have noticed that Tom isn't quite himself these days,' he admitted, serious once again. 'But I've not the smallest intention of prying into his private affairs, if that is what you were about to suggest.'

Elizabeth was sensible enough to realise that it would be pointless discussing the matter further. Richard was generously compliant over most things, but on some issues he was immovable, and interfering in other people's concerns just happened to be one of his particular taboos. He was perfectly right, of course, but that didn't prevent her from worrying, all the same.

She was still pondering over the possible reason for her friend's highly uncongenial state when Richard, with all the expertise of a nonsuch, tooled the curricle between the two solid stone pillars and into Knightley Park, and a minute or two later she saw an antiquated berline pulled up at the front of their house.

'Good heavens! Who on earth owns such an old-fashioned equipage? You haven't invited someone to stay and forgotten to mention it, have you, Richard?'

'I was about to ask you the same thing.' Drawing his curricle to a halt behind the antiquated carriage, he watched two of his servants carrying luggage into the house. 'Down you get. I shall be generous and allow you to have your curiosity satisfied first.'

Elizabeth needed no second prompting. Leaving Richard to take the curricle round to the stables, she entered the hall to find it littered with a wide assortment of baggage, and her normally very efficient young butler looking slightly harassed.

'I apologise for the clutter, my lady, only the visitor has just this moment arrived, and as you omitted to inform me that you were expecting a guest I was in some doubt as to which bedchamber to give her.'

Elizabeth swooped down on the butler's most significant disclosure. 'Her, Medway?'

'Lady Augusta Templehurst, my lady. I've shown her into the drawing-room.'

Although she refrained from uttering any exclamation of surprise, Elizabeth was quite naturally astonished to learn the visitor's identity, and, after issuing instructions for her aunt's baggage to be carried up to the green bedchamber, she didn't waste any time in entering the drawing-room to discover the relative she had not seen for almost ten years comfortably ensconced in a chair near the hearth.

'This is a most unexpected pleasure, ma'am!'

A wicked cackle answered this. 'Shock, you mean. And a gross impertinence to descend on you like this without warning. I am fully sensible of it. Come here, child, and let me look at you.'

Mistress in her own home Elizabeth most definitely was, but she found herself automatically obeying the imperious command, and even went so far as to demonstrate that she hadn't taken offence at being ordered about in such a fashion by placing a chaste salute on one of her aunt's satiny pink cheeks.

'Yes,' Lady Templehurst remarked after scrutinising her niece's features closely. 'You and Jane are most certainly the beauties in the family. The Beresford women were always either outstandingly lovely or muffin-faced—which tells you precisely just how highly I rate the looks of the other female members of the family.'

Elizabeth was unable to suppress a chuckle at this outrageous remark, and realised that Jane had not overrated their aunt's outspokenness. She felt instantly drawn to this aristocratic lady and could only wonder why, as a child, she had been somewhat in awe of her.

'You must be wondering what on earth has brought me here,' Lady Templehurst said when her niece had taken the seat opposite. 'Haven't set eyes on you since the day of your dear father's funeral, and I have the unmitigated gall to invite myself to your home. My only saving grace, I suppose, is that I have always kept in touch with you by letter.'

'Ma'am, pray rid your mind that your presence, unexpected though it is, is not very welcome. I'm delighted that you decided to pay us a visit.'

Richard entered the room at that moment and Elizabeth did not hesitate in requesting him to add his assurance that Lady Augusta's arrival was a delightful surprise.

'Indeed, it is, ma'am,' he obliged with remarkable aplomb. 'Jane talks of you often, and always with affection. I am delighted to make your acquaintance at last.'

'Graciously said, my dear boy.' Lady Templehurst wholeheartedly approved of the handsome baronet whose charm of manner was famed. 'I knew your father quite well. You resemble him greatly. He was a handsome devil, too! You are a very lucky girl, Elizabeth,' she added, transferring her shrewd gaze to her niece. 'I wish my Jane were so fortunate.'

Richard did not miss the searching glance cast in

his wife's direction, and felt certain that Lady Augusta had a very specific reason for her unexpected visit. However, after handing the lady a glass of Madeira, he merely asked how long they could expect the privilege of her company.

'Two days. Three at the most,' she responded, after sampling the excellent wine. 'I have no intention of inflicting my presence on you for any great length of time.'

'You are welcome to remain as long as you wish, Aunt.'

'That is very kind of you, Elizabeth, but I shan't impose on your gracious hospitality for long. I must reach Kent by the end of the week to stay with Jane.' She took a further fortifying sip of Madeira before placing the glass down on the table by her chair. 'My nephew George, the impertinent young jackanapes, had the temerity to request his sister's early return from Bath in order to accompany him and that feather-brained chit he married to Paris. Jane, being a young woman of superior sense, wasn't very enthusiastic at the prospect of spending several weeks in the French capital with her parents, her brother, eldest sister and their respective spouses. And who can blame her for that?'

Elizabeth frowned slightly. 'Why on earth didn't she remain in Bath with you, ma'am?'

'Because I'm a selfish old woman, my dear. I rub along tolerably well with my brother. Much preferred your father, though. Never made any secret of that. Ten minutes in the Countess's company is more than enough for anyone. And with the exception of Jane, who's the best out of the lot of 'em by far, I'm not overly fond of their offspring, either. So I thought I'd take this opportunity, whilst the family is away, to visit the ancestral home one last time.'

She paused for a moment to reach for her glass. 'But, since Jane left Bath I've been thinking that I might like to take her to London. She seemed in a strangely subdued frame of mind whilst she was staying with me, and I thought a few weeks in London might be just the thing to cheer her up.'

Richard regarded their visitor levelly, his expression giving nothing away, but Elizabeth displayed quite open surprise at this disclosure. 'She seemed in excellent spirits during her stay with us, ma'am. I wonder what could have occurred to upset her? Although—' she turned to her husband '—she was somewhat concerned about her friend Lord Pentecost.'

'Yes, she told me all about that.' Like Sir Richard's, Lady Templehurst's expression gave nothing away, but inwardly she was delighted, for Elizabeth had unwittingly told her precisely what she had come here to discover: the Knightleys were in complete ignorance of what had befallen Jane after she had left the safety of their home.

'Never cared for Lady Pentecost,' she admitted, without the least hesitation. 'Odious woman! That's a further reason for visiting the capital. There's someone there I think it might be beneficial to see over that particular matter. You probably know him, Richard—Sir Bartholomew Rudge.'

'I've met him, ma'am, certainly. Who hasn't? Plays too high for me. One of Prinney's set.'

'Yes, he is, but then he always was a fool,' she remarked in her usual forthright manner. 'And he's never improved with age. But if you want to discover something, he's the one to ask. There isn't much that goes on that he doesn't know about.'

After finishing off her wine, Lady Templehurst rose to her feet, with the aid of her ebony stick, and requested Elizabeth to show her to her room in order to change for dinner. 'And on the way perhaps you would permit me to pay a visit to the nursery? I'm longing to meet those children of yours.'

Nothing could have given Elizabeth greater pleasure. Lady Templehurst endeared herself even more by saying everything a proud mother could wish to hear about her offspring, and later, at dinner, proved herself to be an entertaining conversationalist, keeping Richard highly amused with her scathing condemnation of most members of the Beresford family.

After the meal was over they retired to the drawing-room to play a hand or two of piquet, and the evening continued to be a most enjoyable one until Lady Templehurst suddenly announced that she was not feeling well. At first she refused to entertain the idea of summoning a doctor, declaring that the discomfort would pass, but eventually acquiesced, and was comfortably tucked up in bed by the time Tom arrived.

It would have been difficult to say which of them subjected the other to the more searching scrutiny. Tom's eyes, as always, were penetratingly alert, and Lady Templehurst's gaze certainly never wavered from his direction as he entered the room and approached the bed with that smooth, long-striding gait of his.

She had never before heard her niece describe any gentleman as an ill-tempered, infuriating darling, yet she still couldn't help wondering whether Jane might not be in the grip of mere infatuation. Had Dr Carrington turned out to be a suavely elegant Adonis, she might have continued to doubt the true state of her niece's heart, but now, having seen him, she did not. Jane had fallen deeply in love with this ruggedly attractive man, whose light brown, waving hair was overlong, and whose attire, at best, could be described as casual.

'What seems to be the trouble, ma'am?' he enquired, and she discovered, quite surprisingly, that even at her age she was attracted by the throaty timbre of his voice.

'I experienced slight discomfort in my chest. Indigestion, I suspect. I do suffer from it. But Elizabeth would insist upon sending for you.'

He did not respond, but seated himself on the edge of the bed and opened his medical bag to draw out a wooden cylinder about nine inches long.

'What in the name of heaven is that?' Lady Templehurst demanded to know.

'It's called a stethoscope, ma'am.' He placed one end to her chest and listened intently for a full minute. 'It was invented by a French physician, René Laënnec. The story goes that he was consulted by a young woman who betrayed symptoms of heart disease. She was by all accounts a rather stout young lady, and in view of her age and sex he felt he could not resort to the usual method of examination by placing his ear to her chest.'

A wicked cackle rent the air. 'At my age I would be extremely flattered if a young man chose to place his cheek against my scrawny bosom!'

This ignited a spark of amusement in what she considered very attractive grey eyes. 'I recall your niece remarking that you are something of a rogue, ma'am.'

She was suddenly very much on her mettle. 'I assume you refer to Jane. I doubt Elizabeth would ever be so impertinent.' She could almost feel him stiffen, and the emotion which just for one unguarded moment flickered in the depths of his eyes told her much of what she needed to know. 'May I take this opportunity, Dr Carrington, of thanking you for the care you took of my niece not so long ago? Yes,' she added, in response to his all-too-obvious unspoken question. 'She did inform me of precisely what befell her during her journey to Bath.'

'I did precious little, ma'am.' His tone was clipped—dismissive, almost. 'But I'm relieved to hear that she eventually arrived at her destination without suffering further mishap.'

Tom finished his examination without saying anything further, and then rose from the bed. 'Your heart is fine, ma'am, but I'll leave you something to help you sleep. Tomorrow, I'll send over a draught which should help with any discomfort you may feel after meals.'

After he had left, Lady Templehurst became lost in her own thoughts until there was a scratch on the door, and her maid opened it to admit Elizabeth.

'Tom informs me that there is nothing seriously wrong—thank goodness! How are you feeling now, ma'am?'

Lady Templehurst nodded dismissal to her maid, and then patted the edge of the bed. 'Come here, child. I wish to speak with you.' She waited until her command had been obeyed before confessing. 'I had a specific reason for coming here, Elizabeth, which concerns my Jane.'

'I recall your mentioning earlier that there was

something troubling her. I hope there's nothing seriously wrong.'

'I'm afraid there is, my dear… She's fallen deeply in love. She's firmly convinced, however, that the gentleman who has captured her young but certainly not frivolous heart does not return her regard. But she is in error. Now, having met him, there is no doubt in my mind that he is as much in love with her as she is with him.'

It did not take many moments before enlightenment dawned. 'Tom!' Elizabeth exclaimed. 'It's Tom, isn't it? I knew there was something, but I couldn't for the life of me think what could be making him so desperately unhappy. For that is precisely what he has been ever since he returned from Wiltshire.'

'It is quite evident to me that he has confided in no one, which does that young man great credit, of course. But I think it is time you learned precisely what befell my niece after leaving the protection of your home.'

Apart from the occasional exclamation of dismay, Elizabeth sat silently listening to an account of the event which had taken place during her cousin's eventful journey to Bath. When she had learned all, she said, 'I can quite understand why Tom has kept silent. If that became common knowledge, Jane's reputation would be in shreds.'

'Jane assures me that he did not seduce her.' Lady Templehurst's rather wicked sense of humour came to the fore. 'Personally, I should feel extremely aggrieved if I had spent two nights alone in the company of that wholly masculine young man and he hadn't attempted seduction!' She became serious again. 'No, I mustn't laugh. It's wicked of me in view of the heartache those two young people are suffering. What I should like to know is why…? Why, if he does love her, and I'm firmly convinced that he does, has he not made an offer for her hand?'

Elizabeth was silent for a long time, and then said, 'The reason may possibly be because he doesn't think he's good enough for her.'

'In that case he must be brought to see the error of his ways.'

'I'm afraid, Aunt Augusta, where Thomas Carrington is concerned that is far easier said than done.'

Chapter Thirteen

Lady Templehurst didn't regret coming to London. After all, Jane could brood just as easily here in town as she could in Kent. She didn't regret, either, her decision in accepting Sir Richard's very generous offer of the use of his town house for the duration of their stay. It would, of course, have been perfectly possible to stay at the Beresford mansion in Grosvenor Square. Her brother, the Earl, was very generous and permitted any member of the immediate family to make use of his town residence, but, as Lady Templehurst had feared, one of Jane's sisters had already installed herself there with her husband.

It wasn't that she selfishly wished to deprive Jane of her sister's company—far from it, in fact. Unfortunately, though, her sister Lavinia was very like the Countess, needing the stimulation of continual company, and Jane was most definitely not ready, yet, to be thrust once again into the hectic social whirl most of her relations seemed to enjoy.

Raising her eyes from her embroidery, she stared across the room at her favourite niece, who was sitting in the window embrasure, staring down into the street. It would be foolish to try to delude herself into imagining that this visit to the capital would set all to rights, but Lady Templehurst attained a modicum of satisfaction from knowing that Jane had gained some pleasure from their visit thus far. She had appeared to enjoy the few parties they had attended, and her spirits had certainly lifted whenever she had been in the company of Lord Pentecost and Miss Dilbey. However, Lady Templehurst could not be wholly content until her niece began to talk freely of the heartache she was succeeding in keeping hidden from the world at large. Not once had she mentioned Thomas Carrington's name since their arrival in town, and this, Lady Templehurst felt, was far from a good sign.

'You're very quiet, dear,' she remarked, drawing her niece's attention to her. 'What are you thinking about?'

'I was just wondering if you are right, Aunt Augusta, that Hetta and Perry will make a match of it.'

'All the indications are there for anyone to see, my love. I for one would applaud the match. From what you tell me the young Lord Pentecost has gained even more self-confidence since his visit to this London physician. Like his father, he will always require his periods of solitude, and I believe Miss Dilbey is very well aware of this. She's not only extremely pretty, but a very sensible young woman, and I think she'll make him the ideal wife.'

She paused for a moment to set another stitch in the fire-screen she was embroidering. 'I found his disclosures yesterday most interesting. His visit to the family solicitor to reacquaint himself with the contents of his father's will shows clearly enough, does it not, that he is thinking of the future? It is little

wonder that he took precious little interest in his affairs after his father's demise,' she went on, displaying the kind and understanding side to her nature that
few people were privileged to see. 'Not only was he
grieving over the loss of a much loved parent, but he
was battling with the added burden of believing he
might one day go insane. Which is precisely why I've
asked my old friend Sir Bartholomew Rudge to visit
us this morning to see if he cannot shed some light
on that rather puzzling matter.'

Jane remained sceptical. Although she was not well
acquainted with the obese baronet, their paths had
crossed from time to time during her three Seasons,
but he had never struck her as a person in whom one
could place much reliance.

'Sir Bartholomew may appear a buffoon,' Lady
Templehurst remarked, reading her niece's thoughts
with uncanny accuracy, 'but do not be fooled by that
devil-may-care attitude he adopts. He possesses quite
the most remarkable retentive memory. He can recall
incidents from the distant past in minute detail. Also,
little escapes his notice, and what he doesn't know
about what goes on in society isn't worth knowing.'

Jane's attention was once more drawn to the street
below and the fashionable carriage which had just that
instant pulled up at the door. 'We'll soon discover
whether your faith in him is justified, Aunt Augusta,
for unless I'm very much mistaken, your old friend
has just arrived.'

Within the space of a few minutes the door opened
and a rather portly gentleman, sporting a garishly coloured waistcoat, and the most preposterously large
nosegay in the buttonhole of his fashionable jacket,
entered the sunny front parlour. With his round face

wreathed in smiles, and without uttering a word, he
went directly across to Lady Templehurst and planted
a smacking kiss on one of her pink cheeks.

'Couldn't believe it when I received your note,
Gussie, old girl! Thought nothing would ever induce
you away from that dashed watering place. Never
could stand Bath myself! Must say, though, you're
looking well.'

'Which is more than can be said for you, Bart,' she
told him, with all the frankness of a long-standing
friendship. 'Do sit down and take all the weight off
your feet.'

Without betraying any outwards signs of having
taken offence, he did as bidden, but made to rise again
almost at once when he noticed Jane for the first time.
'Sorry, m'dear. Didn't see you sitting there.'

'Please don't get up, sir,' Jane adjured him, fearing
the procedure might prove a strenuous one for a gentleman of his size. 'Might I offer you some refreshment?'

'No, thank you, m'dear. Never imbibe until after
midday.' He turned his attention back to Lady Templehurst. 'What a pleasure it is to see you back in
town. But what the deuce are you doing here in Sir
Richard Knightley's house?'

'He kindly offered me the use of it when I paid
him a short visit not so very long ago, and I must say
I find it infinitely more comfortable than the Beresford mansion, but that is neither here nor there. The
reason I particularly requested you to visit, Bart,' she
said, coming straight to the point, 'is because I believe
you were well acquainted at one time with the late
Lord Pentecost.'

'And so I was,' he didn't hesitate to confirm. 'Considering we had little in common, we were good friends. We were at Eton together and then Oxford. Didn't see so much of him in later years, mind. Turned into something of a recluse. Still, who wouldn't,' he added, 'married to that harpy? Don't think he would ever have got himself leg-shackled if it hadn't been for his brother's death.'

Lady Templehurst regarded him keenly. 'What do you know about that, Bart? I've heard mention that the younger brother wasn't quite right in the head.'

'What…?' He looked completely taken aback. 'Utter rot! Don't know how these silly rumours get started. He was a quiet, reserved fellow, but a bruising young rider. Nothing wrong with the lad until he had that accident. Changed him completely, as I recall.'

'What accident was that?' Lady Templehurst prompted, when her old friend fell silent.

'Oh, a very sad business. Happened during his last year up at Oxford.' He shook his head as though at some private thought. 'Remember it as though it were only yesterday. The late Lord Pentecost was paying one of his rare visits to London at the time. I was with him at White's when he received news that his brother had been hurt. Up to some lark, I shouldn't wonder, and went tumbling down a flight of stairs. Was unconscious for several days, if my memory serves me correctly. Recovered, but was never the same. Would fly off into almost insane rages, followed by moods of deep depression. Probably just as well that he died soon afterwards in that riding accident.'

'Are you by any chance acquainted with the present Lord Pentecost?' Jane asked, after digesting these most interesting facts.

'I've met him. Strangely enough he puts me in mind of young Cedric—same build, same colouring. Noticed it at once when I came across the boy at my club t'other evening. He's even inherited his uncle's excellent seat on a horse, so I understand. Shame poor old Arthur only had the one son. He was fond of children.'

'He may have been,' Lady Templehurst remarked drily, recalling clearly what Perry had told them yesterday, 'but that will he made certainly did his sole offspring no favours. Apparently, Bart, Peregrine cannot touch a penny of his father's private wealth, at least not the capital, until he attains the age of thirty or in the event that he marries, whichever comes first. The problem is that his mother must approve his choice of bride if he chooses to marry before he celebrates his thirtieth birthday, or the money remains in trust for the next holder of the title.'

'Mmm. Bit of a rum deal, I must say,' he was forced to concede. 'Can only think that old Arthur must have been trying to protect his son from money-grabbing harpies.'

'I believe the young Lord Pentecost has too much sense than to be beguiled by a pretty face. He has, however, become wondrous close with a young woman whom I should very much doubt would meet with his obnoxious mother's approval,' Lady Templehurst announced, without the least hesitation, knowing that her old friend could be trusted to keep this information to himself.

He cocked one greying brow. 'Shabby-genteel, eh?'

'No such thing! Good family. Related to the Devonshire Dilbeys. She has no money...at least, only what she can expect to inherit from her uncle. But in every other respect she would suit admirably. She's a very sensible young woman, and she's fond of him, too.'

'If the gel's all you say she is, why do you suppose Sophia Pentecost would oppose the match?'

'I suspect,' Jane put in, once again drawing the baronet's round, childlike eyes in her direction, 'it's because she is unwilling to relinquish her position as mistress of Pentecost Grange. I do not think she would approve of any female Perry wishes to marry.'

'Well, there's usually a solution to be found to most problems,' he announced, after a moment's intense thought. 'Merely need to spike her guns.'

'And how do you suggest one goes about doing that?' Lady Templehurst asked, completely at a loss.

'Dear me, Gussie, old girl. Your years in Bath have addled your wits!' His large stomach shook in response to the fulminating glance she cast him. He still had a soft spot deep down for the woman whom many years before he himself had considered marrying, but he had never repined when she had chosen Lord Templehurst. He had enjoyed the freedom of his bachelor existence.

'You are still someone, Augusta,' he told her. 'It's a simple matter, surely, of rallying enough of your old cronies to the cause? Get enough of 'em to approve the match, then Sophia Pentecost would look nohow trying to oppose it. Why, I might even lend you my support. I've never cared for the dragon-lady myself.'

Lady Templehurst betrayed all the exuberance of an excited child. 'By heaven, Bart! You might just have something there!'

* * *

Jane most certainly thought that he had hit on the very solution, and didn't hesitate in informing Hetta of the ageing dandy's most enlightening visit when she met her in the park that afternoon.

'It must have been this physical resemblance between Perry and Cedric that the late Lord Pentecost was referring to shortly before he died, and the fact that they were both intrepid horsemen. Perhaps it was the fear that Perry, too, might also sustain a serious fall from a horse that concerned the late Lord Pentecost. Needless to say, had Cedric ended his days in a lunatic asylum it would not have been through any inherited defect.'

Hetta, pleased to have the matter cleared up at last, nodded in agreement, and was on the point of disclosing some important news of her own, when she noticed Jane stiffen suddenly. A few moments later a curricle passed them and she watched her aristocratic friend give the briefest of nods in response to the driver's bright smile and cheerful wave.

'From your most unenthusiastic response, I can safely assume that you are not overly fond of the Honourable Simon Fairfax. I cannot say he made much of an impression on me when he visited Hampshire. Rumour has it that since his return from Paris he has been paying court to a wealthy cit's daughter.'

'Then I wish her joy of him, for, as you surmised, I do not care for him in the least.' She had no intention of explaining the reasons for her animosity and quickly changed the subject by asking Hetta what she had been about to say, and was utterly delighted to hear that Lord Pentecost had at last proposed.

'Perry would like the wedding to take place this summer,' Hetta went on to disclose, with a decided lack of enthusiasm, 'but I cannot help thinking it might be better to wait.'

Jane looked at her closely. 'Why? You've no doubts, have you?'

'Not about our regard for each other, no. And I'm certain we would suit admirably. Although I'm more outgoing than Perry, I too like my periods of quiet relaxation, and do not wish to be forever socialising. Only…I know his mother would not approve his choice.'

Jane slanted a look of comical dismay at her. 'Both you and I know that the Dowager would not approve any choice.'

'Perhaps not. But might it not be sensible to wait? When he's thirty he can marry whomsoever he chooses without fear of losing his inheritance.'

'And are you both prepared to wait almost six years?'

'Perry doesn't wish to, and, truth to tell, neither do I. He says he would far rather be happy than wealthy, and I genuinely believe he means it. And as far as I'm concerned… Well, I know precisely what it is like to do without luxuries, so it would be no hardship.' The tiny, heartfelt sigh betrayed her continued misgivings, even before she added, 'I just don't wish to be responsible for depriving him of what is rightfully his, even though I'm certain in my heart that without the money we would be perfectly contented. He has every intention of informing his mother when she arrives in town at the end of the week.'

'Now, that I do consider would be a grave error of judgement.'

'So you do think it would be better if we did wait?'

'In informing your future mama-in-law, certainly!'

Jane experienced a surge of wicked satisfaction at the prospect of outwitting the Dowager Lady Pentecost. 'I think it would be highly beneficial for you and Perry to have a talk with Lady Templehurst. Come to the house tomorrow morning. We have no plans to go out.'

This was certainly true, but during Jane's absence Lady Templehurst had been forced to review certain arrangements, because of Lady Knightley's unexpected arrival in town. She saw no reason, however, for Jane to forgo the evening's entertainment in order to keep her cousin company, and encouraged her to dine with her sister Lavinia at Grosvenor Square as planned.

This suited Elizabeth very well, for, although she had every intention of spending a great deal of time with Jane, she was simply agog to discover how her cousin was going on, and didn't hesitate in broaching the subject the instant Jane had left the house that evening.

'She seemed in remarkably good spirits when she returned from her walk in Hyde Park. I suppose, though, that much of her cheerfulness was due to Hetta's most excellent news.'

'Precisely, my dear Elizabeth. Jane is very happy for them both, but do not be fooled by that display of gaiety. Besides which, she was naturally delighted by your early arrival in town.'

'Truth to tell, I simply couldn't stay away. I know the children will be well cared for in my absence. They have the most efficient and devoted nursemaid in the person of my former maid, Agatha Stigwell.'

Elizabeth momentarily raised her eyes from her

sewing to cast a shrewd glance in her aunt's direction. 'Does Jane suspect that you might have confided in Richard and myself?'

'Suspect?' Lady Templehurst gave vent to one of her wicked cackles. 'She knew without being told—knew the instant I mentioned that I had broken my journey to Kent by spending two nights at Knightley Hall. She might be emotionally damaged, but there's absolutely nothing amiss with the functions of her brain. She's no fool, Elizabeth. By all means speak of your friend Dr Carrington in her presence, for she will not mention his name. And I cannot help but feel that it would be far better if she did open her heart again to someone, instead of continuously trying to keep her misery from surfacing.'

Elizabeth couldn't help but agree, though felt she could bring precious little comfort. Tom was virtually unapproachable these days—reclusive, almost. If it wasn't for his work she honestly didn't think that anything or anyone could induce him to leave his house.

So she would have been surprised, not to say astounded, had she known that at that precise moment her good friend was seated in the library at Knightley Hall, challenging her husband to a game of chess.

Richard had long since realised, even if his wife had not, that their good friend would not place himself in a situation where he might be forced to talk openly about his private concerns until he felt ready to do so. Richard had sensed, too, that Tom would be reluctant to unburden his soul in front of Elizabeth, whose fondness for her aristocratic cousin was evident, and his judgement in this had not been at fault. No sooner had Elizabeth embarked on the journey to London than he had dashed off a note to Dr Carrington inviting him to dine that evening, and had received an immediate and favourable response.

During their meal Tom maintained a flow of pleasant conversation. Anyone observing him might have supposed that he hadn't a care in the world. However, as with Jane, the effort to maintain the display of light-heartedness soon became too much of a strain, and he succumbed to a mood of abstraction, his mind dwelling on events that he would have given almost anything to forget.

'You appear to have lost your concentration, old fellow,' Richard remarked, his long-fingered hand swooping down to remove a hapless pawn.

Masculine eyes then met and locked above the chequered board. 'You know, don't you?' It was more statement than question. 'Lady Templehurst told you, I presume?'

Richard knew nothing would be gained by prevarication. 'She confided in both Elizabeth and myself during her short stay here, yes. But I realised that you were falling in love with Jane even before you embarked on that eventful trip to Wiltshire.'

This admission managed to induce a semblance of a smile. 'I didn't realise I was quite so transparent, Richard.'

'You forget, my friend, I have gone through much the same experience, except my sufferings were not, I think, as profound as yours.'

Abandoning the game completely, Richard leaned back in his chair and sipped his wine, while he watched his companion down the contents of his glass and reach once again for the bottle. Tom was drinking heavily this evening—had been imbibing too freely for several weeks, Richard guessed—and it was beginning to show. His complexion was pallid, and his lacklustre eyes were darkly circled. The lack of concern he had always displayed over his appearance was certainly more marked. The waving hair, which he had always tended to wear long, now reached beyond the collar of his heavily creased jacket; and what purported to be a cravat looked nothing better than a crumpled rag that might have been used for a drying cloth before being abysmally tied about his neck.

'You cannot go on this way,' he remarked, watching yet a further glass of wine being consumed with scant regard for its excellence.

Tom didn't pretend to misunderstand. 'No, I know. I've been trying to drown my sorrows, but it doesn't work.' Placing the empty glass down on the table, he made no attempt to refill it this time. 'I've received a letter from Sir William Dent, inviting me to stay with him in London for a few days in order to attend several lectures he thought might be of interest to me.'

'Then I would accept if I were you,' Richard encouraged. 'A change of scenery might be beneficial. I'm joining Elizabeth in town early next week. You could travel with me in the curricle.'

'Why not?' Tom's sudden shout of laughter had a reckless quality. 'I'd try anything if it helped me to forget.'

'Is that what you want—to forget her?'

The response when it came was little more than a broken whisper. 'No... But how can there be a future for us when she is what she is and I...? Oh, God, Richard! Of all the females in the land, why did I have to go and fall in love with her?'

Perhaps because it was meant to be, Richard answered silently.

He had realised from the first that Tom must have exerted the most formidable control over himself during the time he had spent alone with Jane, since he did not feel himself in any way honour-bound to marry her. And that he had not taken advantage of the situation was proof, surely, of the depth of his regard?

But what of Jane? Much depended on that young woman. If she loved him, and Lady Templehurst had given him every reason to believe that her niece did, then the situation was not hopeless. There might be some opposition to the match, but Jane would not let that deter her if her feelings for Tom went deep enough. Richard was extremely fond of them both, and thought that they would make an ideal match. He decided, however, for the time being, to keep his reflections to himself.

Chapter Fourteen

Richard would not have been in the least surprised to receive a note from his friend to say that he had decided against a visit to the metropolis after all. However, he had done him an injustice to suppose for a moment that, even in his present, eminently unhappy state, Tom was incapable of coming to a decision and sticking to it.

Strangely enough, though, it was this single-mindedness of Tom's—one might almost say this dogged determination to stand by his principles—that concerned Richard most of all, for it could well prove in this situation to be Tom's downfall. Unless someone, perhaps even Jane herself, a well-adjusted female by any standard, could prove to him just how misguided he was in this instance, there wasn't the remotest possibility of a joyous outcome to the present, most unsatisfactory state of affairs.

None the less, when his friend arrived at the hall, promptly at the pre-arranged time, Richard was delighted to see that he had taken his first step along the road to recovery. His appearance was much improved, and he had even gone to the trouble of having his hair shorn to a more acceptable length since the evening they had dined together.

They did not delay their departure. The morning was dry and bright—ideal, in fact, for travelling in an open carriage. Stopping only to change horses, and to partake of a light luncheon at one of the superior posting-houses, they made excellent time until they arrived at the outskirts of the metropolis, where Richard had, perforce, to reduce his speed because of the volume of traffic.

'I'd forgotten just how overcrowded it is in the capital,' Tom remarked, viewing the congestion with avid distaste. 'Unless my livelihood depended upon it, nothing could induce me to remain here for more than a short period.'

'Yes, I know what you mean. Even though Elizabeth and I come here each spring, we are never sorry to leave the noise and stale air behind and return to Hampshire.'

Tom frowned as a thought suddenly occurred to him. 'Now I come to think about it, you are making your visit earlier than usual this year. Normally you arrive in town when the Season is almost over.'

'Oh, didn't I mention it?' Richard looked mildly surprised. 'I offered the use of my house to Lady Templehurst for the duration of her stay in London, and as Elizabeth hasn't seen anything of her aunt in recent years she decided she'd take the opportunity to spend a little time with her.'

An uncomfortable, but thankfully short silence followed, before Tom said, 'Is Jane residing there, too?'

'Why, yes!' The look Richard received would certainly have alarmed any craven member of his sex. 'Now, see here, Tom. It was never my intention to deceive you, but you'll admit yourself we've seen precious little of each other in recent weeks, and to be honest with you it never crossed my mind to mention it before. I did, however, have the intention of taking you to the house first, but if you'd rather we went directly to Sir William's lodgings then I'll quite understand.'

There was no response.

'You're bound to come face to face with her some time, old fellow,' Richard continued, in an attempt to break the awkward silence. 'Elizabeth and I were hoping to persuade her to pay a visit to Hampshire again some time during the summer, but we're not likely to meet with very much success if the poor girl suspects that her presence in our home will keep you away.'

This contingency had not occurred to Tom before, and he was rather taken aback. 'Good Lord! Yes, I'd not thought of that,' he freely admitted. 'I wouldn't wish to make her feel uncomfortable…ever. And you're right, of course. Yes, we'll call at your house first.'

The decision had not been an easy one to make. Tom felt as though he were being ripped in two. He was nowhere near ready to come face to face with Jane again and couldn't hope to stand a better than even chance of keeping his feelings firmly under control. But, at the same time, the thought that, by not seeing her now, he might never again see her in the future was more than he could bear.

She might, of course, have no desire whatsoever to see him—a heart-rending possibility, but one much better faced. After all, he had not been given the opportunity to speak to her in private before he had journeyed with her in the Prices' cart to Devizes, and had seen her a short time later safely ensconced in the hired carriage to continue her journey to Bath. How could he have explained his behaviour of the night before while there had always been someone lingering nearby who might have overheard?

He knew in his heart of hearts that he had made the right decision in calling a halt to their lovemaking—that he'd been right not to have taken advantage of their situation—but there hadn't been a waking moment since when he had not desperately regretted not remaining with her throughout that unforgettable night.

It was in this highly confused state, where bitter regrets warred with the knowledge that he had behaved in the only honourable way, that he stepped down from the curricle as it was expertly drawn to a halt outside the Knightleys' fashionable London residence. Refusing to linger in the rear, he was smartly at Richard's heels as his friend threw open the parlour door. Two pairs of eyes, both sets betraying surprise and uncertainty in equal measures, turned in his direction, but it was into the third pair that he found himself staring…searching.

For several moments no one moved, no one spoke; then Jane, with all her innate grace and well-bred dignity—which afterwards Lady Templehurst, with tears in her eyes, confessed to the Knightleys made her feel inordinately proud to be her aunt—rose from her chair and went towards Tom with her hand outstretched.

'It is delightful to see you again, Dr Carrington. I didn't know that Richard was bringing you with him to town.'

He retained his hold on the slender, tapering fingers for as long as he dared. 'Truth to tell, my lady, it was a last-minute decision on my part.' Why was she being so formal? For that matter, why was he? 'Sir William Dent invited me to attend some lectures with him on the improved treatments of certain disorders.'

'All work, Dr Carrington!' Lady Templehurst remarked, finding her voice at last. 'Do you never relax? I hope you will at least find the time to attend our party here on Thursday evening?'

'I'm afraid I cannot commit myself, ma'am, until I know what Sir William has planned.' He certainly couldn't risk spending an entire evening in close proximity to Jane. Being near her now, and wanting nothing more than to take her into his arms, was sheer torture. How lovely she was!

'I trust my remedy did the trick and that you have not been experiencing further discomfort after meals?' he hurriedly went on, before anyone could force the issue of his attending the forthcoming event.

Jane transferred her gaze to her aunt and the message, *You broke your journey to Kent for the sole purpose of meeting him,* was clearly to be seen in her eyes.

'Yes,' Lady Templehurst responded, as if to the unspoken accusation, before returning her attention to Tom's attractively masculine form. 'It has worked wonders, Dr Carrington. I've had no trouble since. I must get you to make me up a further supply to take back with me to Bath.'

Elizabeth then took command of the situation by offering the gentlemen some much needed refreshments. Richard, however, refused to prolong the agony for at least two of the people present, both of whom were making a sterling effort to maintain a flow of inconsequential chatter, but whose inner turmoil was like some tangible thing felt by all, and he did not delay long in taking Tom to Sir William Dent's house.

When he returned a short time later he discovered the ladies still in the parlour, busily making plans for the forthcoming party.

'You put me forcibly in mind of those three crones in *Macbeth*. What the deuce are you all plotting?'

'I'm not so sure we should tell you after that piece of impertinence,' his wife retorted with mock indignation.

There was a hint of wicked amusement in Jane's eyes, which was a relief to see after the barely concealed flicker of misery there for all to observe when Tom had taken his very formal leave of her. 'I do not perceive how you can avoid telling him, dear Cousin, when it is he who will be making the announcement.'

'And what announcement would that be, may I ask?' Richard demanded with all the suspicion of a man who was about to be persuaded into doing something he would far rather not.

'Oh, the most marvellous news!' Elizabeth exclaimed. 'Perry has asked Henrietta Dilbey to marry him and she has accepted.'

'I get the distinct impression,' Richard remarked, eyeing the three ladies with patent suspicion, 'that there is more to this than I have yet been told... I await an explanation from one of you.'

As was his custom, Tom woke early the following morning. There were no lectures scheduled for that day, and as Sir William had arranged to visit some friends Tom was free to spend his time precisely as he chose. He was on the point of leaving the house to do a spot of sightseeing when Sir Richard unexpectedly arrived.

'Did we arrange to meet today?' Tom wouldn't have been in the least surprised to receive an affirmative answer. So much seemed to slip his mind of late. 'If we did, I am entirely at your disposal. I hadn't planned to go anywhere in particular.'

'In that case, how would you care to accompany me to my tailor?'

'Good Lord, Richard! Haven't you coats enough?'

'I have, but you haven't,' was the caustic rejoinder, but Tom wasn't offended.

'I suppose you're right,' he admitted, with a wry glance at the left sleeve of his comfortable but hardly fashionable jacket. 'One or two new items of clothing wouldn't come amiss.'

Richard, however, had other ideas. By the time they had left the shop Tom was the proud possessor of half a dozen fashionable coats and several pairs of unmentionables, plus new shirts and an ample supply of cravats, prompting him to ask whether his friend was trying to ruin him.

'You're not a pauper, Tom. Besides, you can wear that black coat to our party tomorrow evening.'

'I could if I had any intention of attending, but I have not. And you must surely realise why.'

In the years to come Richard was to look back on that moment as one of the most significant, if not in his life, then certainly in that of his friend. If he had chosen to explain that what had been originally planned as an informal party for no more than three dozen guests had been turned into a ball to celebrate the engagement of Lord Pentecost and Henrietta Dilbey, and had induced Tom to join in the celebration, the future might have turned out to be vastly different. For some inexplicable reason, however, he chose not to pursue the matter, and merely suggested that they repair to his club for some refreshments.

Society as a whole was accustomed to keeping late hours when in town and the rooms at White's at this time of day were virtually deserted. They seated themselves at one of the many vacant tables, and Richard was on the point of ordering a bottle and glasses when the door opened and in walked his good friend Viscount Dartwood.

The Viscount and his wife had visited Knightley Hall on several occasions, and knew Dr Carrington well. There was much news to catch up on since the last time they had seen one another. Both the Viscountess and Elizabeth had given birth, thankfully, to healthy children, so the conversation tended to revolve around the joys of fatherhood, which wasn't of that much interest to Tom who began to take more notice of his exclusive surroundings. Consequently, he was the first to catch sight of the handsome, blond-haired gentleman entering the room, and by the time Richard perceived the red mists of anger in the young doctor's eyes it was already too late.

Tom was out of his chair and planting a fist full in the face of the new arrival before either Richard or the Viscount had a chance to intervene. Richard did, however, manage to prevent Tom from following up his advantage, by grasping him firmly by the upper arms.

'That's enough, Tom! You've floored him. Be satisfied with that.' Richard didn't hesitate in requesting the Viscount, whose eyes betrayed more than just a hint of admiration for the flush hit, to escort their mutual friend outside, and then turned his attention to the waiter who had burst into the room to see what all the commotion was about.

'Nothing wrong. Mr Fairfax merely tripped and fell against the table. Fetch some brandy!'

'Damn it, Knightley! You'll not succeed in protecting your friend so easily. I'll call him out!' Simon Fairfax avowed, getting to his feet with his dignity far from intact.

'I was under the distinct impression that it was you I was protecting,' Richard responded, with all the even-tempered control for which he was famed.

Setting the table to rights, he glanced in the corner at the only other occupant of the room, old Colonel Fitzpatrick, still dozing in the chair. 'The incident will go no further. And you would be wise to forget it, too.' He paused in order to take a pinch of snuff. 'It would do you no good at all if the reason behind this slight altercation became common knowledge.'

The younger man looked not in the least shame-faced. 'So you know about that, do you? Then you must know that it wouldn't do the lady in question any good if the truth leaked out.'

'Indeed it would not. But it would do you far more harm… I would see to that. So I would suggest that you listen very carefully to what I have to say.'

It did not take many minutes for Richard to push his advantage home and make Simon see sense. He then went out to the lobby to discover that only the Viscount awaited him.

'What the deuce was all that about, Richard? Can't say I care for Fairfax myself, but one doesn't indulge in fisticuffs in a gentleman's club. Tom will be barred even before he's made a member if he carries on like that.'

'He had good reason for behaving as he did,' Richard responded, 'but as there is a lady involved I'd rather not explain.' He glanced up and down the street. 'Where is the young hothead?'

'I sent him to cool his heels in Hyde Park.'

Oh, Lord! Richard groaned inwardly. Things were going from bad to worse. He felt certain that Jane had planned to go riding there with Perry this morning, and he could only hope that she didn't cross Tom's path in his present unpredictable mood.

Needless to say it was a forlorn hope. The park, too, at this time of day, was not crowded, for it was long before the fashionable hour when Society at large showed itself abroad. That was precisely why Jane enjoyed her morning rides; she could indulge in her favourite form of exercise without having to stop every few minutes to pass the time of day with her numerous acquaintances.

She was in the process of informing Perry, who had given his full approval for his engagement to be announced at the Knightleys' party, that everything was in hand for the ball the following evening, when she happened to catch sight of Tom heading across the grass in their direction. Had it been left to her, she certainly wouldn't have made her presence known, for even from that distance she suspected, by the tense set of his powerful shoulders and the impatient stride, that all was not well with him. Unfortunately, Perry, following the direction of her gaze, experienced no such qualms.

'Why, it's Dr Carrington!' he exclaimed, before hailing his new physician cheerfully.

Tom stopped dead in his tracks, and had little choice but to acknowledge the pair, one of whom he would far rather not have encountered again quite so soon.

'What, still in the capital?' he remarked to Perry as they brought their mounts to a halt beside him. 'I understood you to say that you didn't care for town life, Lord Pentecost.'

'I have been enjoying this particular visit, which in part is due to you, Dr Carrington. I did go to see your colleague and his opinion was the same as yours. And I have since discovered, thanks to Janie and her aunt, that my late uncle's mental disorder was the direct result of an accident he sustained.'

'I'm pleased the mystery has been solved,' Tom responded, doing his level best not to stare in Jane's direction, but aware that those lovely eyes of hers were firmly fixed on his physiognomy. 'How much longer do you intend remaining in town?' he asked, not out of any particular interest, but in an attempt to converse only with Perry.

'Not very much longer. A week at the most. Mama's arrived in town now.'

Jane could almost hear Tom saying, Then I'm not surprised you're leaving it, and quickly turned her betraying gurgle of mirth into a cough, which succeeded in drawing his attention. Their eyes met, but she was afraid to try to interpret the silent message in those grey depths. She desperately wanted to believe that he loved her, but she needed the answers to several questions before she dared trust her instincts again.

An awkward silence followed, and she was just steeling herself to ask whether they would have the pleasure of seeing him at the Knightleys' ball the following evening when a sporting carriage bowling along the driveway towards them succeeded in capturing her attention. There could be no mistaking the portly royal figure who handled the ribbons with such flair, and Jane was just wondering whether Tom had ever seen their future king at such close quarters before when bouncing across the vehicle's path came a bright red ball, quickly followed by its young owner, eager to retrieve his precious toy.

Above her own gasp of dismay Jane heard the mother's terrified scream, and saw the Regent trying to take evasive action by swerving to the left. The next instant, Tom, with lightning speed, threw himself in the path of the carriage to sweep the child up in his arms. Just how they escaped being trampled beneath the startled team's hooves Jane couldn't imagine, but both ended up lying on the grass, the little boy frightened, but otherwise unharmed.

Perry dismounted and hurried to help Tom to his feet. The mother, gathering her young son in her arms, was sobbing out her grateful thanks, and the Regent, having managed to draw his spirited horses to a halt a few yards away, handed the reins to his groom and came towards the small group.

'By Jove, Dr Carrington!' Perry exclaimed, eyes brightened by the excitement of it all. 'That was an excellent piece of work.'

'Indeed it was, sir! Indeed it was!' His Royal Highness agreed, looking rather shaken by the near catastrophe as he mopped his sweating brow with a fine piece of silk.

Jane decided it was time to offer her help, for she could see that Tom was far from gratified by all the attention he was receiving, and, dismounting, she forced her way through the ever increasing group of onlookers who were gathering around to discover what had occurred.

'Lady Jane Beresford, sir,' she said, reminding the Regent, even though they had met before on several occasions, of her name. 'The Earl of Eastbury's daughter.'

'Of course! Yes, I remember you very well, my dear.'

Jane doubted it, but wasn't offended. Given the number of people introduced to him each year, he could hardly be expected to recall every single one. She turned to the naturally distraught mother and very gently suggested that she take her son home to recover, and then introduced Perry and Tom to the Regent.

'A pleasure to make your acquaintance Dr Carrington,' he said, shaking him warmly by the hand. 'Dashed brave thing you did, sir! Wouldn't have had that happen for the world! Dear me, no! Glad you sent the mother away, m'dear,' he went on, turning to Jane. 'Shouldn't bring children here. Much better to let them play in Green Park. Much quieter there.'

'I might suggest, sir, that you could do with some peace and quiet yourself,' Tom remarked, after casting a professional eye over the future sovereign. 'The unfortunate incident has naturally distressed you greatly. I think a short rest would be most beneficial.'

'Yes, very sensible, Dr Carrington,' he agreed, and remained only for the time it took to offer his sincere thanks once again.

The crowd of onlookers quickly dispersed after the Regent's departure and Jane, sensing that Tom had no desire to remain, would have taken her leave, but Perry forestalled her by saying, 'You will be coming to the Knightleys' ball tomorrow evening, won't you, Dr Carrington? We'd very much like you to be there to celebrate our happy news.'

'I'm afraid not, sir. I've other plans,' he replied, and with the briefest of farewells he walked smartly away.

'Pity he has made other arrangements for the evening,' Perry remarked, drawing his eyes away from the doctor's rapidly retreating form. 'If it had not been for him—and you, of course—I wouldn't be the happy man I am today.'

He cast Jane a surprisingly penetrating stare. 'You must realise, just as I do myself, that my mother must have known the truth about Uncle Cedric all along. It was most unkind of her to keep the facts from me. That in itself is not unusual—she has, after all, not been particularly kind to me throughout my life. But I shall never permit her to be unkind to Hetta. And that is why I agreed to your aunt's suggestion of keeping our intentions secret from her. Once the engagement is officially announced, there is little she can do. And I'm so glad you'll be there to celebrate the moment with me, Jane... I just wish Thomas Carrington could have been there too. I have a deal of regard for that man.'

He raised his eyes in time to see the doctor disappearing round a bend in the path, and a sudden thought occurred to him. 'You don't think I've offended him do you, Janie? You don't think he's annoyed because I chose to consult that London physician after he had told me I had nothing to worry about?'

'No, Perry, I do not,' she responded, making a supreme effort to control the threat of tears. 'I think his decision not to attend the ball has rather more to do with me.'

Chapter Fifteen

Jane didn't regret leaving the party early, but now that she had arrived back at the house she didn't relish the prospect of retiring, either. She wasn't in the least tired, merely heart-weary, something which both her aunt and Elizabeth understood quite well. Neither had made the least attempt to persuade her to remain at Lady Cossington's drum, and she had been grateful to them for that.

After handing her velvet evening cloak to the Knightleys' excellent young butler, she made her way across the hall, but checked at the foot of the stairs. It was unlikely in her present frame of mind that she would succumb very quickly to sleep, so it made sense to provide herself with something to pass the time.

The library here, like the one at Knightley Hall, was well stocked, and she felt certain of finding something to her taste. She did not, however, expect to find the master of the house sitting quite alone in his sanctum, and didn't attempt to hide her surprise.

'Why, Richard! I understood you to say that you were going to your club this evening.'

'That had been my intention, but then I decided I should prefer a quiet evening at home. I have since discovered, however, that one can soon grow tired of one's own company, so can I not persuade you to remain with me for a while?'

She needed no second prompting, and made herself comfortable in the chair on the opposite side of the hearth, while her cousin's charming husband procured her a glass of wine.

'By your early return I can only assume that you gained little pleasure from the evening's entertainment?' he remarked.

'No, I did not,' she freely admitted, seeing no reason to deny the fact. Although Richard had not once broached the subject of her eventful journey to Bath, she felt it safe to assume that he was in full possession of all the relevant facts.

'Truth to tell, Richard, had it not been for Lady Templehurst's desire to visit the capital, I would have been content to remain in Kent. I am, however, for obvious reasons, very much looking forward to the ball here tomorrow evening. Perry's happiness means a lot to me, and I cannot express my thanks strongly enough for allowing my aunt to hold such a large party in your house.'

'You are a devious young woman!' he told her with mock severity, before handing her the wine and resuming his seat. 'Do you feel no pangs of conscience over your part in the subterfuge?'

'Quite frankly, I cannot say that I do,' she responded, truthful to the last. 'I do not think Lady Pentecost deserves any consideration.' She sampled the contents of her glass while her mind wandered back over the years. 'I cannot forget the way she treated Perry when he was a boy. He could never do anything to please her. It is little wonder that he reached adulthood with no self-confidence, although he is much improved now. She did little to make his childhood happy, Richard. And I for one will not idly stand by and allow her to ruin the rest of his life if I can do something to prevent it.'

His attractive mouth curled into an appreciative smile. 'You are a very determined young woman, I see.'

'I can be if I believe in something strongly enough. And I do sincerely believe that Hetta will make Perry happy.'

'I'm inclined to agree with you on that,' he responded, holding her gaze steadily. 'Very few of us meet the ideal mate, Jane, and when we do we should not let the chance of true happiness slip by.' He saw the slender fingers tremble slightly. 'He does love you, you know.'

'Does he, Richard?' She saw little point in trying to dissemble, and betrayed her feelings clearly enough in a long-drawn-out sigh. 'If only I could be sure of that.'

He found the slight catch in her pleasantly melodious voice heart-rending. 'What makes you doubt it?'

'He never once attempted to make contact with me before he came to town, not even by letter. And now, when he has the opportunity to see me, to be with me, he deliberately keeps himself at a distance.' She wanted nothing more than to cry out all the hurt that she had buried deep within for so many weeks, but it seemed she had no more tears left to weep. 'He isn't even going to attend the party tomorrow evening.'

'No, I know. I saw him this morning.' His lips curled into a rueful smile. 'I made the mistake of taking him to my club. And who should also decide to pay a visit at that time of day…? None other than Simon Fairfax.'

This briefly turned her thoughts in a new direction. 'I knew the wretch was in town. I saw him a few days ago when I was in the park with Hetta.'

'Blackguard!' Richard muttered. 'He had the cursed temerity to inform me that he never meant you any real harm, and that he had been put to a great deal of trouble for no reward. Apparently, when he returned to his house, after having searched for you, he discovered that your maid had departed with what money you had in your possession, and your jewel box. He journeyed to Paris in the hope of discovering her whereabouts, but found no trace.'

'Really? How very interesting.' Jane experienced a deal of satisfaction at learning this. 'I wonder if she took my advice, after all?'

She then went on to inform Richard of her former maid's wish to become a milliner. 'The jewellery I had with me, although not my best pieces, might have been sufficient for her needs. And strangely enough I cannot find it within me to begrudge her the booty. If it hadn't been for her, I might never have escaped the infamous Simon's clutches.'

'If it hadn't been for her,' Richard countered, unable to fathom, even with all his vast experience, the workings of the female mind, 'you wouldn't have found yourself in that predicament in the first place. However, if it's any consolation, at least one of the miscreants involved in the despicable affair is now sporting a fine black eye.'

'Ah, yes! Now you come to mention it, I did hear a rumour circulating at Lady Cossington's party that someone had planted Simon Fairfax a facer.' She discovered that, even in her most unhappy state, she had not lost her sense of humour, and laughed. 'Whom have I to thank for it…? You, Richard?'

'Sadly, no,' he was forced to admit. 'It would have given me the utmost pleasure to have obliged you, my dear, but not in a gentleman's club. Tom, however, experienced no such qualms.'

He regarded her in silence for a moment, watching her amusement quickly fade, then said, 'I shall not attempt to make any excuses for his current behaviour, except to say that he doesn't consider himself good enough for you. And you cannot deny that there is every likelihood that you would come up against some fierce opposition from certain members of your family.'

'Do you think I have not considered that, Richard? Of course there would be bound to be some, but I know my father well enough to be sure that he would soon come round, once he realised what a dedicated and intelligent man Tom is.' This time her shout of laughter was mirthless. 'It is ironic, is it not, that I always feared being coveted for my wealth alone, and yet when I do eventually meet the man with whom I could happily spend the rest of my life it is precisely that wealth, if what you tell me is true, which has proved to be the bar?'

'It does not have to be so, Jane.'

'It should not be so!' There was a hard and determined edge to her voice now, one he had never detected before. 'And believe me, Richard, if I could be certain that Tom truly loves me, I would move heaven and earth to make him see reason. But how can I know for sure when he can hardly bring himself to look at me, let alone speak to me?'

Although Richard himself had no doubts, he could quite understand her uncertainty and, deciding that it would not benefit the state of affairs to comment further at the present time, very tactfully changed the subject.

After she left him a short time later, he remained staring down at the empty grate, his mind deep in thought, until the other ladies arrived home, and Elizabeth came in to see him before retiring for the night.

'Did you have an enjoyable evening?' he enquired politely, but knew what the answer would be even before she responded.

'It is difficult to attain any great pleasure, my dear, when one knows how desperately unhappy Jane is. The poor girl tries so hard to go on as normal. She certainly doesn't lack courage.'

'No, she certainly doesn't lack that.' He focused his attention once again on the empty grate. 'I spoke to her tonight about it for the fist time. She never attempted to avoid the issue—nor did she attempt to subject me to a display of feminine tears. She would make Tom the ideal partner. And I'm now firmly convinced that she is as much in love with him as he is with her.'

Elizabeth was not able to duplicate her cousin's admirable control, and unashamedly had recourse to her handkerchief. 'Oh, Richard, is there nothing either of us can do?'

He was silent for so long that she thought he would not respond, but then he astonished her by announcing, 'That, my love, is still far from certain. But I am now prepared to break my golden rule—because I damn well mean to try!'

After attending the first of the lectures the following afternoon, Tom returned to Sir William's hired house. His host had planned to go on to his club, and, although Tom had received an invitation to accompany him, he thought it wisest, given the events of the previous day, if he maintained a low profile at White's for the time being.

For a while he toyed with the idea of filling the time until Sir William's return by going for a walk, but then decided against it, just in case he should happen to come face to face with Jane again. Not that it signified to any great extent if this were to happen: her image rarely left his mind's eye in any event.

He settled in the end for going through the notes he had jotted down during the lecture, and had only just made himself comfortable in the front parlour when the butler announced Sir Richard.

'Good heavens! I never expected to see you today. I would have thought you would have been far too busy with last-minute preparations for your event this evening to pay afternoon calls.' His teeth flashed in an engaging smile of welcome. 'Needless to say, though, it is good to see you. Take a seat. Can I get you a glass of wine, or something else, perhaps?'

'No, thank you, Tom. As you say, I've much to do, so I cannot stay long. I've left the ladies back at the house arranging the last of the flowers.' He paused for a moment to study the shine on his Hessians before adding, 'I know I'm here on a fool's errand, but I did promise to make one final attempt to make you change your mind and join us this evening.'

Tom made not the least attempt to suppress a deep sigh. 'You know why I can't, Richard.'

'Yes, sadly, I do know. But Jane especially wished you to be there to share her joy in the occasion. I am to make the announcement at about eleven.'

'Announcement?' Tom betrayed more than just a modicum of interest. 'What announcement?'

'Well, I know they both wanted to keep it secret until tonight, but I'm sure neither of them would object to my telling you. I'm to announce their engagement. Jane, naturally, is delighted, and it goes without saying that Perry is over the moon at having captured the affections of such a lovely young woman.'

The look of astonished incredulity on his friend's face was almost Richard's undoing, but the knowledge that much depended on his performance now, if there was to be the remotest chance of a joyous outcome to this little subterfuge, helped him to retain his rigid control and not give way to mirth.

'You're hoaxing me!' Tom announced, finding his voice at last. Then he recalled the encounter in the park, and Perry mentioning something about a celebration. 'It cannot be true,' he added, but with far less conviction.

'Afraid it is, old boy. And I must say both Elizabeth and I think they'll make a charming couple. They're very well suited, after all.'

'Well suited…? Richard, you cannot possibly be serious!'

He rose abruptly to his feet and began to pace the room, putting Richard in mind of a caged animal: confined, perhaps, but none the less dangerous and demanding respect, and Richard certainly had the utmost respect for his friend's intelligence. Fortunately, though, Tom, at the present time, appeared to be allowing his feelings full rein, and was not thinking clearly, which, of course, was all to the good.

'Thanks to Jane, I've begun to view Perry in a completely different light. He's an intelligent young man who holds sensible views on a great number of serious topics. He's spent a couple of evenings with me at the Hall, as it happens... Damned good chess player. Nearly beat me on the last occasion.'

'Chess?' Tom stopped his pacing to run decidedly unsteady fingers through his hair. 'What the hell has that to do with anything? She doesn't love him... You know she cannot possibly love him.'

'That I could not say.' Richard experienced more than just a fleeting disquiet. He hated putting his friend through this, but doggedly stuck to his task. 'You must remember that members of my social class do not in general marry for love. Mutual regard usually suffices. There are exceptions, like Elizabeth and myself. But most marry to unite families, and enlarge their estates.'

Tom's only response was a flashing look of disgust, before he resumed his angry pacing, and Richard thought it best to leave before his conscience got the better of him and he told his friend the complete truth.

'I'd better be on my way now. As I mentioned earlier, I've much to do.' He went over to the door, but turned back to add, 'May I at least pass on your felicitations to the happy couple?'

'No, you bloody well can't!' Eyes hard and resentful, Tom glowered across the room. 'Richard, you can't let this happen. You must prevent it! Make her see sense, for pity's sake!'

'I...?' Richard managed to raise his brows in exaggerated surprise. 'What the deuce do you suppose I can do?' He held his friend's angry gaze levelly. 'Oh, no, my dear friend—I'm not the one to prevent it.'

'Then I damn well will!' Tom announced with steely determination. 'She'll marry Pentecost over my dead body!'

Well, that seems to have done the trick, Richard mused with intense satisfaction, and promptly left the room as Tom resumed his angry pacing.

Chapter Sixteen

As Sir Bartholomew Rudge had remarked, Lady Augusta Templehurst remained a personage of some standing. Although her removal to Bath ten years before had succeeded in placing her outside the cream of Society's field of vision, her popularity had been such that just her signature at the bottom of the invitation cards had proved sufficient inducement to persuade many to cancel previous engagements in order to attend the Knightleys' ball.

Sir Richard and Elizabeth, too, had a wide circle of friends, most of whom had been only too pleased to put in an appearance, and, by half past ten the two large adjoining salons on the upper floor, more than adequate to accommodate all the guests, and beautifully decorated for the occasion, were rapidly filling.

Needless to say the joint hostesses were well pleased with the results of all their efforts. It had been no mean feat to organise the ball in so short a time, but the sight of Hetta, charmingly attired in a gown of pale primrose silk, and looking so deliciously happy as she danced with her future husband, made all the hard work well worthwhile.

Since the arrival of the Dowager Lady Pentecost in
town a few days before, Perry and Hetta had, in an
attempt to avoid rousing the formidable matron's suspicions, very wisely seen less of each other. Evidently
their tactics had worked, for although Lady Pentecost
was certainly glancing in their direction she didn't
appear to be taking an undue interest in either of
them, no doubt believing that her son had been merely
courteous enough to stand up with the niece of a close
neighbour.

Which was possibly just as well in view of what
was to take place in less than half an hour's time,
Elizabeth mused, drawing her eyes away from the
dancing couples to welcome yet another late arrival.

The Dowager Lady Fitzwarren, a matriarch of no
small consequence, had just reached the entrance to
the first salon, and was about to exchange a few words
with her host and hostesses, when there was a slight
commotion below. The next moment a tall young
man, whom she would have considered strikingly attractive had it not been for the ferocity of the frown
darkening his brow, came bounding up the stairs. He
brushed past her so forcefully that the Dowager almost cannoned into Sir Richard.

'Where the devil is she?' he rudely demanded to
know.

'About halfway down on the right, talking with her
sister,' Richard responded, completely unruffled—
which was more than could be said for most of those
who followed the new arrival's progress across the
floor, and watched him clasp one slender wrist and
haul the aristocratic young lady behind him from the
room.

Lord Peregrine was definitely momentarily startled,

but then became thoughtful. 'I say, Hett, did you just see that?' he asked as they came together again in the set.

'Yes. I expect most everyone noticed. Very odd behaviour, don't you think?'

'No, not really,' he surprised her by responding. 'Thought there was something wrong. I might never say a great deal, Hett, but I do notice things. Felt there was something amiss with Jane—not been quite herself since she arrived in town. And yesterday, when we met up with Dr Carrington in the park, I realised why... She's in love with him, Hett—I'd stake my life on it. And it wouldn't surprise me at all if he feels exactly the same way about her.'

Hetta was rather taken aback to hear this, but then cast her future spouse a glowing smile of admiration. 'Perry, you're quite remarkable! That would never have occurred to me. But now you mention it—yes, I do believe you're right. My, my! That will cause a few brows to be raised.'

Lady Fitzwarren, still standing by the door, was most certainly looking startled by such unconventional behaviour, and had recourse to her lorgnette as she continued to follow the couple's progress back down the stairs. 'Upon my soul! Weren't that Eastbury's gel...? Your niece, Augusta?'

'Indeed, it was,' Lady Templehurst responded in a level tone as she tried to control the exhilaration she was experiencing at Dr Carrington's totally unexpected, but wholly gratifying, arrival.

'Well, ain't you going to do something about it, Knightley?' Lady Fitzwarren demanded. 'He looked like a fiend! He may do the gel harm.'

'Oh, I shouldn't think so, ma'am,' Richard replied,

still completely unperturbed. 'Lady Jane Beresford is a most redoubtable girl. She's more than capable of handling the situation.'

He might not have been quite so certain had he been standing in his library at that precise moment to witness his wife's cousin being so ruthlessly shaken that she was in the gravest danger of losing the spray of artificial flowers nestling in her beautifully arranged hair.

'Oh, how dare you?' she managed, more than a little breathless from the ordeal. 'How dare you drag me in here and treat me in this odious fashion? It is not to be borne, sir!'

'Don't you adopt that haughty tone with me, my girl!' Tom growled through clenched teeth, and only just managing to suppress the strong urge to repeat the punishment. 'I'll not permit you to go through with it, do you hear? I didn't put myself through hell just so that you could retain your virtue, only to have you throw yourself away on the first sprig who asks you to marry him.'

Jane studied his angry features in silence for a moment. She was still more than just a little indignant over his rough treatment, but she had heard his every word, even if she didn't perfectly understand as yet precisely what he had meant.

'Would you mind letting me go, Tom?' she asked softly, and instantly he released his hold, though, like some vigilant predator, he watched her every move as she wandered over to seat herself in one of the chairs. 'I think you had better explain your reason for coming here this evening,' she added, after subjecting him to a further searching stare, and seeing clearly the continued anger, but also the deep hurt, in his eyes.

'You know quite well why I'm here.' His tone was more impatient than angry now. 'You must not permit the engagement to be announced!'

Her brows rose. 'Why ever not?'

'You can sit there and blithely ask me that? Ye gods!' He took a threatening step towards her, and for one dreadful moment she thought she was in the gravest peril of being shaken again, but then he seemed to check himself.

'All right, perhaps I shouldn't be here at all. Perhaps I have no right to interfere. Just answer me one question… Are you in love with him?'

'In love with whom?'

'Pentecost, of course!' he snapped, swiftly coming to the end of his tether, but her next words proved his undoing.

'No, I'm not in love with Perry, Tom… I'm in love with you.'

'God, Janie, don't!' It was if the words had been torn from him, so painful did they sound. 'Don't you think I feel the same way? Don't you realise that the mere thought of your marrying Pentecost—of your marrying anyone—tears me apart?'

Tom both looked and sounded as though he was in the depths of despair, but Jane most certainly wasn't, and could hardly contain her elation. He loved her. She was certain of that now. And nothing and no one, she silently vowed, would prevent them having a future together!

'But I have no intention of marrying Perry,' she told him, in a voice as clear as glass.

He glanced at her then, uncertain. 'But Richard informed me earlier that he was to announce the engagement tonight.'

Jane was beginning to see a chink of light. She had noticed Richard return to the house late in the afternoon, and he had looked mighty well pleased with himself. If he had been instrumental in prompting Tom to come here, then she would love the wickedly conniving devil for the rest of her life.

'Yes, he certainly is to announce the engagement,' she responded, slightly unsteadily. 'An engagement between Lord Peregrine Pentecost and Miss Henrietta Dilbey.'

For a moment it seemed as if he had not heard, then very slowly he turned to face her squarely, his eyes suddenly probing and dangerously alert. 'But I understood Richard to say…' His features adopted that same fiendish look that had so discomposed Lady Fitzwarren. 'By heaven! I'll have his liver and lights for this!'

'Oh, I think not,' Jane said, with all the calm assurance of one in full command of the situation. Her course not quite clear, and emboldened as she was by the fact that she knew for sure that her future was destined to be at this man's side, she didn't hesitate to enquire, 'When did you fall in love with me, Tom?'

The direct question took him completely off guard. He would have given almost anything to be able to deny it, but it was rather too late for that now—his actions alone this night had betrayed him.

'I'm not sure, Janie,' he replied softly, and went over to the fireplace to stare down at the empty grate. 'I think I knew for certain that day I showed you round my friend's house in Melcham, remember?' He waited for a response, but none was forthcoming.

'You jokingly remarked that the house would not be too large once I had a wife and family… The trouble was that I could only envisage you as mistress of that house. You seemed so right there.'

A soft, reminiscent little smile hovered about her mouth. She remembered that day so well. 'You were far quicker than I to realise in which direction the wind was blowing, Tom,' she admitted. 'I didn't know until the second night in the cottage, but then…'

Her smile faded. There was not a doubt in her mind that he loved her, but there were still things she needed to know. 'Why did you behave as you did that night? Why did you leave me that way, making me feel rejected, too loathsome to be touched? Why did you never once try to contact me during these past weeks? And why, since your arrival in town, have you made no attempt to see me alone before now?'

For several long moments he continued to stare down at the hearth, then, raising his hand, he gestured in the vague direction of the beautifully embroidered bodice of her gown. 'Because of that.'

Slightly puzzled, she glanced at her firm young breasts rising from the *décolletage*. 'Are you trying to tell me that there is something wrong with my figure?'

'What?' He looked totally nonplussed for a second or two. 'Of course not, you foolish creature!' he snapped, with an abrupt return to peevishness. 'You're perfect.' He groaned. 'That's just the trouble.'

'Then what in heaven's name are you talking

about?' she demanded, not in the least deterred by his brusque tone.

'That confounded brooch I gave you.' He experienced more than just a little resentment as he focused his attention on the silver circlet encrusted with pearls that adorned the bodice of her dress, and recalled all too painfully the last time he had seen it. 'You left it on top of the chest of drawers that night. I happened to notice it lying there, and remembered, you see.' But her puzzled expression was proof enough that she didn't understand at all.

'I informed you that it had once belonged to my grandmother,' he went on to explain. 'Perhaps what I omitted to mention was that she swiftly came to regret her hasty marriage to my grandfather. She became bitterly resentful, and even went so far as to blame him entirely for ruining her life.'

'I see,' Jane responded, perceiving clearly now precisely what he had feared. 'And you imagined that I would one day come to resent it, if you had not called a halt to our lovemaking and we had been obliged to marry.'

She didn't bother waiting for a response. Eyes brimful of loving reproach, she rose from the chair and moved slowly towards him.

'Some might consider that very noble of you, Tom. Personally, though, I consider it damnably foolish, not to mention arrogantly presumptuous. What makes you suppose for a moment that just because I come from the same social class as your grandmother I am likely to behave in a similar fashion...? That my nature resembles hers in any way? And what makes you suppose,' she went on, once again not waiting for a response, 'that just because you are prepared to make yourself desperately unhappy you have the right to make my life desolate, too?'

He reached out to her then, and ran one finger gently down her cheek before taking her into his arms. 'Have you been miserable, my Janie?'

'Dreadfully,' she assured him, and all his noble intentions crumbled beneath the strength of her love mirrored in those lovely grey-green eyes. He could exist without her, but knew he'd never be happy.

He kissed her gently at first, almost tentatively, and then, at last finding some blessed release after weeks of suppressing his emotions, with an urgency that left her breathless and in little doubt of his desperate need of her.

'Darling, this is madness,' he murmured, in a half-hearted attempt to regain a modicum of control and make her see reason. Burying his face in her hair, he clung to her, like a man in peril of drowning and holding fast to his only means of survival. 'What of your family? You know they would not approve.'

Loath though she was, she disengaged herself from his loving hold. He needed reassurance, and if she stood the remotest chance of convincing him how wrong he was, he must not only hear it from her own lips but see confirmation of what she was saying in her eyes.

'I shan't try to pretend that there will be no opposition, Tom. My mother and sisters have always harboured the foolish notion that I would one day acquire the title of Duchess or Marchioness. But my father is more level-headed, and I know he will like you. Besides which, you already have a very staunch ally in Lady Templehurst.'

This brought some comfort, but he was very well

aware that there were other considerations to take into account, not least of which was the difference in their financial situations. 'I am not precisely a pauper, Jane, I could afford to keep you in comfort, but there isn't the remotest chance that I could maintain you in the style to which you are accustomed. I know you are a woman of substantial means and if...' his lips curled into a wry smile of resignation '...when we marry your money will come to me, but I shall not touch so much as a penny of it, Jane,' he vowed. 'As far as I am concerned, that money will always be yours to do with as you wish.'

She did not think that now was the most appropriate time to discuss her inheritance. He was a proud man, and would naturally wish to feel that he alone was capable of supporting her. There would no doubt be occasions in the future in which to broach the subject again, and maybe suggest that her money be used to educate their children, and provide any daughters they might have with reasonable dowries. After all, not all men were as stubbornly proud as the one with whom she had chosen to spend the rest of her life.

'I do not want a life of luxury, Thomas Carrington,' she assured him softly, 'only one at your side. So now will you stop searching for difficulties where none exist and, instead, prove to your future wife just what a loving husband you intend to be?'

Unlike her, he could still foresee turbulent waters ahead, but he did not doubt that together they would master the currents and find a safe haven. He had known almost from the first that there was something very special about this young woman, and he had realised that at long last he had found someone with whom he could quite happily spend the rest of his life. Their love had transcended all social barriers, and would remain strong enough to bind them, no matter what tribulations lay ahead.

So he gave himself up to the pleasurable task of proving to her just how sensible she was to place her future happiness in his caring hands, and would have been quite content to verify this conviction many times over had not the library door suddenly swung open to reveal the tall figure of their host.

'There are several persons upstairs in some concern over your welfare, my dear Jane,' he remarked, sauntering towards them, the epitome of a man of fashion. 'Your sister, to name but one, is quite naturally distraught after witnessing your forced departure.'

He cast his friend a look of mild reproach. 'Really, Thomas, you cannot continue to indulge in such behaviour... Brawling at White's, and abducting fair damsels from ballrooms...' He paused in order to inhale a pinch of snuff. 'Remind me to instruct you some time in how to comport yourself.'

'And remind me some time to plant you a facer!' was Tom's threatening response. 'What the devil do you mean by telling me that Jane was to marry Pentecost?'

Sir Richard's expressive brows rose. 'I know I am a few years your senior, Tom, but there is nought amiss with my memory, and I can therefore state with certainty that I never told you any such thing.'

Jane thought it prudent to intervene and, disengaging herself from her still aggrieved future husband's arms, she went over to Richard. 'Well, I for one neither know nor care what you did say, precisely, but whatever it was I thank you, sir, from the bottom of

my heart. You have made me the happiest of females.'

He did not need to hear this: the proof was in her
eyes for anyone to see. 'Then it is well.' He transferred his gaze to his friend to see the same blissful
expression on his face, too. 'Now, all I need to know
is am I to announce one engagement tonight...or
two?'

Tom gave a shout of laughter. 'You might be an
unscrupulous dog, Knightley, but your wits aren't addled... What do you think?'

Richard couldn't prevent a broad smile of satisfaction. 'Then might I be the first of many, I'm sure, to
offer you my sincerest congratulations? You have
succeeded in capturing a pearl beyond price, and I
hope you will have the good sense to cherish her always.'

'That is my intention,' Tom responded softy, slipping his arm gently round his love's shoulders.

Richard continued to regard them in gratified silence for a moment, but then bethought himself of his
duties. 'Loath though I am to play propriety, but in
view of the fact that I am in honour bound to protect
this fair lady's name in the absence of her father, I
must ask you both to accompany me back upstairs.'

Many pairs of eyes turned in their direction as
Richard led the way back into the crowded salon.
Lady Templehurst took one glance at Jane's blissfully
happy expression, and the rather proud look in the
eyes of the man by her niece's side, and unashamedly
drew out a wisp of silk.

Richard waited only for the set of country dances
to come to an end, and succeeded in gaining the at-

tention of all the guests by asking the quartet of musicians hired for the occasion to strike up a chord.

'It gives me the greatest pleasure,' he said, his deep, clear voice reaching the furthest corners of the room, 'to make an announcement—in fact two announcements—this evening.'

An unexpected commotion by the door forced him to pause. The next moment there was a general murmur of excitement and several of the guests who had gathered round began to move apart to enable two portly and flamboyantly attired gentlemen to approach their host.

'I do believe we have interrupted something, Rudge,' the larger gentleman remarked in a jovial aside. 'Sir Richard, are we *de trop*?'

'On the contrary, Your Royal Highness,' he assured him, once again successfully raising his voice above the excited whispers. 'Your arrival is most opportune. I was on the point of announcing the engagement between Lord Peregrine Pentecost and Miss Henrietta Dilbey. And...no less gratifying...the engagement between my good friend Dr Thomas Carrington and Lady Jane Beresford.'

For several moments there was a stunned silence, then, 'Carrington, did you say...? Carrington!' The Regent's plump face beamed with pleasure. 'But I know him! Excellent fellow! Oh, by Jove, yes!'

He led the way in what became rapturous applause and hearty congratulations to both couples. 'Love weddings. Didn't like my own, of course. Dear me, no,' he remarked in an undertone to a young lady regarding him in awestruck silence, before he turned once again to his companion. 'Where are the happy couples, Bart? Must offer my personal congratulations.'

Sir Bartholomew left the future king to ease his way through the throng, and went in search of his old friend Lady Templehurst, who, surprisingly, was amongst the few not to leave their chairs in order to join the crowd of well-wishers congregating down the far end of the room.

'Well, Gussie, old girl? How has the wicked Dowager taken the news?' he asked, raising his glass to scan the throng for a glimpse of Lady Pentecost. 'Don't seem able to locate her.'

'You won't. She fell into a swoon and had to be helped from the room.' She gave vent to one of her wicked cackles. 'Oh, Bart, you could not have timed it better! And bringing the Regent, too! Now she'll never dare to oppose the match. What a complete hand you are!'

'Told you, m'dear, I'd lend you my support. Didn't expect the second announcement, though. Who's this Carrington fellow? Never heard of him, myself, but Prinney seems to know him, right enough.' He regarded her tear-filled eyes in silence. 'Eastbury's daughter and a doctor, eh? Come as a bit of a shock to you, has it, old girl?'

'I would say, rather, an extremely satisfying surprise,' she admitted, astounding him. 'He's the very one for my dear Jane. He loves her too.'

'Be that as it may, I rather fancy it will cause something of a stir.'

'I rather fancy it already has,' was the prompt rejoinder. She then gave vent to yet another of those famous wicked chuckles. 'Now the Regent himself has openly countenanced the match—both, in fact—

there isn't a soul who would dare to oppose either! What an evening this has been! I cannot thank you enough for what you've done, Bart. Why, I'm almost tempted to show my appreciation by marrying you myself!'

'Now, now, old girl. Don't let's be hasty,' Sir Bartholomew advised, suddenly finding his cravat had grown uncomfortably tight. 'Very fond of you, and all that. Always have been. But two engagements in one evening are more than enough to be going on with!'

*　*　*　*　*

MILLS & BOON

The Regency

LORDS & LADIES
COLLECTION

*Two glittering Regency
love affairs in every book*

*Available at WH Smith, Tesco, ASDA, Borders, Eason,
Sainsbury's and all good paperback bookshops*
www.millsandboon.co.uk

REG/L&L/LIST 2

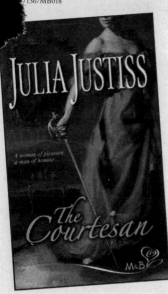

Be whisked
away to
an age of
chivalry, where
passionate
knights and
innocent ladies
face danger
and desire...

The Knight, the Knave and the Lady
by Juliet Landon

Marietta Wardle *never* wanted to be someone's
wife, but Lord Alain of Thorsgeld had
no scruples about compromising her into
marriage...

My Enemy, My Love by Julia Byrne

Kept hostage during a royal feud, Isabel de Tracy
held fast to the memory of tough, yet tender
knight, Guy fitzAlan...